THE
SEVENFOLD
HUNTERS

THE SEVENFOLD HUNTERS

ROSE EGAL

PAGE STREET
PUBLISHING CO.

PAGE STREET
PUBLISHING CO.

First published in 2022 by
Page Street Publishing Co.
27 Congress Street, Suite 1511
Salem, MA 01970
www.pagestreetpublishing.com

Distributed by Macmillan, sales in Canada by The Canadian Manda Group.

26   25   24   23   22   1   2   3   4   5

ISBN-13: 978-1-64567-616-4
ISBN-10: 1-64567-616-1

Library of Congress Control Number: 2022933342

Cover and book design by Melia Parsloe for Page Street Publishing Co.
Cover image © Shane Rebenschied

Printed and bound in the United States

For my three younger ~~peasants~~ sisters:
How many other people in the world can say
their bedtime story got published?

ARTEMIS

THERE WERE TWELVE CRACKS IN THE PAVEMENT OUTSIDE Artemis's house. She'd counted them each around two dozen times, but every now and then she found a new one she'd missed, a tiny imperfection you would hardly notice on a normal day. And if anyone cared to ask how many cars had driven down her street in the last two hours, what exact colors they were, and the sixteen digits of each of their license plate numbers, Artemis could regurgitate every detail from memory.

Just my luck.

She tore her eyes away from the window, glancing down at the cleaning rag that had all but dried in her iron grip, and gave a heavy sigh. Mum was going to have a heart attack when she saw the state of the living room. It was 11:00 a.m. on a Saturday, and the chairs were still covered in mountains of her little brothers' toys and other random things Artemis had found lying around.

Stealing one final glance at the road outside her house, some part of her wished her eyes could manifest a Royal Mail van out of sheer willpower. *Focus.* Mum was going to be done with the bathrooms downstairs any minute now and walk in on her. Artemis's pulse picked up as she sprayed the window with bleach and scrubbed so fast her golden-brown fingers turned scarlet.

There was no way she was going to finish in time.

"So, while I cleaned three bathrooms, the stairs, and the

kitchen, you only managed half a window?" Mum huffed from the doorway behind her with a mop and bucket in her hands. "We're already behind, Jay."

"I'll get it done in half an hour max."

"Don't think I didn't notice how distracted you've been today either." She shook her head. "You can't let your grief take over everything in your life."

Artemis looked to the ground, picking at the edges of her shorts. "Why do you have to bring it up all the time?"

Mum's face softened a fraction. "Jared's car isn't going to appear outside no matter how long you stare at the street."

She hated the pitiful look everyone always gave her.

It was a weird mashup of "Oh, it's so sad your boyfriend died" and "Pull yourself together, girl." And she couldn't stand it. The past six months had been hell, and while her family tried not to say it out loud, Artemis knew they wanted her to start moving on with her life already. It didn't matter, though. She didn't care what they thought. Artemis refused to move past what happened to Jared until she found the answers she needed—she just couldn't tell her parents that.

The doorbell rang before she could find the right words to smooth over the fresh cracks opening in her chest. *Finally.* Her heart leaped to her throat, her feet moving to the door before her brain had a chance to catch up.

Mum stood firm in the doorway. "I'm not finished, Artemis."

She bristled at that; her real name always sounded weird coming from Mum and Dad's lips. She was always Jayda to them. It wasn't like it was anything special, though—everyone in their family called Dad Leroy but his real name was Clifton. Dad's first wife—Artemis's real mum—was the one who originally named her, but she'd been dead for seventeen years now.

"But I have to get the door, Mum."

"Your father can answer it."

She clasped her hands together like she was praying at an altar.

"Please, it has to be me."

Mum analyzed her face for a few agonizing heartbeats. "Okay, you can—"

Artemis didn't let her finish her sentence, flying past the moment the first word left her mother's mouth. She sprinted through the hallway, taking their carpeted stairs three at a time on her way down, and threw open the front door, breathless and red-faced.

The postman blinked at her in shock, his green eyes wide, before holding out a parcel for Dad and a single solitary envelope. *This has to be it.* Artemis snatched them out of his hands and shut the door before running to the kitchen, barreling past Dad on her way to the breakfast table.

"One letter has you forgetting your manners, huh?" He laughed from his position at the stove, his deep voice easily carrying over the onions he had sizzling in his pan. "You should've thanked him for the delivery."

"I promise I'll apologize to him tomorrow."

Artemis wanted to sigh with relief as she held the envelope to her chest. As soon as she first touched it, she could tell it was the one she'd been waiting these past twelve weeks for—from how her details were written in perfect calligraphy on the front to the way it felt so heavy in her hands.

There was no way it could be a rejection.

Dad watched as she leaned backward and took a knife from the cutlery drawer, his obsidian eyes alight with intrigue. Her hands trembled lightly as she placed the envelope in front of her, the gold paper stark against the black countertop. She cut a neat vertical line at the top and slid out a single letter and a dense pack of other papers.

Dad said, "Read it out loud so I can hear."

"Dear Artemis Garrett-Coleman, we are delighted to welcome you to Carlisle Academy—"

Her vision blurred, and hot tears rolled down her cheeks. She made it. The highest grades, passing three separate aptitude tests, and a flawless performance in the entrance exam were all prerequisites to being accepted at the school. Carlisle Academy somehow managed to be stingier than both Oxford and Cambridge combined, and it wasn't even a university.

Quick footsteps echoed from the staircase outside that she didn't doubt were her younger brothers' but Artemis couldn't focus on anything besides the letter in her hands. Dad came over, the faint scent of food clinging to his vest, and wrapped his russet arms around her. "I hope those are happy tears, Jay. I'm so proud of you."

They weren't happy tears, though.

Not entirely.

But Artemis couldn't tell him that because then he would ask why she wasn't elated to be going to one of the highest-ranking schools in the country, why she wasn't dancing on the kitchen table and screaming from the top of her lungs because she'd gotten a full scholarship. In truth, she'd have preferred it not to have come to this. Artemis would've given everything she had and then some to rewind time back to six months ago.

Before she found out the hard way that life was a fickle and precarious thing. That at any moment people could be taken away from you. Sometimes little by little over time or in the blink of an eye.

There were so many things she'd wanted to say to Jared before he was snatched from her, so many things they had left to do, and so many places he'd promised they'd see together. Artemis could never forget what happened no matter how hard she tried. He was the sweetest boy she'd ever met—her first real boyfriend—and she had to watch him die.

Her whole body tensed as phantom snarls echoed in her ears, and images she'd tried so hard to bury flashed through her mind: her tight grip on the rocky mountain face, Jared's mischievous grin as he adjusted his harness, and how their group's rope shook so hard Artemis thought the nylon would snap clean in two and send them all tumbling more than nine hundred feet down the north face of Ben Nevis.

"Mum!" her nine-year-old brothers yelled in unison from the stairs, yanking her from her thoughts. "Jay got into a new school!"

Artemis and Dad looked at each other, the same panic flashing across their faces at the sound of Mum's steps coming down from the living room. He was the first to recover. "Calm down—we always knew your mother was going to find out sooner or later."

"I would've preferred never," Artemis said, a layer of sweat forming at the nape of her neck as her brothers ran upstairs and left her to deal with the fallout. "What am I going to say—"

"I should've known you would help her apply to that place behind my back." Mum's voice was perfectly level as she stood across the breakfast table from them. It was the kind of calm that came before thunder and hail, the silence before a towering wave crashed over your ship and swallowed it whole. "I told you I didn't like that school."

Dad sighed. "That's not enough, Maureen. It's one of the best private schools in the country, and our daughter got in with a scholarship. I'm not going to stand in her way."

"Not enough? I told you my spirit didn't take to that place, and my spirit never lies!" Mum snapped, and Artemis looked everywhere but at her. She wanted to hide in one of the kitchen cabinets behind her, to just squeeze in next to the tuna and baked beans while her parents hashed this out. "There's something wrong in there."

Artemis couldn't tell Mum how right she was.

Most people believed the lies that the school sold them. All the papers and brochures and articles. That it was a residential sixth form in the heart of London, accessible to only the brightest and richest students the world had to offer. No one on the outside knew the true face of Carlisle Academy, what they really did behind those fancy barbed wire gates and looming brick walls.

There was no way on Earth her parents would let her go there if they knew the truth—that aliens were real, they killed her boyfriend, and Artemis enrolled at his old school to find out why.

"I went there and saw the whole campus with my own eyes. There was nothing wrong," Dad insisted. "Show her the little brochure thing, Jay."

Artemis scuttled over with the stack of papers that came along with her acceptance letter and held them out for Mum to see. "Here, look. It's a great school."

There was nothing in any of the pages that hinted at the creatures she'd seen on the mountain. When Mr. Carlisle visited her in hospital after the attack—the first and only time she'd ever seen the CEO of Carlisle Enterprises—he just told her the bare bones about the Nosaru species: They were a parasitic alien race that came to Earth in the 1700s, fed on oxygenated hemoglobin, and used humans as hosts. Some of the things he said still didn't make sense to her, and her list of questions could wrap around all Carlisle Academy's buildings twice and still have length to spare.

"You could show me a thousand laughing children, and my opinion still wouldn't change." Mum shook her head solemnly and reached for Artemis's hand. "Go to this school if you want it that badly, Jay, but I'll warn you: If you don't want to hear, then you will feel."

She'd heard it a hundred times.

It was Mum's favorite proverb, and every time she said it, it was as if Artemis could feel the fates aligning in Mum's favor, star by cosmic star. She wondered if this was how the ancient Greeks felt when an oracle descended from her temple with knowing eyes and a prophecy on her lips or if Mum tasted the foreboding in each of the letters as they formed on her tongue.

While she knew she should speak up for herself, say something courageous and hopeful about how she'd prove Mum wrong, Artemis was well aware that Carlisle Academy was a school that wore many masks, and just because she'd seen one and decided it wasn't so monstrous didn't mean there weren't a dozen others lurking in the shadows that could turn even Medusa to stone.

Everything about the school, the backbreaking training and cutthroat competition, would've sent Artemis running a mile in the opposite direction if it wasn't for Jared. A dull ache hummed in her chest whenever she remembered seeing him laid out in the hospital closest to Ben Nevis, his body pieced together as best as the doctors could. At his bedside, she gazed at his once-vibrant tawny skin and swore she'd get revenge.

Artemis refused to break that promise for anyone.

Though her pulse jumped, she choked down the fear. "I'm going to Carlisle Academy next year, Mum."

Whether you like it or not.

2

ABYAN

ABYAN WAS ALWAYS THE LAST MEMBER OF THE SQUAD TO leave for the summer. Her closest friends had wrapped her in tearful embraces and flown off in their families' private jets, yet she couldn't help but stay a little longer in their dorm. Something about it steadied her. The seven bedrooms, the lingering smell of Hank's awful perfume, and the memories etched into the crevices of every wall. It was the firm arm around her when she stumbled, and the soothing embrace after an especially shitty day.

It was home.

Everywhere she looked, there was an imprint of her squad, the crown jewel of Carlisle Academy, and Abyan wished it had never had to change. She strolled down the hallway where all their rooms were, the light thuds of her slippers echoing all around her.

Kade, Hassan, and Mason's rooms were on the left along with her own, while Hank, Tolly, and Jared's sat on the right. Abyan peered into each one as she passed as if her friends would suddenly manifest from the barren beds and lingering dust mites and tell her they'd stay with her for an extra day or two.

She came to a stop outside Jared's bedroom door, her hand trembling as she reached out. Abyan hadn't set foot inside since he passed away. Kade and Mason hadn't either—all these months later, and it was still too much, too raw, and too cruel. Most people didn't choose to die, she knew that. Jared certainly didn't. Death didn't ask you if you were ready to go or promise to come back later if you said you weren't, but that didn't stop it from feeling unfair.

It didn't stop her from being angry.

Still, it was her last day of Year 13, and she knew she needed to say goodbye. Abtiyo Ayaanle was going to pull up at the front gates any minute now and wonder why she was still in her dorm dressed in a *Doctor Who* onesie and slippers. *It's now or never.* Abyan released a slow breath before turning the brass door handle and stepping inside Jared's room.

The walls were still the same disastrous shade of green, but everything else was all wrong. There was a single bed with no bedding, no posters or pictures on the walls, and the only things that tied the room to Jared were the handful of mementos strewn about the place.

Abyan walked to the window where all their makeshift trophies for the squad's biannual arm-wrestling contests sat in all their glue and duct-tape glory, looking like hideous little Frankenstein's monsters. She smiled a little, remembering how Jared would always act like he was holding a UFC belt or something whenever he won any of the tournaments, not a failed D-I-Y project covered in three layers of glitter.

"You idiot," she said, as though he could hear her from wherever he was now.

"See, I'd have preferred a simple: 'I miss you, Jared' or 'You were the hottest out of all of us' or even an 'I secretly enjoyed your legendary nudist phase.'" Abyan looked to the window and saw him leaning against the wall dressed in the Carlisle Academy uniform, his long hair tied up in his staple man bun.

Her lips curved upward in a traitorous smile despite her best efforts. "How is it that even in my imagination, you still manage to be a dick?"

"Blame yourself." Jared shrugged. "You're the one who made me transcend visible reality with my personality intact."

Abyan rolled her eyes. "I came here to say goodbye, not bicker with you."

"You said goodbye when they buried me six months ago, Yan." He laughed, but there was no humor in it. "You all did."

A lump formed in her throat. "You'd think I'd be better at letting go, Jared."

She'd seen enough graves to last her a lifetime, but the dead never really stayed buried when it came to Abyan. They latched onto her, their chill seeping deep into the marrow of her bones, and she clutched them to her body even tighter, carrying them with her wherever she went. Abyan gladly took whatever parts of those she loved that remained because it was still so much better than being alone.

The cold was only a small price to pay.

"Personally, I think talking to your imaginary dead friend all alone in a semi-dark room is a very healthy coping mechanism." His half smile lacked its usual light. "But if I could get any deader to help you out, I would."

"But you didn't deserve to go out like that." Her voice wobbled over each of the syllables. "Who's going to force me and Kade to start talking again after we argue? Who'll make Hassan wash the dishes on time when it's his day or stop Mason from killing Hank whenever he leaves his dirty socks lying around?"

"You'll be fine without me, Yan."

"No, you should've made it to graduation." Tears filled Abyan's vision. "You should've had annoying little kids and grown old with the rest of us."

Jared's expression was unreadable. "It's not your fault—it's not anyone's fault."

But none of this was *fair*.

She clenched her fists. "I'm so sick of losing people all the time."

Before Jared could reply, the door to The Sevenfold's dorm burst open. Abyan's limbs turned to ice. It couldn't have been the maintenance people because she still had two days before they came to deep clean the dorm. It also couldn't have been Abtiyo Ayaanle, since relatives had to be buzzed into the residential building and escorted around.

"Yan! Are you still here?"

Abyan wiped at her eyes furiously and cleared her throat. "Hold on a second, Tolly."

When she turned back to the window, Jared was gone. She cursed under her breath and ran to her room to find the closest hijab-resembling thing in sight.

Abyan snatched one of the bedsheets from her neatly folded pile and wrapped it around her head as fast as she could, silently praying that Tolly didn't decide to investigate why she was taking so long. She emerged from her room and found his lean figure pacing up and down the living room, a light sheen of sweat across his mahogany brow.

"Did you see the email we got about an hour ago?" he asked, his frantic eyes searching her face for any sign of recognition.

"No, my phone's been charging while I packed." Abyan's brows furrowed. "You delayed your flight for an email, Tolly?"

He started rummaging through his bag for his phone, but everything he managed to pull out was either some random gadget or tangled set of wires. Eventually, he released a frustrated sound and blurted it out. "Ms. Bruno said we have to clear out Jared's room ourselves in the next forty-eight hours or maintenance will throw out everything they find."

Something in her wilted at that.

"What the hell?" she said. "They can't do that to us."

Ms. Bruno and the other senior Carlisle staff were the ones who gave them the green light to keep their mementos not only for the rest of the school year but also over the summer and next year, too, and now they were going back on their word.

This is bullshit.

"We need to talk to Ms. Bruno. It's only been six months—she can't expect us to just get over it like that." He finally found his phone and pressed some buttons before showing her The Sevenfold's group chat. "The others are just as angry. They've all agreed on what we need to do."

Abyan thought for a moment. Tolly was clearly livid, and while she was as well, with his wild eyes and wavering voice, Tolly was in no state to talk to a senior teacher like Ms. Bruno. It would do more harm than good. They needed someone who had a rapport with her and could get them the answers and outcome they wanted.

"I'll go and speak to her, but it has to be alone," she said, and although Tolly opened his mouth to protest, Abyan got there first. "It has to be me. She used to be my form tutor, and your judgment is too messed up right now."

He clenched and unclenched his jaw a total of three times before speaking. "What the hell am I supposed to do in the meantime then, Yan? Twiddle my thumbs? I'm the only one who'll stand up for Jared, so you can't just tell me to sit this one out."

"Just because you two were close doesn't mean you're the only one grieving him," Abyan snapped, his words cutting deeper than she could've ever imagined. "And you sure as hell don't get to decide whether or not I'm doing enough for him."

Tolly blinked at her, remorse quickly filling his eyes. "I didn't mean it like that, Yan."

"I know," she said with a sigh. "But I'm asking you to trust me on this."

They both wanted to do right by their friend, and she hoped Tolly would finally see it that way, too. From the day Jared died, Tolly was the one holding the senior staff at Carlisle's feet to the fire over what happened to him and squeezing out every detail he could. They wouldn't tell them anything at first, only that Jared was out climbing a mountain in Scotland and had an accident of some kind.

It took three weeks before they told the squad what really happened.

He made for their leather settees. "I'll wait here for you, then."

"No, you need to get yourself back on that jet and off to Lagos before your aunt kills you for being late again." She put a hand on his arm. "Leave everything to me."

He deliberated for a couple of seconds, his bottom lip held in a vise between his teeth. "You'll keep the group chat updated?"

"I promise you'll find out the reason for all of this as soon as I do," Abyan said. She released a breath when Tolly nodded in agreement, internally thanking Allah for the bullet she'd just dodged, and pulled him in for a tight hug. "See you in September."

They exchanged their goodbyes, and as soon as Tolly closed the door to their dorm firmly behind him, Abyan sprinted back to her room. She hurriedly unzipped her largest bag and pulled out cargo trousers and a long-sleeved gray shirt. After putting on her combat boots and wrapping a black hijab around her head, she set off to Ms. Bruno's office, quiet fury carrying each of her steps.

Abyan barely registered the journey from her dorm in the residential halls to Ms. Bruno's front door in the main recruitment building. She was too busy trying to think of something coherent to say that wouldn't get her suspended.

Raising her hand to knock, Abyan took a steadying breath and put her anger to the side—she had to be professional, for Jared's sake. If Tolly or any of the others were with her, they'd have already torn the door down and rained fire down on everyone's heads, consequences be damned.

Be calm.

"Stop gawking at me from the door and just come in, Guled!" Ms. Bruno barked, looking her dead in the eye through the small glass window in the door. "I've been expecting you for almost an hour now."

Abyan entered the room, trying not to bristle at how Ms. Bruno butchered her surname. "Am I that predictable, miss?"

"Painfully so." She gestured to the empty seat in front of her. "Listen, Jared's death in action was unprecedented, so we allowed you some leeway to give you all time to process what happened, but you need to start moving past it."

Abyan pulled out the chair and sat down in front of her wide desk. Ms. Bruno's long dark hair was tied up in a ponytail that was so tight it gave Abyan a headache just looking at it, and her office was lifeless and bland, just a desk, a few chairs, and a computer.

"So, you want us to just ignore the fact that our friend was torn to pieces by Nosaru with no one to help him?" Abyan fumed. "We're not robots. We can't just switch off our feelings because you want us to."

Ms. Bruno's bronze eyes flashed with annoyance. "You're not the first squad to lose a member, and you certainly won't be the last. Though it's regrettable that Mr. Leong passed away before becoming an operative, you were given the last six months of the school year to grieve, and there will be no more concessions in your final year at Carlisle."

Abyan couldn't believe what she was hearing. "I don't even know what to say."

She couldn't go back to her squad and tell them this. It would crush them. They didn't drag each other through these last couple of months out of sheer will just to get slapped in the face. They were the best damn squad Carlisle Academy had to offer. Ms. Bruno couldn't treat them like this.

"We expect you all to squash whatever remaining feelings you have in any way you wish over the summer. Come the next school year, The Sevenfold must be focused on training and graduation only."

"I don't care." Abyan welled up again, and all she could think about was how Jared's headstone was ashen gray and that he'd always hated that color. "We won't be emptying out his room, no matter how much you threaten us."

Ms. Bruno sighed. "This posturing will get you nowhere, kid.

You have forty-eight hours to move all your keepsakes somewhere else or you'll find them at the nearest landfill."

"You're the one who gave us permission to keep them there in the first place!"

"And my opinion has changed since. It's as simple as that."

"I don't believe you, miss." Abyan leaned forward. "You can't just change your mind on us now and not tell us why."

It just didn't make any sense. How could the school go from offering The Sevenfold anything they needed throughout the rest of their time at Carlisle, unlimited counseling sessions, and forcing them to take psych evals on the third of every month to telling them to just suck it up and deal with it?

Something else had to be going on.

"This is your problem, Guled—it's your whole squad's problem—you have a nasty habit of sticking your head into things that don't concern you."

Abyan jabbed a finger in her direction. "I've done everything that you've ever asked of me without question since I started here; I eat, live, and breathe this school, so the least you can give me in return is the truth."

"You and your squad will find out why in September."

Her brow creased. "Why can't you tell us now?"

Ms. Bruno quieted, and Abyan could see her thinking over her next words. "Because your newest member hasn't arrived yet."

Abyan's limbs grew numb. "We don't have a new member."

Please, let this be a sick joke.

"They'll be assigned to The Sevenfold on the first day back."

The ground beneath her started to spin. "A third-year transfer from one of the other academies?"

"No." Ms. Bruno shook her head, and Abyan knew she'd hate her next words. "The latest addition to The Sevenfold will be a new recruit."

3

ARTEMIS

ARTEMIS NEVER THOUGHT SHE'D LEARN HOW TO KILL aliens on the first day of autumn term.

Then again, she'd also never imagined that she'd be stuck in a staring contest with her training instructor either. Ms. Bruno's gaze bore holes into Artemis's skin, her eyes definitively unimpressed by what they saw. *She hates me already.* Artemis's pulse picked up the longer the silence between them stretched, and a thin layer of sweat gathered between her clasped hands.

She tried not to look too long at the curved black prosthetic attached to Ms. Bruno's right knee and trained her gaze to the mirrored walls of the room around them. Ms. Bruno couldn't have been more than five foot two, and even in its high ponytail, her dark hair flowed all the way down to her waist.

It's now or never.

Artemis gulped heavily. "Good morn—"

"I didn't give you permission to speak, recruit," her instructor interjected, and before Artemis could respond with the flurry of apologies on her tongue, she turned on her heel and gestured to the door. "Follow me."

"Yes, mi—" Artemis began.

"In silence."

She clamped her mouth shut immediately, what little confidence she had left in her shriveling up in an instant. A wave of uncertainty washed over Artemis as she followed Ms. Bruno through the dark stone corridors of Carlisle Academy.

While her first day was already off to the worst start imaginable, she'd always known it would be an uphill battle at a school like this. Most of the students were legacies, after all. Artemis figured they'd fantasised about being a field operative their whole lives and knew nothing else.

All their hopes and dreams began and ended with Carlisle Academy. Encompassed in the cursive letters hanging above the front gates and wrapped in the gold foil of the school's crest.

She didn't want to entertain the thought of not making the final cut of recruits and being given the choice between the research or intelligence wings of Carlisle Enterprises. *It took so much to get here.* Artemis straightened, squaring her shoulders under the weight of Ms. Bruno's imposing gaze, as they arrived at their destination.

There was no turning back.

"These are VR machines for training simulations." Her instructor pointed at the cubicles lining the dark room around them, the dull whirring of machines filling the air. Artemis squinted, trying to see if she recognized any of the tech, but the dim strobe lights made it impossible. "Come, I'll strap you in."

Artemis swallowed her fear and walked toward her cubicle with her chin high. She squeezed herself into a suit that had wires coming out of it in every direction and put on the VR goggles Ms. Bruno held out for her. Artemis stood stock-still as the machine read her vitals and configured itself with her heavily wired gloves and boots, trying not to let the neon red lights in the walls freak her out.

She needed to prove herself.

Three loud beeps sounded, and Artemis released a slow breath, watching as the screen of her VR goggles morphed into a desertlike terrain.

Scalding air blew across the length of her body and heat

pelted her limbs from all angles. *How is this even possible?* Artemis paused and took in three people a short distance from her, dressed in Carlisle Academy uniforms, fighting several hostiles that she assumed were part of the simulation.

Ms. Bruno appeared beside her in the blink of an eye. "See how they fight? The synchronicity?"

The three of them moved like one body, where someone defended the other attacked, and it was almost like a dance only they knew the steps to. How did they keep track of what the others were doing? They certainly weren't looking at each other—at least not for more than a split second.

It seemed like second nature.

Instinct.

Artemis thought of it like each of them was a different limb on the same body because no other explanation made sense. Were they in the same squad? They had to be. She couldn't help but feel a twinge of envy, its tendrils hidden deep in the cracks between the awe, and she wondered if she'd have the same relationship with her own future squad members. If they'd have her back like this and defend her without a second thought.

Ms. Bruno snapped her fingers, and Artemis gasped as all the simulation bots paused, their arms stuck mid-punch and their legs frozen as they leaped in the air.

The three students in front of them groaned in frustration.

"I don't want to hear any complaints," Ms. Bruno called over before any of them could get a word in. "Come here, I have a task for you."

"You have the worst timing, miss." A stunning East Asian girl with a sharp pixie cut rolled her eyes as she moved toward the two of them. When she glanced at where Artemis stood, giving her a once-over, Artemis blushed and cursed herself internally for it.

One pretty girl and you lose control.

A familiar kind of sickly feeling settled over Artemis as she remembered how Jared could make her blush by just standing near her. It was odd—all these months after his death and she still didn't know if she was allowed to start moving on, if he would hold it against her.

"We can't even train in peace," the other girl in the trio replied, adjusting her hijab with a slender terracotta hand, and as soon as Artemis's gaze landed on the surname etched into her breast pocket, she stilled.

It's her.

Artemis hadn't been at Carlisle Academy long—it was only her first day at the school—but she'd heard enough about her to feel weird in her presence. All the other recruits did was talk about her under their breath, as though she'd hear their words through the bulletproof glass and reinforced steel and rain fire down on all their heads.

Abyan Farax Guled.

That was the name of the leader of The Sevenfold. Her squad was the crown jewel of the school. And she strode across the sand with ease as her eyes bore into Artemis's, searching for something she couldn't place.

Ms. Bruno's hand clamped down hard on Artemis's shoulder, jerking her from her thoughts. "I want you to fight this recruit, Abyan. No questions asked."

Artemis froze and the ice threatened to crack beneath her skin at the slightest movement. "I have to fight *her*?"

A wide grin spread across the face of the brown-haired boy in front of them, and he threw his head back in hearty laughter. The pretty Asian girl hit him in the arm in a matter of seconds. "Stop being an ass, Hank."

"What Kade said," Abyan concurred, shooting Hank a pointed look before turning back to Ms. Bruno. "The recruit looks two seconds away from running away." Ms. Bruno released a sound of annoyance, but the leader of The Sevenfold got there first.

"Technically, it was an observation, not a question, miss."

Their instructor was quick with her reply. "Don't get smart with me, Guled."

"Fine, have it your way." Abyan walked a few paces out into the sand. "I'll fight the damn recruit."

Artemis's stomach dropped to the floor as everyone turned to her and parted like the Red Sea. *Crap.* When she didn't move, Abyan cocked a finely arched brow. "Come on, recruit. I don't have time to wait for you to be done pissing yourself."

Artemis gulped and tried to take her first step, but the machinery connected to her boots was pulling at them, weighing her legs down as though she were trudging across a real sand dune, and she stumbled.

She tried to ignore the snickers she knew came from Hank's lips as she took up her position in front of Abyan, each of her movements more baby giraffe than human. *For God's sake.* She tested the ground, lightly bouncing on her toes.

It was foreign and unsteady.

Nevertheless, Artemis raised her fists and kept her knees bent like in the movies, while Abyan stood opposite her, looking her up and down. The corner of her mouth twitched for a heartbeat, and the fact that Abyan wanted to laugh at the sight of her made Artemis's chest burn with cold rage.

"Are you just going to stand there, recruit?" she asked after a few seconds, clasping her hands behind her back. "What did I say about my time and it being precious to me?"

That's it.

Artemis took her chance and swung; her fist aimed right at her smug face. But Abyan sidestepped it, hands still behind her back, and before Artemis could angle herself for another blow, Abyan's foot found her ankles and swept her legs out from under her.

She landed on her back with a loud thud, and the impact knocked the wind from her lungs. The sand scorched her back as

Abyan stood beside her and offered her a hand, disappointment clear in her eyes.

The piercing gazes of everyone else around her bore into her skin, their judgment weighing on her flesh like a thick tar, and Artemis wanted nothing more than for the sand beneath her feet to swallow her up.

As the two of them walked back to the others, Abyan said, "A word of advice? It's better for you to drop out now." Her tone was more sincere than scathing, and Artemis hated her all the more for it. "If I could do that to you in under three seconds, imagine how much damage a Nosaru could do."

Ms. Bruno chimed in, then, but Artemis didn't have the heart to look up from her feet. "The three of you are dismissed. I need to talk to the recruit alone."

Abyan's brow creased. "But we were in the middle of—"

"I didn't hear myself ask for your opinion, Guled. Did you?" There was a finality to her words, warning them all not to press her further because she was more than ready to strike. "Do as I asked."

Artemis watched as the members of The Sevenfold left the simulation, blinking out of existence in three clouds of scattered blue pixels. Yet the blood rushing in her ears was the only thing she could focus on as shame clogged her throat—she didn't know what to do—her hands were clammy, her mouth suddenly dry.

A stern voice cut through the haze. "I separated you from the rest of the recruits to see what you were made of, but I would kick you out this very second if I could." There was no hatred in her voice, only cold truth. "While you clearly don't have the baseline level of skill needed to excel here, I'm not allowed to get rid of you for some reason."

A chill ran up Artemis's spine. Ms. Bruno seemed senior enough to have significant weight behind her opinions, which meant whoever had tied her hands was even higher.

Yet Artemis steeled herself as best she could. "I'm sorry, I don't know what you're talking about. This is all new to—"

"Enough," Ms. Bruno interjected. "Although you are to remain at Carlisle Academy, don't expect any further special treatment. All recruits are the same and not all make it to the end of the year. Understood?"

Artemis gulped. "Yes, miss."

"We're done here." She snapped her fingers, and everything around them faded to nothingness.

4

ABYAN

"YOU SHOULD AT LEAST TRY BEING NICER TO THE RECRUITS, Yan," Hank said as he pulled on his boots.

Abyan quickly shoved her vitamins into her mouth before she forgot. "A little tough love won't kill them. Just be thankful they won't get hazed like we did."

They were getting ready for their first official mission of the year, and since the rest of their squad would be stuck in traffic on their way back from Heathrow Airport and Kade had to babysit some recruits, they were the only two available for the job.

"No one in the world deserves to get hazed like we did." He shuddered at the memories she didn't doubt were flooding his mind—there was a reason recruits used to call October "Hell Month."

Abyan distinctly remembered her old combat instructors tying her up on the rope wall of the training room and leaving her to free herself in pitch-black darkness. It took hours to get loose, painstakingly untying the knots binding her wrists, and then freeing each of her limbs one by one. And if you asked Abyan, her instructors deserved the hair removal cream she put in their shampoo bottles the next day.

She went to get their weapons and couldn't help the smile on her face. "Remember when they stole your clothes after swimming, and you had to walk back to your room naked?"

"I'd prefer never to talk about that again in my life," Hank replied, tying his laces with a little too much force. "In fact, I say we agree to collectively forget it ever happened."

"Who could ever forget seeing your pale arse running through the corridors and yelling at anyone who accidentally looked in your general direction?" Abyan laughed. It might have been one of Hank's worst memories, but it was also hands down the funniest moment of their first year at Carlisle, and she wasn't the only one who thought so.

"Admit it, you loved seeing me naked," he said, and smirked.

She knew it was his way of flipping the conversation back under his control, but Abyan was in a giving mood. "Oh please, it was traumatic."

"Liar."

"Denial isn't a good look."

She handed him his daggers and began sheathing her own in the holsters at her thighs. She wore a standard combat uniform: form-fitting black trousers and a matching black shirt with her surname etched into the breast pocket. Abyan always made sure her hijab was pinned firmly to her T-shirt—the Nosaru didn't need any more of an advantage.

"One of us is definitely in denial, but it's not me."

Abyan strolled out of their rooms with him in tow. "Whatever."

All squads got their own communal rooms for their second and third years at Carlisle, but since The Sevenfold was the school's prized cow, they had an entire floor of the residential building to themselves.

Being the best of the best had its perks.

"So, what's the WLDO?" Hank asked as they made their way to the parking lot.

They tried their best to ignore the stares of the few students they encountered in the halls, not making eye contact with any of them as they breezed past. It was only ever younger years that pulled this shit with them. Most of their fellow Year 14s never treated The Sevenfold as anything besides competition.

She pulled out her phone and read the file Ms. De Costa sent her. "Suspected Nosaru attack on the M1 just outside London. They caused a seven-car pileup with multiple casualties. Police and ambulances are already on the scene."

Ms. De Costa was in charge of dispensing WLDOs—kill-order missions students were only allowed to start taking in the latter half of their second year—and their lesser counterparts: BLCC orders.

Hank ran a hand through his chestnut brown hair. "I'm guessing the hosts went into the forest for cover?"

They entered the elevator alone and waited for the doors to close. "My thoughts exactly."

"How many were there?"

"It's hard to tell, and even De Costa didn't know for sure. From the damage they caused, I'd say at least four."

Abyan knew she was being conservative in her estimation.

The Nosaru were a social species with a central hive mind connecting them all. They preferred to hunt in large groups and only went solo when situations were dire. There definitely weren't only four waiting for them. Yet if she told the truth—that there could be up to eight hosts in the forest—Hank would insist on waiting for Kade or another member of their squad to join them just to be on the safe side.

While Abyan knew it was risky, she'd never been one to turn from a challenge.

"You sure you can handle four with your rusty skills?" he teased as they exited and crossed the parking garage to where his black BMW awaited them. Abyan couldn't drive yet, and she still didn't know whether she loved or hated being stuck with Hank as her self-appointed driver.

Her eyes narrowed. "I went on holiday for two months, not ten years."

She only went because Habaryaro Bilan forced her to—not in a literal sense, of course, but very few people in the world could withstand the Somali Elder Look of Disapproval, and Abyan wasn't one of them.

Hank cocked a brow and entered the car, turning on the police sirens built into the front. "With sixty-one days without practice, I think calling you rusty is generous. Maybe this WLDO will finally make you accept that I'm a better fighter than you."

She scoffed. "I could beat you any day of the week."

"That's not what the leaderboard says."

"It's literally the first day of school, and I know you have that thing rigged." Abyan hit him lightly as they sped through the empty streets. "Don't get ahead of yourself now, Hercules."

Hank's cheeks reddened at his full name. "See, you know I'm right, and you're trying to throw me off."

"No, I just like getting under your skin." She shrugged, her smile growing as his blush deepened. Abyan leaned forward as much as her seat belt allowed and pretended to examine his face. "Aw, look at you—you're blushing,"

His grip on the steering wheel tightened. "It's called vasodilation, not blushing."

Abyan gave an exaggerated sigh though her chest swelled in triumph. "Fine, I'll stop. I don't need you pouting in silence again."

"Hey, I wasn't pouting." He pointed a finger in her direction. "I was brooding—there's a difference."

"Oh, you were brooding?" She crossed her arms. "I see."

"Yeah, in a very sophisticated and manly way, contemplating life and stuff. I don't expect you to understand."

Abyan cocked a brow. "Why not? I'm the manliest man I know."

"But—" Hank spluttered, confusion taking hold of his features. And although she tried her hardest, Abyan couldn't contain her laughter, almost doubling over in her seat, and he eventually joined in.

"This is literally why no one believes you get straight As," she said as she sobered.

The car slowed a fraction and their eyes met, sea-green to warm-brown, a smile lingering on both their lips. "I'd be hurt by that, but we all know you only insult my intelligence because you love me."

"Sure," she drawled.

"It's okay to admit that I'm your favorite person, Yan. It's physiologically impossible to resist my charms." His tone was exaggerated and teasing, but there was something in the way he looked at her that made her heart flutter.

Hank's eyes lingered on Abyan like they always did, long enough for her breath to catch as she watched him trail the length of her body for no more than a few seconds. Astaghfirullah. Abyan straightened in her seat abruptly. And the air only returned to her lungs when he turned his attention back to the road, yet a tiny part of her wished he hadn't—Abyan wanted to be suffocated under the weight of his gaze, and she hated herself for it.

She should've known better.

"We have to finish this mission quickly. I'm not missing Asr," she decided to say, still not looking directly at him. Asr and Maghrib were always tricky, since most missions usually fell in the time for either prayer or overlapped between both. Winter was a pain especially as the days were shorter, and she had less time between prayers.

Last year, De Costa looked ready to fight her for asking to sit out four missions in a row because she refused to miss one or the other. Luckily, Abyan was always ready to whip out the religious discrimination clause of the Carlisle Academy handbook, so the squad wasn't penalized for the mission forfeits.

"Relax, we'll get back in time insha'Allah." He sighed. "We wouldn't have had to rush if you didn't take so long accepting the WLDO from De Costa."

"It's not my fault," Abyan argued. "It was like she didn't want me to take it."

"What?"

De Costa had kept trying to dissuade her from accepting the WLDO. It was strange because when Abyan was helping with the welcoming ceremony for the new recruits a few days ago, De Costa complained for hours that there was already a huge backlog of low-level WLDOs the operative squads didn't have time for which were defaulted to the academy. There'd been a huge increase in Nosaru activity worldwide, and she said she needed all hands on deck to clear them out.

Abyan focused her attention back to Hank. "I don't know why, but she kept pushing me to forfeit and accept a random BLCC order instead."

Even though Abyan was confused at the time, she demanded to be allowed to do her assigned mission. It was so rare to get solo missions without their designated operative squad shadowing them, and not to mention, WLDOs were worth double the percentage points of BLCC orders for their overall grades.

There was no way she was letting it slip out of her hands.

Hank's brow creased. "Do you think something's up?"

"I'm not sure, but I wouldn't be surprised if there was," she replied, twisting the gold ring hanging from her neck. "Too many things are changing at Carlisle."

"Agreed," he said, pulling up at a police blockade.

They showed the officers their IDs, which proudly declared they were from Carlisle Academy. All law enforcement knew Carlisle students and operatives were the ones who dealt with all the weird balaayo they came across. Carlisle Enterprises had deep underground ties to every branch of government, and operatives were treated as government agents in all official settings.

She and Hank were told to proceed on foot and silently made their way through the scores of people, police, and cameras, into the cover of the forest.

Abyan counted at least five body bags as they passed and whispered a quick prayer that all the injured pulled through. Although several officers and bystanders watched them as they abandoned their jackets and vaulted over the barriers, Abyan was too focused on the Nosaru lurking in the trees to care.

She pulled out the tracker from her pocket. It was a small, phone-sized device that scanned for electromagnetic radiation—radio waves, more specifically. Many organisms emitted radio waves, but Nosaru produced enough that it could be easily detected by their radars.

Hank covered her back, sword raised, as they waded through the forest, the water-logged soil swallowing their steps. Abyan skimmed the trees as she moved in the direction of the green blob on her radar.

A host.

She soundlessly unsheathed her sword, Gacan Libaax, and crept closer to the blob, only to see five more just like it appear and close in on them. Abyan quickly slipped the tracker into her back pocket. "They're coming straight for us."

"There goes the element of surprise," Hank said just as six men emerged from the greenery, black eyed and teeth bared.

Three went for Hank and the rest went for Abyan. She wasted no time hurling a dagger at one of the men running at Hank, and it struck true, piercing the gap right between his eyes. A small flicker of pride danced in her chest even though it was far from her best shot. Damage to the central nervous system paralyzed hosts, giving you long enough to finish them off properly, and made sure you weren't overrun when engaging multiple hostiles.

"How's that for rusty?" she asked, turning to face the others.

"Lucky shot," Hank's strained voice came from behind her, and not a moment later, one of the men coming for her fell to the ground, a knife protruding from his skull.

Abyan's whole body buzzed, a rush of pure adrenaline

thrumming in her veins. Of the remaining two Nosaru, the dark-haired creature lunged at her while the other blond one hung back and kept his eyes trained on something just over her shoulder. He was trying to ambush Hank. She hurried to finish off the dark-haired host before the other got the chance.

That thing wasn't going anywhere near him.

She sidestepped from the Nosaru's grasp, and he swiveled to face her. Abyan rushed forward, thrusting her blade outward, aiming for the meat of its stomach.

Yet the host managed to dodge the blow just in time, leaping to its side, and hurried toward her before she could retract her arm. The creature swung, but she blocked the blow with her free arm, a grunt escaping her lips at the impact.

Abyan punched him square in the nose and then hit him across the head with the pommel of her saber, giving the host no time to recover, and it staggered back. Just as she stepped toward it, the creature quickly turned on his heel and sprinted for the closest tree, running up its length and flipping himself over her head faster than she could blink. He knocked the sword from her hand and wrapped his arm around her neck, his grip only getting tighter by the second.

Her heart hammered in her chest.

She couldn't reach Gacan Libaax, couldn't even edge it toward herself with her foot. The unmistakable sound of the host's fangs cutting through his gums and elongating sent Abyan's pulse into overdrive. She had only three seconds left until unconsciousness took her, and a couple more before death quickly followed.

She desperately reached for the hidden dagger at her thigh, and the moment her grip on the smooth metal was firm enough, she plunged it deep into his skull.

The host's body crashed to the ground, and she wasted no time diving for her sword and putting the creature down for good.

Abyan swiveled to Hank's direction, thinking her last hostile had to have gone for him. But he was just looking at the two remaining Nosaru, his brows furrowed in confusion. And when Abyan's eyes landed on them, she blinked twice just to make sure she wasn't hallucinating.

"They're trying to kill each other," Abyan whispered, watching as the blond Nosaru launched a bone-splintering punch across his pale, brown-haired enemy's jaw and stabbed him deep in his stomach with one of their stray daggers. A low groan left the injured host's lips as the blond Nosaru twisted the blade, taking his head in both hands and snapping the fallen host's neck.

How is this even happening?

The remaining Nosaru snarled at them once, but before he could attack, Hank flung a knife at his head. The blade lodged itself firmly into his eye socket and the host crashed to the ground, his body slumped across his foe's.

This didn't make any sense.

Nosaru were unique in that, as an endangered and sentient species, they never killed one another. Abyan learned it in her first Nosaru Fundamentals lesson. Their purpose on Earth was to repopulate and, while they did get into the occasional skirmish, killing a fellow member of their species was the worst taboo.

Hank turned to her. "I don't think they were attacking humans on the M1. I think they were fighting each other, and the people just got caught in the middle of it."

Abyan blinked again at the carcasses. "What the hell is going on?"

5

ARTEMIS

CARLISLE ACADEMY WAS MORE MAZE THAN SCHOOL.

The endless corridors and torturous number of stairs made the simple task of finding Dr. Telford's office harder than scaling Scafell Pike in pouring rain. The architect who designed the recruitment building must've really hated them all, Artemis concluded.

Though the school was home to almost 400 students and 150 staff members, having state-of-the-art technology and the finest security systems on the market, the recruitment building didn't have a single elevator.

After going to the wrong end of the building, courtesy of the generous Year 13s, she managed to muster up the courage to ask for directions, Artemis eventually arrived at Dr. Telford's door, sweat-stained and heaving.

She knocked and waited, though her knees were shaky and her backpack was getting heavier with every passing second. Artemis bent over and desperately tried to fill her burning lungs. She'd run at least a mile going back and forth around the school, and hell had no fury like muscles scorned.

She crossed her fingers and silently prayed Dr. Telford wouldn't be too angry with her for being almost half an hour late to their meeting. As she straightened, a thin white woman opened the door. "You must be Artemis."

Her voice was soft and deeper than she expected, and her

auburn locks were firmly tied atop her head. Green eyes and ginger hair—just like Artemis's birth mum. Some people just couldn't wrap their heads around basic genetics and always looked at Artemis weird because her hair changed from auburn to brown with the light while her skin stayed very much brown. The ginger jokes were one of the reasons she had to be homeschooled and still never failed to get under her skin.

"I'm sorry I'm late, Dr. Telford. I got lost on the way here."

Artemis wiped at her brow with the sleeve of her shirt and hoped she didn't look half as disheveled as she thought she did. The mental image of her face all pink-tinged and shiny made her skin crawl. First impressions were the only ones that counted, and so far, she'd flopped every single one.

God, she was such a mess.

"Oh, I can tell." She stepped to the side and gestured for her to enter. "First days are always hectic, but don't worry, you'll adjust quickly."

"I really hope so." Artemis set her bag down and eased herself into a chair.

Books lined every wall—fancy leather ones, too, and a few quotes she recognized as Stephen Hawking's were painted onto the ceiling in beautifully curved calligraphy. The room was a world away from the stale stone walls and dark wood floors of the rest of the school. There was something . . . homely about it, a warmth Artemis couldn't put her finger on.

Dr. Telford handed her a water bottle before taking a seat opposite her, and Artemis's throat was so dry, she almost snatched it straight out of her grasp. "How was your first training session with Ms. Bruno? Have you met any of the older students yet? I know they like to have a bit too much fun with their games on recruits."

Artemis paused with the bottle half raised to her lips, her eyes darting between it and Dr. Telford's concerned eyes. "Training was great," she finally settled on saying. "Ms. Bruno said she saw a lot of potential in me and has high hopes for my future here."

The lies flowed easily from her tongue as she remembered her instructor's real words when they were alone in the simulation. Someone was protecting her, and Artemis wanted to know who it was. She didn't have any connections at the school and had only spoken to Mr. Carlisle once.

Why was someone so willing to keep this door open for her? Artemis had half a mind to check for cameras in her dorm—there was no telling who her mysterious protector was, what they wanted from her, or what lengths they were willing to go to in order to get it.

"That's good to hear." Dr. Telford leaned back in her chair, a small smile resting on her lips. "Did Mr. Carlisle tell you of the tests you are to receive here when you met with him?"

Her heart skipped a beat. She'd been hoping he would see her progress and change his mind about it. Ever since she left the hospital back in Scotland, Artemis had made sure to eat right and get some semblance of normalcy back after the incident.

"He did, but I don't think I need them anymore."

Dr. Telford's brow creased for the briefest moment before she recovered. "We'll do your first one today and see how it goes from there, shall we? If you really have got to a point where they're no longer needed, I'll be able to tell from the results in a few days."

Artemis thought on her words. When her results came back normal, Dr. Telford would see she was right all along. "Okay, then."

She nodded. "Great, I'm glad you're on board."

"Can I ask a question?"

"Ask all the questions you like, Artemis. I'm your mentor here, after all."

"Can't the operatives handle all the missions on their own?" It had been nagging her ever since she set foot in the school. "I'm sure they don't really need us."

Dr. Telford laughed a little. "While the operatives can indeed 'handle' it, we'll always need more because some will inevitably die, retire, or get seriously injured. And do you know why we start recruitment so young?" When Artemis shook her head, she continued, "The human cardiovascular system works at the best level it will ever work at before we hit the age of twenty, so these precious years are the most ideal time for recruits to acclimate to harsh training regimens. Similarly, the brain's processing power peaks at the age of eighteen, so what better time to introduce recruits to vast amounts of new information and stimuli they've never seen before?"

"So, you need us for our good years, and that's it?"

"I wouldn't put it like that at all." Dr. Telford looked personally offended by her words. "Think of it like this: Carlisle Enterprises is fighting a war on behalf of humanity, and we need soldiers who are at their optimum to win it. That means enlisting them when they haven't yet had time to learn any bad habits like laziness and alcoholism. It means giving the administration three years to instil Edward W. Carlisle's original values of synergy, discipline, and integrity, and ample time to separate the wheat from the chaff so that only the strongest candidates move on to become operatives."

Artemis's ears perked up at the founder of Carlisle Enterprises' name. Half of the hour-long welcome assembly for the recruits that morning was dedicated to the eccentric nineteenth-century millionaire, and even she had to admit he was fascinating.

He was plastered all over the school in one way or another. His portrait hung over the school's main entrance, his famous sayings were etched in aurelian on the walls all over campus, and the original company sign of Carlisle and Sons from the late 1800s was framed above the residential building.

"We were told about him this morning," she explained. "They said he lobbied for the first three Napoleonic Wars."

Dr. Telford smiled in approval. "Yes, it was a cover for his mercenaries to fight Nosaru in Eastern Europe largely unnoticed.

That was the first time the Nosaru had ever formed a united force against us and, ultimately, what led Mr. Carlisle to creating the academy to stop it from happening again."

"I guess he's succeeded so far, then," she joked, and Dr. Telford chuckled. Yet once the room quieted, Artemis fiddled with her hands as the question she truly wanted answered shakily assembled itself on her tongue. "How did Mr. Carlisle—the current Mr. Carlisle—know?"

Her smile faltered. "Know what?"

It had burned in the back of her mind for months. Back in the hospital near Ben Nevis, Artemis put the question to Mr. Carlisle many times, and he dodged it at every turn so swiftly she started doubting her own need for answers.

Each of his words were enveloped in an effortless smile, laced with quiet charisma, and admittedly, it was the most honed smoke-and-mirrors tactic she'd ever seen. He had a comeback for everything she said, and none of them ever seemed to answer her directly—always skirting around the question, lightly grazing the matter at hand.

"How did he know Jared and I were on Ben Nevis that day? That we'd been attacked by Nosaru while climbing the north face with our group?" The questions flew from her mouth, thick with confusion, and Artemis still couldn't wrap her head around it. "It's impossible."

"I'm sure he had his reasons for—" Dr. Telford began, but Artemis didn't want to hear any more lies and half-truths.

"Mr. Carlisle and his operatives got there before the ambulances, Dr. Telford." Artemis clenched her fists to hide their trembling. "You can't expect me to believe that was a coincidence."

Who would've thought the day she found out aliens were real, and that everything she thought she knew about them was a lie, would be the day she lost her closest and only friend? Memories of the five Nosaru hosts scaling the mountain beneath them with only their bare hands struck her like a harsh bolt of lightning, merciless and scathing, and the sound of her boyfriend's screams ricocheted in her ears.

You're not there anymore.

You're safe.

She squeezed her eyes shut and repeated it over and over in her head until the noise faded away, and her heart stopped hammering in her chest.

"Jared must have sent them an emergency evacuation request when he first saw the Nosaru coming for you. He was a member of The Sevenfold, one of our best students, and would always be prepared in case of trouble." Dr. Telford's voice became softer as she spoke, and Artemis wanted to believe what she was telling her.

She really did.

But it wasn't the truth.

She shook her head. "He couldn't send any requests because all our electronics were left at base camp by accident."

Artemis knew she should've been angry with him for forgetting. They would've needed something to contact the outside world with if things went awry on the mountain. Mum always said: "Trouble nuh set like rain," and Artemis understood it was better to be over-prepared than under. But she was climbing the tallest mountain in the UK with the miracle of good weather and her loving boyfriend by her side.

There was nothing that could sour her mood that morning.

"He must've still had his phone on him. Otherwise, Mr. Carlisle couldn't have gotten there in time to save you," Dr. Telford assured her. "When you lose someone you love, it's easy to want a person to blame for your loss. Anger is the second stage of grief, and it's perfectly understandable for you to be feeling this way."

Artemis furiously rubbed at her face. "I don't believe you."

She only sighed. "Your feelings are valid, Artemis, but they're also misplaced. Direct all your anger and hate toward the Nosaru who took Jared away from you, not the people trying to help rid them from our planet."

More lies.

Artemis figured she wasn't going to get anywhere with Dr. Telford and composed herself as best she could, casting her mind away from Jared and Ben Nevis. No matter what, she was going to find out exactly what happened on that mountain and what role Carlisle Academy played in all of it. There were too many unanswered questions for her to just let it go.

"You're right," she said, and her mentor's eyes brightened at the victory.

If Mr. Carlisle was hiding anything, Artemis didn't think Dr. Telford would know about it anyway. Although she was a senior staff member, she wasn't a member of The League—the elusive board of Carlisle Enterprises—and from what Artemis had heard, most of Mr. Carlisle's dealings were with his fellow board members. Apparently, one was more likely to catch a unicorn grazing in the front gardens than see him ever set foot in the academy.

"We should get started on your tests now before you have to go for your fourth period class." She stood to retrieve medical equipment from the corner of the room. "We'll do a simple blood test and record your height and weight today. Though it's normal to feel apprehensive and wary in unfamiliar environments, I'm sure your squad will help guide you through everything when you meet them this afternoon."

Artemis asked, "My squad?"

The rest of the recruits told her they only chose their squads at the beginning of their second term. How could they put her in a squad without the rest of her year group? She didn't know anyone yet and hadn't said more than three sentences to anyone besides the receptionist.

"Due to your particular circumstances, it was thought that you would perform better with a group of students who could act as mentors as well as friends to help you adjust in this new environment—the finest students in this school, as a matter of fact."

Her stomach rolled. "Which squad?"

She already knew what Dr. Telford was going to say.

"You are to take Jared's place in The Sevenfold."

6

ABYAN

"Honey, I'm home!" Mason Carlisle swept into The Sevenfold's dorm and threw his luggage on the floor.

Even though Abyan was still covered in mud from their WLDO earlier, she didn't hesitate before leaping into his outstretched arms. His navy shirt and gray jeans would be ruined, but she figured if your dad was a billionaire CEO, two articles of clothing wouldn't matter too much.

"You took your time coming back, didn't you?" she joked, squeezing him as hard as she could. "I always knew you hated us deep down."

"Not to sound dramatic, Yan," came his muffled voice, "but I ran faster than both my uncle's pet cheetahs combined just to see you guys, so I won't stand for this slander."

She released him, realizing their reunion was incomplete. "Where are Hassan and Tolly?"

Their year group had most of the afternoon off, but all Year 14 squads needed to be present for fifth period training, and of course, those idiots had to go and pick the first bloody day of school to be late. The whole squad could've been punished for training tardiness, and there was nothing Abyan could do about it.

Mason shrugged, his purple hair glowing in the dim light of the wet afternoon. "All I know is their flight was delayed in transit. My cab had already left when they landed at Heathrow." He put a cool hand on her cheek, scanning her face. "You look tired, Yan. Have you eaten?"

She replayed the events of the day in her head and realized one thing was missing: lunch. Abyan gulped, acutely aware of Hank standing behind her. Forgetting meals wasn't anything new. She didn't even remember what it was like to have a regular sleep and food schedule anymore.

"You haven't been here five minutes, and you're already worrying about me." She plastered on a smile so big and fake, she could damn near feel Mason inspecting its wonky seams and cheap lining. "We have something important to tell you."

Before Mason could prod her further, Kade's dark pixie-cut materialized between them. Abyan couldn't help but feel grateful for the intrusion—she could never keep up a lie for long when it came to him.

"Thank God you're here, Mason," Kade said, exaggerating the emotion in her voice as he spun her around. "The straights were suffocating me—it was torture."

"I can only imagine your pain, comrade." Mason's features were a perfect picture of manufactured horror, from his widened blue eyes to the way his mouth fell open. He rested a hand on her shoulder. "Thank you for your service."

Hank laughed and put an arm around him. "You do realize me and Yan can hear you, right?"

They did that weird sideways bro hug, and Abyan couldn't help but savor the moment a little. The smiles on her friends' faces, their easy conversation. What she and Hank needed to tell them was going to turn everything on its head.

Some part of her wondered how bad it would really be if she kept it to herself, if she ignored what went down on their WLDO. Maybe it would never happen again. What she saw might've been a fluke.

She could've just been making a big deal out of nothing.

Or maybe she wasn't.

The Sevenfold gathered in Kade's room.

It wasn't the smallest of the seven bedrooms, but with all of them concentrated around her bed, it shrunk by at least a half. Kade and Abyan sat cross-legged on the bed as Hank and Mason pulled up chairs.

Abyan couldn't pinpoint the exact moment this became their war room. Yet whenever they needed to discuss anything serious, they found themselves there, surrounded by sappy rom-com posters, *Les Misérables* fan art, and enough pink to make you nauseous, and she wouldn't have had it any other way.

Abyan's chest twisted when she remembered there was one person who'd never come to another squad meeting. One pair of annoyingly squeaky combat boots they'd never hear again.

They'd moved Jared's favorite leather armchair into Kade's room soon after he passed so they would always have a part of him with them when they were deliberating, and though it had been months, not one member of The Sevenfold could look at it for more than a split second. It just sat there tormenting them, but no one had the strength to throw it out.

"Did you fail your WLDO?" Mason asked.

Abyan couldn't help the scoff that left her lips. "No, it's done."

"It's what happened during the mission you need to know," Hank replied, nodding at Abyan to continue.

Almost simultaneously, the rest of The Sevenfold edged closer to where she sat. She let out a deep breath before speaking. It was the sun setting in the east and the sky turning green at the same time. If any other person had told them what she was about to say, she knew they would've thought it was a lie.

Hell, Abyan wouldn't have believed it either.

"We took a WLDO for a Nosaru attack on the M1," she started, recounting what happened during the mission. "But the last two didn't fight us—they turned on each other instead."

Abyan still couldn't make sense of why they would do such a thing, and when she glanced around at her squad, all their expressions mirrored her own.

Mason shook his head. "Nosaru fight all the time, though. They were probably just annoyed one of them messed up and led you right to them."

"They weren't just fighting. They were trying to kill each other."

"Impossible."

Abyan sighed. "We saw it with our own eyes. One of the hosts snapped the other one's neck and then tried to come for us. There were six of them originally, and Hank thinks they were fighting in the forest and accidentally caused the car crash."

It took a moment, but Kade broke the silence that had swept over the room. "This doesn't make any sense."

"That was my first reaction, too."

"So, the humans were just collateral damage?" she asked.

"Yeah, and what we can't figure out is why they were trying to kill each other in the first place," Hank said, looking directly at Abyan.

It was innocent enough, but there was always an undercurrent to their shared gazes—one that hummed to the touch and crackled with enough energy to send a shot of electricity up her spine. She tore her eyes from his before any of the others noticed and used it as their joke fodder for the rest of the year.

Kade's eyes lit up. "Were they first gens?"

"No, third or fourth."

Ora, Soros, and Aefa—the three Alpha Nosaru who first came to Earth—were pregnant, and their offspring became known as the first generation. But soon after the birth of the second generation in 1805 the third original, Aefa, was killed by Edward W. Carlisle, and all her progeny died with her. The other surviving second gens then bred in the subsequent years, and there were now four waves of Nosaru infecting the planet.

Though the only definitive way of knowing which wave a Nosaru was from was through checking their genome, Carlisle operatives were trained to make educated guesses using speed, strength, and other behavioral indicators. Those in the forest were weaker, less disciplined, and easier to beat than spawn from earlier generations.

Kade raked a hand through her hair in frustration. "Older Nosaru were making them kill each other for some reason."

"We need to figure out what's happening here." Abyan cracked her knuckles, her heartbeat far too fast for her liking. Something was changing. She could feel it in her bones, and she didn't like it one bit.

"Do you think we should tell someone?" Mason asked.

"No way." She'd thought about it, but she'd never put her team at risk. "We don't know what we saw."

Abyan didn't want any problems from higher-ups. If it was something above her rank she wasn't supposed to see, she'd prefer no one ever finding out she knew in the first place. It was less trouble that way. Interrogations and depositions would waste her time when she needed to be focused on graduating.

"Then we'll keep an eye out on our next WLDO," he said. "If it happens again, we'll know what you saw wasn't a onetime thing—just pray it isn't a bloody Peeping Tom."

Abyan's heart almost stopped in her chest at the thought. Peeping Toms were bullshit. There was no need for some of the already rare solo BLCC orders and WLDOs to be secretly observed by operative squads and reported back to the school, but Carlisle was extra like that.

A third, unofficial category of missions.

"Okay."

Hank cut in, frustration etched into his perfect features. "We can't just wait around to be assigned a solo operation. It could take months."

Some part of Abyan agreed with him. Ninety-five percent of academy missions were supervised by shadows, 3 percent were

Peeping Toms, and the remaining 2 percent were solo missions. Just 2 percent.

The Sevenfold still hadn't been told who their shadows were going to be for the rest of the year, and they definitely didn't need nosy operatives finding out what they saw. It was risky gambling everything on the slim chance of getting a solo mission when they'd already received one earlier in the day, but there weren't many other viable options.

Mason spoke first. "Should I set up a Triumvirate meeting?"

"Absolutely not." Abyan stared at him in disbelief, everything in her wide eyes questioning whether he'd lost his damn mind.

It was too much and too soon.

The other two squads that made up the academy's top three, known as the Triumvirate since decades before Abyan was born, were hawks and would no doubt jump at the chance to finally beat The Sevenfold at something.

"How about we just wait it out for a few more weeks?" Kade's voice flowed over them like a cooling stream. "We don't know what missions De Costa will give us, and who knows? We might even get lucky."

The room seemed to calm at that, as if all her friends released a collective breath. Abyan thought about it, glancing around the room and looking at each of them in turn for their verdicts, though she lingered on Hank for a heartbeat longer than the others.

Just trust me.

The second he gave her a nod of agreement, she spoke. "We'll wait."

———————+———————

The top five squads in Year 14 trained separately from everyone else.

They were assembled in one of the Year 14 training rooms, devoid of any equipment—just rubber flooring and bulletproof two-way glass. Sixteen points separated The Sevenfold from their closest competitors, The Trojans, on the group leaderboard, followed by The Renegades two points later.

They all had a different instructor from the other twenty-five squads in their year. Sir Marland stood well over six feet, his brown hair was short, his full beard close-cropped, and the glare he was giving Abyan and her partially present squad was enough to make her want to shed her own skin and give it to someone else to wear.

They'd been standing there for a good five minutes, and he had yet to say a word. The only sign of emotion coming from him was the sea of red creeping up from the base of his neck. Veins were protruding from places Abyan didn't know veins could protrude from, and it took a conscious effort to keep her shoulders square and her hands still at her sides.

The Trojans were laughing under their breath at them, but they were stupid to think Sir Marland wouldn't come for their heads, too. His anger was like a ballistic missile, and if The Sevenfold was the intended target, everyone else in the room was in the blast radius, too.

No one was escaping without a scratch.

Shaydaanka iska naar. Abyan released a silent breath. *He won't hold it against us.* How were they supposed to control flights, for God's sake? She was so going to kill Tolly and Hassan whenever they decided to grace them all with their presence.

Hank stood eerily still while Kade and Mason were getting restless, subconsciously switching their weight from foot to foot and rolling their shoulders so many times Abyan was getting fidgety herself.

Hank looked to her and mouthed, "We're so screwed."

"Might as well get our shahadas out of the way now, I guess," Abyan whispered back.

She'd been so careful about it, timing the whisper to be in tune with the whoosh of the air-conditioning, so Sir Marland wouldn't hear it and finally explode on them. But Hank had to ruin it all with his snort.

The sound was a bass drum at a funeral, a deafening scream in a midnight cemetery, shattering the taut silence holding the room hostage. Her eyes bulged at the noise, and Hank's body froze over. Sir Marland zeroed in on them, and she stood stock-still, afraid to even breathe too loudly.

Now, they were most definitely screwed.

"Is something funny, King?" Sir Marland's thick Mancunian accent echoed through the room, and Abyan nearly jumped out of her skin. Her foot was halfway to stepping in front of Hank instinctively before her mind stopped it.

He cleared his throat, his cheeks reddening. "No, sir."

"I'll tell you what's funny," Sir Marland walked right up to where the four members of The Sevenfold stood, close enough for the scent of his aftershave to burn Abyan's nose, "the fact that half your squad thinks they can skip my class!"

His voice rose with every word, and she forced herself not to flinch.

"You see, I was going to go easy on you all, but since some of you think this is a joke, I'll go with plan B." He pulled out his phone and pushed a few buttons, taking a seat in the corner of the room.

After a few agonizing minutes of waiting, the door opened and several people walked in. They assembled in front of them in five groups of varying sizes. Adult squads. Her eyes widened. Operatives. They'd already graduated from Carlisle and now worked for the organization out in the field. Abyan clocked Sir Marland's plan straightaway: He was going to make them fight each other, squad versus squad. The only problem was that the smallest adult squad had six people, and The Sevenfold currently had four.

"You'll each be fighting one of these operative teams," Sir Marland announced, moving to the center of the room. "Four points to the squad who can beat the operatives. If no one manages to win, two points will be given to the squad that lasts the longest, and all the others will be docked two points for being useless disappointments."

His gaze landed on Abyan. "The Fourfold will go first and face Squad 2528."

The rest of the adult squads moved to the side and left the six members of Squad 2528 in the red circle right in the middle of everyone.

Abyan figured there was no point asking Sir Marland to get two of them to sit the fight out. He wanted them to suffer. She gave the squad a once-over: six men, all taller than she was, varying builds. Abyan walked to the ring with a slight limp she tried to hide, barely noticeable to anyone who wasn't paying close attention.

It was fake, but the other squad didn't know that. They were going to aim for any weak spots they saw. At least this way she could control the outcome. She stood in front of the biggest one; the man towered over her and was built like a bloody juggernaut. *Audhubillah, muxuu cuna?* Abyan went into fighting stance, one foot forward and both fists raised.

Sir Marland's whistle blew, and all hell broke loose.

Her opponent went for her left side where her fake injury was, but Abyan was expecting it and shifted all her weight to her right leg, rotating on the ball of her foot, and landed a bone-splintering right hook to his jaw.

He staggered back for a moment, and Abyan's eyes darted to her teammates. Mason and Hank were fending off four of the men as a coordinated unit, while Kade was fighting the last member of Squad 2528, matching him blow for blow.

Kade's opponent wasn't keeping an eye on her, so Abyan kicked the back of his knee, and the second he buckled, no longer having the security of his left leg, Kade hit him across the jaw with the back of her foot in a high axe kick.

Before she could check if Kade's hostile was fully down, Abyan's legs were swept out from under her. A grunt escaped her lips as her body connected with the ground, but Abyan didn't feel the impact. Her muscles neither ached nor shook.

She flipped herself over her head before her opponent could angle himself for another attack, landing on her feet. Energy coursed in her veins as the guy rushed forward for an elbow strike. Abyan blocked it with her forearm and punched him across the face with her free hand. He stumbled back a few steps, ugly red welts already forming on his cheeks.

The poor guy wouldn't have a good side for a while.

Kade capitalized on his lapse and aimed a palm-heel strike straight at his nose, and the deafening crunch was enough to tell everyone in the room she'd struck true. Still, Abyan closed the gap between them and bounced on her back foot, spun her body around, and brought her heel down on the guy's head.

Something cracked, and she really hoped it wasn't anything important.

The man crashed to the ground, and she and Kade promptly went to help Mason and Hank, who only had two hostiles left. One of the men had Hank in a headlock, so Abyan punched him square in the kidney, and his grip must've loosened enough because the next thing she knew, the guy was on the ground and Hank was beating him senseless.

When it was clear the man wasn't getting up, she held a hand out to her friend, trying not to focus on the bright red line around his throat. The rest of her squad soon joined them, since Kade and Mason were done with the last member of Squad 2528.

The Sevenfold faced Sir Marland, red-faced and panting, and he looked at them like they'd just pulled out his guts and wore them as jewelry. The other adult squads had the same look of shock and horror, but Abyan didn't care.

They'd won fair and square.

"Well, it looks like the Fourfold have won," Sir Marland said, his voice hollower than before. "While you may have gained four points, you've also been docked two for each missing squad member, resulting in a net gain of zero points."

Abyan's jaw dropped. "That's bullshit and you know it."

"Give me any more back talk, Guled, and I'll dock four more."

The warning in his eyes was enough to make any protest on her tongue dissolve in an instant. This was her last year at Carlisle. Abyan was going to get her black belt and graduate come hell or high water, and if she had to bury both her pride and dignity to achieve her goals, then so be it.

She shut her mouth and went to the corner of the room with her squad, quietly seething. If every training session with Sir Marland was going to be like this, it would take nothing short of a miracle for them to do well.

The corner of Sir Marland's mouth twitched, and Abyan knew nothing good would follow. "I suppose I should've mentioned this earlier, Fourfold, but meet the operatives who will be shadowing you for the rest of the year."

Her stomach lurched as she followed the very tip of his index finger to the squad they'd just defeated. *Bloody hell.* The sheer force of the glowers each member of their shadow squad was sending The Sevenfold was enough to tell Abyan exactly how the rest of the year would go.

Operative squads all had a certain mean streak when it came to shadowing students, but this was different. They'd bruised Squad 2528's egos. Now their shadows were going to nitpick every single mistake The Sevenfold made, give them the worst combat reports, and try their best to make this year as difficult as possible.

Abyan clenched her hands into fists so tight her knuckles paled, the magnitude of the odds stacked up against her squad dawning on her fast.

The Sevenfold would have to work ten times harder to stay on top.

7

ARTEMIS

Artemis stared at the door to The Sevenfold's private floor of the residential building. According to Dr. Telford, all her things had been moved from the recruit dormitories, but she already missed her tiny first-year room, ugly magnolia wallpaper and all. It was small and safe, and she would've gladly stayed there all year.

Although Artemis had a half day along with the rest of her year group and could've gone to her new room hours earlier, the same fear that stopped her before was still very much coursing through her veins, and she stood frozen at the door like an ice sculpture. Every time her hand touched the handle, she retracted it a second later as if the brass burned to the touch.

Her first and only encounter with The Sevenfold kept replaying in her head. Abyan's words. Hank's laughter. Kade's pity. And now Artemis was going to be in their squad taking Jared's place—a mismatched piece forced into the only empty spot in their puzzle.

They were going to hate her.

She drew in a long breath and let it out slowly, reaching out with a trembling hand. "C'mon Jay, you can do this."

Her whole body jerked like she'd been shot with a hundred-thousand-watt Taser at the ding of the elevator behind her. The steel doors slid open silently, and Kade strolled out with three large bags in her hands. She was just as beautiful as Artemis remembered from training earlier, and her brown eyes widened a fraction as she took Artemis in.

That's not a good sign.

"You're our new recruit?" she asked, setting the bags down. Artemis nodded, not trusting her voice yet, and a thousand different emotions crossed Kade's face before she found her words again. "Do you want the truth or a lie?"

Artemis braced herself, fashioning her hands into tight fists and wrapping herself in armor strong enough that nothing Kade could potentially say would cut through. "The truth, please."

"No one in the squad wanted a new member, let alone a recruit," she explained, eyes sympathetic. "Everything will get a whole lot worse for you here before it starts to get better."

Artemis's stomach dropped at that. "I don't understand why they'd be angry at me of all people for this. I didn't ask for any of it."

"I know," she said. "Mason and I will try to get the others to understand, but it's one of those things that need time, you know?"

Great, just great.

Artemis's shoulders slumped as she deflated under the weight of Kade's words and her own dread. Her voice sounded lifeless. "Thanks for letting me know anyway."

"Hey, I didn't get your name, recruit." She stuck out a hand. Artemis knew an olive branch when she saw one and took it without a second's hesitation. "Asako Nakamura, but my friends call me Kade."

"I—I'm Artemis," she replied, trying not to fixate on how soft Kade's hand was. She'd been expecting calluses from all the training or scars from fighting the Nosaru, yet her skin was like silk in her grasp and a tiny part of Artemis missed her touch the moment they broke away.

"Before you ask," Kade said, picking up two of her forgotten shopping bags from the floor. "I'm from L.A, my parents are Japanese, and no, I didn't transfer from the Tokyo branch."

"People really think you came from the Tokyo branch even with your accent?" Artemis asked. It was very clearly American, and although Carlisle Enterprises had two academies on each continent, Tokyo would've been the last place on Artemis's list of guesses.

Kade scoffed, "Didn't you know all Asians have to come from either the Tokyo or Ankara branch? It's just impossible for us to be from anywhere else. The world would literally spontaneously combust."

"I would say I can't believe it, but . . ." she trailed off with a shrug. She'd had her fair share of encounters with people demanding where she was from and "London" not being a good enough answer.

"Yeah." Kade leaned forward and put her finger into a small hole in the wall Artemis hadn't noticed, lifting it up to reveal a keypad. "Sorry you had to wait so long. Training with Sir Marland was a nightmare, so I decided to buy some comfort food for the squad."

"It's okay. I didn't mind." She decided not to tell her that she hadn't known the door was still locked and was too scared to turn the handle, opting to pick up the remaining bag and help her out instead.

"The code is 2-4-6-0-1," Kade told her, as she punched in the numbers. "It's from my favorite musical: *Les Misérables*."

Artemis didn't know much about musicals and only shrugged as they entered The Sevenfold's headquarters. She held her breath as Kade led her through the living room and into the kitchen.

Once they set the plastic bags down, Kade turned to her. "Do you want to help set the food up after I give you the grand tour?"

"Sure."

Artemis looked around the kitchen and took in the brown cabinets, two microwaves, and all the other common things strewn about the countertops. It was painfully ordinary, she concluded. Though she wasn't expecting laser beams to be mounted on the walls or anything, this small degree of normalcy was more than a little comforting.

"Well, you've seen the kitchen and living room, that only leaves the bedrooms." Kade grinned, flashing her perfect teeth, and heat engulfed Artemis's cheeks. *Stop it.* She flooded her brain with memories of Jared, how she used to run her fingers through his long hair, his muscled arms around her shoulders, and that smile that catapulted her to the stars.

Kade led the way, her rough combat boots squeaking on the tiled floor. She took her to a corridor with seven doors, three on one side and four on the other, and stopped before the first door on the right. Artemis's heart pounded in her chest. This was it. Where she'd be staying for the best part of three years.

"This is your room." While Kade tried to act cheerful when she said it, she heard the unspoken words that followed. Jared's room. Artemis would be sleeping in her dead boyfriend's bedroom, and there was no way to get out of it. "Hank and Tolly are your neighbors, and on the other side are Yan's, Hassan's, and Mason's rooms—in that order—and mine is at the end of the corridor."

Her chest ached at the thought of stepping inside Jared's room and seeing it empty of everything that marked it as his, all traces of him scrubbed away. She wondered if it would remind her of him, if the walls were still painted his favorite shade of green like he once told her, and if the mattress still clung to his warm, woodsy scent.

"I don't want to go inside yet," Artemis quickly said, almost tripping over her words.

"That's cool. It's your room, go inside whenever."

A lump formed in her throat as they shared a long look.

Though Artemis didn't say it, she hoped Kade saw the gratitude in her eyes. Jared's parents hated her for convincing him to climb Ben Nevis and getting him killed. She wasn't even allowed to attend his funeral and didn't know if she was ready to be living in his room.

She already hated herself enough.

Kade's voice cut through her thoughts. "Can I ask why you don't want to go in?"

Her brow creased. *He didn't tell them.* "I'm his—I *was* his girlfriend for three months last year."

"Really?" Kade's voice trailed off. "Did he know you were his girlfriend?"

"What's that supposed to mean?"

"A lot of girls thought they were something more to him, too." She gave her a sympathetic smile, though there was a touch of suspicion in her face. "He was, and I say this with so much love, a complete asshole."

Jared never spoke about his other life.

He'd told her he was an art student at UCL and hardly ever shared anything with her that she didn't have to coax from him. It was like pulling teeth. Artemis knew it was weird, but he was the first boy who'd ever shown any genuine interest in her, so she convinced herself it was because he had trust issues.

She didn't have it in her to be angry at him when Mr. Carlisle told her the truth—it was hard to be annoyed with a dead person. He probably had his reasons, she figured; maybe he was just waiting for the right time to tell her he was also a full-time alien hunter.

It wasn't your standard icebreaker.

Artemis wanted to ask her more questions about him. The boy she knew was sweet and held doors open for her all the time—he was the perfect gentleman in every sense of the term. Nothing even resembling an arsehole. But Kade's eyes were getting sadder by the second, and she had a feeling that even if Kade smiled her highest kilowatt grin, the joy wouldn't move past her lips.

As they made their way to the kitchen to get started on the food, Artemis tried to change the subject. "You said your surname was Nakamura, as in Hanshiro Nakamura?"

"So, my dad's a member of The League." She shrugged like it

was the most normal thing in the world to have a parent sitting on the board of a multibillion-pound empire like Carlisle Enterprises. "If you treat me extra nice because of it like everyone else, I'll spit in your food when you're not looking and enjoy watching you eat it."

Artemis laughed. "That's probably the most disgusting thing anyone has ever said to me."

"Why thank you, Artemis. I do try." She flicked nonexistent hair from her shoulder and retrieved some bowls from the cupboard while Artemis began grouping the food into categories: chocolates, crisps, biscuits, and fizzy drinks, opening them all as she went. Kade put all the bowls and cups in a line, and they both poured the junk foods into them.

"We make a good team, recruit." She put a hand on her hip, her eyes glinting with something that made Artemis's heart race.

She cleared her throat and cursed her flaming cheeks. "I think so, too."

"God, you're adorable." Kade sighed just as her phone buzzed. "Tell me if you're gay now, so I don't get my hopes up. Straight-girl crushes are torture, and I'm not wearing my masochist underwear today."

"I'm bisexual," she spluttered, after taking a moment to make sure she heard her correctly.

Kade grinned like a Cheshire cat. "Thank God, I couldn't deal with another straight person in the squad."

"Another straight person?"

"I'm pansexual, Mason's bi, but he's only here for boys and nonbinary people, Tolly's asexual, Hassan is . . . complicated, and—"

"So, everyone here's gay?"

Maybe she'd like being part of The Sevenfold, after all.

"No, we have Hank and Abyan." She made her way to the door, speaking over her shoulder. "They're our token straights, but you didn't hear that from me."

"Where are you going?" She hadn't known her for very long, but the longer Artemis spent talking to her, the more relaxed she felt about being there. The others might not be so bad after they got over the initial animosity and awkwardness. Maybe Dr. Telford was right, and she could actually do it—be a part of The Sevenfold.

Maybe Kade even wanted to be her friend.

"Mason, Hassan, and Tolly are at the door with a ton of bags, so I have to let them in."

"Mr. Carlisle's son?"

He'd told her he had a son called Mason enrolled at the school when she was in the hospital, though he didn't mention anything about him being in The Sevenfold. Then again, it made sense the CEO's son was in the best squad in the school.

Nepotism and all that.

"Don't worry, he's not what you think he is." Kade laughed, her hand resting on the door handle. "You'll like him. Everyone does."

Artemis didn't know what to do with her hands, so she clasped them together, trying not to think of the sweat gathering in her palms. She didn't have to wait long before three boys came barreling into the room, each of them with several bags tucked under their arms and September rain soaking their clothes.

"Did you miss me?" one of them said, lifting Kade clean off the floor. He was a tall, lightly muscled Black boy, and he held some contraption in his hand Artemis couldn't make sense of.

"You know I did, Tolly." Kade squeezed him once more and took the metal thing from him as she broke away. "What the hell is this?"

"It was my wireless speaker," the other boy said, not looking up from the Rubik's Cube he was solving at lightning speed. She guessed he was Hassan, and he had sun-kissed tawny skin and midnight hair. "It was acting up, and instead of fixing it like I asked him to, he decided it needed a damn autopsy."

Tolly only shrugged. "The wiring was fundamentally flawed."

Artemis drowned out the conversation, not looking away from the third boy who'd come in with them. Though his hair was bright purple, not copper-dotted brown like his father's, the resemblance between Mr. Carlisle and his son Mason was still startling. They had the same straight nose, electric blue eyes, and full lips. It didn't take much to guess that he probably had people throwing themselves at him from every direction.

She watched them all hug and fawn over each other, excitedly talking of things that happened in days past. The newcomers didn't notice she was standing not six feet from where they were huddled.

It's like I'm invisible to them.

There was a pang in Artemis's chest, and it tore through her body; she wanted to be small—tinier than a droplet of rain—and let the wind billowing in through the open window carry her far away.

The door to The Sevenfold's rooms opened again, and Hank and Abyan walked in. Artemis immediately straightened, smoothing out the nonexistent creases in her shirt, though neither person paid her any mind. Hank wiped rain from his tanned brow, holding a white pharmacy bag in his hand.

"What did the doctor say?" Mason asked as they all embraced.

Hank rolled his eyes. "It was nothing. He just gave me some painkillers."

The Sevenfold glossed over Artemis like she was a boring piece of furniture. Completely irrelevant. Not even worth a second's acknowledgment. Her eyes burned at the realization. She didn't know what to do; she couldn't force people to like her.

Hassan glanced up from his Rubik's Cube, his dark gaze finally landing on Artemis and then Kade. "Isn't it a little too early for a booty call, Kadrian?"

Oh my God.

"She's not a booty call, dumbass," Kade snapped, gesturing to where she stood. "Her name is Artemis, and she's our recruit."

"As in *the* recruit?" Tolly asked, his lip curling in disgust. "You should quit while you're ahead, recruit. You can't just take Jared's place and expect us all to welcome you with open arms."

Artemis's throat was suddenly dry.

Yet she couldn't say anything with every member of The Sevenfold bar Kade looking at her with a mixture of hatred, morbid fascination, and curiosity. She wanted to run away. To get on a train straight back to Birmingham and forget about Carlisle Academy and the Nosaru, but she couldn't.

Jared.

Artemis had to stick it out.

"He's right," Abyan said, giving her another once-over. "I've seen you fight. There's no way you'll be able to keep up with us."

Hank agreed, "We won't stay in first place for long with her on the team."

"She didn't choose to be here, remember?" Kade said. "And it might be rocky in the beginning, but we'll get through it. All Artemis needs is some extra training."

Artemis's heart stopped. "With who?"

The only members of the squad who weren't looking at her funny were Mason and Kade, so it didn't leave many options. Artemis would've rather eaten a bowl of rice grain by grain than be stuck with any of the others alone. They'd just criticize her every mistake or make snide comments—she could already hear their phantom snark biting her ears—and she didn't know how much of that she could take.

Kade grinned with all the light of the sun. "You'll be training with all of us."

8

ABYAN

DE COSTA WAS TAKING THE MICK.

Abyan tapped her phone furiously, so focused on making sure her strongly worded email was just the right balance between passive-aggressive and polite that she didn't notice the hush that fell over the Year 14 dining hall as she entered. Hassan grumbled under his breath at her side, but she only scoffed.

Idiots.

You'd think none of them had ever seen a recruit before with the way they were acting. She ignored the whispers and led Artemis to The Sevenfold's usual table at the back, while Hassan went to get their food.

Their tuition only covered breakfast and lunch, so they had to pay for dinner and whatever else themselves, which wouldn't have been so bad if a single muffin from the cafeteria didn't cost three pounds.

Abyan wasn't like all the rich kids that filled Carlisle to the brim. Her family was working class—Abtiyo Ayaanle was a cab driver and her cousins lived in a three-bedroom council house. Though she qualified for free school meals, under the scrutiny of people whose families owned castles and had three different suffixes after their last names, her little red ticket all but burned to the touch.

When The Sevenfold was first formed, the others would always ask why she'd never buy anything, and Abyan always said she wasn't hungry even when her stomach was grumbling loud enough to hear from the other side of the hall.

She lost fifteen pounds in the first two weeks.

It was just so much harder to sneak off with her ticket when she was forced to be around them all the time. One day, Hassan came to the table and set one plate of spaghetti Bolognese in front of him and the other in front of her without a word.

Abyan tried to thank him afterward, when they were alone, offering him her ticket to repay the debt, but he wasn't having any of it. It seemed so stupid now that she thought about it. Why would a millionaire need a free meal ticket?

She turned her attention back to the recruit. Artemis had her head on the table, and green bruises from training were already forming on her arms. She was exhausted and Abyan couldn't blame her, as Ms. Bruno was a harsh instructor on good days and that afternoon was far from good. Maybe she'd woken up with the same migraine as Abyan. It felt like her head had been split clean in two when she woke up, and although she'd taken two ibuprofens every four hours, she had yet to feel a change.

Her phone screen started to blur.

When Abyan could no longer see her six-paragraph-long email, she set the phone on the table. She gently nudged the recruit with a finger, making sure she was fast asleep, and then cupped her mouth lightly with both hands before beginning to read. Surah Al-Fatihah seven times followed by Ayatul Kursi.

After each recitation, she wiped her palms over her head and hoped Allah would succeed where the ibuprofen hadn't; she'd booked the gym for the whole squad that night and wasn't going to let a migraine ruin her plans. She didn't fight off five other squads in the booking office just to be sabotaged by her own body chemistry.

Hassan set the food on the table and waited for her to finish Ayatul Kursi before speaking. "Are you okay, Yan?"

"It's just a headache."

"Yeah, only your fourth migraine this week." He looked pointedly at her. "You need to get it checked out."

"Stop worrying about me, Hassan. The ibuprofen's already kicked in, so there's no need for any doctors," she lied effortlessly and showed him her phone, though she couldn't shake the nagging feeling in the back of her head that told her this wasn't going to be her last migraine either. "De Costa needs to stop trying to make us do missions at five, I'm not missing Maghrib for anything."

"Sounds like Sunni problems to me." He slurped his Capri Sun, a teasing gleam in his brown eyes. "Can't relate."

Abyan tried to stop the smile creeping across her face and hurled a saltshaker at him. "Dickhead."

He easily dodged it, speaking with a forkful of pad thai in his mouth. "Violence isn't the answer to your disagreements, you know. You should debate people in the marketplace of ideas."

"That's a bit rich coming from you, wouldn't you say?" Hassan had a certain reputation at Carlisle, and most people would've rather sat in a bath full of hungry piranhas than cross paths with him on a bad day.

He shrugged. "Sometimes the marketplace of ideas is someone's face, and the debate is an uppercut."

"You're ridiculous." She sighed and lightly shook the recruit awake—her food was getting cold. Artemis mumbled something distantly related to a thanks before digging in, her eyelids still heavy with sleep. If she thought these first few days at Carlisle were bad enough, it was only going to get worse.

As she took in the recruit's exhausted form, Abyan almost felt a little sorry for her. She didn't deserve the frosty welcome she received. Yet the squad neither trusted nor really liked Artemis because she was a living, breathing reminder of what they'd all lost: Jared.

And their consolation for losing a member of their family? His secret *girlfriend*: awkward, unremarkable in every way, and utterly useless. A pale shadow of the brother they once had, and an ever-present, painful reminder of his absence. They all felt it to a degree, though some of them could hide it better than others.

"Artemis, you said you met Jared three months before he died?" Abyan asked, raising her fork to her mouth. She'd been bursting with questions ever since Kade told her the recruit was Jared's girlfriend. "How exactly did you guys meet?"

Artemis sobered immediately. "He was buying coffee in Starbucks and accidentally knocked into me. I dropped my drink, so he offered to buy me a new one, so we started talking from there."

That didn't make any sense.

"Jared does—" She stopped to correct herself. "Jared didn't drink coffee. He went as far as banning us all from bringing it into the dorm because he said the smell made him nauseous."

The recruit blinked. "He usually had a cup of coffee whenever I saw him."

Hassan leaned forward, skeptical. "Carrying a cup of coffee is different, though. Did you ever see him drink it?"

Her brows furrowed as she thought, while Abyan and Hassan shared a look. "I don't know."

Although Abyan opened her mouth to probe the recruit further, she paused at Hassan's hushed voice. "Don't turn around, but Steph's coming right for us."

"Who's Steph?" Artemis asked.

She sighed. "The leader of The Renegades."

"The most man-hating lesbian you'll ever meet in your life," Hassan said at the same time.

"She prefers to be called a committed misandrist."

Stephanie Marshall was the daughter of the biggest non-League shareholder of Carlisle Enterprises, and you either loved her or you hated her. There was no in-between. Abyan waited for the thump of her boots to reach their table. Steph's skin was a couple shades darker than her own, and she had an Afro wide enough to blot out the sun and so radiant it could take its place.

Abyan offered her a smile. They'd been close friends once, after all. "What do you need?"

"Why do you always assume I want something?" She pretended to act insulted, but at Abyan's pointed look, she caved. "Okay, okay. My squad has Recruit's Flu, and we can't do our solo BLCC order tomorrow morning—"

"No way," Hassan cut in, his dark eyes narrowing. "We're not using up our only trade for them."

Yet Steph acted like he wasn't sitting across from them—like he didn't even exist—and never looked away from her. "You'll be in and out in half an hour tops, and we'd be happy to take any mission you want in exchange, no questions asked. Please, Yan, you know I'd do the same for you."

Squads weren't allowed to choose what missions they were assigned, and forfeits for any reason incurred penalties of varying severity. But Year 14 was special in that the school gave each squad a single trade for the whole year, a mission for a mission.

No conditions, no penalties.

Abyan mulled it over in her head. Hank was still trying to convince their squad they needed to call a Triumvirate meeting with the other two squads in the top three: The Trojans and The Renegades.

But if they took this mission, The Renegades would owe them if it ever came to a Triumvirate meeting. And The Sevenfold might be able to confirm the weird Nosaru behavior using this BLCC order.

It was perfect.

"You owe me," Abyan settled on saying. She tried not to look at Hassan or the recruit. Was it so bad to want to do something nice—and mutually beneficial—for an old friend? The Renegades sure as hell didn't want the 5 percent grade and 7-point leaderboard penalty of a forfeited mission, and The Sevenfold needed an easy win.

Steph pulled her in for a hug. "Thank you, Yan. I mean it."

This was exactly what they'd been waiting for.

———+———

The squad wasn't happy about her decision at first.

Abyan didn't know whether her persuasive skills had drastically improved since Year 13 or common sense finally prevailed over their anger, but when she put it to a vote, Mason, Tolly, and Hank sided with her while Kade and Hassan still disagreed. She didn't bother asking the recruit—it wasn't like Artemis knew enough to have a useful opinion anyway. It didn't matter, though, because while Abyan had hoped everyone would come around eventually, she had the majority necessary to formally accept the BLCC order.

The details were sent over not a minute after their acceptance— the target of the BLCC order was a first-gen Nosaru, and the host's human name was Matteo Valente: a few months shy of nineteen, six foot two, with dark hair and eyes. It was a three-person mission, which wouldn't have been a problem if the three people De Costa picked weren't Abyan, Kade, and Hassan—the only two members of the squad who didn't want this mission.

Evidently, the universe hated her.

The three of them had to jump on the Central Line, with trench coats covering the daggers and tranq guns strapped to their bodies. Abyan only thanked Allah that it wasn't a WLDO. Swords were hard enough to hide in public, and it didn't take any mental strain to imagine all the panicked phone calls the transport police would've been getting of the crazy sword-wielding Muslim loose on the underground.

"We shouldn't even be here," Hassan muttered, glaring at Abyan as they came upon Mile End Place.

They were the first words he'd said to her all day.

She bit back the snarky reply itching its way up her throat and decided to go for the franker approach. "Well, it's too late to back out now."

With Sir Marland still breathing down their necks in training, docking points left and right and being so much harder on The Sevenfold than The Renegades or The Trojans, they couldn't afford a mission forfeiture penalty.

Her friends would see she was doing this for all their sakes soon enough.

Mile End Place was an alleyway in the ass end of East London. It led into a bunch of old cottages Abyan guessed were nineteenth century, surrounded by three cemeteries.

Matteo Valente was supposedly hiding in number 26.

Shivers wracked her body as Abyan undid her coat and slipped it off, the icy morning wind tearing through all four of her shirts. She did a quick check of her weapons, counting all twelve of her daggers and flipping the safety off both her tranqs. The darts contained a tranquilizer specially synthesized by Carlisle Enterprises five times the strength of ketamine—it was the only known sedative successful on hosts.

"So, what's the plan?" Kade asked.

It was simple: Capture Matteo and bring him back to Carlisle in one piece. Nothing they hadn't done a hundred times before. Normally Abyan would go over the step-by-step plan for a mission until they all knew every detail like the backs of their hands, but this BLCC order was on short notice, and it was hard to go over anything with people who refused to talk to you. She glanced at the radar on her wrist, her heartbeat slow and rhythmic, and released a breath at the single blob on the screen.

"The front window's already open so you and Hassan go that way. I'll take the back door and make sure he doesn't escape."

They nodded at each other once before splitting up.

Abyan threw her jacket into nearby bushes and crept to the back of the house. The garden was overrun by weeds, gangly and tall, and stinging nettles covered the fences. She stepped around the rusty bikes and wheelbarrows, careful not to disturb anything that might alert the host to her presence, and knelt at the back door.

She slipped a pin from her pocket, but her hand froze in midair, hanging in the space in front of the lock, at the sound of voices. She raised her head a fraction before ducking back down and saw Matteo with another man she didn't recognize. It took her a second to realize why she could only barely understand what they were saying: They were speaking in the Nosaru tongue.

Still, she pressed her ear to the rotting wooden door and strained to catch their words. She could hear a commotion coming from the front of the house. Kade and Hassan. Yet if Matteo was with Abyan, who were they fighting? She glanced down at her radar and saw several massive green circles on the other side of the building. An ambush. Abyan's heart pounded, her mind racing to figure out how she could've gotten it so wrong.

The radar couldn't distinguish between two Nosaru close in space—they'd just show up as a singular circle. But they should've been able to detect more than two.

Abyan wanted to kick herself.

There was some kind of tunnel under the house. It had to be more than six feet deep, otherwise they would've picked up the radio waves. Allah ba'ay. She had to help her friends. Just as she edged backward to bust the door open, the host said something that made her stomach drop to her feet.

Abyan pressed her ear to the door again, focusing all her efforts on deciphering the words. "Ora gave us her orders. If we fail again, Khalo will get the package before us."

Khalo.

She hadn't heard that name since she was fourteen.

A chill shot up the length of her spine, and it wasn't from the cold. Abyan squeezed her eyes shut, as though it would stop the memories flooding her mind, each one a different bullet to her heart.

Kade called out her name, her voice desperate. They couldn't hold off the Nosaru for much longer. Yet Abyan's limbs refused to move; they might as well have been melded to the grass beneath her feet.

Her whole body trembled.

He was still alive.

Of course, that shaytaan was still alive.

"Quick, we must leave," Matteo said.

Their footsteps moved in her direction, so Abyan quickly rolled into the cover of the weeds. Though one of the hosts made to bolt away from the house, Matteo lingered for some reason, sniffing the air with confusion written clear as day across his face. What was he smelling? Abyan held her breath as he took several steps closer to her, her fingers wrapping tighter around her dagger with every muddy squelch she heard.

The second host pulled Matteo by the arm. "What's wrong with you? There's no time to waste."

Abyan watched the first gen blink twice as if shaking himself awake and then turn tail and run with the other Nosaru in tow. She sprang to her feet, adrenaline humming in her veins, and rushed to follow them with daggers in either hand. They had to know where Khalo was, and Matteo Valente was going to lead her straight to him.

Hassan's voice cut through her revenge-filled haze. "Yan!"

She stopped in her tracks, every swear and curse she knew leaving her lips as she watched the two Nosaru get farther away from her. Abyan's grip on her dagger tightened until she couldn't feel her fingers anymore, but she turned on her heel and sprinted back to her friends.

Several hosts surrounded them on all sides, bodies were strewn about the floor, and she and Hassan were out of daggers. The moment she stepped into the house, Abyan heard it. The light click of a camera. It was faint, almost swallowed by snarls and grunts, but there was no mistaking it. The dread in her stomach only grew when she caught movement in the corner of her eye, filling each of her organs and shutting them down one by one.

This was no ordinary BLCC order.

It was a Peeping Tom.

9

ARTEMIS

Abyan clearly had a very different idea of team building.

When she first told Artemis to come along to see Ms. De Costa, she thought it had to be a trick. There was no way Abyan was being serious. But Artemis figured this might've been her way of extending an olive branch—maybe she was being nice? It was hard to tell when it came to her. Her eyes were always guarded, and her mind was a jigsaw Artemis could never seem to piece together.

Still, she jumped at the opportunity. It was her first week at Carlisle, and even though recruits wouldn't start being assigned missions for a couple of months, she wanted to start learning their ways sooner rather than later.

Artemis had been following her through corridor after corridor, and they hadn't said two words to each other. Part of her thought that even though this trip with Abyan was slightly awkward, sleeping in Jared's room was torture, and she was still glad to be away from it for a while.

She'd spent every night tossing and turning, switching between staring at the ceiling and two blissful seconds of sleep that were swiftly overrun by nightmares of that afternoon on Ben Nevis: the snarls of the Nosaru at her back and her boyfriend's ear-splitting screams. Artemis lost count of the number of times she woke up a sweat-stained, trembling mess, but while the night was merciless at best, the day brought its own perils and was no more forgiving.

The lively conversation in the kitchen always died as soon as she entered, and her squad eyed her warily while she ate breakfast as if her pancakes would pounce on them the second they let their guard down.

A few of them did, at least, try to talk to her, but the ice in the room had seeped into every corner, making even the warmest of words brittle and cold.

"Where are we going?" Artemis asked, gathering all the courage she had left.

She was nowhere near as tall as Abyan's five-foot-nine frame and struggled to keep up with her long strides. The squad had a very noisy meeting the night before. Artemis heard it from the kitchen, all of them swearing and shouting over each other. Though they never told her what it was about, she knew it was bad when they ate breakfast the next morning in stone-cold silence.

"To get another mission off De Costa." When Artemis's brows furrowed, Abyan explained further. "Protocol states that De Costa is the one who decides which missions go to which squads, but she used to be my old instructor before her hip injury, so I'm hoping she'll give us another WLDO and ignore our Peeping Tom."

Artemis laughed. "WLDO as in the name Waldo?"

Abyan tried to suppress her smile and failed miserably. "It stands for White League-Approved Death Order, but that's a mouthful, and no one has the energy to say all those words."

"And the BLCC orders?"

"BLCC is said like the colour black, but it stands for Black League-Approved Conceal and Capture. Those are usually for Nosaru needed for testing in the research wing."

They went into a hallway full of fancy plaques and framed pictures. Artemis had heard stories about it: the Hall of Operatives. It was where the legends of Carlisle were honored, and images of famous squads lined the walls, with summaries of their historic missions detailed below them. One picture—one face, more specifically—caught her eye, and Artemis stopped in front of it.

Mr. Carlisle.

He had a wide, earnest smile on his face and stood next to two men and three women, one of whom she recognized as Ms. Bruno. Yet in the picture, she didn't have a prosthetic. Mr. Carlisle looked around nineteen, and his eyes shone so brightly that even Artemis could feel their warmth. No matter how hard she tried, she couldn't picture the boy in front of her growing up to become the cold, stoic man she'd come to know.

"The Cardinal Six was the best squad to ever come out of this place, you know," Abyan whispered, awe clear as day in her eyes. "They had to change their name to Squad 1115 when they became operatives. You can't have trivial names after you graduate."

Artemis peered closer to the picture. "Who are they?"

"Mr. Carlisle; Hank's parents, Rosemary Mulligan and Percy King; Omar Murad, Hassan's uncle; Mariam Sepetu; and Ms. Bruno." She listed them off one by one, and it took Artemis a moment to clock that Abyan had them memorized.

There was something in the way she looked at the pictures, the light caress of her fingertips on the glass, and the hunger in her eyes. Jealousy. Artemis could understand it, though. Every student at Carlisle probably wanted to be legendary like The Cardinal Six.

"Ms. Bruno lost her leg, and Omar died in their last mission together as a squad." Abyan wasn't looking at her anymore. It was like she'd forgotten Artemis was standing beside her. "No one knows what happened on that day. It should've never been possible."

Artemis said, "You must really look up to them."

"I did." It was like the life drained out of her. Her smile, the softness of her voice, the excitement—all of it disappeared in the blink of an eye. "We won't reach their level for . . . obvious reasons."

She's talking about me.

Abyan started walking again, and Artemis hurried to catch up. She wanted to say something bold like in the movies. Something defiant. Something that would make her feel less useless and take her mind away from how badly she wanted to go home.

They came upon De Costa's office, and Abyan didn't bother knocking as she entered. "Hey, Ms. De Costa."

De Costa greeted them with a welcoming coffee-stained smile. Her graying dark curls were tied atop her head, and the formidable stack of papers on her desk gave Artemis a headache just looking at it. "Asking for a mission, Guled? I'm almost certain this is against the rules."

"You're getting too stingy in your old age, miss," Abyan teased, grinning wider than Artemis had ever seen. "Have you thought about early retirement?"

"The only way I'm leaving this place is in a coffin, you little shit," De Costa scoffed. "Keep talking like that and you just might find yourself all tied up in the gym again."

Abyan tapped her chin, looking straight at her former instructor. "Yeah, I wonder how I got up there in the first place."

"And I wonder how all my hair mysteriously fell out the day after." De Costa turned to Artemis suddenly, pointing to a small bald patch just behind her ear. "You know, part of it never grew back after that."

Abyan only shrugged. "Honestly, it's a case for MI5."

Artemis's brows furrowed, watching as they stared each other down for a few seconds before bursting into laughter. *So, all of that really happened?* God, this place was something else.

"Just one WLDO, that's all I'm asking for," Abyan said once their laughter faded. "No one needs to know."

"Your Peeping Tom yesterday was a travesty. I read the report Squad 2528 submitted twice, and there wasn't a single word of sincere praise in all five pages of it." She looked between them, and Abyan's body turned to stone in the moments before she gave a heavy sigh. "But fine, only because I love a good comeback. I have eight outstanding BLCC orders up for grabs, all of which must be shadowed by operative squads, and no WLDOs. You can take your pick of the lot."

Abyan raised a brow. "There were four WLDOs available the other day though."

"Don't ask me." De Costa shrugged and turned her computer screen to face them. "It's above my pay grade."

This didn't feel right.

Abyan seized the mouse, examining the missions. Her eyes landed on something for one of the BLCC orders and widened a fraction; it was such a minuscule movement, Artemis would've missed it entirely if she wasn't paying close attention. She tried to quickly scan the page to find what shocked her so much, but Abyan had already clicked onto the next one, her face never changing as she flew through the rest.

"Thank you, miss." She straightened, smoothing her shirt, and Artemis could see her trying her best to act calm. "We'll just take whatever we're assigned next and hope for the best."

De Costa had broken the rules for them, and Abyan just shrugged it off. She eyed them warily but said nothing as the two of them walked out. Abyan saw something on that computer that scared her, and Artemis wanted to know what it was.

"What did you see?" she asked. Abyan couldn't meet her gaze, and she knew whatever she'd say next would be a lie.

"Nothing."

———————+———————

Artemis skidded to a halt outside room B1-A9—her curls falling into her face as stark white lights nearly blinded her—and found Hank leaning against a wall on his phone and Ms. Bruno staring right at her from beside him.

She was in so much trouble.

"You're three minutes and seventeen seconds late for my class, Garrett-Coleman."

She still hadn't got her breath back. "I'm sorry, I got lost trying to find this place."

It wasn't a total lie. The foyer they were in was located on the second basement floor of the recruitment building, and Artemis hadn't even known there was a second basement floor until that day. All the walls and floors were pitch black, with dim white lights lining the ceiling.

"Where's everyone else?" Artemis asked, looking around for the other recruits.

She couldn't have been *that* late.

Ms. Bruno opened a door in one of the black walls she hadn't noticed. "It'll just be you today. Hank will give you the rundown of your task, while I'll be keeping my eyes on you from above."

Before Artemis could get a word out, Ms. Bruno disappeared and slammed the door shut behind her. Hank immediately pushed off the wall he'd been propped up against, shedding his air of nonchalance in a split second, and pulled Artemis to the far corner of the foyer. His green eyes were guarded, and his brown hair looked like he'd run his fingers through it one too many times.

"Look, I tried to convince Ms. Bruno that putting you in The Choker is a bad idea," he began, whispering so no one else could hear, and Artemis's stomach twisted into knots. "But in all honesty, I'm pretty sure she hates your guts and would 100 percent feed you to her Dobermans if it wasn't illegal."

"That was . . . oddly specific." Artemis gulped. "What's The Choker?"

Hank had laughed at her pitiful skills on the first day. The memory was burned into the back of Artemis's mind, so having him try to help her now felt weird. Did Abyan ask him to keep an eye on her? They seemed pretty close back in the dorm. He was always looking at her, and she was always pretending not to notice. Artemis couldn't help but wonder if he was only helping her now to make sure she didn't fail and drag The Sevenfold's grade average down.

Hank didn't really care about her well-being.

"It's a corridor that's just over two hundred yards long, and at the end, there's a tranq—a gun that shoots a special tranquilizer for hosts." He pointed at the double doors across from them. "You get put in first and then approximately three seconds later, a host is released to follow you in. The goal is to make it to the end of The Choker and reach your weapon first, so you can put the host down before it gets you."

Artemis put her head in her hands. "Oh my god."

A live host? And she was supposed to somehow fight it off with less than a week's worth of training? There was no way she could do it. Artemis wouldn't make it ten steps before the Nosaru caught up to her.

"Hey, don't freak out." Hank snapped his fingers in front of her. "The host you'll get will be a fourth gen, and it'll be partially sedated because The Choker is a test for second- and third-years and you're still a recruit."

"This is insane." Her throat closed, and it was like someone lit her chest on fire. "There's no way this is happening."

Artemis's breaths came short and shallow. Hank put a hand on her shoulder but looked flustered, red creeping fast across his face the more stressed he got. "I'm so not good with nervous people, recruit." The words tumbled out of his mouth at breakneck speed. "I never know what to say to fix things. Yan freaked out like this on me once when we were recruits, and I panicked and told her about when I ate a stick bug as a kid."

She blinked. "Why on earth would you eat a stick bug?"

"They're really long, so I thought it would make me taller." He held his hands up. "Seven-year-old me thought it was a great idea with very sound reasoning behind it."

Artemis wanted to laugh but remembered what she was going

to have to do in a matter of minutes. *Focus.* She forced herself to inhale and exhale until her racing pulse had slowed enough for her to think properly.

The Choker was just two hundred yards.

The host would be partially sedated.

Her stamina wasn't too bad, and daily training meant her muscles were in decent shape. Artemis didn't have to do any kind of fighting as long as she kept enough distance between herself and the host to reach the weapon in time.

Her voice was small. "What if it gets me?"

"It won't," Hank assured her. "Ms. Bruno and I will be on the rafters above you, and I'll have a gun trained on the host at all times; the second it looks like it'll overpower you, I'll shoot."

Her frazzled nerves calmed a fraction at the determination in Hank's emerald eyes. Ms. Bruno probably wanted the fourth gen to drain her dry, but Artemis had a feeling Hank wouldn't let anything bad happen to her.

She nodded. "Thank you."

A yellow light flashed three times above the double doors, and she steeled herself. That could only mean one thing. *It's time.* Artemis forced air in through her nose and out through her mouth, all the while reminding herself why she was at Carlisle Academy, before walking in the direction of the light.

She placed her hand on one of the doors leading to The Choker and whispered to herself, "You're going to be okay."

"Good luck, recruit," Hank called before disappearing like Ms. Bruno did.

When she was given the all clear, Artemis pushed it open and ran like her feet had been lit on fire. She had a three-second head start and didn't plan on wasting a single one.

I can do this.

The Choker was all black like the foyer, with high walls and no ceiling, only two rafters on either side about 65 feet up where Ms.

Bruno and Hank watched like spectators in the Colosseum. Artemis wouldn't have been able to see anything around her were it not for the tiny red lights on either side of the floor showing the way.

She didn't hear any door slide open, but the gargling noise behind her was unmistakable. The fourth gen had been released. Artemis wanted to look back and see, wondering if it was twitching violently like her textbooks said and if the host was male or female. If it looked hungry or not. Yet almost as soon as it entered The Choker with her, the host started sprinting, and the only thing louder than its thunderous steps was the pounding of Artemis's heart.

She was going to be sick.

Her muscles burned as she forced her limbs to go harder. The Nosaru was gaining on her fast; there was no way a partially sedated host should be this quick, but surely Hank wouldn't lie to her?

The fourth gen's snarls grew louder, and suddenly she was back on Ben Nevis with cold rock under her palms and the morning sun on her cheek. She peered down and saw five Nosaru bounding toward her group with death in their black eyes, the very same snarls and growls she heard from this fourth gen leaving their lips.

Snap out of it, Jay.

Although she whimpered at the memory ripping through her mind, tears stinging her eyes, she didn't stop running. They'd just passed the halfway point, and Artemis's chest swelled when she saw what lay on the table at the end of The Choker.

The tranq gun.

Before she could celebrate, her combat boot snagged on something beneath her and she fell forward, plummeting to the ground on her hands and knees. Though the impact shook her bones, Artemis's veins pulsed with so much adrenaline she didn't feel a thing.

She didn't know how far behind her the Nosaru was, but she threw her whole body to the closest wall and watched as it tried to grab at the empty space she'd left behind.

It was a youngish woman with tan skin and pitch-black hair. They took each other in for a heartbeat before she growled, her upper and lower fangs extending to their full length. Artemis fixed her eyes on the tranq and made a break for it. She didn't have to look back at the host to know it was close, too close for comfort.

Its fingers grazed the back of Artemis's shirt.

Yet the tranq was almost within reach—she just needed more time. Though Artemis's legs shook, sweat drenching every part of her, she pushed on. Another swipe from the Nosaru skidded across her back, and she yelped in shock.

Just a few more seconds.

Artemis leaped forward and grabbed the tranq as soon as she was close enough, swiveling on her back foot and shooting the host three times in its torso. The fourth gen collapsed at Artemis's feet not a moment later. She panted, desperately trying to fill her lungs, a deep ache in each of her muscles setting in at a record pace, and looked up at the rafters.

Artemis didn't know what she was expecting, maybe a "Well done" or a simple nod of approval, and instead, she found Hank and Ms. Bruno murmuring to each other, their eyes wide.

Ms. Bruno noticed her staring. "You're dismissed, Garrett-Coleman."

What the hell did she do wrong now?

10

ARTEMIS

EVERYTHING HAD BEEN WEIRD SINCE THE CHOKER.

Hank barely made eye contact with her and Ms. Bruno's scowl only ever deepened when Artemis crossed her line of sight.

I did my best and it still wasn't enough.

She sat alone in the middle of the living room, her textbooks splayed out before her, and decided to focus on the things she could control and push everything else to the back of her mind. Her subjects for the year were maths, physics, and economics, and while Artemis's first lessons weren't so bad, some of the things on the syllabus did give her pause.

The only reason she was in the living room and not holed up in Jared's bedroom was because Kade let it slip that they would all be busy until third period, and Artemis was sick of those four walls and the ghost that lived within them.

The light squeak of the front door opening snapped her out of her thoughts and her mind raced, desperately trying to figure out how she could get out of the room without drawing attention to herself. *Jesus Christ.* Artemis's eyes locked onto the clock that hung from the slate-gray wall, and her brows furrowed when it read only ten thirty—halfway through second period. She began soundlessly gathering her things as voices echoed down the hallway.

None of The Sevenfold should've been back yet.

Someone sighed. "She's over there worrying about some

WLDOs when we have much bigger problems on our hands. That Peeping Tom cost us eleven points, and if we keep going on like this, we'll be out of the Triumvirate faster than you can blink."

Kade.

"I really think Yan might be reading too much into it," came a guy's voice. It was Mason, she recognized, and the sound of the textbook she held slipping from her grasp was loud enough that his heavy footfalls instantly began making their way to her.

"Agreed, the WLDOs could mean anything." *Crap.* Tolly. Out of all The Sevenfold, he hated her the most. She had no idea what she ever did to Tolly for him to despise her so much besides exist in the same general vicinity.

"Hey, recruit." Ocean-blue eyes and bright purple hair greeted Artemis when she looked up from her papers. Mason and Kade sat on either side of her, and the second Mason's gaze landed on all the notes strewn about the mahogany coffee table, he groaned. "It's literally the first week of school, Artemis. The last thing you should be doing right now is work."

She smiled, trying not to focus on the dirty look Tolly was giving her from the doorway. "I like being prepared."

Mason picked up her Nosaru Fundamentals book and flipped through the pages. "Okay, Ms. Prepared," he began, his eyes electric, "there are thousands of other animals that use hemoglobin to transport oxygen around their bodies, so why do hosts only target humans?"

This is too easy.

"Well, we're the only known species that has compatible antigens with Nosaru, so our antibodies don't recognize them as foreign entities, and our immune response isn't triggered, meaning that they get to carry on living within us."

"Good answer, Ms. Prepared," Kade replied, and Artemis couldn't help but laugh at her freakishly accurate version of their Nosaru Fundamentals teacher's annoying voice. "Are living humans their only viable hosts?"

"No, they can raise humans from the dead, but the human can never become sentient again as they're not alive, and the host then lacks the characteristic quadruple heartbeat. It only has a double heartbeat as the human heart no longer works, and the Nosaru's contraction is the only thing observed."

"Wrong." Mason offered her a knowing grin as her cheeks burned. Tolly shook his head at her, and it only made Artemis want to disappear more. "You should've paid more attention to the wording of my question. I asked if living humans were their only *viable* hosts."

Tolly took a few steps toward them from his position in the doorway. "Nosaru rarely use dead humans as hosts because their bodies can't make fresh oxyhemoglobin. They're stuck with what's left in the body, and because it's only a finite source, they only ever enter a newly deceased vessel when there are no other options. So, yes, living humans are their only viable hosts."

Mason raised both hands. "Truly splendid, Mr. Aghahowa."

Tolly rolled his eyes as Mason joined in with Artemis's fit of giggles. Carlisle was so weird. She didn't know why everyone always danced around the elephant in the room. They all knew what the Nosaru really were—what regular people knew them as: vampires.

Only no one said it out loud.

"So, what were you talking about when you first came in?" she asked once their laughter died down. The WLDOs had to be what Abyan saw the other day on De Costa's computer; she had to have told the rest of The Sevenfold what she saw.

"Just Triumvirate drama," Mason said, and Artemis wanted to groan in frustration. "It's the name for the top three squads in each year—as in the Roman Triumvirate."

She decided to play along for now. "But the original Triumvirate didn't have the best endings."

"So, Julius Caesar had an impromptu acupuncture session,

Gnaeus Pompey's head became a really insensitive welcoming gift, and Marcus Crassus came down with one hell of a sore throat," Kade said as if it were the most normal thing in the world. "It's meant to be some weird metaphor, since the best squads are always stabbing each other in the back to stay on top."

"Right." Artemis dragged the word out, the nagging feeling in the back of her mind growing too strong to ignore. She had to say something. "And what about the WLDOs? I heard you guys talking about that, too."

Everything paused.

Artemis looked at Kade and she turned to Mason who looked at Tolly. Maybe Artemis had gotten too comfortable? The room went so quiet, she was sure they could hear her heart hammering against her rib cage. *Please don't hate me.* The last thing she needed was for her only allies to abandon her as well.

"Don't do it," Tolly warned. "We can't trust her."

Mason gave a heavy sigh. "Not this again."

Tolly clenched his jaw. "She doesn't deserve it."

Artemis fiddled with her papers, not knowing what to do with herself, and watched from the corner of her vision as they glared at each other, a silent battle ensuing in the depths of their eyes. When Tolly stalked out of the room, she knew Mason had won the war.

"You're part of the team now, Artemis. We need to have absolute trust in each other." He shed his easygoing exterior and eyed her with such intensity, she could feel her thundering pulse in her throat. Though it was hidden in his words and intricately laced between the letters, it became crystal clear what he truly meant: He was offering her a lifeline.

A window into the squad.

It was a test of trust.

"I understand."

I won't tell a soul.

After a couple torturous seconds, Mason cleared his throat

and brought her into the fold. "When you were with Abyan in De Costa's office, she saw that all the outstanding WLDOs had been downgraded to BLCC orders—that's never happened before. And with Nosaru starting to display behavior we've never observed before, like killing each other, she thinks the academy is up to something."

"I kind of see her point."

Other recruits told her Nosaru didn't kill one another on purpose. Nosaru killing their own was like lions eating grass because it just didn't happen. She thought it was a strange coincidence that right when they started murdering each other, all the WLDOs suddenly changed.

"I'm not too sure. I love Abyan more than air, but she tends to overanalyze everything," Mason said, and Kade nodded in agreement. "Even if she's right and something's up, we still need more evidence than one or two WLDOs changing to accuse the school of anything."

Artemis thought for a moment. She hadn't been at Carlisle long enough to have any sentimental attachment to it, like he did, that could sway her to believe it was just by chance these things coincided. "So, what are you going to do?"

The more she thought about it, the fishier it got, and it came to a point where Artemis couldn't stand the stink anymore. She had to find out more. Maybe the WLDOs were part of something bigger. What if it was all connected somehow? Artemis didn't believe in coincidences when it came to Carlisle Enterprises—there were too many eyes, too many moving parts in the organization for anything to be down to simple chance.

"Nothing," Mason said. "We'll tell Yan to let it go for now, and you should forget I ever told you this."

There was no chance of her forgetting. She needed to find a way to get Abyan to trust her like Mason did. Abyan probably had a plan to find out what Carlisle Academy was up to, and she wanted in.

Artemis burst into Training Room 18A. "I'm so sorry, Kade. We were let out of economics late, and—"

"It's fine." Kade waved a dismissive hand and gestured to the seat next to her on the bench. "I'll give you a minute to catch your breath before we start."

Artemis mumbled something vaguely resembling a thanks before sitting down. She forced in several slow breaths to try to temper the burning in her lungs, at least a third of her soul dying each time Kade heard her pant like an elderly Great Dane.

Once Artemis had gotten her breathing under control, she peeled off the sweaty red shirt that marked her as a recruit, not missing how Kade's eyes lingered for a split second longer than necessary on her black sports bra.

It's probably nothing.

Don't make it weird.

Artemis got to her feet, clearing her throat. "So, what are we doing today?"

"You'll be doing mostly cardio to build up your stamina," Kade replied, her pale cheeks a touch redder than when Artemis had first walked in. "But I've reviewed your training records, and you also need to do more weights, since your body's fat-to-muscle ratio is too high."

Her brow creased. "Dr. Telford said my weight was normal for my height though."

"An average fat-to-muscle ratio isn't a bad thing for regular people. You just need to decrease it at Carlisle to have any hope of winning a fight with Nosaru." Kade led her to a treadmill and pulled out a stopwatch. "If we get all the cardio out of the way quickly, I can start teaching you self-defense." She leaned over the treadmill, resting her arms on the plastic. "Just letting you know that anywhere is free game when we're fighting, but I have a Not-in-the-Face rule, okay?"

Artemis laughed. "Don't worry, I'd never damage the merchandise."

"I'm glad you understand the severity of the situation." Kade gave her a wink that did things to Artemis's pulse she'd never say aloud and mirrored her wide grin. "Okay, I want to time your mile again first to compare it with your last attempt."

Artemis willed her flaming skin to cool as Kade configured the treadmill. When everything was set up, Kade started the stopwatch, silently observing her as she ran. Artemis learned a lesson from watching the other recruits during their group training sessions and deliberately chose not to start off with a huge burst of energy at a high-speed setting to show off, instead taking her time and keeping an even pace.

The last thing she needed was to injure herself.

Artemis let Kade and the training room, with its bright lights and exposing mirrors, fade to black around her as she pumped her legs harder. Finishing her mile was the only thing that mattered. She ignored the groans of her muscles, how her legs already trembled, and her skin burned like fresh embers that needed only a soft breath to catch light.

I can do this.

Kade glanced at her stopwatch once Artemis was finished. "Twelve minutes."

She groaned, breathing heavily as she rested her forehead on the machine. "I was trying my hardest."

"Last time, your mile was twelve minutes and thirty seconds, so this is technically an improvement," Kade said, offering her a reassuring smile. "You're doing great."

She sat down on the treadmill, crossing her legs under her. "You'd think I'd be better though. I used to spend hours chasing my younger brothers around back home."

Kade chuckled lightly. "How old are they?"

"Nine—they're identical twins," Artemis replied, something in her chest twisting when she realized that she'd never been away from them for longer than two days until now. "Do you have siblings?"

She shook her head, the corner of her lips tipping up. "None by blood but about five by unfortunate circumstance."

The door opened, interrupting them, and Hassan strolled in. He dumped a duffel bag in the middle of the room and handed Kade one of the two sheathed swords left in his hands before speaking. "Freshly sharpened," he told her. "This is the last favor I'm doing for you, Kadrian."

Artemis couldn't help herself. "Is that where your nickname comes from?"

Kade glared at Hassan before turning to her. "Yeah, we had a simulation training session back when we were recruits, and I was doing so well holding the bots back that none of them were making it past my line."

"Ms. De Costa was our instructor back then, and she called Kade's line 'Hadrian's Wall' as a joke, so I called her Kadrian from there," Hassan continued, pushing his black waves back from his face with a devious gleam in his midnight eyes. "Kade was a happy medium for everyone."

Kade pulled out her sword in a flash of steel and pointed to the engraving at the base. "In other news, meet Éponine," she announced, so Artemis leaned in to get a closer look. She gestured to Hassan. "Show her yours, too."

Although he released a heavy breath, he drew his blade and presented it to them. "Meet Sword."

"You named your sword Sword?" Artemis asked, incredulous.

He made a sound of indifference. "That's literally what it is, isn't it? I don't understand why we have to name them like they're a pet or something."

He does have a point.

"A clean cut across the neck, severing the spinal cord, is the only way to kill a host," Kade explained, sweeping Éponine across the air in front of her slowly, and it wasn't hard to imagine a dead host falling to his knees before her. "And if you can't manage that for some reason or other, then causing extensive damage to their brain with a dagger can disable them completely."

Artemis drew in a shaky breath. "Good to know."

Hassan cocked a brow, looking between the distance on the treadmill and Kade's stopwatch. "How did she do on her mile, then?"

"Twelve."

Artemis didn't want to look either of them in the eye.

"Twelve minutes for a mile?" He shook his head. "See, I thought you *might* need these extra training sessions as a plus, but I didn't think you needed them this badly, recruit."

Anger flashed across Kade's face. "Stop—"

"I'm not being a dick on purpose." He held his hands up in mock surrender. "I just want her to understand that she's a literal cannonball tied to all of our ankles, and we have to run a damn marathon in a few months." Hassan turned to Artemis, then. "We're only helping you now because there's no way to get rid of you, and if I'm being honest, I think this is a lost cause anyway."

Kade tried to salvage the situation. "Ignore him, your goal is nine minutes by January for the mid-year fitness tests. That's four months from now, so you still have a lot of time to get better."

Though they both waited for her reply, Artemis was busy sifting through the barrage of emotions in her chest. There was hurt, fear, and a hundred other things she couldn't place, but the blinding moon that eclipsed them all was anger. Red hot and all-consuming. So much fury churned in her body that she had no clue what to do with it.

Her hands shook.

Artemis was so tired of The Sevenfold hating her and treating her like crap for no reason. She'd been nothing but nice to them. And they'd all been extra mean, bar Mason and Kade, after their failed mission as if it were somehow her fault and she was sick of it all.

All she ever wanted was to be their friend.

"I get that you're all disappointed and upset about your Peeping Tom, and this year just got a whole lot more real for you guys," Artemis started, her voice strong despite her fear. "But I'm sick of having all of you take it out on me when I wasn't on the mission. I hate to break it to you, but the Peeping Tom was a failure because of you, not me."

Kade swooped in, then. "You're right, and if anything, it was Yan's fault. We could've passed that Peeping Tom in our sleep with our hands tied behind our backs if she hadn't messed everything up."

Abyan?

"Her head isn't in the game anymore," Hassan agreed. "All she cares about is graduation, and we all know why."

Artemis cocked her head to the side. "What do you mean by that?"

"Never mind, it's not important. Let's go back to training," Kade replied, and the look in her eyes told Artemis it was final, yet even an outsider like her could see the cracks in The Sevenfold burgeoning with every passing day.

And something told her the Peeping Tom was only the beginning.

11

ABYAN

THE SEVENFOLD ASSEMBLED IN TRAINING ROOM 103 AND waited for their shadows to grace them with their presence. It was their official introduction with Squad 2528, and although Abyan tried not to show it, she couldn't shake the unease creeping its way across her skin.

Abyan knew her squad had already pissed off their shadows at training with Sir Marland on the first day of school. Squad 2528 had gotten their revenge by shadowing what was supposed to be a solo mission, so the only thing she needed to know now was whether their shadows would be satisfied with their pound of flesh or if they'd rather claw at The Sevenfold until not even bones remained.

Her team had been sitting in the corner of the training room for over half an hour, the familiar burn of pins and needles humming in Abyan's calves, but Squad 2528 had yet to show. Their shadows were taking the piss, and there wasn't anything she could do about it.

The blue-tinged lights above them made Abyan's head hurt, her annoyance growing with every passing minute. Their shadows would have a good laugh once they saw Artemis sitting with them. Abyan wouldn't even blame them for it. If The Sevenfold didn't work their asses off this year, they could kiss the Triumvirate and first place goodbye.

Hank bumped her lightly in the shoulder. "Get out of your thoughts."

"They were important thoughts," she replied.

He gave her a half smile. "Well, I'm flattered you were thinking about me, Yan, but this obsession you have is becoming a problem. We have to keep things professional for the sake of the team."

"See, this is why I would walk past you if you were on fire," she said without missing a beat. "I'd literally only stop to roast marshmallows."

He put a hand on his chest, his voice so dramatic you would think he was straight out of a low-budget drama. "Et tu, Brute?"

Abyan rolled her eyes. "I hate you so much it causes me physical pain, Hercules."

"Okay, now that really hurts." They both chuckled, and Hank leaned a little closer. "There's something you should know about the recruit, Yan," he whispered after a short pause, and Abyan's ears perked up in an instant. "Something happened when she was in The Choker that I still can't wrap my head around. It's been bugging me for days."

Abyan asked, quiet enough that the rest of the squad didn't overhear, "What was it?"

"I was ready to squeeze the trigger on my gun the second the host started gaining on her, but Ms. Bruno stopped me," Hank explained. "Artemis reached out for the tranq at the end, and she was so close, except the host was practically scuffing her heels. The host tried to grab at her a third time and it would have succeeded, too, if it didn't pause mid-grab."

"It *paused*?" Abyan wasn't sure she heard him right. "How could the host pause?"

"It was only a split second, the kind of pause you'd miss if you blinked at the wrong moment. And it gave the recruit enough time to reach the gun and put the host down." He rubbed at his brow. "I thought I was seeing things at first—that it was just my eyes playing tricks on me. Then I saw the shock on Ms. Bruno's face, and I knew she'd noticed it as well."

Why would the Nosaru falter mid-strike?

Abyan bit the inside of her cheek as she thought for any logical reason that made sense. "It had to be a strange reaction to the sedation drugs or something, right?"

"Could be," Hank replied. "I thought the host was moving way too fast for the drugs to have been working properly anyway, so it could've been a bad batch of meds that was making it act so weird."

Before Abyan could reply, Mason interrupted them all. "I won the raffle for the League Night house party!" He passed the phone around so everyone could read the email. Abyan looked to Hank with a question in her eyes, her mind still stuck on his revelation about the recruit, but he shook his head a little and she got the message loud and clear.

Don't tell anyone.

Act natural.

She turned her attention back to Mason, pushing Hank's suspicions to the back of her mind. There was nothing surprising or coincidental about his announcement—the backdoor deals made to decide who was hosting the party outshaded even the shadiest underground meetings.

"You won the raffle in your last year here, as well." Artemis grinned. "You're so lucky."

Mason didn't hesitate. "Bribery is an art form, and don't let anyone tell you otherwise."

Though Artemis's jaw dropped at his nonchalant admission, Abyan shook her head. "You're a literal criminal."

"Did you hear that, Artemis?" He raised a hand to cup his ear. "It sounded like overwhelming bitterness, but Jesus Christ, it was just so distant I couldn't quite make it out."

"Prick," she retorted, trying to suppress the yawn creeping up her throat and failing. "You're so lucky I'm too sleep-deprived to waste any more energy on you."

Hank chuckled. "Yeah, thanks for that, Hassan. It's literally the first week back, and you're already on the maintenance guy's shit list for waking him up at 3:00 a.m."

"You're acting like it was my fault," Hassan grumbled, fiddling with his Rubik's Cube. "I can't control when my GI tract decides to act up."

"Just because there's ice cream in the freezer doesn't mean you have to eat it."

Hassan scoffed, "I'm lactose intolerant, Hank, not dead inside."

He and Kade still hated her for what happened on their BLCC order, Tolly was disappointed in her, and Abyan knew Mason and Hank were as annoyed as the others—they were just the best at hiding it.

She'd blamed everything on Artemis, but it was going to be no one's fault but her own when the squad's rep went down in flames. Though Abyan stared right at Hassan, he did everything he could to avoid her gaze. Kade was even worse, turning her back to Abyan and whispering something under her breath to Tolly who was sitting beside her.

How was she supposed to know Matteo Valente was no ordinary first gen? Abyan had never thought in a million years that Khalo would still be alive, let alone back in London. Her blood boiled at the thought of how long he'd been walking around with so much blood on his hands.

She clenched her jaw, and Hank must've sensed her tensing up because his arm landed firmly on her shoulders. She knew it was a warning. Abyan took several silent breaths because the last thing she needed was for her squad to notice and start asking questions she wasn't ready to answer.

The door to the training room slid open, silencing the scattered conversations around her. Abyan immediately shot up from her seat. The rest of The Sevenfold mirrored her movement, standing at attention, and watched as an older white man entered the room.

She didn't recognize him from their first training session with Sir Marland. Did that mean Squad 2528 had seven members rather than the six they'd already kind of met? The man looked like he was in his early forties, had his dark hair buzzed short, and his abs strained his T-shirt so much it looked one sharp movement away from bursting at the seams.

He stood in the center of the room and gave them each a once-over before speaking.

"At ease, Sevenfold," he began in a surprisingly posh voice, and the whole squad relaxed their postures. "You can call me Harry. I'll be your main point of contact in all things concerning your relationship with your shadows this year."

It was a fake name obviously, yet Abyan was more interested in why he wasn't with his squad before. Did he know his team were beaten? And by third-year students, no less? Everything about him, from his intense eye contact to his assured stance, screamed that he was the leader of Squad 2528.

"I've spent the last couple of weeks going through each and every one of your old combat reports dating back to when you first started at Carlisle Academy." Harry looked at Abyan then, and her brows furrowed on instinct. *That can't be good.* "One of my main conclusions was that although each of you are capable in your own right, you rely too much on Miss Guled."

Abyan couldn't stop herself speaking. "What the hell is that supposed to mean?"

"I didn't stutter, Guled." Harry crossed his arms. "You come up with the mission plans, and you direct every move your squad makes when engaging hosts—you say jump and the rest of your squad asks how high. It begs the question: What would The Sevenfold do without you? Could they maintain their position in the school? Or would they fall apart?"

Kade snapped, "We're all as good as each other. Any one of us could lead."

There was a pang in Abyan's chest at the venom in Kade's voice, and she couldn't bring herself to look at her friend's face. This was all Harry's fault. He didn't know what he was talking about. Harry had not only insulted every member of The Sevenfold but also thrown live C4 right into the newly formed cracks in the team.

"So you say, Nakamura, but there's still no evidence of it." He shrugged. "It's become clear to me that some of you are just going through the motions here. You're all legacies bar Garrett-Coleman and Guled, and I figure that you don't care too much about the Nosaru but do care a whole lot about what Daddy thinks." He looked at each of them one by one before he stopped on Hassan. "Isn't that right, Murad?"

Hassan's body was so tense even Abyan held her breath as he spoke. "Who do you think you're—"

"Or is it a wider family thing?" He zeroed in on Kade. "You want to place first so badly because Mummy and Daddy did it and so did their parents before them, Nakamura, and you don't care how you do it."

She took a step toward him. "You don't know anything about me."

"I was shocked to discover that a number of you never wanted to be here in the first place." Harry took slow steps around them and paused in front of Tolly. "Aghahowa here is one second away from transferring out of this place on any given day, so tell me: Is this what you call a squad?"

Tolly stood straighter than Abyan had ever seen, his anger rolling off him in waves. How did Harry know all of this? Tolly told her she was the only person he had ever confided in about his wavering resolve, and she sure as hell hadn't told anyone else.

If Harry cared he'd ruffled so many feathers, he didn't show it and moved on to Hank. "Everyone loves a bit of vengeance, don't they? The righting of past wrongs. Yet wanting to do right by your father's memory isn't going to cut it anymore, King."

Oh no.

Mentioning his dad never ended well. Abyan placed an arm across Hank's chest in a split-second, stopping him mid-lunge. She held him back with all her might—all six foot three inches of him—as his thunderous pulse reverberated through her skin. "Don't give him the reaction he wants, Hank," she managed through gritted teeth. "He's trying to get under your skin."

Hank clenched his jaw, swearing under his breath as he forced himself to calm down. Their shadow knew exactly what buttons to press to make each member of The Sevenfold snap, and Abyan was sure he was enjoying the show.

"Ragnar Mason Carlisle, the heir-apparent himself." Their shadow raised his hands as he came upon his latest victim, his hollow claps filling the air. "What would the dear old man think of his only son if he didn't follow in his footsteps? He's never liked you much anyway, right? But I think it's safe to assume that would be the final straw."

Mason's fingers twitched at his side.

Harry loomed over the recruit, his final victim, and Abyan braced herself for the bite of his words, yet . . . they never came. He simply looked at Artemis for several heartbeats, the silence around them stretching for miles, then sighed in disgust, and somehow that was worse than anything he could've said because the recruit went tomato red, swallowing heavily with her glassy eyes.

Don't you dare cry, Artemis.

That was exactly what Harry wanted.

"This is a piss-poor excuse for a squad." Their shadow went back to the center of the room. "Most of you aren't here for the right reasons, and it shows in how you carry yourselves. If you're really serious about getting the best possible reports from me, you can't proceed like it's business as usual," he warned. "I'm not harsh on students for the sake of being harsh or because I enjoy it—you have Ms. Bruno and Sir Marland for that. I pride myself on being fair, so you still have a chance to improve if you show that you've taken what I've said on board and act accordingly."

Abyan didn't buy his Nice Guy schtick for a second.

The briefest glance at how each member of her squad now looked at the other with a touch of uncertainty told her everything she needed to know.

Squad 2528 wasn't going to ruthlessly tear her team to shreds with damning after-action report after another, slowly chipping away at The Sevenfold's reputation over time—a torturous death by a thousand cuts. Instead, Harry was just going with the good old divide and conquer tactic, fanning the flames of discord between them until the whole squad crumbled.

Her eyes darted between Harry and her friends, quickly realizing her squad was splitting in too many places to count, and she didn't know how to fix it.

Ya Allah.

Abyan didn't even know where to start.

12

ABYAN

ABYAN HAD BOOKED ONE OF THE GYMS FOR THE SQUAD, BUT with all that had happened with Harry, tensions were running high, so she had to call off group training and go by herself. A whole hour had passed since she entered the gym, yet she still hadn't found the motivation to use any of the equipment.

She'd spent the entire day alternating between training different groups of recruits with Ms. Bruno, and every single one was worse than the other. How naive of her to think her day couldn't get any worse after spending all morning vomiting her guts out. She'd made honeyed shaax for her sore throat and raised her thermos to her lips, glaring at the closed door of the training room.

Abyan didn't usually shout so much in training sessions, but it seemed all the recruits had set out to test her patience that day, and with everything that was going on, it was wearing dangerously thin.

The endless sea of insufferable rich shits only raised her blood pressure with their terrible attitudes and nauseating senses of entitlement. She overheard countless students with bruised egos whispering about how they'd ask their parents or other relatives to get her expelled, and it was only the first week of term.

Sure, Carlisle didn't run in her blood. She didn't have a ton of money or a mansion in the suburbs with her family's name carved into the front gates like most of them. Her ties to the Nosaru were personal, she owed them a debt, and the school was her only way of getting what she needed.

Khalo had somehow crawled out of the woodwork after all this time, and the thought of finally seeing his head roll at her feet was one of the only things keeping her going. Abyan didn't care how she did it. Only that she'd eventually find him, no matter how long it took, and he would get what was coming to him.

Legacy, pride, ego—none of that mattered.

Once Abyan got what she came for, she was done. She'd been carrying the guilt for so long, weighing atop her head like a cursed crown, the ice had melded with her skin and its bite was all she ever felt.

Mr. Carlisle knew why she wanted to become an operative. She'd told him everything at the police station he found her in when she was fourteen, and he was more than happy to help. So, if anyone had a problem with her, they'd have to take it up with him and The League directly.

Abyan squeezed her eyes shut. Her head was pulsing, and the gym lights might as well have been the surface of the sun. Another dose of ibuprofen was off the table, since only two hours had passed since her last one. Abyan cursed under her breath because this sure as hell wasn't normal, but she prayed it was only temporary.

She didn't have time for her body to give up on her.

Abyan took another swig from the thermos, and the ginger and xawaash soothed her anger. Just one more bloody year. Then, she'd be an operative, free to take whatever WLDOs she wanted and go to wherever she needed to find her answers with nothing holding her back. That was the bargain she'd struck with Mr. Carlisle all those years ago: one year in therapy, three at the academy, and then the freedom to kill those who wronged her.

It was supposed to be simple.

The gentle scratch of the door against the carpeted floor jerked Abyan from her thoughts. She sprung from her seat on the hammer spring machine and ducked behind the dumbbell racks. Whoever walked in could probably see the outline of her body if they were to look hard enough, and in her shorts and tank, with her curls tied back in a ponytail, Abyan prayed it wasn't a man.

Her heart jumped to her throat as silence smothered the room, and her eyes frantically darted to where she'd left her clothes. *Bloody hell.* Her hijab and uniform were in a bundle too far for her to reach without being seen.

The person cleared their throat. "Uh, Yan? You in here?"

Audhubillah, it *was* a man.

"Close your eyes," she yelled back.

Mason quickly replied, "Sorry!"

She rose from her crouch, her muscles protesting the slightest movement, and ran over to her clothes. Abyan quickly changed into her uniform and gave Mason the green light to open his eyes when her hijab was firmly around her head.

He offered her an apologetic smile. "I didn't mean to barge in like that, but you weren't replying on the group chat or answering my calls. I wanted to see how you were feeling."

There was nothing to talk about.

Kade and Hassan were still feeling some type of way toward her, and Abyan's patience for their pettiness was running out. They needed to get over the Peeping Tom and stop holding it over her head. The past was the past. And with Harry trying to stir the pot with his nonsense, Abyan didn't know what to do next. She couldn't ignore what he said or Kade would blame her for every negative combat report they got, and she couldn't try to hash out their beef because Kade also refused to talk to her.

It was all going wrong.

They needed Jared—if he was still alive, he'd lock the two of them in a room until they sorted things out. Her bottom lip trembled. Jared would've known exactly what to do. Abyan pinched the bridge of her nose, squeezing her eyes shut until she was sure she wouldn't lose it in front of Mason.

This was supposed to be The Sevenfold's year, but everything was spiraling out of control.

Abyan lost track of what Mason was doing, suffocated by her own thoughts. Had he said something and she missed it? The next thing she knew, he was pulling her in for a hug. "You don't have to keep everything in all the time, you know," he whispered. "The strongest people are always rotting away on the inside."

"It's all my fault, Mason." Her eyes burned. *Screw him and his stupid feelings.* "Our first Peeping Tom of the year, and I messed everything up."

"Hey, it's not all your fault," he said, looking her right in the eye. "Things go south sometimes, and we just have to deal with it."

Abyan sighed. "I wish we could all go back to normal."

A couple of seconds passed, and uncertainty flickered across Mason's features. "I think . . . something was up with you on that mission, Yan." Her mouth opened in shock, but he got there before her. "You don't have to explain it to me, but as your friend, it's my job to tell you that it's messing with you too much."

Her tongue turned to stone at the thought of telling him the real reason why she froze up on the Peeping Tom. Abyan just couldn't make the words come out. Suddenly the gym around them disappeared and she was a kid again, confused and wondering why bodies had so much blood in them and why it was sticky and smelled so weird. Her hands shook at her sides as she desperately tried to center herself again before she was trapped in the memory.

You're not there anymore.

You're not there anymore.

You're not there anymore.

Mason put his hands on her shoulders, his voice panicked. "Yan?"

"I'm fine, I'm good," she managed, though her voice quivered. "If I told you I'm working on it, would that be enough?"

"More than enough." He hugged her again, and she almost

disappeared into his frame, since he was built like a bull and almost a full head taller than she was. "I'm sorry for bringing it up."

Yet Abyan was far from fine.

"We could all move past what happened if Kade and Hassan just got over it, don't you think?" She pulled away and paced, unable to think of anything else. They were holding the squad back for nothing. "You said so yourself, mistakes happen and shit hits the fan. I don't know why they keep holding that mission against me when we have our shadows breathing down our necks and a bloody recruit to train."

Mason tried to reason with her. "They're not angry about losing itself. It's *how* they lost that's got them all worked up." Abyan opened her mouth to protest but he continued, "You abandoned your squad, Yan, and that's a valid reason for them to be angry."

"I abandoned the squad? You weren't even there." The words flew from her mouth at lightning speed, sharp and poison-dipped, absent thought or regard for how much damage they'd do. "You didn't even want to be a field op in the first place! Everything Harry said about you was true."

Mason's mouth fell open a fraction before he recovered. "What are you talking about?"

"I made one mistake and everyone's on my case about it, for what?" She jabbed a finger in his direction. "I refuse to listen to you talk down to me when you're only here because of your dad. You don't have a real dog in this fight—this is theater to you but it's my *life*. This school is all I have left, so I don't need you to tell me anything."

"Alright, Yan." Mason inhaled sharply, not meeting her gaze, and the hurt in his voice made all the fury in her veins turn to dust beneath it. "Have it your way."

He left the training room before she could figure out how to mend all that she'd broken.

Shit.

Abyan had been avoiding Mason like the plague ever since yesterday, but it was hard not having him around—she missed him telling her how anything remotely bad that happened in his life had been predicted by his tarot lady, how he'd sing so loudly she could hear it from her room all the time, or how he always made her watch boring period dramas with him after training.

She knew she needed to apologize but couldn't make the words come out yet.

It didn't take long for the rest of the squad to pick up on the awkward vibes between them in the dorm either, but no one said anything, which somehow managed to make things ten times worse. Eventually, Abyan decided she couldn't take it anymore and dragged Hank away to test one of her theories about the school.

She raised a hand to knock on Mr. Oluwole's door.

Hank whispered, "Are you sure you want to do this?"

There were two assistant headteachers at Carlisle, and Mr. Oluwole was undoubtedly the more approachable one. As the school's test project—the only squad to ever be put together by Carlisle instead of choosing each other—they were each assigned senior faculty members to be their mentors and monitor their progress.

Mr. Oluwole was Abyan's mentor, and she didn't necessarily mind; he was nice enough, always stopping to speak with her in corridors outside of their weekly meetings, and was their best shot at figuring out what was going on with the Nosaru.

"This is the fifth time you asked me that, and my answer still hasn't changed," Abyan said.

When she reached forward, Hank's hand shot out like lightning and held her wrist gently. Abyan tried to ignore how warm it was and how the calluses felt so right against her skin as she looked up at him, raising a defiant brow.

"This isn't something we can come back from, and they'll be keeping a close watch on us after we leave." He searched her eyes for any sign of doubt but was met with steadfast resolve. Abyan was well aware of the consequences, but she needed to know the truth, and Mr. Oluwole's reaction would tell her everything.

"I know what I'm walking into," she assured him. "Trust me, I've thought this out from every possible angle."

"Fine." Hank released her wrist and adjusted his glasses.

She offered him a teasing grin. "Stop worrying so much, Hercules. I might have to start calling you Mum if you keep this up."

He smirked. "That's not the parent I would've preferred."

Abyan elbowed him in the ribs and knocked on the door. "You're disgusting and I hate you."

"Thank you, but lying is haram," he wheezed, just as Mr. Oluwole called them in. The assistant headteacher was well-built, his muscles straining his navy dress shirt, and his tie was all but eclipsed by his large frame. He offered them a welcoming smile as they took seats in front of his polished desk.

"Ah, two of my favorite students," Mr. Oluwole said, rubbing his hands together. "Tell me, Abyan, how was your holiday?"

The smile she gave him was sincere despite her suspicions. "It was great, sir. I hadn't been there since I was thirteen, and it was nice to be back home for a while."

"That's good to hear. I'm happy you experienced your homeland again. I haven't been back home in years, since it's always so busy here, so I guess I must live through you, eh?" he joked, and they laughed together in earnest as Hank looked between them both, not so subtly waiting for the subject to change. "You must tell me everything."

"Another time, sir," Abyan replied, genuinely regretting that she couldn't relive her memories with someone who could relate. "Hank and I came to ask you something."

He seemed to realize Hank was sitting beside her and leaned

forward. "How are you, Hercules?"

His reply was curt. "Good, sir."

"So, what did you want to ask?"

Hank spoke first. "Ms. De Costa said there were no more WLDOs available, and we just wanted to know why that was."

"And if it's going to be a permanent thing," Abyan added.

Mr. Oluwole cleared his throat, adjusting in his seat. "There will be no more WLDOs for the rest of the year—they are being phased out. The academy is moving onto other, better things."

"Why?" Hank asked.

"That's classified information above your rank," he warned. "You two would do best to forget about the WLDOs."

Abyan and Hank glanced at one another, both thinking the exact same thing. Someone at the school not only knew about the dodgy Nosaru activity but was also keeping the reason behind it from everyone else.

She nodded. "Thank you for telling us, sir. We'll just take BLCC orders from now on."

"I'm glad you're embracing the future." They moved to stand, but Mr. Oluwole stopped them. "Stay behind, Abyan. We have matters to discuss. Hercules, you may go."

She cursed internally. The BLCC order. Hank's eyes briefly met hers as he rose, but they both knew he couldn't stay because this was one person they could never disobey.

The second the door closed behind Hank, Mr. Oluwole spoke. "How is your health? Are you adjusting well to being back at school?"

He took out a pen and notepad. It was always the same kind of questions, just different variations. She used to try lying to him when she was a recruit, but somehow he always knew the truth.

"I'd say I'm adjusting well enough." Abyan paused, thinking on Hassan's words before she took their Peeping Tom. Maybe he was right, after all. "But I'm getting these migraines, and sometimes

I'll suddenly feel light-headed or nauseous—I don't know why it's happening."

He wrote something down. "You've been taking your vitamins, right?"

She nodded. "Yes, sir."

"I don't think it's anything serious, but you should see the doctor on campus to make sure of it." Abyan knew she should've gone to the doctor sooner, but with her symptoms, she was probably going to need a blood test, and there was nothing she hated more than needles.

"I'll do it as soon as possible."

Mr. Oluwole shook his head, looking at some of the papers on his desk. "I'm assuming you know the report from your BLCC order wasn't favorable."

There it was.

"I take full responsibility for it. It was my fault for being unprepared. My skills were rusty having been away from combat for so long." The last thing she needed was for the squad to be punished more for what she did.

They were hanging onto first place by the skin of their teeth.

While Mr. Oluwole didn't look entirely convinced, he let it slide. "Make sure it never happens again, Abyan, or there will be consequences. The Sevenfold cannot afford to fail another mission."

She nodded and stood, knowing when she was being dismissed. Warning was clear in his eyes, but he didn't need to tell her twice.

Abyan knew what she had to do.

13

ARTEMIS

THOUGH KADE GAVE HER A SUPPORTIVE SMILE BEFORE SHE
left Artemis outside Lab 12, Artemis didn't miss the second of
hesitation in her step. The flash of uncertainty in her brown eyes.
She knew it was because Kade didn't want to go back to their dorm
with everything so weird after the fallout from their Peeping Tom.

It was the reason she'd all but jumped at the chance to do
something as boring as walking the squad's recruit to third period.
Artemis didn't necessarily mind, though. The tense air that hung
over The Sevenfold's dorm was stale and suffocating, and it wasn't
doing any of them any good—Abyan was alienating the squad one
by one, first Kade and Hassan, now Mason, and no one knew how
to fix it.

They were all just tiptoeing around the giant elephant in the
room.

The door next to the group of recruits in front of Artemis
opened, and Ms. Bruno's unmistakable bark sliced through the
hallway. "Hurry up! Does it look like I have all day?"

All the recruits shuffled into Lab 12 in single file, grabbing lab
coats, safety glasses, masks, and disposable gloves before sitting at
their designated workstations. Artemis's was the farthest on the
left, and a stack of papers rested facedown next to her visor and lab
tools. Yet as she took in the range of scalpels and forceps, an uneasy
feeling settled over her.

Regular training with Ms. Bruno was hard enough, so Artemis couldn't help but wonder what on earth they were going to have to do now.

Ms. Bruno stood in front of the huge white board, dressed head-to-toe in protective equipment, and waited for them all to take their seats before speaking. "I warned you that not all of you would remain by the end of the year," she announced. "Today is your first test, and I'd like everyone to thank Garrett-Coleman for bravely volunteering to go first."

"F-first for what?" Artemis asked.

Ms. Bruno acted like she hadn't heard anything, instead bringing a large container over to Artemis's workstation and calling for the rest of the class to follow her there. She placed her gloved hand on a metal container that had at least eight different hazard signs and "WARNING!" in neon red on all its sides.

Jesus.

She looked at the class expectantly. "Can anyone tell me what the first two stages of Nosaru development are?"

A voice chimed in from somewhere in the back. "Larva and pupa."

"Exactly, and Nosaru are weakest at these stages because they need a constant supply of oxyhemoglobin, just twenty seconds without it and they'll die." Ms. Bruno gave the metal container three quick raps with her knuckles. "In this box, there's an Omega Nosaru—they don't progress past the pupal stage and can't molt into higher organisms like their alpha and beta counterparts."

Artemis squared her shoulders. "What do you want me to do with it?"

Ms. Bruno lifted the metal lid to reveal a clear glass containment box with a pink-white pupa the size of a closed fist sitting inside it. The Nosaru had an IV drip connected to a small pouch of blood labeled "O-Negative" protruding from its side.

The Nosaru moved inward and outward rhythmically, like it

was pulsing, and it didn't have eyes or anything—in fact, there were no defining features on it at all besides the linear ridges all across its skin.

"I want you to kill it," Ms. Bruno said bluntly. "Simply removing the IV cord won't cut it either, so don't even think about it. You've each been given a scalpel, and I'll direct you on how to make a precise incision into the upper-left quadrant of the Nosaru's head region. That way the rest of its body will be undamaged for the dissection afterward."

"That's not fair on us, miss. We haven't had any time to prepare."

"Not fair? I'll tell you what's not fair: spending three years training someone to kill infected human hosts who can't squash an overgrown bug," Ms. Bruno snapped. "This pupa looks innocuous now, but it can reduce its size to smaller than a tapeworm just so it can squeeze into those little blood vessels of yours." She pointed at the glass cage. "It'll then go back to its full size in your chest cavity and insert a small tube into any artery it wants so it'll have an endless supply of food, and all the hormones and neurotransmitters it secretes into your system will turn you into its personal plaything."

Artemis's jaw dropped. She hadn't had that many Nosaru Fundamentals lessons yet and didn't know the specifics of host invasion. "Why do hosts drink blood if the pupa drinks from an artery?"

Ms. Bruno looked at her like she was the dumbest person she'd ever seen. "It's a side effect of host invasion. The intense hormone secretion for more oxyhemoglobin by the Nosaru pupa is what leads to hosts drinking blood even though the pupa doesn't directly benefit from it."

One of the boys next to Artemis spoke. "I could crush that thing in two seconds."

"I don't doubt that, Thompson." She almost smiled. "For those of you who successfully neutralize the Nosaru pupa, you'll find a copy of Edward W. Carlisle's original notes on how to perform a step-by-step dissection from the year 1798. I expect you to follow them to a tee. Those who refuse to perform any of the tasks will be cut from the group and expelled."

Murmurs spread around her class as those words left her mouth.

Eight of the thirty students in foundation training were cut on the first day of school, and none of them wanted to be the next names on the list. Artemis quickly scanned everyone's faces to find most of her classmates' eyes electric, with minds she didn't doubt had been hardened to the task at hand, but a couple were trying their hardest to avoid looking in the general vicinity of the Nosaru and looked like they were moments away from throwing up.

"Garrett-Coleman, you're up." Ms. Bruno moved the box to a machine that kind of looked like a stove hood, but it had small square openings in the glass that Artemis figured she had to put her hands into in order to protect the rest of her body.

Though her stomach lurched in anticipation, Artemis joined Ms. Bruno at the machine. She slid her hands into the gap in the glass and practiced moving them in the tiny space. Artemis was going to prove her wrong and kill the pupa without hesitation—she would prove to everyone that they should never have doubted her.

"You're not cut out for this business, recruit," Ms. Bruno murmured just loud enough for Artemis to hear as she put her arms into the second gap beside her and began to remove the glass encasing the Nosaru. "You're still untouchable as far as expulsion is concerned, but there's nothing stopping you from bowing out on your own."

Her guardian angel was still looking out for her, and Artemis didn't know whether to laugh in Ms. Bruno's face or cry. *I'm not going anywhere.* She tried to control her breathing as the Nosaru started to move around, fire scorching the surface of her skin, and the closer her scalpel got to the Nosaru, the itchier her skin got.

Artemis wanted to claw at her flesh until it peeled away under her nails.

Sweat gathered across her brow as she cornered the pupa and held it steady with a hand. Ms. Bruno said something else to her, but all she could focus on was her pulse thundering in her ears. Artemis's sight grew blurry, though her eyes never left the Nosaru in front of her, watching as it slid out of her grip.

She tried again to swipe at it in the correct spot but just missed it.

What's wrong with me?

It shouldn't have been this difficult. Dark spots appeared in her vision, increasing in size and number with every passing second. There had to be something in the air. Artemis stumbled backward, plummeting to the ground before she could steady herself, and the only person she could think of before the darkness overtook her was Jared.

I'm so sorry.

14

ABYAN

THE MORNING SKY WAS UGLY.

Abyan had been staring at it for a good hour and thought her conclusion was well founded and supported by all the evidence she'd amassed lying on the cold stone roof of the residential building. The sun was all right, she figured. It was doing its thing converting hydrogen to helium, but there was this ghost of a fog that spread across the skyline, and knowing London, it was probably just smog from all the vehicle pollution.

Nitrous oxides, tropospheric ozone, sulfur dioxide, and whatever.

Usually she'd be staring out into the busy high street a few roads over, but Abyan didn't want to move a muscle. She wasn't even supposed to be on the roof. It was off-limits for all students, yet she'd picked the lock ages ago and made it her haven, planting a flag in the ground and marking it as her own.

Twisting the gold ring around her neck, she wondered when she was going to get up. She and Tolly were meant to be meeting the others for a mission. Yet after falling out with Mason yesterday and the dynamics of the squad still being off from the Peeping Tom, the last thing she needed was to be stuck with her squad for hours.

Although Abyan knew she'd overstepped when it came to Mason and wanted to apologize the second the dust settled from her words, Kade and Hassan weren't going to let what happened on their Peeping Tom go until she told the truth about Khalo.

The whole squad knew about Abyan's history with the Nosaru, what was taken from her—they just didn't know the specifics. She balked at the idea of reopening her wounds even the slightest amount, as all these years later they only ever ached and festered.

Healing was never an option.

Mason's words a few days back were a warning, and she would've thanked him if half her mind wasn't slowly slipping back in time, tripping on the shards of her repressed memories. Though she'd tried searching through Carlisle's database of first gens, Khalo's page was sparse, and the last time he was tagged by Carlisle's systems was just over two years ago in France.

Bastard.

Although she told herself to get up, listing all the reasons why she shouldn't be lazing about in her mind, each time she searched for the strength to move, she came up empty. That was depression for you, she supposed.

Abyan was diagnosed when she was fourteen and knew all its tricks well enough, but that didn't stop moments like these. Moments where all she could think about was how shit everything was: Carlisle Academy, the world, her life, the stupid sky.

The weight of it was crushing.

She knew it was going to be a bad depression day the moment she woke up. Most of the time, Kade or Hank were around to distract her with everything and nothing, yet Abyan thought it was cruel enough to force them to deal with her problems on a regular basis and decided to let them be free of her for once.

They weren't the magic cure to depression, of course. Friends helped keep her mind from being consumed, but it still gnawed away at the edges, never letting her forget for a second. The only difference was sometimes it whispered, and other times it screamed.

Tolly stepped onto the roof, squinting at the morning light. "I thought you'd be up here."

Abyan didn't look away from the clouds. "Sorry, I was just thinking."

"About?"

"What Harry told us the other day," she lied effortlessly. It was so much easier than telling the truth. "I don't know how he knew all of that stuff about us."

He waved a dismissive hand. "He was taking cheap shots to get us to turn on each other."

"He must've been keeping tabs on us for a while to know all of that shit," Abyan mused. "It's kind of weird when you think about it."

Tolly sat down next to her, his gangly legs stretched out before him. "What he said about me . . . you didn't tell anyone how I was thinking about leaving here, right?"

"I would never," she confirmed. "Have you made up your mind, though? Because you're going to have to squeeze me into your suitcase if you're really going to the Dakar branch."

"When my parents were alive, they told me to transfer out but I wanted to stay here," he admitted. "I chose to stay for my friends— six idiots who had my back through thick and thin." Tolly met her gaze then, a small smile on his lips. "I'd never had that before."

Abyan cocked her head to one side. "And now?"

"I lost my best friend, and it got a little messy for me up here." He pointed to his head. "But we're family, and I'm not going to run away just because things got tough."

She wrapped him in the tightest hug her heavy bones could muster. "We love you, okay?"

Tolly smiled as she pulled away, but the light didn't reach his eyes, and he inhaled deeply before speaking. "Something about the way Jared died isn't adding up for me, Yan. He left without telling any of us to go and climb a bloody mountain? And he had a secret girlfriend? Hassan said he was drinking coffee with her all the time. Since when did Jared see a girl more than twice in a row or let coffee come within smelling distance of him?"

"I've been thinking the same thing ever since we found out," Abyan said, racking her brain. "Artemis even said he wore his hair down when he was with her and let her run her hands through it—does that sound like Mr. My-Hair-Is-My-Temple Jared Leong to you?"

Tolly shook his head. "It's like he was a different person."

Both of their phones buzzed at the same time, curses flying from their lips as they scrambled to their feet and hurried to the parking garage. They were so screwed. The rest of the squads had arrived for their mission while the two of them were running catastrophically late.

Damn it.

De Costa had finally given them another solo operation to redeem themselves. Unfortunately for Abyan, it was a recon mission.

Abyan hated recon missions.

They shouldn't have counted as operations because all students ever did was tiptoe around a hive planting bugs and cameras so operatives could gather intelligence. Still, it wasn't like Abyan could say no or anything. Though only De Costa and Harry knew what happened during their Peeping Tom, and the squad had stayed tight-lipped about it, rumors of The Sevenfold's fall from grace had already spread around the school.

Her friends needed a win.

She and Tolly shared a determined look before exiting his Rolls-Royce and joining their squad. Abyan gave her daggers and tranqs a quick check, though she knew she probably wouldn't need to use them because the last thing you needed in a recon mission was to disturb the hive and start a brawl.

Deadly force was always a last resort.

The hive was in Wood Green, in a block of apartments that looked perfectly normal from the outside: intact windows, no mold, and a clean exterior. But there were no humans in them.

Every single one of the six floors was contaminated with hosts. It was one of the biggest third-degree hives Abyan had ever seen.

The creatures largely led double lives, with full access to their humans' memories, but the cravings for blood led them to hives sooner or later to get their fill before they went back to playing house.

Abyan took a moment to take the building in, scanning its length.

As a squad, they had fifteen cameras and thirty bugs. Mason and Hassan would take the east face of the building with their share of the surveillance equipment, Artemis would stay in the car, and Kade and Tolly would take the west face, leaving the south for Abyan and Hank.

She crept to the back of the building with Hank in tow and looked up at the metal staircase hanging above her head on the outside of the complex. "Can you—"

He was already pushing a rubbish bin toward her. "One step ahead of you, Yan. There's no way you're standing on my head again."

"You really need to let that go, Hercules." She hoisted herself on top of the bin and climbed the ladder. "Big Diomede was two years ago, and last time I checked, there weren't any wheelie bins in the Arctic."

He climbed up, joining her on the first landing of the staircase. "I think you should stop downplaying my traumatic experiences."

"Hey, I ended up *saving* us from that polar bear, remember?"

"Only after leaving me mildly concussed."

She grinned despite herself. "I think the key word there is *mildly*."

The final tests at the end of their first year at Carlisle were meant to challenge them both individually and as a squad; they changed each year but somehow Shaytaan was always available to mastermind them.

There were different ones for each squad, and The Sevenfold was split into three groups and dumped on Big Diomede, a remote Russian island in the Bering Strait, just south of the Arctic Circle.

She was stuck with Hank, and they were given a med kit, a

fishing pole, a week's worth of rations, and thirty days to find the other members of the squad and reach the evac point in one piece.

"Remind me never to get stranded with you ever again," he whispered as they planted their first few bugs. "Somewhere there's a polar bear who got a taste of my blood and is just waiting to catch my scent again so it can finish the job."

Abyan pouted, poking him with a finger. "Poor you, how will you ever survive without going to a barely habitable, remote island in the middle of nowhere?"

"Seriously, it was the only thing on my bucket list."

The bundle of bugs in Hank's hand slipped from his grasp, knocking against the windows of the hive. *God.* The two of them stood frozen, and Abyan's breath caught in her throat as she waited for several agonizing heartbeats with her eyes glued to the drawn navy curtains.

Once she was certain they hadn't disturbed the hive, she let herself exhale and rolled her shoulders. "They didn't hear—"

The glass window behind her shattered, the shards flying all around her, and rough hands wrapped around her waist and pulled her inside. Abyan landed on the ground with a heavy thud, wet liquid from the ground soaking her clothes.

Rotting body parts littered the floor around her, dark red blood stains were smeared on the walls, and around ten hosts surrounded her, frothing at the mouth with their fangs bared.

Stay calm.

Hank yelled her name, but she didn't have a way to escape.

They were everywhere.

Abyan drew both her tranqs, internally cussing herself out for not bringing something bigger than a bloody handgun just in case. The Nosaru rushed forward from all sides, and she shot at the horde, emptying both her clips in under five seconds. Hank materialized next to her, giving her cover as she reached for the extra ammo strapped to her thighs. Once her guns were loaded, she pushed forward and left a trail of bodies in her wake.

Only one Nosaru was left by the time they were both out of ammo, so she ran forward and hit the female host with two jabs to its right cheek before landing a bone-splintering uppercut to the creature's chin. Hank hurled a dagger between its brows when it crashed to the ground, and the host never got back up.

Abyan looked at him. "We need to find the others."

If she and Hank were burned, then so were the other members of the squad.

He drew another blade. "You go west, I'll go east."

She nodded and ran out of the apartment, turning left with a dagger in her hand. The central foyer area that connected the apartments was darker, so she couldn't make out the murky figures—any one of the countless shadows could be harboring hosts just waiting for the right opportunity to pounce.

Abyan crept forward a few steps, and several hosts ran out of the stairwell next to her. Her body jerked and she jumped back, hurling daggers until she ran out. More hosts spilled out of the other rooms, but she had no ammo in her tranqs and no more daggers left.

The hosts were only getting closer.

Her eyes darted from corner to corner, but she couldn't see Hank—she couldn't make out anyone from her squad in the semidarkness.

A pair of hands wrapped around her waist before she registered anything and pulled her into the next apartment over. She lost her footing and fell to the ground, yet Abyan's yelp died on her tongue as she took in the host in front of her: a few months shy of nineteen, six foot two, with dark hair and eyes.

The same host from her Peeping Tom.

Abyan tried to raise her empty gun, but the host simply shook his head disapprovingly, as if she were a child, the light bouncing off his inky locks. He looked at her intently, scanning her body. *Is he checking for injuries?* "We both know that weapon is no threat, human."

She froze.

A host had never spoken to her before.

He sounded so normal she almost wanted to pinch herself.

"Matteo Valente"—she took a breath, internally cursing herself for how shaky her voice sounded.

The edge of his mouth twitched. "How astute."

"If you're going to kill me, just do it already." Abyan gathered the last of her wits and sat up straight because she wasn't dying on her back. "Your kind aren't known for playing with their food."

"Such an ungrateful creature," Matteo muttered, crouching next to her with feline grace, and his dark stare cut right through her. He leaned in close, sniffing the air around her like he did during the Peeping Tom. "What have they done to you?"

"What are you talking about?" she demanded, rising to her feet and putting enough distance between them that she could finally breathe freely. "Why did you save me?"

He was a bloody first gen. There was no way Matteo couldn't control the fourth gens outside still trying to break through the door and get to her. He stepped away from her and moved toward the window, opening it with a hand.

"I should not have let you live, on that we agree." Matteo took a step toward where Abyan stood, the scattered rays of light casting shadows across his olive skin, and she instantly moved back.

Abyan's brows furrowed. "You could compel the other hosts to stop, but you're choosing not to."

A small smile flitted across his lips. "There are things afoot you can't even begin to imagine, human."

The door behind them slammed open as The Sevenfold burst in, drenched in blood that Abyan desperately hoped wasn't their own. She whipped back around to face the host who'd saved her, but he'd disappeared, the open window the only evidence he was ever there in the first place.

She didn't have time to dwell on the Nosaru's words and yelled for her friends to follow her through the window. They'd messed up royally—a disturbed hive was bad news for everyone, especially since all those hosts now had The Sevenfold's scents.

Once they all managed to get out of the hive and were close enough to their car, Tolly gave a five-second count. Abyan turned to ask what the hell he was counting for, but the deafening boom of the hive collapsing answered the question for her.

Debris sprayed in every direction, smoke and flames fanning upward into the clouds, and the sirens in the distance told her Carlisle Enterprises was going to have its hands full trying to keep a lid on this.

They were so screwed.

15

ARTEMIS

THE SQUAD HAD TO MEET ABYAN IN THE SCHOOL'S PARKING lot, and of course she didn't tell any of them why. The Sevenfold had another meeting yesterday after their BLCC order that Artemis wasn't included in, though it wasn't as noisy as all the other ones she'd overheard. They'd all seen that hive go up in flames, and Kade told them all in the car that she and Tolly had found the explosive device in the basement already rigged to blow.

The most Tolly could do was delay the inevitable.

Three men in dark suits knocked on the door to The Sevenfold's dorm an hour after their return to Carlisle, flashing their intelligence wing IDs to silence any dissent. They asked to speak privately to all the squad except Artemis, so the six all left without a word. They returned a couple hours after, and Artemis wasn't sure what was going to happen until the squad started bringing all their blankets and mattresses over to Kade's room.

No one wanted to sleep alone that night, it seemed.

And, as usual, Artemis wasn't invited.

As she made her way down the stairs of the main building, her left leg vibrated, and she fished her phone out of her pocket. Artemis didn't have to look at the Caller ID to know who it was. Being homeschooled didn't leave many opportunities for making friends.

"Hey, Dad."

"How's my girl?" Maybe it was hearing his familiar gravelly

voice or the patois that rolled from his tongue so effortlessly, but the steps in front of her suddenly went fuzzy, and before she knew it, the first tears rolled down her cheeks.

She hadn't spoken to him since she started at Carlisle. Mum made sure to call her every day and send his love, but he'd been working crazy shifts on the new runway expansion of Heathrow Airport and hadn't found time to call her yet.

"Good." She cleared her throat, gripping the railing. "I'm good." Her chest ached at the lie, and the words clung to the lining of her throat, leaving a bitter taste in her mouth when she shook them loose.

"Have you been crying, Jay?"

She cursed internally. He always knew what was wrong with her—it was like a sixth sense. "No, Dad, I'm just on my way to the library to get books and stuff."

Artemis could never tell him how bad being at Carlisle really was. That she'd cried herself to sleep every night since she fainted in Lab 12 because she was so crap at everything—because Ms. Bruno and everyone else at Carlisle hated her. Just thinking about how her so-called squad made it their mission to make things awkward for her and how Kade was the only one who noticed how much she was going through made her want to sob.

As much as she hated to admit it, Mum was right about this place.

"That's good, I want to see you get an A in all of your subjects," he said after a short pause. Artemis couldn't help releasing a silent sigh of relief as he didn't prod further. "Don't waste this scholarship, now. Keep up with your revision, and don't let anything make you lose focus on your goals."

"Yeah, I know." She laughed and only dared to roll her eyes because he wasn't in the room with her. "Oxford or Cambridge. Trust me, I'm focused."

"I don't want any boys. Do you understand?"

Artemis could see him wagging his finger as if he were standing in the stairwell with her, and she couldn't help giggling. They'd had this talk countless times before she officially moved into Carlisle and throughout the car ride there, and he still wouldn't let it go.

She could just about make out Mum in the background saying, "Tell her when I send you to school, I send you to learn."

"You don't have to worry about that," Artemis assured them before saying her goodbyes.

Most of her squad didn't like her, so why would anyone else?

Artemis tried not to think so much about what they thought of her because it didn't matter in the grand scheme of things. She was there for Jared and nothing else. That was what Artemis reminded herself any time things got tough, and it was enough to keep her going. She had another appointment scheduled with Dr. Telford soon to go through her test results, and thinking of the real reason why she was at Carlisle was the only thing that steadied her wavering spirits.

Everything would be fine.

The parking lot was empty when she arrived, but The Sevenfold assembled around their school-issued Mercedes soon enough. Artemis just hoped this meeting wasn't about her. She already had more enemies than friends at Carlisle and didn't need any more names added to the list.

"Does anyone know what this is about?" she asked, looking around the group. Abyan was the only one missing, but before any of The Sevenfold could reply, she materialized between two cars.

Tolly spoke first. "So, why are we here, Yan?"

"Our first squad test is today," she explained. "It's Stronghold."

He made a sound of frustration. "After what happened yesterday, we should be training twice as hard, not wasting time on a stupid test."

"The school wants us to keep our heads down and mouths shut." Abyan shrugged like it was the most obvious thing in the world. "De Costa told me that more operatives are being deployed to London to figure out what went down the other day, and some of our instructors are off on a classified mission, so we need to roll with this for now and see what happens."

The rest of The Sevenfold nodded in agreement, but Artemis was still lost. Abyan spared her a single glance before rolling her eyes. "Just get in the car, recruit. Everything's already loaded. We'll explain on the way there."

Hassan and Mason sat in the front, Artemis was sandwiched between Kade and Abyan, while Tolly and Hank were in the back. "So, what's Stronghold?"

"Ten of the best squads in our year were called up today, and the five squads on either team are randomly selected by a computer beforehand," Abyan told her. "It's like capture the flag except there are three places in the forest we're going to called Strongholds. There are three rounds, and in each one, your team has to defend a particular Stronghold and hold it until the next round."

"How do we defend it?" Artemis's stomach turned at the thought of fighting five seasoned Year 14 squads after less than two weeks of training. She was an average fighter on her best day—she wouldn't last long in one-on-one combat with a third-year.

"We have these specialized guns that shoot darts laced with a temporary paralytic agent," Mason chimed in from the driver's seat. "The first few shots aren't so bad, but if you get hit enough times, you won't be able to move at all."

Abyan must have seen that Artemis was a second away from jumping out of the moving car. "Try not to panic. Just stay behind me and follow my lead."

She nodded, though she couldn't really feel her limbs anymore. "Thanks."

"Be careful out there, everyone. Both The Renegades and The Trojans are on the other team, and they'll definitely be gunning for us."

By the time they got there, it was already dark out, and the shadows and towering trees swallowed her team up whole. They could barely see one another as they spread out into the forest, and each of them wore trackers observable by all students on the radars attached to their wrists.

"Thirty feet until the Stronghold is reached. The red team has already taken it," Tolly's voice sounded from Artemis's earpiece. He'd remained in the car and watched everything from his laptop; each squad was allowed one member to be their eyes in the game and notify them whenever anything changed.

Artemis gripped her small pistol to her chest as she followed Abyan through the greenery. A stick cracked beneath her boot, and she didn't have time to blink before Abyan threw her behind the closest tree and shot out into the shadows three times. More shots fired in the same direction from the other members of The Sevenfold spread about the forest, and once she was sure the enemy was down, Abyan turned to her.

"Not another noise, recruit," she whispered, eyes hard. "You have to watch where you put your feet, or you'll give us away again." She didn't wait for a reply, pressing forward, and Artemis made sure to triple-check her footfalls as she went after her.

"Fifteen feet until the Stronghold is reached," Tolly's voice crackled in her ear. "You have twelve concentrated in the middle and six spread on either side."

"Left tree," Abyan said, her voice barely a whisper.

Artemis caught her meaning and made for the tree, four darts whizzing behind her as she sprinted. Shots rang out around them, sounding more like loud pops than the gunshots heard in movies. Abyan ducked behind a tree, took one look at her tracker, and then shot multiple times in front of them, several satisfactory thuds and curses sounding a few seconds later.

"Stronghold is gridlocked. The score is 10 to 4, to the reds." At that, Abyan pushed ahead without her, finishing off the remaining members of the red team.

Wind whipped through Artemis's hair, and she watched the

blue dots converge on the Stronghold on her radar as the reds retreated, none of them wanting to sustain any more damage so early on.

Once the noise died down, Artemis figured it was safe to come out of hiding and made her way to where her team was waiting, guns raised and ready for any incoming attacks.

"Stronghold has been taken, and the score is 16 to 11, to the blues," Tolly said. "It's now at point B, one hundred fifteen feet east, fifty feet north."

They spread out again, and Artemis's hands sweated so much her gun nearly slipped from her grasp. The rest of the squad had disappeared somewhere between her third and fourth existential crisis so she hurried to catch up with Abyan, but she couldn't make out anything beyond leaves and bark. Though she looked around frantically, her heart in her throat, Abyan had gotten lost in the shadows.

"Go seven feet to the left, Artemis," Tolly said.

The forest was so silent each of her shaky breaths felt like they could be heard for miles. She followed his directions, her index finger poised on the trigger of her gun, but Artemis still couldn't see anyone.

"Sixteen feet north, then you'll find the others."

She rushed forward, adrenaline coursing through her veins as she went farther into the forest. Still no sign of The Sevenfold. There was a line of trees ahead of her, and the second Tolly told her the squad was on the other side of it, she picked up her pace. Yet all her muscles tensed when she burst into the clearing, her breath catching.

There was no way she was getting out of this.

"Looks like the puppy's lost her way." Dark hair, tan skin, that devilish smile—she knew his face: Lucas Yi, leader of The Trojans.

He sighed before raising his dart gun as if, even in winning, he was already bored of it all. The five members of his squad behind him all aimed for her, too, and Artemis squeezed her eyes shut, drowning out the noise from her earpiece as she braced herself.

Shots fired around her, and Artemis's body jerked. Although she touched a different limb at every pop, none of the darts hit her. Cracking open an eye, she saw The Trojans firing into the trees in different directions, and several of them were hit, their movements increasingly slow. Artemis wanted to laugh out loud in sheer disbelief and cry at the same time.

The Sevenfold.

Abyan and Hank emerged from different sides of the clearing, but shots were still coming from the greenery. She held a gun in either hand and ran in Artemis's direction, firing at the retreating Trojans every step of the way.

Abyan whisper-yelled at her the second she was close enough, "Run, Artemis. Run!"

It took her a few moments to shake her bones to life, but as soon as she did, Artemis headed straight for the tree line. Once she was safe, she checked herself again, patting every part of her body down for darts. She wasn't hit. Artemis released a silent sigh when Abyan emerged from the branches beside her, and she would've hugged the life out of her if she didn't see all the darts protruding from her body.

Artemis counted six.

All on her right side.

While Mason didn't say how many it took for full paralysis, with the way she was limping, Artemis was sure she'd hit the threshold. She hurried to Abyan, putting her arm under her shoulders and carrying all the weight of her injured side.

Artemis gulped. "You came back for me."

"I don't leave people behind," she managed through gritted teeth, hopping on her good foot, a weapon still in her free hand. "Why would you walk right into their hands? I told you to follow me."

"The Stronghold has been taken. The score is 27 to 18, to the reds," Tolly said. "It's now at point C, fifty-three feet west and sixty-six feet north."

He'd set her up.

That was the only reason she ended up with The Trojans. Tolly had to have known they would be in the clearing—he led her right into a trap, and Abyan had paid the price. Just as she was about to defend herself, Abyan's phone buzzed. She blinked twice before reaching into her pocket and pulling it out, her eyes bulging at the message.

"We need to go back to Carlisle right now."

Thank God.

"Why?"

"It doesn't say—"

"Twenty-five high-ranking operatives have been killed by Nosaru in Vauxhall, and they stole the highly classified cargo they were transporting," Tolly said, and Artemis's eyes bulged.

"Not again, Tolly," Abyan murmured, speaking to herself since there wasn't a reply feature on their earpieces. Artemis's phone was on silent, but when she checked, sure enough, she'd received an alert from Carlisle, although it was nowhere near as detailed as what Tolly had.

It was like Tolly knew what Abyan would say and was quick to defend himself. "I didn't hack the teachers again, Yan. It was the school email this time."

She and Abyan shared a look, remembering how several of their teachers had left for a mission that afternoon, both of them too stunned to say a word. The same question shone in their eyes, the words nestling on the tips of their tongues, but neither dared to say it out loud.

How could this have happened?

16

ABYAN

ALL CLASSES WERE CANCELED ON MONDAY MORNING.

The Sevenfold were on edge from what they'd heard during their Stronghold match yesterday, and coming home to see the entire school on lockdown did nothing to settle their nerves. When Emergency Protocol One was activated, all students were confined to their rooms, and with its barren stone hallways and curling stairwells, Carlisle Academy might as well have been a haunted eighteenth-century sanatorium.

Teachers guarded the entrances and exits, with some of them positioned on the roof to keep an eye on the surrounding streets. Though only a Carlisle student would catch it, operatives were posted all over Notting Hill, dressed in plain clothes, with all their weapons artfully hidden as they walked up and down the high street like ordinary pedestrians. The only difference was they looked at anything but the shops and their shiny winter sale signs.

Abyan made her way to Mr. Oluwole's office. He'd emailed her to say their weekly meeting was still on despite the heightened security around the school, and she didn't know whether she was annoyed at how extra he was being or grateful for the distraction.

Last night wasn't supposed to happen.

The Sevenfold knew more about what went down in Vauxhall than the other students thanks to Tolly's hacked emails: The convoy carrying the cargo was ambushed on the A202 in the middle of

Vauxhall Bridge by hosts, all twenty-five operatives present were killed, and the cargo was stolen.

The string of expletives in the emails made it clear whatever the payload was, it held an importance none of them could begin to understand. But what could Carlisle have that would cause this much panic? The emails didn't say, and her imagination wasn't helping. It could've been anything from a nuke or two to the cure for Nosaru invasion the company had been trying to synthesize ever since they crash-landed on Earth in the eighteenth century.

The creatures were changing.

Getting smarter.

The Vauxhall attack had to have taken months of planning, and weeks of surveillance on the intelligence operatives. It was a level of discipline Abyan had never seen before—intense coordination, near impossible by Nosaru standards, and meticulous calculation.

Even the intelligence operatives who spoke to her in the squad's three-hour-long interrogations about the hive explosion were shocked by what they'd witnessed. She didn't tell them about the host who'd spoken to her, nor did she breathe a word of it to her friends because she knew he was the one who'd planted the bomb in the hive.

There was no one else that could've done it.

Yet the reason why Matteo did it still escaped her. Nothing added up when it came to him; he was a first gen but couldn't control the lesser hosts and refused to kill her when Abyan was a sitting duck. Everything about him flashed red and bared teeth, but part of her wanted to know more despite the danger.

He held all her answers.

Though she was certain she was right when she said something was different about the Nosaru after her WLDO, she also figured it was more than a simple change in the wind—a huge shift in how the creatures operated happened right under their noses, and no one knew where to start: the bodies or their mistakes.

Abyan only remembered the pills in her pocket when she paused outside Mr. Oluwole's office. *Stupid multivitamins.* She forced them down before knocking, and entered the moment she was called in, taking a seat in front of his desk.

"Good morning, sir."

"Good morning, Abyan." He offered her a smile that couldn't quite cover the stress etched into the fine lines of his brow. "How are you feeling? I know Emergency Protocol One isn't something you're used to."

"I'm fine, sir. The school's doing what needs to be done." She shrugged, trying her best to act normal. "I can't help but wonder what caused the lockdown though. No one's told us anything."

Abyan didn't know how far she could prod before she gave herself away. He was the assistant headteacher. He had to know more than he was letting on. And if they were all in mortal danger, she preferred to know exactly how bad the situation was.

Why were operatives still prowling Notting Hill a day after an attack in Vauxhall? Did they think the Nosaru were going to hit the school as part of a bigger plan? She had so many questions, yet the blank look Mr. Oluwole was giving her told her he didn't intend on answering any of them.

"That's not something students should concern themselves with, but rest assured, the matter is being handled. Classes and training sessions will resume as normal on Wednesday."

How could she not concern herself with it? Abyan almost scoffed out loud. They knew—or had some idea, at least—what the single biggest threat to mankind was up to, and they were hiding it at everyone's expense. She guessed they had a good reason for it and probably knew best, but that didn't make the pill less bitter or any easier to swallow.

"Understood."

"Last time we spoke, you complained of headaches and nausea. Have you seen the doctor yet?"

It had been around a week since she and Hank met with him, and Abyan still hadn't gone to the doctor. The headaches weren't so bad anymore, the bouts of nausea were few and far between, and she didn't want to waste anyone's time.

Her period was close, and everyone knew uteruses had their moments sometimes and messed up your body chemistry, so she decided to tough it out. There was no point seeing a doctor when her symptoms would clear up in a few days naturally.

"It's not as bad anymore. I think they'll go away on their own soon enough."

"Still, I think you should see a professional," he said, leaning back in his chair. "You haven't said anything about the newest addition to The Sevenfold. If you have something you would like to say on the matter, now is the time."

Mr. Oluwole was disappointed in her.

She could see it in his face.

Abyan was always the one who had to deal with all the pressure and expectations of the squad. Whenever they did well, everyone lauded The Sevenfold with equal congratulations and praise, but when their grades dipped by even the smallest percentage points, she carried both the judgment and responsibility to correct their failures by herself, always sharing the glory of their highs with the others and drowning in the embarrassment of their losses alone.

"Artemis can't fight. She freezes up when she's scared, and I don't know how she's still here or why she's in my squad." While Abyan tried to hold herself back, the words wouldn't stop as she met Mr. Oluwole's surprisingly sympathetic gaze.

He stroked his full beard. "Her training reports are not where we expected them to be, but the school has faith that she'll improve. Some students take longer than others to come into their own."

She wouldn't improve.

Though Artemis was nice enough, nothing about her was cut out for a place like Carlisle Academy, and Abyan half wanted to ask how she even got past the application stage. Abyan was the only non-legacy student in her year back when she was a recruit. Everyone else either knew one another already or had heard of each other's families while she was an outsider.

They would talk about things she'd never heard of like Ascot and the Ashes, and she would avoid them all like the plague. There was no point trying to build bridges with people you had no common thread with. She could empathize with Artemis's situation in that way. It wasn't easy navigating a rough sea like Carlisle Academy when you were isolated on a rubber dinghy and everyone else was in a military-grade submarine.

On Wednesday, they would have to walk into training with a recruit, and Abyan cringed at the thought. Sir Marland still had a vendetta against The Sevenfold, but even he wouldn't be able to keep a straight face the second he saw them.

How did they expect her to keep the team on top with a recruit weighing them down?

If she didn't know any better, Abyan would've sworn up and down the school was punishing them. Yesterday's Stronghold match was nothing but a grim reminder of how the rest of the year was going to go. Carlisle kept a close eye on each squad's performance, and Artemis's run-in with The Trojans had to have cost the squad dearly.

They were lucky it was cut short.

"With all due respect, she's only holding us back," Abyan deadpanned. "She doesn't belong here."

"The school believes in her abilities, so she must remain." He sighed. "The decision is out of my hands."

"It feels like you're setting us up to fail, sir."

Mr. Oluwole clearly disliked Artemis being with them just as much as Abyan did. He probably would've kicked her out ages ago if his hands weren't tied. Yet it left the question of who wanted Artemis there if it wasn't him. Was it Mr. Williams? Abyan couldn't figure out why the headteacher would want her to stay at Carlisle. What could he possibly need an emotional, useless, and directionally challenged recruit for?

"You know who else said those exact words to me not too long ago?" He smiled and Abyan cocked a brow. "John King, right before his Year 14 squad test."

Her throat dried up in an instant. Hank's older brother was a legend. He'd never failed a mission in his life, his face was plastered all over the school, and though he'd only graduated three years ago, he already had a place in the Hall of Operatives and a shiny plaque with his name on it. Whenever John visited Carlisle, you would've thought it was Beyoncé or something with the way people flocked to him, practically falling over themselves to catch a glimpse.

"He did?"

He nodded, the light gleaming off his deep brown skin. "Right after I gave him Mission Epsilon, he sat where you're sitting now and told me he couldn't do it. That we must've wanted him to fail. How could he protect a bus of schoolchildren from one hundred Nosaru with only eight other people?"

Abyan had no idea how he managed it.

Third year squad tests were always demonic, but everyone could admit Mission Epsilon was one of the hardest ever given. Though the hosts all had collars that'd zap them into the astral plane if they got too close to the kids, that was only a last resort—using the collars would've been a failure for John's squad.

The ten primary schoolers didn't know what was going on either and the driver wasn't even in on the mission. The poor things just saw death rise from the hills of the Scottish Highlands and run straight for them.

"I'll tell you what I told him: A true Carlisle operative would be able to handle whatever task we give them. If something we throw at you is enough to make you shake in your boots, then perhaps you aren't cut out to be here, after all, because for every terrible situation we put you in, the Nosaru have ten that are a thousand times worse."

Abyan set her jaw. "I understand."

"You're looking at the addition of Garrett-Coleman like an impenetrable wall, when really, it's a window you're just too afraid to look through."

War yaa ilaah yaqan.

She had to resist the urge to roll her eyes. "Thank you for the advice, sir." She made to stand. "Can I go back to my squad?"

He dismissed her with a wave of his hand, and Abyan immediately headed for the stairwell. There weren't any bugs or cameras on the highest flight. Once she reached it, she stared at the golden Carlisle Academy symbol etched into the marble stone ceiling, wondering exactly how many secrets were being held in the walls around them.

Abyan pulled out her phone as soon as the coast was clear and called the only person who would listen to her. "Hank," she said, not letting him get a word in. "The school is lying to us about something big."

17

ARTEMIS

THE RESEARCH WING OF CARLISLE ENTERPRISES REMINDED Artemis of a hospital from one of those futuristic movies. The building was white and ashen gray on the inside, with glass bridges connecting one side to the other and giant mirrors on every wall. A huge tank filled with fish of all sizes sat square in the middle of the ground floor, and Artemis paused for a moment in front of it to take in the array of colors.

Doctors walked around in white coats, the nurses in blue scrubs, and the security guards in all black with guns the size of small children strapped across their chests.

No matter how hard she tried, Artemis couldn't look away from their weapons. Her gut told her they were loaded with something packing a far deadlier kick than a simple tranquilizer, and she never wanted to see the business end of their barrels.

East Wing.

She had to get to East Wing. Dr. Telford would be wondering where she was if she lingered any longer, and the last thing she wanted was to be late for her appointment twice in a row.

As Artemis sped through the halls, following the detailed directions on her appointment letter, a tiny bulb of excitement blossomed in her chest. Dr. Telford was going to cancel all her tests. Artemis could feel it in her bones. Her previous blood test results had to have come back by now, and she'd have seen that further testing wasn't necessary.

Mr. Carlisle, the rest of the faculty, her parents—none of them needed to worry about her anymore. She was keeping her head down and focusing like they all wanted.

Artemis hadn't even let Emergency Protocol One faze her, training with Kade and Hassan in their living room, since all the gyms were locked down, and did all her homework in spite of it all because hardly anyone around her really believed in her. Most of them were waiting for the day when she finally called it quits and headed home with her tail tucked between her legs and her head hung low, but Artemis knew they'd all be bitterly disappointed.

She was going to prove them all wrong.

Turning into East Wing's foyer, Artemis smiled warmly at the waiting receptionist. "Hi, I'm Artemis Garrett-Coleman. I'm here to see Dr. Telford."

The dark-haired woman pointed to the closed door at the end of the corridor to her right. "Head that way. The nurse will see you first."

Artemis thanked her before making her way down the corridor and entering a room with several beds shrouded with aquamarine disposable curtains. A sunburned nurse approached her, pen and clipboard in hand, and asked, "Artemis Garrett-Coleman?"

She looked around before answering, not seeing Dr. Telford anywhere. "Yes, that's me."

"Please put your jacket and shirt in here," she handed her a plastic bag, "and take a seat on that empty bed in the corner and Dr. Telford will be right over."

Artemis did as the nurse asked and didn't have to wait long for Dr. Telford to come and pull up a chair beside her hospital bed. "So, Artemis," Dr. Telford began, opening a beige folder with #HTS1806B written in the corner, "I can see you're itching for your results, so you should know your blood test came back normal aside from a slight vitamin D deficiency."

She released the breath she was holding. "I told you it would."

"I know, but you shouldn't relax just yet," she warned. "I spoke with Mr. Carlisle about you, and while he's pleased the results don't cause any immediate concern, he thinks it would be best to run a few more tests to provide a more holistic view of where you're at. Then, we can move on from there."

"You said if my results came back promising I wouldn't need any more."

Artemis didn't know whether Dr. Telford was having a severe case of selective amnesia, but she remembered her exact words during their first meeting like it was yesterday. Mr. Carlisle told her himself that the testing was always optional and would only be conducted with her express consent—they were supposed to pull her out the second she didn't want to take part, yet the more Dr. Telford spoke, the less *optional* it sounded.

She shrugged. "You'll have to take it up with him. He's put you down for a larger blood draw today and a biopsy during our next session, so you'll need to come down to the research wing again on that day."

Artemis gritted her teeth. "What if I refused to do it?"

What they were trying to force her to do had to be illegal. Though she'd been warned Carlisle Enterprises had a foot in all government agencies and a finger in every judge's pocket, there had to be someone free of their hold.

"I've been instructed to tell you that in the event of your refusal to submit to testing, your place at Carlisle will be taken away."

Dr. Telford couldn't look at her as she spoke, settling on staring at her papers instead. Artemis didn't know what to do. Her hands were tied. She hated the idea of being Mr. Carlisle's personal lab rat, but she still had to find her place in The Sevenfold—she still had to do right by Jared.

She couldn't leave now.

"Fine."

Artemis had a feeling Dr. Telford was lying about the real purpose of the examinations. She wasn't an expert in medicine, but even she knew people didn't get biopsies as part of a routine health check, and the size of the empty blood bag next to her was enough to know that this was no ordinary blood draw.

Mr. Carlisle was keeping something from her and had ordered Dr. Telford to keep her quiet and docile while they poked and prodded her with their instruments, and Artemis had eaten it all up.

He'd told her they were on the same side back in Scotland, and she was stupid enough to buy his lies. She couldn't believe she'd been so naïve as to think they were trying to help her. As she gazed at Dr. Telford across the desk, Artemis's nails dug so deep into the skin of her palms she was sure she'd pierced the skin.

"Wonderful." Dr. Telford gave her a thin-lipped smile and stood, needle and tube in hand. She stuck the needle in her right arm, and Artemis watched the maroon liquid rush into the waiting bag. "You'll be giving just one pint of blood today, which is enough to make you feel tired and dizzy, so be careful over the next few days."

Artemis didn't reply.

She doesn't really care about me.

When it was over with, Dr. Telford spoke again. "You won't be going back to the academy on your own. Transport has been arranged for you and Hassanain to take you back to your dorm safely."

Artemis cocked a brow. *Hassanain?* But Dr. Telford turned on her heel and disappeared before she could ask who it was. She leaned back in her bed, her eyelids already feeling heavy enough that Artemis didn't care about the ache in her arm, yet the sound of the curtain next to her head being pulled to the side jolted her from her haze.

"I thought that hag would never leave," Hassan said from the bed next to her. "I hope she steps on a burning Lego."

She couldn't look away from the bandage on his arm, identical to the one on her own. "They took blood from you, too?"

He nodded. "They said they'll be taking it from the whole squad once every six months this year."

"But why?"

"Don't know and don't care." Hassan pulled his legs up to his chest, his free hand squeezing his Rubik's Cube like a stress ball. "I begged them not to do it here, you know? I told them they can have whatever they want as long as I don't have to set foot in another hospital."

Artemis paused for a second, taking in his hunched shoulders and the sweat along his brow, and wanted to kick herself for not realizing it sooner: Hassan was scared. "So, they forced you to come here?"

He took in a shaky breath, eyes darting around. "They had to sedate me because I told them I wasn't coming anywhere near this place. I only came to when Telford already had her hooks in you."

Artemis hauled herself off her bed, the fatigue clinging to her bones making it a Herculean effort, and pulled Dr. Telford's forgotten chair next to Hassan's bed to sit in. "Why do you hate hospitals so much?"

Hassan snapped, "I don't want to talk about it."

"Okay, I'm sorry," she said, glancing at the floor. "I just . . . want to be your friend."

He looked at her like she was insane. "I haven't said a nice word to you since you started here, and you want to be my *friend*?"

"You and the others are mean sometimes, but that doesn't mean I have to be the same back." Artemis looked at the ground. "I get that you're all still hurting from Jared's death."

"You're not what I expected, recruit." His tone was less mocking. "I'll give you that."

A comfortable silence took hold of the room, yet Artemis couldn't get her brain to quiet. There were too many unanswered questions. She wanted to know what the school was hiding from them all and why they were all being kept in the dark; Artemis knew she couldn't be the only one in the squad who found all the secrets impossible to stomach.

Hassan had to know something else.

"I've been thinking . . ." she trailed off, not knowing how her words would be received. "What if they've found the cure for Nosaru invasion and are inoculating us all in secret? That could be why they're testing us, right? To see if we'll have side effects or not?"

"You sound just like Yan, recruit." He groaned. "You should be telling her all these theories, not me, then you can combine forces like the Powerpuff Girls or some shit."

You might be onto something there.

She straightened, the plan she'd just formulated in those precious seconds making her heart race. "That's actually not a bad idea."

The only way for them to find out the real reason behind everything that was going on was to get inside information about the inner workings of Carlisle Enterprises, and no one was ever going to give them that willingly. They'd have to take it by force. Yet Artemis knew she couldn't convince The Sevenfold to go along with what she planned when most of them were lukewarm to her at best, but Abyan could.

Artemis would've been lying if she said she remembered any of the journey back to their dorm. The car ride, the two operatives who escorted them there—none of it registered over the anticipation humming in her body.

She needed to find Abyan.

She staggered into their living room as movement echoed from the kitchen, and Abyan soon strolled out, pulling off oven mitts.

"Is anyone else home?" Artemis asked, breathless.

She shot her a questioning look. "The whole squad's here."

Artemis choked down her fear and walked right up to her. "I know you think the school is up to something, and I'm just as suspicious," she said. "You don't trust me yet, and that's fine because what's more important is understanding what's really going on."

She was quiet for a long time, silently studying her. "What do you have in mind, recruit?"

Artemis wanted Abyan to trust her—she *wished* she did. It wasn't the same getting Abyan's true thoughts from third parties between dismissive waves and flippant remarks, and Artemis knew the two of them were onto something.

The others just needed to see it, too.

"We need to hack into Carlisle's systems," she said, and glanced in the direction of the bedrooms, "but there's only one person here who can do it, and he's not really my biggest fan."

"Hacking into the school is reckless and dangerous."

Artemis shrugged. "It's not like that's ever stopped you from getting what you want before, is it?"

"I can't make Tolly do this for you." She shook her head. "Something like this has to be a team decision."

Abyan pulled out her phone and sent a text before heading out of the room without a word. Artemis's own phone pinged not a second later, showing a message to the squad's group chat: "GROUP MEETING."

So, she walked to Kade's room slowly, each step tentative, as if she expected one of the others to tell her she wasn't supposed to be there at any second.

The Sevenfold had already assembled by the time she got there.

"The recruit has a proposition for us." Abyan addressed the squad, leaning against the wall with crossed arms. She angled her head in a way that told Artemis to stand up and take the floor, and it took Artemis a second to get her limbs to work.

Artemis gulped at all the expectant faces around her: Hassan trying to keep himself awake on the bean bag, Hank and Mason watching her with a curious glint in their eyes, Kade's supportive smile that told her she was doing great, and Tolly's immortal glare.

She took all of it in the palm of her hand and clenched her fingers into a tight fist. "The school is up to something, and we've all got our suspicions. From the WLDOs to the weird testing that we're being forced to do, I think . . . I think we should stop asking them nicely for answers and take them ourselves."

Kade tilted her head to the side. "So, how do we do that?"

"We should hack into the London branch," she announced, looking at each member of the squad in turn. "The intelligence and research wings have all the information we need."

Something like respect shone in Abyan's eyes. "Let's keep it simple," she said, her voice carrying all the authority Artemis wished she had. "Raise your hands if you want to do the hack—we should be unanimous on this."

Slowly but surely each member of the squad raised their hand, yet the smile taking hold of Artemis's lips died when Tolly looked at her in disgust and said, "I'm not doing anything for her."

Mason tried to save the situation. "Come on, give Artemis a break."

She was done taking all the flack for something that wasn't her fault. "I know you all miss Jared and wish he were here instead of me," she said. "I wish he were here, too, okay? But as much as I hate myself and as much as I regret what happened on Ben Nevis, I know it's not going to bring him back."

Though Artemis's eyes burned, she kept them trained on Tolly. "I'm sorry that he's in the ground and I'm here—I really am, more than you could imagine—but I'm part of this squad now, and I'm not going anywhere. You have to deal with it because I'm not going to be the emotional punching bag anymore."

Her body shook as she desperately tried to control her breathing and a voice startled her. "She's right." It was Kade, and Artemis wanted to hug the life out of her. "Whether you like it or not, Artemis is one of us now, and you should treat her as such." Her brown eyes briefly connected with Artemis's, the promise that she was on her side even if everyone else wasn't clear as day in their depths, before she focused on Tolly. "Sure, you might not trust her fully yet, but shouldn't she be given the chance to earn it?"

He released a heavy sigh at that, no doubt sensing the tide around them shift fully against him. "Fine, I'll do the damn hack."

Artemis met Abyan's gaze from where she was still propped up against the solitary wall a little far off from where everyone else was clustered. Something about her face, the knowing tilt of her jaw, the tiny upturned fraction of her lips, told Artemis that Abyan had entered the room with a series of predictions and gotten every one of them right. *Well played, Abyan.* She'd known they were going to do the hack the second the words had left Artemis's lips.

18

ABYAN

MASON'S HAIR STUCK OUT LIKE A SORE THUMB, AND AGAINST the backdrop of gray October mist and the muted colors of the pedestrians around him, he was a bolt of purple lightning. He raised his mug to his lips, never once looking away from his phone. Just like she expected. Abyan pulled up the collar of her trench coat and closed the distance between them, sliding into the seat in front of him outside of his favorite coffee shop.

He began, "How did you—"

"Coffee at 10:00 a.m. outside Jenny's," Abyan said, recalling the details like she'd known them all her life. "After your tarot reading on the first Friday of the month."

Mason's mouth fell open a fraction at that.

She gently grabbed his hands over the table, their surprising warmth seeping into her icicle fingers. "I'm so sorry for what I said to you in the gym the other day," she said. "I didn't mean it."

Mason's blue eyes never left her face once, the rest of his features insufferably impassive. "Which part are you apologizng for exactly, Yan? The part where you said I was only here for my sperm donor or when you implied that I didn't care about our squad as much as you?"

Her heart twisted at his words.

"I'm sorry for all of it," she said, pushing her hurt to the side. This moment wasn't about her. "I was being defensive and let my anger do the talking for me."

Abyan wished with everything in her that his lips would pull up at corners into that ridiculously perfect smile of his, that she'd hear his boisterous laugh and giggle at how its bass shook his entire body along with it. She didn't want to lose him over a few careless words. It was her own fault, Abyan supposed—no one held a gun to her head and forced her to shatter two years' worth of friendship in under a minute.

He'll never forgive me.

Mason opened his mouth, but Abyan was faster. She took out the thermal container from her bag and placed it in front of him. "I brought a peace offering." She bit the inside of her cheek as he loosened the lid and peered inside. "Google said it was Norway's national dish, and I thought it would remind you of your mum, but please don't ask me to pronounce its name—I don't want to upset the Viking spirits."

A tiny laugh escaped his lips, not more than a second long but it was enough to lift Abyan's hopes to the stars. "Fårikål."

"I hope it doesn't taste bad," Abyan said. "I may or may not have added some . . . extra things in there."

He grinned fully, and she knew then that all the light in the world couldn't come close to the sight before her now. "Did you just call my national dish unseasoned?"

"Have I mentioned how much I love you?" she asked, doing her best to hold back a laugh. "If you ever need a kidney, just know I have two."

"Well, all my organs are on the table for you except my liver—I don't think its halal anymore."

"That's . . . not how that works." Abyan giggled. "Does that mean we're good?"

Mason pointed to her bag. "That depends entirely on whether or not you brought a spoon along with you."

Abyan took out the spoon she'd wrapped up, handing it over. She glanced at her phone, unable to look at Mason tasting her fårikål, to see a call from an unknown number coming in. "Give me two seconds," she told him before getting up from the table and picking up. "Who is—"

A gruff voice deadpanned, "You're being tailed."

"What the hell do you mean?" Abyan's gaze darted all around, flitting across all the passing faces and lingering a little on every shadow she saw. "Why would anyone follow me to a coffee shop, Harry?"

More important, why was he keeping tabs on her? This wasn't a BLCC order or WLDO. Something in her whispered that Harry knew the squad had been snooping around the school, that they were catching onto whatever was going on, and he'd been ordered to keep watch over them all.

She almost wanted to thank whatever host was dumb enough to follow her.

Now she wouldn't be caught unaware.

"A first or second gen by the looks of it," Harry replied. "You and Mason need to split up and take different routes back to the academy."

She kept looking around. "Give me a description of what to look out for, at least."

"Tall, lean build, dark hair, and fairly young." Harry's voice crackled in her ear. "Didn't get a good look at his face."

Wait.

Abyan clenched her jaw. "Leave him to me."

She hung up the phone and walked back to Mason with brisk steps. She knew which host was following her—Ya Allah, he was like a sentient version of alien herpes, and she was going to find out once and for all why he wouldn't leave her alone.

Mason handed her back the thermal container, nothing but the bones from the lamb left, and raised a brow at her expression. "Did Hank get a girlfriend or something?"

Abyan narrowed her eyes. "Harry's been watching us. He

caught sight of a first gen tailing us and said to split up and get back to the academy as soon as possible."

"He's funny if he thinks I'm leaving you alone." Mason got to his feet and instinctively reached to his side, cursing under his breath when he found no sword or dagger. "We'll have a better chance if we're together."

"It was a direct order, Mason. We can't just ignore it."

He clicked his tongue. "Bastard."

Abyan gave him the first gen's description and then pulled him in for a quick hug, and he squeezed her tight enough that she thought her ribs would break. "Good luck out there, Ragnar."

Mason kissed the top of her hijab. "Get back to us in one piece, okay?"

Abyan pulled away. "I'll try my best."

She turned on her heel and proceeded down the street, pulling up her collar as though it would hide her from wherever Matteo was watching her from. Couldn't Harry have told her where he was? Nevertheless, she kept her eyes peeled as she maneuvered through the bodies and crossed into Brompton Cemetery.

It was huge, more park than cemetery, and there was enough space that Abyan could catch sight of her tail with ease. She thanked Allah for the October cold, as the place was pretty much empty when she entered.

Time to come out, Matteo.

She continued to the older graves, past the crumbling Victorian archways, and turned on her back foot abruptly, catching the barest hint of a shadow flitting behind one of the tombs. Abyan stalked toward where she'd seen the shadow, stopping a couple paces ahead of it. "I know it's you, Matteo. There's no point hiding."

When she received no reply, Abyan threw all caution to the wind and peered behind the tomb with her heart in her throat. It was empty. There was no way Abyan could've gotten it wrong—she could practically feel him nipping at her heels when she entered the cemetery. She bit the inside of her cheek as she took in her surroundings again, her heart in her throat, and forced herself to rethink everything.

He's here somewhere.

A twig snapped behind her, but Matteo had both of her arms locked at her back before she could blink. He whispered next to her ear, his upper fangs skimming the side of her face. "So close yet so far, human."

Although Abyan tried to pull against his iron grip, the only thing she succeeded in doing was almost dislocating her shoulders. "Let me go!"

"A rabbit who willingly draws out a wolf is a dead rabbit." His hands pressed deeper into her flesh. "Consider yourself lucky I am not here to kill you."

She bit out, "Why are you following me then?"

"I do not answer to lesser organisms." She could feel his smile against her skin and recoiled in disgust. "You should have stayed in that establishment with your paramour and eaten your food."

Abyan inhaled, relaxing all her muscles, and kicked him in the shin with the heel of her foot. The instant his hold loosened by the slightest amount, she caught him in the jaw with a roundhouse kick and put some much-needed distance between them.

"How's that for a lesser organism?" she spat, itching to show Matteo exactly how much damage she could do. "You won't win a fight against me, so answer my questions and I might let you live."

Matteo shook his head, the whites of his eyes going black. "Humans and their insufferable pride."

Shit.

A figure appeared behind the first gen, materializing from the cracked headstones and leaning autumn trees, dressed in black cargo trousers and a navy T-shirt. "Don't move a muscle, Valente." Harry had a pistol trained on the back of Matteo's head, but Abyan knew it would be no use in a matter of seconds. "Leave the girl alone."

"I would think twice about pulling that trigger if I were you," Matteo warned. "My associates would not like it."

Abyan couldn't tear her eyes away from the six hosts that now encircled them. She reached for her sword and wanted to scream when Gacan Libaax was nowhere to be found. Her stomach turned—she'd seen them all before: three waitresses from the cafe she'd been sitting in, the old man who'd been drinking coffee behind her, and the two men she'd passed on the way into the cemetery.

Matteo had known they'd caught onto what he was doing.

"If I were you, I would walk away," he said, the smirk on his lips driving Abyan insane. "No one needs to die on this day."

There was a chance Harry's dart could hit Matteo before he either dodged it or the other hosts descended on them all. It was small but still possible. Yet Abyan got the feeling that her shadow wasn't one for risks—she had no weapons and Harry only had the one pistol in his hand. It wouldn't be enough to take on a first gen with six hosts under active generational control.

By the time they'd managed to kill these six, ten more could appear.

It would be a losing battle.

Abyan and Harry shared a look, the same grim resignation in their eyes, before he sheathed his gun. Matteo nodded once before slinking away to whatever dank hole he crept out from, his group of inferior hosts protecting him from all sides.

She couldn't believe it.

They'd let him win.

19

ARTEMIS

ARTEMIS BROKE THE ONLY RULE SHE WAS GIVEN.

Her fist flew through the air, her muscles humming with adrenaline, and she couldn't have stopped the momentum even if she'd known what was coming.

Kade didn't block the blow or move fast enough to sidestep it, and Artemis's knuckles collided with her cheek with a resounding thud. She pulled back immediately as Kade held a hand to her face.

"I'm so sorry," Artemis said, extending her hands in caution as though Kade were a tiger waiting to pounce. "I didn't mean to hit you in the face. I just didn't think it would land or that you wouldn't get to it in time or—"

Kade laughed a little, wincing at the pain. Her cheek was getting redder by the second. "I've been hit harder, Artemis."

"So, you forgive me?"

"With a face like that, how could I not?" She winked and heat flooded Artemis's body right down to her toes. "Besides, it was my fault for lowering my guard and leaving that side open."

Kade sat on a bench and handed her a towel and water bottle while taking the same for herself. Artemis splashed water on her face and wiped at her body—they'd been training for about an hour and were both exhausted.

Sweat glistened across Kade's exposed collar bone, and while Artemis didn't dare look any lower, Kade caught her staring before she could look away. *Crap.* Artemis's eyes bulged and she wiped at her face, focusing on anything but the gorgeous girl next to her.

The last thing she wanted to do was ruin their friendship.

"You're thinking about him, aren't you?" Kade asked, and although Artemis wasn't before, she sure as hell was now. "I'm sorry if this is too weird for you."

She looked down. "No, it's not that. It's just . . . don't you think about Jared, too? Like how he would feel about this and stuff?"

"Of course I do, but he's not here anymore and he wouldn't want us to spend the rest of our days in repressed misery—that would be like borderline homophobic." Kade shrugged. "Don't get me wrong, I loved him—even though he was an ass—but I've come close to dying so many times that now I just think that life is meant to be lived to the fullest, Artemis."

"So, you really think he'd be okay with this?"

"God's honest truth? I do," she admitted. "And if Jared's watching us now and really doesn't like it all that much, I guess he can just fight me in the afterlife."

Artemis didn't know how to respond to that. It wasn't what she was expecting. Maybe she'd underestimated the relationship between Kade and Jared—she joked about him like he was right in the room with her while acknowledging that he was six feet under in the same breath. Maybe Kade was right. Jared would've probably wanted the two of them to be happy and might've even preferred Artemis move on with someone like her.

Kade nudged her lightly. "Gay panic is adorable on you, by the way."

"It's not my fault!" Artemis slapped her hands to her face. "You look at me how you do, and I completely forget how to act."

"What can I say? I have a thing for pretty girls who can punch me in the face hard enough to make me see stars." There was a teasing gleam in her eyes. "Even if it was a lucky shot that only landed because nausea has me by the neck right now."

Artemis cocked a brow. "How long haven't you been feeling well?"

"It started at the beginning of term, but it was bearable, you know?" she admitted. "Now it's constant. I just want to throw up all the time and the worst part is the migraines. God, it feels like my head's being split clean in two most of the time."

Artemis thought back to two weeks ago. Abyan hadn't been feeling well either, and she remembered her talking about having really bad migraines, too. Artemis had caught Hassan throwing up several times as well, but she wasn't sure if it was just because he kept scarfing down whatever flavor of ice cream he found in the freezer. Artemis wasn't close enough to Mason, Hank, or Tolly yet to know if they'd been experiencing anything similar, but she made a mental note to keep an eye out for any more uncanny similarities.

"What do you think it is, Kade?"

She waved a hand. "It's probably just a weird version of Recruit's Flu. It's always going around at this time of the year, and Yan's already coming out the other side of whatever this is, so I'll probably be fine in about a week, too."

Artemis hadn't seen Kade and Abyan exchange a single word since their failed Peeping Tom, but the two of them hugged the life out of each other after their interrogations about the hive explosion. She'd thought they'd made up until the next morning, when they went straight back to pretending they didn't exist to one another.

"Have you—"

"If you're about to tell me to make nice with her, the answer is no," Kade interrupted. "Aside from Hassan, no one else understands it: In two years of friendship and fighting together, I've never had a reason to doubt whether Yan would have my back . . . until that Peeping Tom." She raked a hand through her hair. "Something she saw or heard made her leave her team for the wolves, and she needs to tell us for our own safety. It's not just about her anymore if she's willing to sacrifice us all for whatever it is she's hiding."

That was understandable, Artemis supposed.

"I appreciated your support the other day for the hack." Artemis chose her words carefully, fiddling with her fingers. "I didn't think anyone would agree with me."

"You were onto something," she replied. "I didn't see what Yan saw at first, but it's starting to get too weird to ignore. The way they tried to shut us all up after the hive explosion was when I knew it for sure."

It wasn't as if they'd actually succeeded in hacking Carlisle yet, as days had passed since Tolly agreed to hack into the London branch of Carlisle Enterprises, but so far, all the research and intelligence wings' expensive cybersecurity was proving difficult to breach even with his freakishly good computer skills.

He'd set up programs that ran night and day to try and crack the system's fortress of a firewall, but so far they'd had no luck. Apparently, it was unrecognizable from the school's, and she figured it made sense—the research and intelligence buildings held all of Carlisle Enterprises' secrets, and they weren't there for just anyone to stumble upon.

Artemis gave a frustrated sigh. "I've tried floating the idea of getting answers elsewhere if the school's so set on keeping us all in the dark, but Abyan refused."

"Elsewhere?"

"From the hosts," she explained. "They could explain what's happening on their end of things and help us piece everything together; call me crazy but I don't think killing every Nosaru we come across is productive."

They didn't have to be enemies with the Nosaru 24/7, but with Carlisle Academy, it was always war from beginning to end. Weren't they all tired? She'd only been there a few weeks and was already sick of it.

Some hosts were more useful to them alive than dead.

"Don't you think the school stuff is more important, though?"

Kade asked, tilting her head. "We could find out what all the testing is for first and then figure out the Nosaru side of things afterward."

Artemis thought on her words. "I suppose so. I've asked a dozen times, but Dr. Telford never tells me the real reason why I'm getting all these tests."

"We could steal your file and see what's inside."

Her brows furrowed. "There's no way she'll let us anywhere near her research office unless we have an appointment."

Kade held out a hand for her and Artemis took it without hesitation. "Leave that part to me, Artemis."

20

ABYAN

NO MATTER HOW HARD ABYAN TRIED, SHE COULDN'T STOP thinking about Matteo. There was no rational explanation for whatever he was up to. After they let him get away, she'd directed all her anger at Harry because it was his fault for bringing a knife to a gunfight and leaving them vulnerable.

Abyan hated him.

In fact, she hated him just as much as Matteo.

They were both so focused on keeping her in the dark. Was the truth really such a hard ask? She couldn't even vent to Hank or Mason about it because she'd decided it was better if they didn't know for now—that way they'd have plausible deniability if shit ever hit the fan and Harry left her to deal with the fallout alone.

Her phone buzzed against her thigh, snapping her out of her thoughts. She looked at all the pages of The Cardinal Six's *Red Eagle* mission transcript splayed out in front of her, having half a mind to just put her phone on silent so she could focus. She'd waited so long in the hopes that it would be declassified for everyone to finally be able to read, and her brain had already wandered enough.

Red Eagle didn't sound too bad if you ignored the fact that the device The Cardinal Six had to retrieve was kept on a remote island in the Pacific, populated by up to a hundred Nosaru with black-market weapons. Thankfully, Mr. Carlisle was a master strategist and figured out a way to both get the device and protect his friends.

Sebastian Carlisle wasn't just the best operative of his time.

He was in a league of his own.

Abyan sighed as her phone vibrated again, so she tore her eyes away from all the pages around her and finally took out her phone. The text message made her want to scream and cry out at the same time. Tolly's programs had been running night and day to find a way to crack Carlisle Enterprise's systems, and they were all well aware that nothing short of an act of God or a crazy amount of luck would see them on the other side of that firewall and all the layers of encryption beyond it.

She'd told him to let her know first the second anything changed, yet the message she held in her hands told her they'd done the impossible, that they were one step closer to unraveling whatever was happening under their noses, and that Tolly was nothing short of a miracle worker.

They'd finally breached Carlisle's systems.

Abyan leaped from her bed, running straight to his room. Three computer screens shone blindingly bright in the darkness, and in her hurry, she stubbed her toe twice and tripped on the sheer amount of random shit on his floor.

Tolly furiously typed, hitting keys faster than she could blink, and as she neared where he sat, Abyan watched hundreds—maybe even thousands—of files being moved from place to place by whatever program he was using.

They'd really done it.

She blinked, edging a little closer, but just as she'd accepted what was happening, the screens went blank. Every window bar one suddenly disappeared, and Abyan couldn't stop the words flying from her mouth.

"What the hell just happened?"

"We've been kicked out by their additional safeguards." He

scratched the back of his head. "But I think we stole more than enough information to find out what's going on with the Nosaru, though. There's over ten thousand files here."

It took her a second to truly realize what they'd done.

Abyan laughed, incredulous, and gave him the biggest hug she could muster. "You did it!"

As she pulled away, he spoke. "I think you should make up with the others, Yan."

"No." She gritted her teeth as her heart twisted. While she knew what it would take to get them to forgive her, she didn't want to do it—some skeletons were better in the closet than out.

"It's ruining the squad, and the three of you are so much better than this," Tolly challenged. "I know I'm not Jared, and I'm not good at his United Nations Kumbaya shit, but you and the others need to get over whatever you have going on between you."

Abyan opened her mouth to reply, yet the words died on her tongue. He was right, of course, but she didn't want to admit it and stormed out of his room. The weight of what she had to do grew too much, and she couldn't take another second of it. Abyan gathered her wits in the corridor before grabbing a pair of shoes and finding Hank in the living room.

She just wanted to forget.

"I'm going to get some air," she told him, pulling on her boots. "Can you drive me?"

Though it was only October, and the real winter hadn't started yet, Abyan was wearing a thermal undershirt and the thickest jumper she owned. And since everyone protested her turning up the heat anymore, she'd had to use Mason as a human radiator for most of the morning.

Abyan had to tell him about the hack, had to tell everyone else about it, too, but she just needed five minutes to get her brain together first. To bring some order to the chaos raging in there.

Hank took one look at her shuddering form and held out his

much larger hoodie, an emotion she couldn't place flitting across his face. "John stole my BMW, and I don't even know how he got in here and took the keys. Can you believe that asshole left a note saying to use his busted-up Rolls Royce? He knows I wouldn't touch that crap with a ten-foot—"

"I don't speak trust fund, Hercules," Abyan said, as she slipped on his hoodie. Four layers of clothing, and she was still cold. "Do I have to take a bus or not?"

It was at times like this when she wished the school allowed them to visit their families. Abtiyo Ayaanle lived only a thirty-minute brisk walk from Notting Hill, so she wouldn't need to take a bus, but home visits were off-limits no matter how close your relatives lived.

According to the school it was *unfair*.

Hank looked at her, then, his emerald eyes taking in each of her features and softening at the sight. "Why don't we go to the roof and talk?" He got to his feet, his towering height bringing his head dangerously close to the ceiling. "Just you and me."

A voice in Abyan's head whispered to turn him down, that she could handle it all and didn't need Hank's help, and she'd almost agreed until he chimed in, "Fair warning, Yan, I'll one hundred percent annoy my way through whatever wall you're in the process of building around yourself right now."

Abyan gave a heavy sigh and made an exaggerated show of hanging her shoulders in defeat as she made her way to the door with him in tow. "One of these days, I'll make good on all the times I've threatened to strangle you."

"Personally, I can't think of a better way to die." Hank didn't blink twice as they made their way. "They call it a 'crime of passion' because it's all heated and intense, you know? And I'm so down for all of that."

She gave him a withering look. "I just want to know what I did to deserve this."

Hank followed her up the steel staircase that led to the roof, the metal creaking under his weight, and laughed a little. "And all I want to know is what *I* need to do to deserve the honor of being slowly asphyxiated by you."

"You're supposed to be cheering me up, Hercules." Abyan rolled her eyes. "Not forcing me to hear about your weird fantasies."

He sat down next to her on the ledge, taking a moment to watch the pedestrians below. "It's the time of the year that's getting you down, isn't it?"

The anniversary.

Abyan had been so wrapped up with the school's mystery, with Matteo and the hack, that it had slipped her mind. The date she always dreaded. Ya Allah. Hank was the only person who understood what it was like because his own anniversary was a week after hers—a weight she wished with everything in her that she could take off his shoulders.

Abyan bit the inside of her cheek until she drew blood. "Winters are always hard."

"The closer we get to November every year, I get funnier and you get quieter," Hank admitted, rubbing his knuckles. *I should tell him to stop.* Last November, he'd rubbed them until they were red and raw, yet Abyan didn't want to overstep. "We visit some graves together and then carry the bodies back with us."

This year, they'd have a new one to add to the list.

Jared Leong, treasured son and friend.

"I keep wondering if it'll always be this way." Her eyes glazed over. "I think about Jared and my family all the time and everything that could've or should've happened. They say it gets easier, and I'm just like: when?"

Hank inhaled a shaky breath. "I'm the same with my dad. I have so many questions about what exactly happened on his last mission, why my stupid mom was always so busy with The League that she didn't get him the help he needed when the survivor's guilt got to him so bad, and there's never any answers." He paused when his voice started to tremble. "Just a hole that gets bigger and a knife that only ever twists."

That was exactly how it felt.

She remembered the night they told each other their sob stories on the roof like it was yesterday. It was the first week of November; the anniversary of her family's deaths was so close, Abyan could hear their screams in the distance if she listened hard enough.

Hank was the first person she'd ever willingly told about what happened, and he listened carefully, holding her when she needed to be held. And once it was over with, he looked at her with glassy, solemn eyes and said a sentence Abyan would never forget: "The day my dad died was the day my mum died, too."

Abyan cleared her throat, wiping at her face. "If I hypothetically wanted to hug you right now, Hercules, would you agree to forget it ever happened?"

"Did you say something, Yan? I thought I heard a sound coming from your direction. Then again, it could've been a coyote or Bigfoot, maybe even the fading spirit of a young Victorian chimney sweep, taken from this world too soon." His tone was still teasing even as he swiped at his own eyes, and Abyan couldn't help the strangled half laugh, half sob that left her throat as she hugged him from the side and he wrapped his arms around her shoulders.

They stayed like that, comforted enough by each other's embrace that they could almost forget the bodies they carried on their shoulders, and Abyan jumped at the vibration in her pocket. She pulled it out, checking the notification on her screen.

A new BLCC order.

Although they were investigating the school, The Sevenfold still needed to keep up appearances. She wanted to roll her eyes the second she realized it was a shadowed mission—Harry would be with them assessing the whole thing. *Great.* When her eyes landed on the name of one of the three Nosaru on the BLCC order, her heart stopped.

Abyan showed Hank the screen. "It's him," she said. Robert Collins, the name of the human infected by the first gen known as Khalo. She'd almost given up hope that his name would pop up on a mission while she was at Carlisle. "Bloody hell, Hank. It's really him."

Hank went quiet for a second. "Don't take the BLCC order."

"What do you mean 'Don't take the BLCC order?'" Abyan pulled away, her blood pressure skyrocketing. "How can you even say that after everything I've told you?"

Her eyes stung, but she blinked back the tears. How dare he? Images of that night flooded her mind, the blood, the screams, Khalo's smile. Goose bumps raced across her flesh, and every hair on Abyan's body stood on edge. She couldn't let him get away. This was so much bigger than she was.

Why couldn't Hank see that?

"That's exactly why you shouldn't take it, Yan," he said softly. "You're too close to it. You don't know how you'll react when you see him, and you could put the team at risk."

Her jaw dropped. "I'd never put the team at risk."

"Not when you're thinking straight, that is, but if you see Khalo, you might not be."

"I'm not forfeiting it, Hank." Abyan hit the accept button without a moment's hesitation. "You're either with me on this or you're not."

It had been four years, and her revenge was long overdue.

She owed Khalo blood.

21

ABYAN

THE SEVENFOLD LOADED INTO THEIR SQUAD'S BLACK Mercedes, but Abyan pulled Artemis to the side before she could join the others. "Are you sure you know what you're meant to do?"

While the recruit nodded, it did nothing to reassure her. "Stay back and don't stray from the group," Artemis said. "I won't engage any Nosaru by myself, and I'll shout your name if anything goes wrong."

"I didn't want you on this mission," she said as a heavy sigh left her lips. "This is above your rank."

Artemis looked down. "I know."

"We'll handle the Nosaru. You just need to stay out of our way." Abyan placed a hand on her shoulder and hoped Artemis didn't think her words came from a bad place.

She wasn't trying to be mean.

Abyan just didn't want anything happening to her friends and preferred to call a spade a spade. There was no point lying to her about what she was. Artemis had only a few weeks of training at best, was an almost-average fighter, and the Nosaru would've had a field day with her.

Artemis gulped. "I understand."

This was Abyan's first chance at revenge.

She'd been waiting years for an opportunity like this, and the recruit wasn't going to ruin this for her. Not when she was so close.

The sight of Khalo's perpetually smug face made Abyan's stomach turn the first time she opened the BLCC order. Now, she couldn't wait until she was finally able to stomp it till it was a mess of mangled flesh and brains beneath her steel-toed boot. She prayed the other two who were there, Losar and Dalis, knew she was coming for them, too.

They would all pay soon enough.

"I'm serious, recruit. Don't try and play hero." Abyan looked her dead in the eye, and when Artemis nodded, they entered the car together.

Abyan had been over her plan with the squad more times than she could count, but only Hank knew she intended on killing Khalo herself. Although BLCC orders were for capture rather than execution, Abyan couldn't care less what the rules said. Khalo was going to die the second she laid eyes on him, and she would bear whatever consequences her superiors saw fit with her head held high and her heart at peace.

She'd already braced herself for their inevitable negative combat report from Harry. There was no way Abyan would let Kade or anyone else take point on this mission—it was too important to her. He'd be in King's Cross station with them, judging her every move, and Abyan wished she had a shred of fear as to what he'd think about her but she didn't.

She didn't get a wink of sleep last night. Ghosts of the past haunted her, their gray and hollow forms asking her over and over again why she was the one who got to live, and Abyan could never say anything back.

She didn't know why either.

They pulled up in front of King's Cross station and exited the car. It was closed due to the suspected Nosaru activity within, but they still had to keep their blades hidden under long coats and their tranq guns in black briefcases in case a civilian saw them.

They weren't trying to give anyone a heart attack.

Harry was already outside waiting for them, dressed in black combat attire. "I don't need to explain how important this mission is, do I?"

"No, we understand," Abyan said through gritted teeth.

He gave them a stern look. "Don't mess it up."

Abyan bit back her snarky reply and pushed forward with her squad in tow.

King's Cross had always been one of her favorite train stations. The sweeping white spiderweb structure in the middle and the arched canopies over the platforms never failed to make her want to stop and stare.

Seeing such a huge place devoid of people as The Sevenfold made their way up the frozen escalators made it look like a scene straight out of one of Hassan's beloved horror movies, and an involuntary shiver ran down Abyan's spine.

She held her gun firmly with Gacan Libaax sheathed at her back as she led their group through the station, scanning every inch of the place in search of hosts.

When they turned the final corner, they stopped dead in their tracks, each of them freezing as the noise hit them all simultaneously. The crash of a body flying into a bin, the rough snarls bouncing off every wall, and the shrill screams of the injured.

There were way more than the three suspected Nosaru in the BLCC order waiting for them. Abyan held a closed fist high enough for the whole squad to see as she moved forward through the hallway, her steps silent as the wind, and poked her head out.

Sixteen hosts.

There were fourteen of them battling across the platforms and on the tracks between. Khalo and what she figured was another first gen were fighting each other near the gates at the far end, though Abyan could barely make out their blurred figures in the half light of the station.

She turned back to her squad and relayed exactly what she saw using hand signals because train stations had one hell of an echo and a whisper might as well have been a scream.

The Nosaru were preoccupied with one another, and they had the chance to catch them by surprise—the last thing they needed was to announce their presence by accident.

"Call it in," Mason signed.

Abyan shook her head, acutely aware of Harry lurking next to them. This was her only chance to get Khalo. Calling operatives in would snatch it right from her grasp, and who knew if the hosts might've escaped in the time it took them to get to King's Cross?

"Calling it in would be a mission forfeit," Harry interjected, his face annoyingly impassive.

She steeled herself. "We can handle it ourselves."

They wouldn't be calling anyone.

Abyan instructed the team to follow the BLCC order and keep three alive while killing all the rest. Once each member of her squad made it clear they understood her orders, Mason, Kade, and Hassan broke away and went back in the direction they came from to the opposite platform with Harry trailing behind them, so the Nosaru would be boxed in when they attacked.

She told the recruit to stay in the corridor as they waited with bated breath for Mason to flash his small torch three times from the northwest stairwell on the opposite side of the tracks, and as soon as they saw the signal, they moved in.

Abyan fired two shots at the dark-haired female Nosaru closest to her, and a sharp grunt escaped her lips before she slumped to the ground. The rest of the creatures wasted no time turning their focus onto The Sevenfold, blood staining their lips as they each let loose a chorus of growls before leaping onto the platform and charging at them.

As Abyan unsheathed her first dagger, she saw Khalo 130 feet from her still fighting the other first gen, not paying any attention to everything else happening around them.

A Nosaru came at her. He was in his mid twenties—or at least his features and build said as much—and Abyan jumped back as he swung for her. She deflected his second blow and twirled on her back foot not a moment later, sending a powerful kick to the left side of his jaw.

A groan came from somewhere behind her that was unmistakably Tolly's, and Abyan gave him the briefest glance over her shoulder before returning to her host. She'd caught a glimpse of two dead Nosaru splayed out on the ground around him, but Tolly had sustained an injury to his calf, and another host was coming straight for him.

A hundred and seventy-eight degrees clockwise.

Sixty-three degrees up.

Abyan exhaled and threw the dagger in her hand behind her before sidestepping the male host's next attack and landing an uppercut to his exposed chin. She hurled her second dagger at his brow, and he was out before he hit the ground.

She glanced around the station, and although Mason's team had killed four so far, Harry's pursed lips told her he was less than impressed with what he saw. Abyan's sub-team had put down five with one tranquilized—but that wasn't what made her heart drop to her feet.

It was Khalo.

Khalo being cuffed and held by Kade and Hassan.

Abyan cursed under her breath at the sight. The cuffs injected him with a hormone to counteract the one first gens secreted for their generational control to work; it meant that Khalo wouldn't be getting reinforcements any time soon and that Abyan had lost all hope of a distraction to slip past the others and kill him herself.

Still, she wasn't going to give up now.

As Tolly went to help Mason with the last of the hosts, Abyan drew Gacan Libaax from its sheath and closed in on her target. It was just Kade and Hassan, she told herself, and if bad came to worse, Abyan knew she could beat both in a fight.

Nothing mattered more than putting Khalo down.

"What are you doing with that, Yan?" Hassan asked, gaze darting between her determined eyes and the sword at her side. "It's a BLCC order."

It's a damn WLDO to me.

Raising her sword, Abyan decided to give them a chance to make this easy. "Step aside, I only want the host."

Kade and Hassan exchanged a look of confusion and she said, "But why? Killing him would be a mission failure for all of us."

"Don't make this any more difficult than it already is." Her voice shook. "This is personal."

The two of them angled themselves in front of the host, everything in their faces telling her that if she wanted Khalo, she'd have to get through them first. *Shit.* Abyan released a frustrated breath, sheathing her sword—she didn't want to hurt her friends. They just didn't understand, and maybe Abyan didn't want them to because some things weren't meant to be shared with everyone.

Why couldn't they see that?

Abyan charged forward as Kade and Hassan did the same. *Damn it.* She dodged Hassan's punch and managed to catch Kade in the side with her fist, but Abyan didn't give her time to recover and hit her across the jaw with an elbow strike, sending her crashing to the ground.

Hassan blocked her kick, a mixture of fury and panic flashing across his features. "You're turning on your own team, Yan!" He landed a punch to her gut, and Abyan was winded for a moment, stumbling back a few steps as fire erupted all over her abdomen. "You're meant to have our backs, and you keep throwing us to the side without telling us why."

I'm sorry.

Abyan clenched her jaw, shoving the pain to the side, and sidestepped his next blow. "You wouldn't understand!" She landed a palm-heel strike to his midsection and then a sharp punch across his cheek when he doubled over. "I need to do this, and getting in my way won't end well for any of you."

Hassan hit the floor, slamming a fist to the ground in anger, yet Abyan's attention snapped to Khalo—or where the first gen should've been. Where he was not two minutes ago and very much wasn't anymore.

Abyan swore, scouring the train station from where the rest of the squad were still fighting the remaining hosts and where Harry was staring at her so intently that part of her wanted to disappear.

Movement farther in the tunnel caught her eye, and Abyan sprinted toward it without thinking. *You're not getting away again.* Her lungs were on fire, and though she could only make out the barest hint of Khalo's silhouette in the faint light of the tunnel, she pushed on.

Bright lights shone in the distance and Abyan cursed, speeding up as much as she could before Khalo could duck into one of the service exits. While the station was closed, trains that had no alternative tracks could still pass through, though they never stopped to drop off passengers.

The gap between them was widening, and the yellow beams were only drawing nearer. *No.* She wasn't going to give up. Maybe she could still make it. Someone was screaming something behind her, Abyan couldn't tell what it was over the train's blaring horn and her own thundering heartbeat.

Khalo was right there.

Only a few more feet and she would have him.

An arm wrapped around her waist just as the train reached them, her eyes catching the briefest tuft of Khalo's hair disappearing off into the distance as she was pulled into the closest service exit. Hank's eyes were wild as he checked to make sure she was okay, his hands resting gently on her shoulders as she hunched over and screamed as loud as she could.

It tore at her throat, scraping and scratching her flesh, but Abyan didn't care. The noise was swallowed by the train, but all she could feel was everything being ripped away from her all over again. The agony was too much—she wanted to claw it out of her own chest. Her eyes flooded with tears as she fell to the dust-covered ground, and Hank held her as sobs wracked her body, never once saying he told her so.

"It's okay, you're okay," he said, stroking her arm. "We'll get him next time."

It wasn't okay.

She'd had Khalo right in front of her, and he slipped through her fingers. Their mission was blown, the civilians on the next train would see the dead Nosaru strewn about the station the second they passed through, and Carlisle was going to have to deploy operatives to stop word of what took place from getting out.

The Sevenfold had failed, and now her squad was going to ask why the hell she turned on them and who Khalo was to her, and Abyan didn't have the slightest idea what she was going to tell them.

22

ARTEMIS

THE SEVENFOLD FLOPPED THEIR MISSION IN KING'S CROSS, and Artemis still couldn't believe it. She'd done as she was told back in the station, making sure to stay in the hallway as her squad took on the hosts, and silently observed how each of them fought.

None of them were banking on Abyan going rogue.

Artemis had watched in horror as she turned on their friends, letting Khalo slip from grasp. Yet that wasn't the most bizarre thing about the mission—it was Harry. Not once did he move to stop the mutiny in The Sevenfold even though it meant that the first gen escaped. All he did was stare at the fight, face utterly unreadable, and stand in the shadows of the platform.

The whole squad was shaken after the BLCC order, but Abyan was more so than everyone else, staring off into the distance at nothing and everything as she walked out from the tunnel.

Artemis wrung her fingers as she entered the kitchen, too lost in her thoughts to notice the whole squad was already there, save for Abyan. Piles and piles of notes on their hacked files were scattered around the countertop—so far they'd discovered that Carlisle Enterprises was working on not one, but three Nosaru infection cures: a vaccine, a surgery, and an electrotherapy. While they hadn't got far enough into the files to find anything on the abnormal host activity they'd witnessed, Artemis knew they were close.

"We need an intervention," Kade said, putting her hands on her hips.

The rest of the squad eyed each other warily, but Artemis could see where she was coming from. With their failed mission, The Sevenfold would officially be the second-best team at Carlisle when the leaderboard updated the following Monday, and as much as some of them didn't want to admit it, the fault landed squarely on Abyan.

It wasn't the easiest pill to swallow.

"That's going a little far, Kade," Hank said, trying hard to keep his demeanour relaxed, but Artemis could see how tense he was. "Don't you think?"

Artemis took a seat at the breakfast table beside Mason and watched the squad draw their lines in the sand and turn on each other, not knowing how she could possibly make the situation better.

Kade took a step toward him, and everyone in the room twitched simultaneously. "If you would just tell us what she's hiding, then we wouldn't have this problem. We lost first place because of her. How can you be okay with this?"

"It's not my secret to tell." His eyes blazed, red creeping fast up his neck. "If you really cared about Yan, then you'd respect her wishes instead of trying to pressure her into telling you something she obviously isn't ready to."

"Hey, we might not be talking right now, but I love her just as much as you do." She jabbed a finger at him. "Don't *ever* question that, King."

Though there was still a good ten paces separating them, Hassan stepped in the gap, keeping his eyes on both Kade and Hank. "What she means is, we've given Yan as much time as we could—we all guessed something bad happened to her family, but now she's jeopardizing us all and refusing to tell us why. How are we supposed to trust someone like that?"

"They have a point." Tolly shrugged. Artemis's eyes widened. She would've thought that, along with Mason and Hank, Tolly would be on Abyan's side in this. "We can't turn a blind eye anymore."

Mason shook his head. "Do you hear yourselves right now? This is Yan we're talking about. She's had our backs through so much, and now you guys are all trying to squeeze her secrets out of Hank for what? It's like I don't know who you are anymore."

"We're not doing it for shits and giggles." Hassan was quick with his reply. "She attacked us, and you're all acting like it's nothing."

Mason released a heavy breath. "She shouldn't have done that, but I'm sure she had her reasons. We just need to give her some time to let us in. I know Yan too well to just assume the worst of her like you guys are doing."

"Oh give me a break; if anything, I want to help her." Kade's hands shot up in exasperation. "It's not right for her to suffer on her own."

Artemis swallowed, knowing this was a family dispute and her dissenting opinion wouldn't be welcome. "Wouldn't it be best if Abyan were to decide that, not you?"

Hassan's intense gaze zeroed in on her, but whatever words he was about to say died on his tongue as Abyan walked into the room and poured herself a glass of water, oblivious to the past fifteen minutes. They all looked at each other, none of them knowing how to go about speaking to her now that she was there.

Her brows furrowed as she glanced around the room, her glass half raised to her lips. "Did someone die while I was out or something?"

Mason slurped his coffee, looking at where Kade and the others stood. "I just think it's funny how certain people in this room were talking about you just fine before, but something seems to have gotten their tongues all of a sudden."

Kade's jaw dropped as Abyan turned to her with a cocked brow, but she composed herself quickly enough. "We want to know what's been up with you, Yan. Yesterday's failure was your fault. You had some kinda history with that first gen, and you need to tell us what it is."

Abyan's grip on her glass tightened. "I don't *need* to tell you anything. Try minding your business for once, how about that?"

Her eyes bulged. "You literally hit me in the face and put the team—your friends—at risk! And now you want us to just ignore it, and what? Baby you until you decide we're worth opening up to? How far do you want the squad to fall before you suck it up and get the job done like you used to?"

Kade's voice rose with every word, and the instant she edged toward where Abyan stood, Hassan and Hank moved between them. "Suck it up?" Abyan laughed humorlessly. "You really don't know anything, do you? I guess that's what I get for expecting a spoiled brat who's never struggled a day in her life to have some empathy."

Artemis slapped a hand over her mouth, and Mason's entire body tensed beside her. Kade leaped forward, yet Hassan was quick to pin her against the countertop.

"Why don't you stop being a weak little bitch and quit feeling sorry for yourself for once?"

"Weak?" Abyan screamed, tears filling her eyes. "He butchered my whole family, and I had to watch!" The cup in her hand shattered, the pieces flying in every direction, but if she cared about the glass or the shards piercing the skin of her palms, she didn't show it. "You can all finally stop playing your little whodunnit."

Silence engulfed the room, and Abyan fought to control her breathing. A few century-long seconds passed before Kade tried to speak. "I'm sor—"

"No, you're not." Blood dripped down her hand, yet she didn't look at it once and turned away from the damp cloth Hank held out to her.

Hassan opened his mouth, but she cut him off before he could get a word out. "There's the answer you've been waiting for all this time. I hope it was worth the wait." She took the cloth Hank offered her earlier and walked to the door. "Recruit, let's go. We have training scheduled."

Abyan didn't spare her a glance as she stalked out of the room at lightning speed, and Artemis jogged to catch up with her.

They marched all the way to Gym 2 in stone-cold silence. Abyan's face gave nothing of her true feelings away, and Artemis didn't know how to bridge the chasm between them without falling headfirst into its depths.

"I'll meet you in the ring," Abyan said, her voice hollow. "Just give me a second."

Artemis nodded and walked over to the red ring in the center of the room, peering at Abyan from the corner of her eye all the while. Artemis's heart hurt just looking at her. She had a hand pinching the bridge of her nose, her eyes tightly squeezed, and the second her bottom lip started to tremble, Artemis threw all caution to the wind and went over to where she stood.

She couldn't watch anymore.

"Come here." Artemis wrapped her in an embrace and held Abyan as she finally let it all out—sobs wracked through her body, and not once did Artemis let her go, not when her knees gave out or when she repeatedly tried to tell her she was fine through her hiccups.

She held her for as long as she needed.

"Thank you, Artemis." She pulled away, eyes red rimmed. "I mean it."

"Don't worry about it," Artemis assured her. "If I'd known the names of the hosts who killed Jared, I'd do the same thing you're doing. I wouldn't stop for anything in the world."

She nodded, and the weight lifting from her shoulders was clear enough to see. "The others just don't get it. One day, I was the oldest of four siblings with two amazing parents, and the next I was an orphan with nothing but three names on my list and a promise to make good on." Abyan wiped the stray tears from her cheeks. "I love my friends so much it hurts but . . ."

As she trailed off, unable to say the words, Artemis finished the sentence for her. "Your revenge comes first."

"It was the deal Mr. Carlisle and I made when we first met," she confirmed. "There were three first gens at my house the night my family were killed: Khalo, Losar, and Dalis. Mr. Carlisle showed up at the police station and promised me revenge. All I had to do was take a year of therapy and come here to become an operative, then I could hunt the bastards who killed my family."

Artemis said, "I hope you catch them."

And she meant it with everything in her.

"I can't wait until we get rid of them all for good," she replied darkly. "Their entire species."

Though Artemis nodded in agreement, she realised that Abyan could never find out about what she was planning with Kade because she'd never agree to sit down with any host.

From now on, they were on their own.

23

ABYAN

ABYAN PREFERRED THE ROOF TO HER DORM BECAUSE IT was quiet, empty, and somewhere she could just sit and think without the burden of her squad or expectations.

It was just her and the wind up there.

While it had only been a couple hours since her revelation, the wound had yet to scab over—and now that everyone knew her past, it was suffocating being around them. The rest of the squad tried their hardest to hide it, but Abyan knew they pitied her.

The poor orphan girl who watched her whole family die. It was something she'd never wanted to be defined by. Though Abyan made sure to excel in training, her studies, and everything else in her life to ensure that people saw her before her history, it seemed like what happened to her was hot on her heels no matter how fast she tried to run away from it. And everyone was always so much more interested in the beast with a thousand teeth than the girl who managed to escape it.

She put her head in her hands and swore in every way she knew how in both English and Af-Somali, glad for once that the only witness to her outburst was the evening wind. Abyan was so tired of everything. Since the start of the year, it had been disaster after disaster, and she couldn't catch a bloody break.

Why did it always have to be her?

Abyan knew she was losing her grip the second she started

crying in front of the recruit. The damn recruit of all people. Abyan had so much to do—they still had thousands of files to sift through in the hopes that they might find out what Carlisle Enterprises was up to. The seven of them had each taken a thousand to start with and relayed anything promising back to the group.

How was she supposed to look anyone except Hank in the eye when she eventually returned to their dorm? They'd all seen too much. They knew too much. Peeled back her layers with the harshest of hands, not caring in the slightest that they caused fresh scars over the old, and now they expected her to be okay with it?

She wanted to laugh.

"Yanny dearest," came the voice of the only person she wouldn't lob her shoe at at a time like this. "Wherefore art thou, Yanny?"

Abyan let herself fall back from her seated position, looking up at the sky, and answered with a voice six feet below the jubilance of his, "Call me that again and I'm throwing you off this roof, Hercules."

"You know, I feel us getting closer in spirit every time you threaten me with bodily harm. I can tell that it really comes from the heart." He sat down next to her and placed a tub with a spoon poking out of it between them. "Here, I brought an olive branch from the others to smooth things over."

There's no way ice cream is fixing this.

"Whatever." Abyan dug into the blue-sprinkle-covered chocolate fudge. "I don't care about Kade and Hassan's drama. All I want to do is figure out where Khalo is so I can end this."

Hank cocked a brow. "You think they're the only ones at fault here?"

"They got in my way on our BLCC order," she insisted. "If it wasn't for them, Khalo would be dead by now, I'd have my closure, and we could all focus on everything else."

"Is that all you care about?" He shook his head. "What about your friends, Yan? They weren't right to pressure you into telling them about him, but you're the one who turned on your squad. You make it so hard to defend you sometimes."

She recoiled from him. "So, you think it's all my fault then?"

"No, that's not what I meant and you know it—"

Abyan pulled herself up, ignoring how each of her limbs felt like they carried the combined weight of several planets, and made to leave. "I don't have to listen to any of this. I have training to get to—"

Hank's arm snaked around her waist and pulled her back, one hand on her forearm to stop her breaking his hold. "I'm sorry but you need a reality check, Yan, and the others don't have it in them to tell you because they know it'll go in one ear and out of the other." His grip loosened a fraction, and she finally faced him. "But you'll listen if I'm the one who says it: You need to stop tossing your friends to the side at the drop of a damn hat whenever it suits you. Have you ever thought that maybe we could help you take down Khalo and the others? You keep wanting to take on the world by yourself and it's ruining everything."

The intensity in his face turned her to stone, and she couldn't help but think back to her conversation with the recruit. The squad or vengeance. Did the choice have to be so binary? Hank was offering her a lifeline to mend her relationship with their friends, but this was too personal for Abyan to share with them.

No one understood where she was coming from.

"Like I said before, I have training to get to." She stepped away from Hank, her voice a touch softer than before. "I just need some time to process everything, okay?"

Abyan left the roof before he could find another way to stop her and headed straight for the gyms with her head more crowded than ever. She needed time away from everyone. Just a minute to think everything through. She'd originally booked Gym 13 for The Sevenfold weeks ago, but she had no intention of telling anyone else about it anymore.

Now Abyan would have a few hours to herself to get all these dumb feelings out of her system. Her old therapist would've said this was a prime example of her favorite defense mechanisms—isolation and repression—but Abyan didn't care.

The door to the gym slid open when she punched in The Sevenfold's unique code, yet her sigh of relief stopped midway in her throat the second her eyes landed on the person waiting for her within, leaning on one of the mirror walls.

"You're late." Harry stalked toward her. "We need to talk."

Abyan crossed her arms. "I came to train."

"That's fine." He shrugged, his nonchalance only grating on her further. "We can talk and train at the same time."

"Whatever."

He pulled off his dress shirt, revealing a simple black vest. Harry had a full sleeve of tattoos on his right arm she hadn't seen the last time they met. It was made up of a bizarre mix of Catholic symbols, quotes, and old rock band references. He noticed her staring as they walked to the punching bag in the corner of the room.

"You're surprised I have tattoos," Harry stated, resting his hands on the bag.

Abyan raised her already bandaged fists. "People in your tax bracket aren't usually fans of ink."

A small chuckle left his lips. "What are we fans of, then?"

"Dodging taxes, oppressing the poor, inbreeding—"

Harry's eyes widened. "Inbreeding?"

"I said what I said."

He laughed as Abyan landed blow after blow on the punching bag. She didn't have time for him. Why couldn't she have a couple minutes of peace? All Harry wanted to do was berate her for messing up their BLCC order and rub their negative after-action report in her face. Abyan didn't want to know what his opinion of her was or hear about how it was all her fault that The Sevenfold was now second best.

They moved to the ring beside them to spar.

Abyan wasted no time closing the gap between them and

aiming a straight punch to his jaw. She knew he'd block it easily—
it was only meant to skip past the stupid thirty-second wait for
who was going to hit first—yet some part of her had hoped the
blow would land out of sheer pettiness.

"Did you know your personal file has a triple seal on it?" Harry
asked, blocking her next jab effortlessly. "That means only The
League can access it."

Abyan didn't know that. Thinking of the board members of
Carlisle Enterprises snooping through her most personal details
was enough to make her skin crawl, yet she tried to mask her shock,
rearranging her features into a perfect picture of impassivity. "You
know what's in it, don't you?"

"What makes you say that?"

"You're . . . slippery."

There was no way Abyan would tell Harry he was a conniving
snake to his face. However far the syllables itched their way up her
throat, she'd never say it out loud. The Sevenfold still needed to
scrape their way back to first place somehow, and as much as Abyan
hated to admit it, Harry was the only one who could help them.

"I'll take that as a compliment." He raised a brow. "I would've
never chosen that BLCC order for your squad had I known about
your conflict of interest. In the future, your missions will be more
mindful of it."

Her conflict of interest.

She'd never heard it put like that before. All clinical. Some part
of Abyan told her she should be angry, he was minimizing her past,
but she wasn't. It was a simple conflict of interest to him and much
more to her.

Abyan didn't reply immediately, catching him off guard and
landing a punch on his left cheek instead. "So, when is our report
coming? I'm guessing you ripped us a new one."

"I can't tell you that," he said, taking a step back from her. *Looks
like the fun's over.* "The report won't be what you think. I made a few

choice omissions about your mutiny that you need to appreciate because it won't be happening again."

She straightened. "Why would you cover for us?"

"The BLCC order was my fault for not knowing everything about you, so I took responsibility for it, but we all know you intended on breaching protocol to kill Khalo that night, and your whole team would've covered for you."

"What's your point?"

"It strikes me that if they were willing to cover for you then, they've probably done it before." Harry took a step closer to her. "I think you and The Sevenfold have been breaking the rules for a while, and I'm warning you to stop—you're too young to be pulling these kinds of stunts, and this path is going to lead you nowhere good."

Abyan sighed. "And here I was thinking we were becoming friends."

"I'm serious, Guled."

Abyan tried not to think about how Tolly had a couple thousand classified documents on his laptop on the highest floor of the residential building not two minutes away from where they now stood. "I understand." She paused, carefully thinking over her next words. "What about Matteo Valente?"

Harry took a moment before answering her. "He hasn't been found yet."

"I think I know what he wants," she told him, and continued the second she caught the flash of curiosity across his features. "I could help you catch him, but it has to be together: I get my answers and you get yours. That's the deal—no bullshit or hidden agendas."

"An off-books mission?" he asked, and when she nodded he said, "Let's say I agreed to this plan of yours, what would you have in mind?"

Abyan smirked. He wasn't getting anything out of her that

easily. "I'll send you coordinates to meet me at tomorrow morning. You'll find out the rest then."

"Have it your way, kid." He picked up his shirt and made his way toward the exit, but he stopped in the middle of the doorway. "You were wrong about what you said earlier."

"How do you mean?"

"I'm not rich—I mean, I wasn't born into wealth." Harry turned to face her, one foot still out in the corridor. "You aren't the only person one of the Carlisles have brought in from the cold."

She didn't know what to say to that. Harry was old, so he had to have been at the academy when Mr. Carlisle's father was in charge. This was a breach of conduct, she realized. He shouldn't have told her that, and Harry clocked it a second after Abyan did and left the gym before she could get a word out.

She tucked his minor slip into the back of her mind for later. Tolly was confident that his hack couldn't be traced to him and that they had nothing to worry about. Harry wouldn't find anything amiss around The Sevenfold. Yet two could play at this game, and Abyan wondered how far she'd have to dig to find out more about him and Squad 2528.

Something told her it wouldn't be difficult.

24

ARTEMIS

A HUSH FELL OVER ARTEMIS'S FIRST PERIOD ECONOMICS class. Kade popped up in the small square window of the door and knocked three times before walking in. Their teacher's eyes widened as she whispered something to him, and the next thing Artemis knew, she was being escorted to the door with Kade in tow.

Once they were alone in the corridor, she turned to Artemis and spoke in a hushed voice. "We need to get out of here," she said, handing her a tiny earpiece. "We're going to the research wing to get you your answers."

Her brow creased. "When did you plan all of this?"

Kade pulled her by the hand. "Well, things are still awkward in the dorm after the whole Yan thing, and scheming is my third favorite pastime."

Artemis put her earpiece in with her free hand, fluffing her curls around so no one could see it. "So, how exactly are we going to break into Dr. Telford's office? I've only been to the research wing once."

"I'm due for my blood draw in about two hours," she explained. "That's our window to get in and out. We'll need a distraction for the receptionists so you can slip past without them asking any nosy questions—it should be fine as long as you act normal."

Artemis remembered her time in the lobby of the main

research building. They hadn't scrutinized her beyond a thorough up-and-down appraisal, and she got the feeling that all the guards and security were more for the Nosaru test subjects or possible intruders than anyone in a Carlisle Academy uniform.

There was just one problem.

The two of them came to a stop outside Kade's black Mercedes as Artemis asked, "Wait, what's going to be our distraction?"

"I think the better question, recruit," came the unmistakable voice of Lucas Yi, strolling out from behind the shadows of the parking garage, "is, *who* is going to be your distraction?"

Artemis's body bristled, remembering what he'd tried to do to her during the Year 14 Stronghold test. *Looks like the puppy's lost her way*, he'd said mere moments before pointing his tranq at her face with the rest of The Trojans, ready to shoot her without hesitation or remorse. If Abyan and the others hadn't come back for her, Artemis didn't know what would've happened.

Lucas couldn't be trusted.

More important, Artemis didn't like him one bit.

"Why him of all people, Kade?" She couldn't help the annoyance in her voice. "He's a . . ." she tried to think of something terrible to call him but came up blank under his dark stare, "very bad person."

"You're right," Kade confirmed, opening the front passenger door and gesturing for Artemis to get in. "He's an asshole, but he owes me, so he's agreed to help us out this one time."

"Watch it, Nakamura," Lucas said, getting in the back. "Now, I don't want to know anything about whatever you guys have got going on. I'm just there to flirt with some old ladies so you can get in and then I'm gone."

"Shut up, Yi." Kade started the car and reversed out of her spot. "I'm already sick of your voice."

Artemis clamped a hand over her mouth and watched as the two of them bickered for the entire drive across London. Kade looked five seconds from snapping Lucas's neck by the time they pulled up outside the research wing, but Artemis didn't let their drama make her lose sight of her goal.

Answers.

Why she was having the tests, what the school wanted from her, and what exactly Mr. Carlisle saw in her that no one else did. Her personal file would shed light on all of it. Every time Artemis had met Dr. Telford, she'd held that midsized brown binder in her hands with #HTS1806B written under Artemis's full name.

Was it her reference number?

Did the other members of The Sevenfold have one?

She had no clue, yet she was sure as hell going to find out one way or another. Artemis refused to sit back and take whatever crap the school put her through anymore. *Enough is enough.* Nothing, not even Kade and Lucas's argument or the lingering animosity in their squad, could sway her from what she needed to do.

Artemis stepped between her two companions. "Where to, Kade?"

"Dr. Telford's office is the second door on the left of the first floor. It's next to this tiny storage room for medical supplies—you can't miss it," she said, turning away from Lucas. "We'll be able to talk to each other through our earpieces. Wait here for a few minutes while I go inside and let them know I'm here for my blood draw, and then I'll tell Lucas when to come in. Once the receptionists look distracted enough, I'll give you the go ahead to join me."

"Sounds good." Artemis nodded and Lucas agreed.

Kade gave them one final breathtaking smile before heading for the entrance at the end of the road. Clasping her hands in front of her, Artemis tried to focus on her breathing.

Everything will be fine.

Unless . . . it wouldn't.

What if she messed up and gave their plan away by accident?

"This isn't the time to lose your shit, recruit," Lucas warned, his inky locks falling over his brow. "We don't have the luxury of getting cold feet here."

Artemis released a heavy breath and tried to distract herself from her nerves. "What made you owe Kade enough to do this for her? This isn't your average favor."

"We were together back when we were recruits, and I messed up," he admitted. "She's never liked me much since." He scratched the back of his neck. "I mean, she literally tried to run me over once and missed—that's how bad it was."

Something in her chest twisted knowing that the two of them had been in a relationship before, but Artemis ignored it. "So, there's no feelings there anymore?"

"None whatsoever." He chuckled as if she was crazy for even bringing it up and then winked. "But I'd still take a round or two with her if she'd let me."

Artemis's lip curled in disgust. "Don't talk about her like that, you pig."

Just as he was about to reply, Kade's voice crackled in her ear, and at the way Lucas jolted, Artemis knew he'd heard it too. "Can you both hear me?"

She held a hand to her burning chest. "Yeah, loud and clear."

"Captain Shithead, you're up," Kade announced. "We're lucky there's only one receptionist today, so you shouldn't have to do too much to keep her occupied."

Lucas grumbled something under his breath and stalked off to the entrance, leaving Artemis alone next to their car. She didn't know what to do with herself as the seconds passed and paced up and down, praying that no one looked her way and saw how suspicious she was acting.

Kade chimed in soon enough, "Did he say I ran him over? He always tells people that, and it's so annoying. All you need to know is that he deserved it." She grinned a little despite her nerves, but Kade interrupted her before she could reply, "Oh, the receptionist is laughing at one of his jokes, Artemis. Here's your chance—meet me on the foyer of the first floor."

Here we go.

Artemis started walking toward the huge white building, not making eye contact with anyone on the way there. "Stop doing that thing with your shoulders. I'm looking at you from the window, and you look like you just tripped an old lady and ran away."

A shaky laugh left her lips. "Just to be clear, I would never trip an old lady."

"So you say," she teased.

Artemis could almost see her doing her head-tilt thing that said she was right and you were wrong, but Kade was waiting for you to realize your stupidity on your own.

She entered the research wing, trying her best to act like she was there for a normal appointment. Lucas leaned over the front desk, giving the redheaded older woman seated behind it the eyes, and she looked entertained enough with her wide smile and hushed laughter.

Artemis slowly picked up her pace, feigning an air of nonchalance as she passed the ginormous fish tank and stood on the escalator. She made sure to keep her head down in case someone recognized her.

A pale arm snaked hers the instant she stepped onto the foyer, leading her to the corridor of offices. "You took your sweet time, didn't you?"

Artemis mumbled an apology before asking. "How do we know Dr. Telford's not already inside?"

"They notified her as soon as I arrived for my blood draw and I said I needed the bathroom, so she's probably waiting over there for me to be done," she assured her. "Everything should be fine."

That sounded plausible enough.

Once they reached her office, Artemis peeked through the glass pane in the door, sighing when she saw it empty. She turned the cool handle and turned to Kade. "It's locked. What do we do now?"

She snapped into action, not a flicker of panic in her brown eyes, and took two bobby pins out of her hair. "Go and keep watch.

I'll have it open in a few seconds."

Artemis ran to the end of the corridor they'd come in through and cast a long glance around to make sure no one was headed for them. At the faint click from Kade's direction, Artemis jogged toward her and flung the door open.

"Be quick, Artemis," she warned before leaving her alone. "We don't have much time before she gets suspicious."

Artemis's eyes darted in every direction, looking for anything resembling a filing cabinet. A large brown one sat on the far wall, and she opened each drawer, carefully searching the names in the corner for her own. Every muscle in her body was held taut as she read, her heart dropping lower and lower the more files she read and the more drawers she pulled out without seeing her name or reference number anywhere.

The door flew open, and Kade's face was red, her eyes wild. "She's coming back—I don't know how she knew, but she'll be here in five minutes tops, Artemis. We have to go right now."

"But I haven't found my file yet," she pleaded. "This can't have been for nothing."

"I'm so sorry—I really am—but we can't stay any longer."

I'm not leaving.

"Please, I just need . . ." She spun on her back foot, heading for the desk, since she couldn't see any more files on all the huge bookcases lining the walls. It had to be here somewhere. Artemis knew in her gut that it was in this office, right in front of her.

Kade swore, keeping an eye on the corridor outside through the glass pane. "We've just run out of time."

She ducked as the sound of clicking heels echoed through the hall. Dr. Telford. Bile rose in Artemis's throat, but she continued with her search despite her fear. She pulled out the stack of papers from the desk, a few files of random students and scattered blood results, yet she sucked in a sharp breath when she came to the last file in the stack.

Artemis Garrett-Coleman.

#HTS1806B.

Although it wasn't heavy like the one Dr. Telford usually carried, Artemis didn't let it faze her. She opened it up praying to see something, anything that would give her some clarity, yet all her hope withered at the first page.

It was blank.

And so was every page after it.

A file full of blank pages—it had to be a decoy, she realized. But if this was a fake meant to throw her off the school's scent, where was her real file? Kade's sigh of relief was the only thing that jerked Artemis from her shock, and it was a second before she, too, heard the second voice in the corridor telling Dr. Telford how he'd been experiencing chest pain and hurt all over and needed immediate help.

Lucas bloody Yi.

At the sound of their retreating footsteps, the two of them bolted from the office and split up, Kade to the nurse for her blood draw and Artemis as far away from the research wing as humanly possible. But no matter how hard she tried, she couldn't shake her unease.

How did Dr. Telford know she was coming?

25

ABYAN

"A ROOF, GULED?" HARRY SNAPPED, HIS VOICE BREAKING UP a little as Abyan pressed her phone to her ear. "You sent me coordinates for some random roof in Wembley?"

Abyan resisted the urge to hang up. "You brought the sniper?"

"Yes," he confirmed. "Now I want to know why, and you're going to tell me or I'll call this whole operation off."

The days that had passed between when she'd struck this deal with him had been nothing short of torture. Abyan hated the awkwardness in the squad—it infected everything like some sort of deadly friendship-eating fungus, and she couldn't stand it anymore. Things had only gotten worse since everyone had forced her to tell them her secret and she was glad to be away from their prying eyes, if only for a short while.

They only ever held pity and regret.

Two things Abyan had very much had her fill of.

She sighed, focusing on Harry again. "You've been looking for Matteo for weeks and haven't found anything because you haven't given him the right bait."

"He doesn't need bait," he said. "He's not some mindless animal."

"That's why you've failed so far, don't you see?" Abyan slowed her pace as she moved between the desolate buildings around her, everything about their cracked and dirty walls was setting her nerves on edge. "Think about it: Magpies are highly intelligent birds, but they can't resist shiny objects. You didn't give Matteo anything shiny enough."

Harry went quiet for a moment. "I don't see anything shiny around this place. Unless you're talking about the scrap metal and barbed wire fences, that is."

"It's me," she clarified. "I'm the bait."

It was the first time she'd left the school grounds alone since she'd apologized to Mason. If Matteo was going to show up, there was no better time to catch her than now. He had this weird fascination with her. It made Abyan's insides turn thinking about how a first gen was obsessed with her for reasons she didn't entirely understand, and she was thankful that the mystery wouldn't be hanging over her head for much longer because her plan would work.

She knew it would.

"You think because Valente stalked you once that he'll do it again?" her shadow scoffed. "There's no way he'd be so stupid."

"For some reason, I confuse him," Abyan said. "And you know what they say about curiosity and the cat."

"If he shows, all I need is a clear line of sight within range and he'll be tranquilized in two seconds flat."

"Then, we'll take him to a secondary location, cuff him so he can't control any other hosts nearby, and finally get what we came for," she concurred. "There's no way he can escape."

Harry's voice changed, then. "You've got movement between the cars up ahead."

Abyan's eyes zeroed in on the scattered cars parked across from her, yet there were no dark tufts or knowing black eyes to be seen. She hung up the phone and placed a tentative hand on the dagger at her side as she scanned the area again.

She'd chosen this place deliberately.

A desolate parking lot, flanked on either side by old buildings and empty warehouses, where Harry would have an excellent vantage point and Matteo could see her clear as day. She'd switched between four trains to get there when it would typically take two, and Abyan had taken side street after side street so this wouldn't look like the trap it was until Matteo was already here.

Focus.

Goose bumps raced across her flesh as the icy afternoon winds licked at her skin. Abyan couldn't help the shudder that ripped through her as she crept forward, watching all around her for any sign of the movement Harry spoke of. Had Matteo caught sight of him? She'd been hoping that Harry at least had the competence to take cover and not make his presence obvious.

Matteo may have been reckless, but he wasn't an idiot.

Abyan drew one of her daggers as she moved between the shoddy cars around her—they had missing tires and doors, and she figured they'd been stripped a long time ago of whatever parts held value. She couldn't see him anywhere. Abyan went to the scattered bushes, filled with abandoned shoes and litter, and made sure to keep an eye on her surroundings as she searched them for any sign of a six-foot-two first gen.

Where are you?

She stalked over to the entrance of the abandoned building opposite her, figuring that she might as well cover all her bases before giving up. Her phone rang, the sound splitting the tension in the air asunder, and Abyan jumped out of her skin as she picked up.

Harry said, "Don't you dare go into that building."

"Why not? If what you saw was actually him, then this is the only place left to hide," she whispered back, muscles still on edge. "I didn't come this far just to give up."

"It's a trap, Guled. He's trying to hide from me and do whatever to you—"

Abyan ended the call, putting her phone on silent as she entered the building. She knew exactly what this was. Some part of her even respected Matteo a little for giving her a challenge because an easy win wouldn't have been nearly as satisfying. The one thing Abyan knew for certain was that Matteo was sorely mistaken if he thought she was simply trapped in there with him, defenseless and unassuming.

She wanted to laugh.

It felt like a game of cat and mouse in a way, how they circled one another. Abyan could feel him watching her as she passed through each room, filled with graffiti, rubbish, and enough rodents to make her lunch rise to her throat. His gaze weighed on her skin like a heavy oil, and she released a slow breath, her grip on her dagger so tight her fingers had gone numb.

The door she'd just passed through slammed shut behind her, and Abyan crashed onto the ground as her feet were swept out from under her. Matteo's smirk greeted her when her eyes snapped up. "You truly thought I was foolish enough to walk into this trap of yours?"

Abyan was on her feet in a split second. "I got you here, didn't I?"

She raised her fists, one foot in front of the other, and Matteo mirrored her. He wore a white shirt and ripped jeans, his black waves were tied back in a way that almost reminded her of Jared, and he gazed at her with a lethal glint in his eyes that made her breath catch.

"Is this the part where we stop dancing around each other and you tell me what's going on?" She pushed forward, aiming a jab at his face, but Matteo's hand came up a heartbeat before the blow connected, and he managed to misdirect her fist.

He managed to catch her across the jaw, the entire side of her face burning. "That would require me to care for you to understand what is happening, but that particular field remains barren in your regard."

When Matteo tried to elbow strike her, she slapped his wrist down, not giving him a moment to recover before swinging her own fist across his face. "I'm not going to let you follow me around like some stray animal."

Matteo stumbled back, shaking his head. "You act as though you have a say in the matter."

She scoffed, sheer disbelief making her momentarily lose focus. "I could kill you—it wouldn't take much. My world would be better for it."

Matteo grabbed her by the shoulder and kicked the back of her heel, the wind escaping her lungs the second she crashed onto the hard stone floor. "Humans . . . so loud and catastrophically wrong." His eyes trailed her body from head to toe. "It's nauseating."

Abyan gritted her teeth, forcing air in through her nose. "What do you want from me, for God's sake?"

She lay flat on her back, balancing all her weight on her right foot, before throwing a kick into the back of his knee. Matteo buckled and that was all the opportunity she needed to send him plummeting to the floor beside her. Abyan wasted no time straddling him, the point of the dagger on his throat warning him not to make a move.

"Tell me the truth." She pressed the blade a little deeper into his olive skin. "Tell me right now."

"You assume that I am stalking you with deadly intent," he bit out, breathing heavy. "That is far from reality."

So, he was *protecting* her?

Abyan's brows furrowed. "I'm tired of your riddles."

"You should remove yourself before things become difficult for you." A fire lit across his features, and Abyan resisted the urge to plunge her knife in deeper. "The forces at play are beyond your understanding."

"I won't repeat myself." Their gazes met, a clash of ice and fire—fury and its perfect mirror image. "Answer my question."

Yet Matteo clearly had no intention of doing so as the whites of his eyes became as black as his irises. *Shit.* Abyan couldn't kill him when he still held everything she wanted to know in that fortress head of his, but before she could think of a solution, a shot rang out from somewhere behind her, hitting Matteo square in the shoulder.

She whipped round to find Harry standing in the doorway, red-faced and weapon in hand.

Finally.

He spoke first. "I told you not to enter this building."

26

ARTEMIS

Hassan was the only one in the living room when Artemis came back from second period. He sat with his head tilted back, his black hair splayed out on the top of the settee, and an icepack rested on his eye. He held a vape pen to his lips with one hand while the other held an iPad with his set of the hacked files up for him to read with his good eye.

Artemis came to a stop in the center of the room and struggled to find something to say. She didn't know if it was her place to ask what happened to him, but alternating between staring at the yellow-toned glare of the light above them and the Persian rug under her feet wasn't how she saw her second proper conversation with Hassan going. She *wanted* to make friends with him, yet it was hard to build that bridge with someone whose only emotions toward you peaked at mild annoyance.

Screw it.

She said the first thing that came to mind, wringing her clammy fingers behind her back. "Are you okay?"

"She speaks," Hassan deadpanned before blowing O-shaped tufts of smoke from his lips. Though her cheeks burned, he continued before she had a chance to reply. "Trust me, recruit, the other guy looks worse."

"I'm sure you get bruises from training all the time."

He took the icepack off his face, revealing the black eye in all its blue and purple glory. "It's not from training."

Artemis's brow creased. "Then, where—"

"If, hypothetically speaking," Hassan interrupted, "I'd beaten the shit out of Lucas Yi and gotten us a tiny inglorious conduct penalty of five points, do you think I should tell the others first or wait for them to find out on their own?"

Her mouth fell open. "I can't believe you had a fight with Lucas."

"It was for a good reason." He shrugged. "He's a prick—I hate pricks."

"You need to tell the others right away. They're going to be angry with you, but they'll get over it quicker if you tell them sooner rather than later."

"Agreed," he said, and Artemis relaxed until she heard his next words. "I'll lie about where I got my bruise and wait for them to find out on their own."

She shook her head. "It's your funeral."

"Happy thoughts only, recruit." The corner of Hassan's mouth perked up, and Artemis found herself taken aback at how handsome he was even with his black eye. Not that Artemis had ever considered him unattractive, yet it was so much easier to admire his angular jaw line and full lips when he wasn't trying to be so intimidating.

"So, what's with the Rubik's Cube?" Artemis pointed to where it sat on the settee beside him with its fading colors and array of scratches. "I don't think I've ever seen you without it."

He drew in a long breath from his pen, blowing it up to the ceiling like a medieval dragon. "I have ADHD and don't talk much, that's the truth, Officer Garrett-Coleman. The cube helps me channel all my extra energy, so I can focus on other things."

"Oh, he remembers my name!" Artemis teased, while carefully tucking this new information away in the back of her mind. "I'm touched, really."

"Very funny."

Artemis sat down on the seat opposite him but shot up not a moment later once her eyes landed on the latest text on her phone. How could she lose track of time like this? She grabbed her combat boots from the corridor and ran back to the closest seat as she desperately tried to force her feet inside.

Hassan pointed his pen at her, raising a midnight brow. "You have somewhere to be?"

"A meeting with Abyan and Mr. Williams."

He gave a low whistle. "Rest in peace, recruit."

Artemis didn't have time to reply and sprinted out of The Sevenfold's dorm. Artemis and Abyan's meeting with the headteacher was about what happened at King's Cross, and she'd been dreading it for days. Nothing good was going to come of it. She knew it in her heart. Artemis finally skidded to a halt outside the recruitment building, her curls falling onto her eyes, and came face-to-face with Abyan.

"Just in time." She made a sound of annoyance and took off with Artemis in tow.

Artemis didn't want to bring up what happened during their BLCC order or the tense events that followed, but the all-consuming silence that hung between them as they meandered through the stone halls of the school wasn't doing them any favors.

Abyan cleared her throat. "I forgot to tell you, but you've done well on our missions—better than I expected anyway."

"I only followed my orders." She shrugged.

"Some people can't even manage that."

"It was nothing, really."

She smiled a little. "Just take the damn compliment, recruit."

Artemis held her hands up in mock surrender. "Okay, okay."

She still didn't feel like the praise was warranted though. All Artemis did was crouch in a corridor and sit in the car, watching everything take place like she had front row seats for a movie, but with a heavy box of crippling fear instead of popcorn and sky-high anxiety to wash it down. Getting complimented for simply sitting on the sidelines was like receiving a participation medal, as if Abyan was only saying it so she wouldn't feel bad about being the weakest link of the team.

Even though The Sevenfold had accepted her as part of the team now, they didn't have any faith in her—they'd been together for almost three years, while she'd been there for just over a month. Artemis wasn't stupid enough to think she wouldn't have to work for their trust. It was just frustrating being both in the loop and out of it at the same time, a bizarre state of limbo she wasn't accustomed to and didn't want to linger in.

Abyan took a sharp turn. The gray stone walls became warm chestnut wood with candles and portraits lining the length of the hall, and a plush carpet swallowed the heavy thuds of their feet.

Though the rest of Carlisle wasn't shabby by any means, it still paled in comparison to Mr. Williams's section. Walking from the older part of the building to this side was like being in the middle of White City Estate one minute, then surrounded by the high-rise condos of Canary Wharf the next.

It was a part of the campus Artemis had never seen before, not even on the introductory tour of the building, and she had a sneaking suspicion it wasn't by accident. Cameras high on the walls followed them as they walked through the open glass doors to where a receptionist sat, typing away at her computer.

"You must be Mr. Williams's three o'clock," said the woman. "Go on in, he's running slightly late, but he'll be with you soon."

They both nodded and entered his office, taking seats across from his polished mahogany desk. There were paintings and a ton of medals adorning the walls. Artemis couldn't sit still and alternated between bouncing her leg and tapping her fingers, not noticing she was fidgeting so badly until Abyan's hand shot out from the corner of her eye faster than she could blink, latching onto her wrist.

"Stop it." Abyan's words came out through gritted teeth. "Just relax, take deep breaths, and think of dancing rabbits or something."

Artemis blinked. "Rabbits don't dance, Abyan."

"Never mind." She shook her head but couldn't stop the laugh that left her lips and echoed throughout the room.

Just as Artemis was about to reply, the door behind them opened, and someone strolled in. The second she turned her head, her heart stopped, her body freezing up so much the ice threatened to crumble at the slightest movement.

Mr. Williams was a shorter man, with pinkish skin, and a well-kept goatee, but the man standing before them had copper-dotted brown hair, an effortless smile, and a twinkle in his blue eyes that was all fire and no warmth.

Mr. Carlisle.

"Sir." Abyan shot up from her seat, and Artemis followed suit, scrambling to her feet.

Mr. Carlisle wore a deep navy suit and one solitary wedding band on his ring finger. Did he know how many questions she had for him? They were perched on the tip of her tongue, twitching in anticipation, and ready to spring forward the moment her lips gave them way.

"Please, take a seat, girls." He unbuttoned his blazer before sitting. "We have matters to discuss."

They followed his command, and Artemis found herself wringing her fingers, unable to focus on anything but her lunch steadily rising in her throat. He leaned forward, eyes alight, and Artemis had to pinch her palm twice to snap herself back into reality.

"It's my understanding that your team was assigned a BLCC order on the third of October that didn't go as planned."

Abyan clasped her hands. "Yes, sir. There were sixteen Nosaru hosts in King's Cross, not the three we were expecting, and they were in the middle of a fight when we arrived at the station."

Mr. Carlisle shrugged, but there was a fluidity to his movements that unnerved her. "So, why didn't you call it in? I'm sure the operatives would've gladly taken care of it."

"I thought we could deal with the situation ourselves and our shadow agreed."

"Logic would suggest that distracted Nosaru should've been easier to kill."

Artemis had to keep from releasing a sound of frustration. "You don't understand, sir. They weren't just brawling in the station—they were slaughtering each other."

Mr. Carlisle didn't look shocked like De Costa was when Artemis told her what happened on their BLCC order. If anything, the way he tapped his chin while staring off in the distance, his eyes fixed on a point farther than Artemis could see and his mind adrift far beyond, made her think he was expecting it.

Mr. Carlisle watched as Abyan opened her mouth to jump in but closed it again, and he cocked a finely arched brow. "You can tell me, Abyan. There's no need to be afraid." Though Artemis could see her internal battle, Mr. Carlisle wasn't giving up so easily. "I can't help you if I don't know everything that happened."

"I saw the same behavior on a WLDO I took on the first day back at school." Abyan swallowed heavily. "This isn't an isolated incident, sir."

What?

"Tell me what happened on the mission."

She tried to hide her confusion, straightening in her seat. Abyan hadn't told her about any WLDO—she probably hadn't trusted her enough back then, Artemis realized. They hardly knew each other at the beginning of term. Still, Artemis waited with bated breath to find out exactly what went down on that mission.

Abyan took a breath before diving into the story of King's Cross station as well as what took place during her and Hank's WLDO, telling them of the warring first gens and the almost faction-like divide between the Nosaru, and Mr. Carlisle didn't interrupt her once.

When she was done, he spoke. "And are Ms. De Costa and Harry the only other people who know about these events?"

That's the first thing he asks after learning all of that? Artemis had yet to pick her jaw up from the floor. Everything Abyan had seen on that WLDO lined up with what happened in King's Cross and all the strange Nosaru activity from the past few weeks, yet Mr. Carlisle didn't seem to care all that much.

She might as well have told him the sky was blue that morning.

"They only know about the BLCC order."

He gave a heavy sigh. "If what you're saying is true, I think it's best you forget it happened."

"What?" Abyan blinked, and Artemis found her face mirroring hers. "Why would we do that?"

"From what I can tell, your mission was a success. You brought back three Nosaru for testing as your BLCC order demanded, and you deserve to be commended for that," he said, resting his arms on the desk. "We'll take care of what you saw internally. In the meantime, try to put it out of your mind and speak of it to no one. Do you understand?"

Abyan clenched her fists under the table, and for a second, Artemis thought she was going to punch him square in his condescending face. "Yes, sir."

Artemis echoed her, but as they stood to leave, he stopped them. "Not you, Garrett-Coleman. I would like to speak with you privately."

Artemis's eyes darted to her side, and while she dutifully lowered herself back into her chair, knowing she couldn't refuse Mr. Carlisle himself, she saw Abyan hesitate for the briefest moment before taking her leave. She gulped as her only ally left the room, her stomach dropping to her feet as Abyan's footsteps grew fainter.

Mr. Carlisle smiled, his teeth looking sharper than before. "We meet again."

27

ABYAN

Abyan had never seen a black site before.

Officially, it was for Harry's squad to recuperate between missions, yet unofficially, it was for the capture and *persuasion* of hosts. Although he never called the house where she now stood anything but 26 Jones Street, they both knew what it was, and the hair on Abyan's arms stood on edge as she walked through the soundproofed corridors.

The four bedrooms of the house had been converted, with all of them being split in half down the middle, one side being a small holding cell and the other with a table and chair that Abyan assumed were for Harry and his squad's benefit.

She stopped outside of Matteo's room. "Has he answered any of your questions?"

"Not since we brought him in," Harry replied from beside her, a vein in his neck jumping. "It'll change today though."

Abyan glanced down at the dark duffel bag draped across his shoulder. "What's in the bag?"

"Something that'll make our friend over there a little more cooperative."

Torture?

Nosaru weren't human, and they didn't think and feel like regular people—she'd been taught exactly how they were. They didn't deserve sympathy. Killing them meant getting rid of the parasite and setting the human their vessel had once been free, so it was more noble than it looked on the surface.

Harry wouldn't be doing anything wrong.

"This isn't the time for doubt, Guled," he snapped, and unlocked the door before she could get a word out.

Abyan took a moment to steel herself before following him and coming face-to-face with the first gen that had been plaguing her for far too long. Matteo's hair was matted, dried blood had crusted across his angular jaw, and his wrists were cuffed around the iron poles of his cell. In that position, the only thing he could do was move the cuffs up and down since the gate lay between him and his wrists.

A form of torture, she realized, as Harry took out a small portable power station from his bag. Matteo tried to move out of the way as Harry approached him with two cords from the power station connected to small clamps, but there was nowhere for him to go. Harry clamped each of the first gen's hands and then returned to Abyan's side and placed the box between them on the floor.

"The rules are simple, Valente," Harry said, seating himself on a chair next to his power station. "We're going to ask you some questions, and if you don't answer to our satisfaction, you'll get ten thousand volts straight through you. Understood?"

Matteo remained silent, nothing but hatred in his eyes.

"That wasn't a satisfactory answer." Harry leaned down and flipped one of the switches of the box on and off. Matteo's body convulsed, veins jutting out of places she didn't know veins could jut out of, and he cursed once he recovered, panting heavily. "I said, am I understood?"

The first gen's lip curled. "Yes."

"Why did you blow up the hive on the day we first met?" Abyan asked first. It had been bothering her for weeks. "I know it was you."

If she hadn't known him any better, Abyan could've sworn Matteo laughed. "Revenge."

"Against your own kind?"

He grew quiet again, and Harry wasted no time sending another ten thousand volts to him. "Answer her before I lose my patience."

"It was one of Soros's main hives," he panted. "My original tasked me with its destruction."

The two Nosaru originals were fighting? Abyan's brows furrowed. "Why would Ora make you do that? The two alphas have been attached at the hip since the third one was killed hundreds of years ago."

"They had a disagreement—I do not know the cause of it, so you can electrocute me all you like." Matteo glared at Harry. "Did you not wonder why my people suddenly turned on each other? Why I could not control those hosts when you and I were in that hive?"

It made perfect sense.

Abyan's jaw went slack for a second before she recovered. The originals had cut off the hive mind so their separate groups of offspring could no longer communicate with each other. But why? Abyan couldn't figure out what could've caused this divide for the life of her.

What could fracture a three-hundred-year-old alliance?

It was impossible for Carlisle operatives to distinguish between hosts who were sired from either Ora or Soros, the two remaining alpha females who first landed on Earth. They didn't have samples of the originals' genetic material, and each successive wave of their offspring had a more messed-up genome than the one that came before them. From what they knew, there was no scientific or behavioral difference between the two: Hosts from either original could interact and control each other.

She asked the other question that had been on her mind for weeks. "Why have you been stalking me if it's not to kill me?"

"Contrary to what you have convinced yourself of, human," Matteo said, "you are not as special as you think."

Harry zapped him. "We'll try that again."

Matteo's eyes rolled backward and his body fell limp against the metal bars. *Shit.* Abyan's voice was frantic. "Did you kill him?"

"Relax." Harry went over and checked his vitals. "He's just unconscious. I'll see if anything's really damaged when he comes to. In the meantime, you need to head back to school and—"

"But—"

Harry didn't let her finish, his tone final. "I'll let you know when you can come back here."

"Fine." Abyan gritted her teeth. "I'll go."

She would be back soon enough, whether Harry gave her the okay or not.

Nothing was going to stand in her way anymore.

———————

It was League Night.

Mason had spent weeks planning his party and had run a million of his ideas past them all over the last couple of days. Abyan should've been ready an hour ago, but it was eight in the evening, and she was still in bed. God, her hair was still in dub dubis, and even getting up to brush her teeth that morning took much more effort than it should've.

There was no way she could go to the party like that.

She hadn't heard from Harry in days and had already made plans to slip away in the coming days when she was feeling better to get what she needed from Matteo. The rest of The Sevenfold still had no clue what she'd been up to, and she wanted to keep it that way for a little while longer because they'd be furious with her and she didn't have time to deal with it all.

Their ignorance was so much better.

She closed her laptop for the first time in hours, adjusting her position in the bed and rubbing the blue-light burn from her eyes. Seven hundred fifty-eight. That was how many of her thousand files she had left to go through. *Damn it.* The pain in her eyes felt like it cut straight through her brain.

And it wasn't like she'd discovered anything major to make it all worth it. All she'd gotten so far were failed cure trials, lab reports that made no sense to her, and random mission reports from operatives in at least four different languages.

It was like finding a needle in a bloody haystack.

As she didn't have the heart to break it to Mason himself, Abyan pulled out her phone and sent a quick text to Hank explaining that she wouldn't be coming along. Not two minutes later, three brisk knocks sounded at her door. She quickly wrapped a shalmad around her head, her arms feeling like stone slabs, before telling him to come in.

"I come bearing ice cream," Hank called in an overexaggerated and barely recognizable British accent, a world away from his usual Chicago baritone. "As sustenance for thy stomach."

Abyan let her head drop to her pillow. "That was bad, even for you."

He cocked a brow, stopping just before the bed, green eyes teasing. "I don't think it's smart to slander me when I'm the one with the goods."

"You would hold my chocolate fudge ice cream hostage and let me die a slow and painful death?" she asked. "I need a new best friend."

Hank held out the tub and spoon. "Unfortunately for you, you're going to be stuck with me until we're at least eighty."

"I'm depressed, Hank." Abyan seized the ice cream, her mouth watering at the sight of the blue sprinkles. "Let me wallow in my misery in peace."

Something in his face changed, and he crouched down to her eye level. "I'm staying back here with you to keep you company."

"No, it's okay," she assured him. "Go and have fun with the others."

"I'd be having the opposite of fun over there without you," Hank said. "It would be like deep 'My dog just died, my car broke down, and my wife's taking my kids and the house' level distress."

"Not the kids and the house." Abyan would've laughed if she had it in her. "I'd have taken the yacht, and the cars too."

His mouth fell open. "You're the worst wife ever, Yan."

"Well, maybe you should've been a better husband."

He chuckled then, retreating to the doorway, and she hoped he knew that she was grateful for whatever this was. Her doctors used to tell her the usual shit about making her depression better like getting some sun, exercising, and whatever, but Hank was so much better than all of that with his corny jokes, stories, and boundless patience, each a ray far better than any distant star could ever gift her.

He was her own goddamn sun.

"Do you want me to tell you another embarrassing story?" he asked, sitting down in the middle of the open doorway and leaning against the frame. "I'm like ninety-nine percent sure I've already told you all of them, but I'm happy to go through the All-Stars again."

Abyan nodded. "Do the one about when you sleepwalked naked into that old lady's yard."

"I'll even tell it in my British accent for you." He winked. "Consider it a best-friend privilege."

"God, please no."

He cleared his throat. "On the tender summer morn of yonder—"

She threw a pillow at him before he could react, and it landed square on his face. "I'm not afraid of going to jail, Hercules."

"Okay, fine." He held his hands up. "If you were that intimidated by how much better my accent was than yours, you could've said so in the beginning."

"I'm too tired to argue with you." She closed her eyes, nestling into her bed and pulling her covers up higher. "Can you please just start the story?"

A couple of seconds passed before he began. "It all started on my thirteenth birthday. I'd drunk a lot of soda that day, and everyone in my family knows that if I drink more than like two cans, I have these weird dreams, so it was already a recipe for disaster and—"

His phone pinged, cutting him off, but Abyan was in that comfortable limbo between being asleep and awake and didn't want to ruin it by opening her eyes.

A sharp breath left his lips.

"I need to show you something." Hank rose from his position and helped her sit up on the bed. Abyan wiped the fatigue from her face as he tapped the screen. "I was looking through the files Tolly hacked a few days ago and found this. Granted, I wasn't sure exactly what it meant until now, which is why I didn't tell you sooner."

"It's empty." Abyan's brows furrowed at the blank page in the folder for the floor plans of the London branch.

"Carlisle Enterprises has this feature in their systems that doesn't allow anyone to copy files from the main server to external ones for security purposes—you'd have to log into Carlisle's system and use a second classified passcode to access them normally. Tolly's hack was the only known time anyone has tried to steal information from the organization in years, and they're alerted whenever anyone tries to, so I spoke to my cousin in the intelligence wing."

"Hercules," she warned. "We don't need Salim to come sniffing around."

"It was purely hypothetical, trust me," he said. "He got back to me just now and pretty much admitted that Carlisle was compromised by multiple sources on the night of our hack. He said they had people check to make sure nothing was taken, but I guess no one really cares about boring floor plans."

Earlier, Tolly had told her some of the files had some kind of lock that restricted them from being copied in any way, even from within the system, and the only way to get them during their hack was to remove them from the database entirely with a third classified passcode. He only did it for a handful of promising files, but Abyan definitely didn't remember floor plans being one of them. Hank's eyes were wide as saucers, and Abyan's mouth hung open.

They'd given the Nosaru the chance to steal whatever they wanted.

The original floor plans for the entire London branch of Carlisle Enterprises—the recruitment, intelligence, and research wings—had all been taken. They showed all the classified lower levels, the hidden exits and entrances, and the places where they stored their most confidential information.

Abyan blinked. "The Nosaru are planning an attack on Carlisle."

28

ARTEMIS

MASON'S PARTY WAS MIND-BLOWING.

Though that wasn't much coming from her, Artemis supposed, since this was her first one. EDM music boomed in her ears, the bass of the speakers thrumming in her veins, and hot bodies pressed up against hers as she moved through the crowd.

The bottle of tequila she clutched in her hand almost slipped out of her grasp so many times Artemis lost count. While she wasn't drinking herself, the rest of The Sevenfold were thoroughly off their faces. Kade was up on a table dancing like it was her last night on Earth, and Tolly had passed out on the sofa.

She was almost glad Hank and Abyan weren't there.

Artemis had made up something half-plausible about what Mr. Carlisle had said to her during their meeting and knew Abyan didn't believe a word she'd said. She could see it in her eyes. Yet what Artemis had to tell the squad would've changed everything, and she didn't want to ruin her relationship with everyone when they'd just started to accept her.

Mr. Carlisle's words were vague, each one carefully plucked from his mind just when it was ripe enough, but Artemis wasn't stupid. She could see the true meaning through his elaborate fog, and it made her stomach lurch.

He kept asking her to go over what happened during their past missions, and Artemis naively thought he was simply double-checking to make sure her and Abyan's recollection of the events were the same. It was only when he specifically asked if she could remember anything strange or out of the ordinary happening that her heart stopped in her chest.

Strange or out of the ordinary.

That was his exact wording the first time he'd asked her the question after the attack that killed Jared, too, and "You mean besides being chased up a mountain by bloodthirsty alien vampires?" she'd wanted to reply at the time, but she didn't have it in her.

He wore a charcoal-gray suit that morning, and it was pouring rain outside—the droplets flung themselves at the closed windows of her hospital room with so much force that Artemis could barely hear herself think over the noise. Though she told Mr. Carlisle the truth on both occasions, she knew he didn't believe her this second time round. He wanted a different answer, the suffocating intensity in his eyes said as much, but Artemis couldn't give it to him.

Nothing strange happened during their BLCC order or recon mission.

When she and Jared were attacked, all Artemis could register in that moment was her fear. The crippling, ice-cold terror that settled beneath her flesh and only intensified the closer the Nosaru got; she shut her eyes, and one moment their labored breaths were mere inches from her ear, the next, their screams filled the air as they recoiled, running farther down the mountain to get away from her.

They went for Jared, and he tried to swing at them with his metal picks. The rough movement shook the lengths of rope connecting them all and threatened to send every one of them plummeting to the ground. Artemis's heart stopped, watching in horror, but both of her hands might as well have been superglued to her picks. She couldn't move. Jared's blood was smeared across their mouths, dripping down their chins, and she couldn't control the scream that ripped through her body.

The Nosaru hissed and fell from the mountain face as they lost their footing. Artemis and the remaining climbers had to make their descent with four of their dead friends' body parts hanging from the very same rope they were attached to, weighing them down.

By the time they got down, Mr. Carlisle was there with his vans and operatives, while the ambulances they'd called came almost forty minutes afterward. She remembered how he kept trying to ask her questions, but she was in shock, barely even managing to breathe properly let alone form a coherent reply. In Belford Hospital, she told him exactly what took place, and the moment she got to the hosts' screeching before they all fell, Mr. Carlisle's jaw dropped a fraction.

It was the most human reaction she'd ever seen from him.

A hand shot out of the mass of people around her, pulling her out of the crowd and jerking Artemis from her thoughts. "You okay, Artemis? You look like you've seen a ghost."

You have no idea.

Though her words were slurred, the concern in Kade's face calmed her racing heartbeat a fraction, and Artemis released a slow breath. "I'm fine."

She held her hand. "Come and dance with me."

"I'm good over here," Artemis said, squeezing her hand so she didn't take this as a full-on rejection. "Really."

"Fine, be boring." Kade gave an exaggerated huff and took the bottle of tequila from her before going off to dance. Artemis's feet hurt and she didn't have any alcohol in her system to make her forget it, so she went over to where Mason and Hassan were sitting.

"Can I have a half-and-half margherita pizza?" Mason slurred into his phone. "Yes, half margherita and half margherita."

Hassan snatched the phone from his grasp. "Make it boneless."

Artemis's phone vibrated as she collapsed onto the settee beside them. She pulled it out, expecting a late goodnight text from Dad or something, not a message from Abyan that made her shoot up from the chair.

Something was very wrong.

———————

It was three in the morning by the time they got back from the party. As the only sober one in the group, Artemis had to drag every member of The Sevenfold one by one into the taxi she'd hailed.

While their drunken ramblings were entertaining enough, she couldn't shake the unease Abyan's text triggered in her chest. None of her friends were particularly light, and she was pretty much carrying all their weight as they stumbled across the pavement, tripping over their own feet and a thousand imaginary obstacles on the way to the car.

Artemis was red in the face by the time she'd gotten them all in with their seat belts firmly fastened, and she just prayed none of them threw up. The boys all slept on one another, and Kade rested her head on Artemis's shoulder. She only hoped Abyan wouldn't be too disappointed when she saw what a sorry sight they all were.

Her message was simple: "MEETING NOW." It was sent to their group chat, and she had no idea what Abyan was going to tell them. Maybe she'd figured out Artemis's dirty little secret and had decided to tell them all what she'd been hiding.

Hank opened the door for them the moment they all staggered out of the elevator, but the breath still hadn't returned to Artemis's lungs from hauling the rest of The Sevenfold out of the taxi. Abyan came up behind him. Her hair was wrapped in a silk scarf and in Bantu knots beneath the cloth. She wore a necklace that had a gold ring hanging from it and a glower that could turn anyone's courage to dust beneath its weight.

"Are *any* of you sober?" she asked as she and Hank helped them to Kade's room. One quick glance into the living room showed a massive pile of papers—satellite images by the looks of them—and an assortment of junk food wrappers strewn about the room.

"Just me." Artemis adjusted Kade's arm around her shoulder.

The bed was king-sized, so they deposited their drunk friends onto it, making sure to take their shoes and socks off so Kade didn't pop a blood vessel the next morning. Abyan ran a hand down her face and growled in frustration, and Hank clenched his fists.

"What's wrong?" Artemis asked, her eyes darting between them. Hank opened his mouth to speak but stopped himself, turning to look back at Abyan. A silent conversation passed between them before he faced Artemis again.

"We need to show you something."

She followed them into the living room which looked like a Category 5 hurricane had torn through it. She picked up one of the papers on the floor and studied the picture it showed. It was a satellite image of Holland Park. Another one she caught sight of was Marble Arch, and it didn't take long for Artemis to realize they were all pictures of areas surrounding Carlisle Enterprises' buildings.

"Why do you have these?" Artemis raised a brow. There wasn't anything particularly special or important about any of the places, and she couldn't help but wonder what had shaken them so much.

"The Nosaru are planning to attack the London branch," Abyan said, picking up some of the papers. "They stole the unredacted floor plans for all three facilities during our hack, and we've only just discovered it."

"We have to tell someone, then." Her jaw dropped. "This is our fault."

Hank nodded. "That's exactly what I've been saying this whole time."

"We can't do that because then we'll have to admit it was us who hacked Carlisle in the first place and handed all our secrets to the Nosaru on a silver platter," Abyan explained. "We have to fix this mess by ourselves."

"This is so much bigger than us now, Yan." He ran a frustrated hand through his hair. "How can you not see that?"

She shook her head. "It's not bigger than us! We can save the London branch. Do you think your brother would chicken out like this? Everyone says we're the best of the best, and here's our chance to prove it."

She was playing a dangerous game.

Artemis asked, "What if you're wrong?"

"I'm not." Abyan's certainty would've rubbed off on her too if Artemis wasn't so terrified. "If either of you believed in our squad half as much as I did, we wouldn't be having this conversation."

"Have it your way," Hank said, red spreading fast up his neck. "If this goes south, it's on you."

"That won't happen," she replied. "We know where all the suspected hives closest to the main buildings of Carlisle Enterprises are."

Artemis asked, "So, they're in Marble Arch, Holland Park, and Greenwich?"

"Luckily, they're only first-degree hives."

"What are we going to do?"

Abyan crossed her arms. "We're going to hit them first."

29

ABYAN

Hank blinked. "You kidnapped a first gen."

"You've said that three times already." Abyan pinched the bridge of her nose. "It's not that hard to believe."

He opened the door leading to Matteo's cell and poked his head in for a sum total of two seconds before closing it and turning to her. "When you told me you'd been hiding something, this isn't exactly what I pictured."

"Harry helped me so you can't yell at me for going rogue on everyone," she was quick to say. "Plus, we only did it because there was no other way."

They weren't even supposed to be there—Harry had no idea she broke in. Then again, it was his own fault for not giving her the green light to visit sooner. Abyan would've preferred to have come alone, but letting Hank in on her secret was the only thing she could think of that would distract him from how annoyed he was with her about the hive attacks she was planning.

Hank shook his head like he couldn't believe she was being serious. "What do you mean?"

Abyan took a sudden interest in the charcoal carpet. "Do you remember when we got separated back in our recon mission in Wood Green?"

"The first or second time?"

"Second." When he nodded, Abyan continued, "I was pulled into

218

a room by the first gen in that cell, Matteo Valente. He saved my life and escaped just before you and the squad burst in. He's also the host that escaped us during our Peeping Tom weeks ago, and he's the one who blew up that damn hive during our recon mission."

"This doesn't make any sense," he said, and Abyan told him about what Matteo had revealed to her about the Nosaru originals, the confusion in Hank's face only increasing. "If the originals are fighting, why would this first gen go out of his way to 'protect' you?"

"That's what I've been trying to figure out."

His eyes narrowed as he ran a hand through his messy hair, and Abyan could see the cogs in his mind turning in their green depths. "You should've told me about this earlier, Yan."

"I know," she admitted. "I'm sorry for not keeping you in the loop."

Hank asked, "So, we're here now because you think he knows something about the attacks on Carlisle that the Nosaru are planning?"

"Exactly," Abyan said, hand on the doorknob. "My gut tells me he's hiding something."

She breezed into the room with Hank behind her, something in her calming at the sight of the anti-hormone cuffs on Matteo's wrists. He sat on the floor of his cell, cross-legged, with his wrist locked around the iron bars to stop his arms from moving too much. *We're safe.* Yet even though Abyan had Gacan Libaax sheathed at her back, and she knew Hank wouldn't let anything bad happen to her, every muscle in her body was still on edge.

Matteo sniffed the air again, looking up at them with a swollen eye, his cheeks littered with dozens of scars and marks that weren't there when they last spoke. "Two of you."

"What do you know of the attack your kind are planning on Carlisle Enterprises?" Abyan got straight to the point, clamping the wires on his hands as Hank plugged in Harry's power station in the corner of the room. "Be honest, we don't want to hurt you."

She didn't know why she was being nice.

It's not like hosts appreciated that kind of thing.

"It has to be Soros's doing." Matteo's voice was rougher than she remembered. "My people would not do such a thing."

"Let me guess." She crouched down next to him. "Because you're the good kind of parasitic alien, and you don't want to do anything bad to us humans," Abyan mocked, "you're not like those other girls."

Matteo's hand shot out like lightning, his fingers squeezing her neck so tight she couldn't think, and he pulled her close enough that their faces almost touched across the metal bars and whispered, "Oh, there are many things I would like to do to you." His breath fanned her face as she struggled to breathe. "Do not mistake my current circumstances for weakness, human."

Abyan's chest burned, her mouth opening for air but coming up empty each time, and she didn't realize Matteo had let her go until he shuddered violently and fell to the side, convulsing. *Hank.* She gasped, the air finally filling her lungs, and cradled her aching throat.

"Yan!" Hank was at her side in a second, checking over her. "Shit, did I get you, too? I'm sorry, shocking him was the first thing I could think of."

She croaked. "I'm fine."

He pulled Gacan Libaax from Abyan's sheath and went for Matteo. "I'm gonna kill him."

"No!" She held him back with what little strength she had left. "He's too important to kill right now."

I have to offer him something shiny enough.

"If you answer some questions honestly, Matteo, we will let you go." Abyan held the first gen's gaze so he knew she meant her words. "I swear it."

Hank turned to her, furious. "Have you lost your mind?"

"I will only answer two, providing they will not result in harm to me or my people," Matteo rasped. "What would you like to know?"

There was one question that she wanted answered more than anything now. "Why are Ora and Soros fighting after all this time? I know you lied about not knowing anything about it before."

"Ora wants to leave this cesspit of a planet and join the rest of our people who have flourished elsewhere on a world with a non-sentient species for us to occupy," Matteo said. "Soros wants to stay and invite the rest of our people here to colonize Earth in its entirety."

Holy shit.

It took Abyan a moment to find her words. "But how did they find out about where your people are? Their original scout ship was so damaged when the originals first crash-landed here, and Carlisle operatives have all the pieces of it under lock and key."

"We managed to take back part of our ship—humans would refer to it as a form of radio, but we know it as something else," he explained. "You've heard of Mission Zero?"

The Cardinal Six's final mission where everything went wrong. Sebastian Carlisle's only failure.

"The payload we stole from your operatives contained components of the radio that had been partially repaired, and we secured the rest of the parts over the years," he said. "The final piece was repatriated two months ago."

Almost exactly when the Nosaru started killing each other.

"No matter what materials we tried to use to return our radio to its full functionality, nothing on this planet worked; so we could receive messages easily enough but not send any back. We found a channel with a looped message for all the old scout ships who had yet to return telling us the good news and that we finally had a home again."

Something still wasn't adding up. "That doesn't explain why Ora and Soros would be fighting if there was no way to send a message back."

"Ora has the radio now and Soros wants it." Matteo shrugged. "There is a piece of the ship that we think can be repurposed to repair the damage done to it in the crash, but then again, Soros is searching for the part as well."

"What does this all have to do with me, then? How do I fit into your plans?" Abyan didn't try to hide her exasperation. "Why are you protecting me?"

He held out his cuffed hands. "I answered two of your questions."

Abyan cursed internally but made no move toward him. She shared a look with Hank and was glad to see he was on the same page as she was—Matteo was too valuable to release. Harry's squad didn't know about what he and Abyan had been up to so they couldn't help find him again if he slipped away now, and she and Hank wouldn't be able to do much alone.

She couldn't let their only lead go.

Matteo must've sensed the shift in her and banged against the bars of his cell, his matted dark locks falling into his face. "You have to honor our deal!"

"I don't take orders from maggots," Abyan snapped, grabbing Hank by the arm and leaving the room. Once she was sure they were alone and the door to Matteo's prison was firmly shut behind them, Abyan spoke. "Do you think he was telling the truth?"

"I wish I thought he was lying." Hank's voice was hollow. "It explains everything we've been seeing this year."

Abyan thought for a second. "I think we should ask your mum about Mission Zero, since she was there."

"No." Hank didn't even blink. "That mission is why my dad got so messed up in the head, and she's just as useless now as she was then. She'll just shut down if you ask her about it."

Of all the members of The Cardinal Six, only four were still alive: Mr. Carlisle, Ms. Bruno, Mariam Sepetu, and Rosemary Mulligan. Abyan had figured Rosemary would be the easiest bet, since she was a member of The League and openly despised Mr.

Carlisle—she'd tell them the truth. Yet the last thing she wanted to do was open this particular wound for Hank, so she didn't argue her point further.

He looked at her expectantly. "You know what I'm going to suggest we do about what Valente told us, right?"

Tell someone.

"I'm scared, Hank." Though Abyan's voice was small, she didn't care. She was finally being honest. "What if we're not supposed to figure any of this out and coming clean means painting a huge red target on our backs?"

"The school wouldn't do that to us," he told her, his eyes softening. "We could tell De Costa, if that makes you feel more comfortable."

De Costa was the only member of staff Abyan trusted. "Fine, but only about the radio and the war. We can't mention the hive attacks at all—I'm not throwing Tolly under the bus like that when we all asked him to do the hack."

Hank's face was conflicted, but he eventually caved. "You're sure you still want to go through with that?"

"We don't have any other choice." Abyan glanced at the time. "Shit, we need to get back home."

They hailed a cab and ran all the way up to their dorm, and every step of the way Abyan prayed with everything in her that they weren't too late. Once they were inside, Tolly emerged from the doorway. "Come on, guys. We're going to miss it!"

Through his surveillance of their teachers' emails, he'd discovered that a few senior faculty members like Mr. Oluwole and Ms. Bruno were headed to a meeting in the research wing. They were supposed to listen in on it together, so Abyan put her and Hank's discovery aside for now and followed Tolly into his room. He sat at his desk with all three of his computer screens covered in feeds from the research wing's CCTV.

After what happened last time, Tolly had planted a back door into their security systems that only he had access to. It was deep in their layers of code, tripling the encryptions and safeguards needed to breach it. She tried her hardest to ignore all the gadgets and machine parts littering the floor as they pulled up chairs beside him and clicked through the cameras, searching for the meeting.

All the muscles in Abyan's body tensed the second Tolly clicked on one of the conference rooms' feeds. The room was packed to the brim with every high-level Carlisle official in the UK. A gasp escaped her lips when she caught sight of Commander Macleod, dressed in his standard combat uniform decorated with all his medals. Mr. Carlisle sat at the head of the huge oval-shaped table; his mouth was moving but no sound came through the camera.

Tolly's hand was immediately on the mouse, clicking everything and anything to try and get audio. The research building was covered in state-of-the-art IP security cameras that recorded both sound and visuals—there had to be a way. She didn't know what button he hit, but they could suddenly hear Commander Macleod speaking, gruff Scottish accent and all.

"If you're in any doubt, here's audio of an American soldier's distress call just before the fall of NATO's air base in the Carnic Alps."

Abyan didn't even have time to order her thoughts before deafening explosions and gunshots filled her ears. "Mayday, mayday, mayday, this is Lieutenant Christopher Jones from the Aviano Air Base. We are under attack by some—" There was a loud crash in the background, and the lieutenant's panicked voice was cut off. "We don't know what or who they are, they look like us but they're too fast and strong to be human. It's unlike anything I've ever seen before, they're biting out throats and drinking blood. We need urgent assist—"

A snarl they'd all heard a thousand times entered the recording, and Abyan had never wanted to block her ears more than when Lieutenant Jones gave out the most blood-curdling scream she'd ever heard. Her heart was in her throat, and she only realized she was gripping Hank's hand when it was too late. The Nosaru had taken a NATO base in Italy. But why? She couldn't imagine what reason they could possibly have to do that.

Commander Macleod paused the recording and rose from his seat, his silver hair gleaming. "That was nine days ago. Just this week the HMS *Cressida*, an elite warship, and Fort Irwin in California were also destroyed by Nosaru."

Mr. Carlisle leaned forward, an emotion she couldn't place flitting across his eyes. "And you're telling me no one can figure out why this is happening?"

The Commander clenched his jaw. "No, sir. We're working on it night and day."

"Work harder, Commander," Mr. Carlisle said. "I want another report within the next forty-eight hours."

They're looking for their missing parts.

Hank turned to her, his features frozen in shock. Half of Abyan hated that they even saw this. Observing the meeting was meant to give her some kind of peace, knowing her superiors had the situation handled, but it only showed they were just as confused and out of their depth as everyone else was. Her stomach dropped to her feet as she realized if they didn't get this situation under control and do it quickly, the unspeakable would happen.

The Nosaru were going to win.

30

ARTEMIS

For someone as big as he was, Mason moved faster than anyone she'd ever seen.

The obstacle course had eight exercises, and Artemis had maintained her lead for all of two seconds before he pulled ahead on the rope wall. The biting morning air licked at her exposed skin, yet despite the cold and her aching limbs, she didn't once stop.

Artemis hauled herself up over the rope wall and dived into the long rectangular pool beneath, only realizing the current was going against her once she was already in the water. There had to be some kind of machine under the pool manipulating the waves to make it as difficult as possible to swim through. She inhaled a deep breath, noting how Mason was struggling with the balancing obstacle up ahead, and pumped her limbs forward.

Her muscles shook against the water, each wave pushing her back with so much force Artemis thought she'd be swallowed by the current. She pushed herself harder, her legs propelling her forward, and didn't stop no matter how strong the water got—the second her hands touched the edge of the pool, Artemis dragged herself out and fell onto her stomach, letting her body adjust for a second before she moved onto the penultimate obstacle with shaking limbs.

Two towering balance seesaws lay spread out in a triangular formation a short distance apart with two legs of rope, one between each beam, hanging from the wooden rafters above. It was easy enough to figure out what she had to do. Run across the first seesaw without dropping, jump onto the rope and land onto the next seesaw, then continue until she reached the second rope that led to the mud pool she'd eventually have to crawl through.

Mason cursed as he failed on the second beam yet again, landing on the thick net several feet below. *I can win this.* For once, she'd beat a member of The Sevenfold at something. The mere thought cranked her determination into overdrive, all her million different aches and pains fading into the back of her mind, as Artemis set her sights on the first of her beams.

She climbed up the fifteen-rung ladder and released a slow breath as she crept across the seesaw, the wood trembling with every movement and threatening to send her tumbling. Artemis held her arms out, spreading her surface area as much as possible. She passed the halfway point on the beam, and it dipped, propelling her forward. She had no choice but to jog down the rest of its length, using the momentum to launch herself into the air, grabbing the waiting rope, and landing comfortably on the next seesaw.

Artemis didn't dare look back to check where Mason was.

She could feel him hot on her heels.

"Come on, Jay," she told herself, her teeth chattering. "You can finish before him."

Artemis set her jaw and continued, her legs trembling as she edged forward on the beam with precise movements. When the balance shifted and tipped her forward, she used the rope to propel herself onto the landing of the last obstacle in the course: the mud-water crawl.

She jumped into the mud on all fours as Mason's heavy footfalls landed on her ears, letting her know that he was finally done with the beams and ready to give a run for her money for the last leg of their training session.

The lattice of thick rope above her head as she crawled made sure there was no illusion of comfort. She had to be as low as possible to avoid getting snagged by it, and with mud already in her nails, hair, and mouth, Artemis wanted nothing more than to be done with it all.

She pushed herself up the instant she felt grass beneath her soaked fingertips and ran to the finish line with a lopsided gait and an inferno in her chest. Artemis didn't care where Mason was at that point. The only thing that mattered was that he wasn't in front of her. She collapsed at the red finish line, landing on the ground with a resounding thud, and flipped onto her back as Mason jogged toward her, a lingering smile on his lips.

"Well done, Artemis!" he cheered, taking a seat on the grass next to her, all long limbs and hard muscle. "You've improved so much since the beginning of the year."

She laughed. "All the extra training's finally paying off."

"I'm so proud of you," he said earnestly. "I know it hasn't been easy this year and that we haven't been the most welcoming people in the world, but it's nice to see you proving everyone wrong."

Artemis thanked him, and a comfortable silence befell them as they looked out at the forest around them and listened to the sound of birds and other wildlife. She opened her mouth and then closed it three times, trying to find the right words and failing, before giving herself one last internal pep talk and biting the bullet.

"I feel like we haven't spoken about everything that's happened with the hack and the school stuff . . ." she trailed off, and after a short pause, she asked, "What do you think about your dad? He's clearly wrapped up in something big, and I think we all know he isn't the good guy here."

Mason went real quiet, more quiet than she'd ever seen. "Have I ever told you about my mum, Artemis?" He didn't pause long enough for her to move past her confusion and answer. "She lives back in Lillehammer, but I'm only allowed to see her in person for two weeks a year."

Her brows furrowed. "Why?"

"Because my sperm donor thinks she makes me soft and will cancel any ticket to Norway I try to buy or get me put on some no-fly list so I can't see her," he explained, anger taking hold of his handsome features. "He's the reason I got sent here after secondary school, not the ten performing arts schools I'd applied to."

Artemis thought back to what Harry had said about each member of their squad when they'd first met him, about how some of The Sevenfold never really wanted to be there.

She'd always known on some level that someone as kind as Mason was fundamentally out of place in Carlisle—he was a daffodil at the foot of a smoldering volcano, beautiful in a tragic kind of way, with the only certainty being that he too would be engulfed in fire eventually.

It was a question of when rather than if.

Then he'd be just like everyone else at Carlisle, cold and thorny. Even Kade whom Artemis adored, maybe in a slightly more than platonic kind of way, had a certain sharpness to her that was clear enough to see.

Artemis pulled herself out of her thoughts. "You wanted to do performing arts?"

He nodded. "When I used to think of my future, I saw myself carrying Oscars and Tonys, and now I have tranqs and daggers because Sebastian called up each school I applied to and told them to reject me in exchange for a very *generous* donation."

Her mouth fell open, but Mason got there first. "One of the perks of being a billionaire, I guess, is that you get to see pretty quickly how most people's morals are measured in the number of zeroes after a comma on some shiny check," he said. "So, no, Artemis, I don't care about Sebastian Carlisle being the bad guy now because he's been the bad guy my whole life."

"I'm so sorry you had to go through that," Artemis said quickly. "I wasn't trying to accuse you of anything."

"Don't worry about it. You had no idea." He waved a dismissive hand. "Plus, the Shit Dad Club isn't that bad. We exchange childhood traumas and list all our abandonment issues for fun."

Artemis chuckled at that.

He rose and held a hand out to her. "Let's get you home so you can eat something before your meeting with Dr. Telford. You literally look like you're about to faint."

"I'm *starving*." She looked at him for a second before taking his hand, and a warm feeling Artemis couldn't place settled over her as they walked back to his car. Were they officially friends now? He'd always been kind to her, and Artemis hoped this was only the beginning of their friendship, that he'd be there for her and vice versa like he was for the others in the squad.

She was done being on the outside.

———————+———————

Artemis's meeting with Dr. Telford was an incisional biopsy this time. Her hands trembled at the thought. Artemis knew what a biopsy was and was already formulating an escape plan, because there was no way she was letting them stick needles into her and cut away pieces of her tissue for God-knows-what.

She racked her brain, trying to remember what she passed as she was led to her hospital room. There were two operatives on either end of the corridor outside and one man standing in front of her door, staring at her intently. There was no way she could get out. *Wait a minute.* Artemis's eyes drifted to the window as she feigned disinterest; she was only two floors up.

She could make that jump.

The window was just under six feet from her. If she really legged it, the guard wouldn't be able to get to her in time. Artemis couldn't be a part of this anymore. She almost wanted to laugh, picturing Mr. Carlisle's face when he found out his precious science project had escaped him.

Her mind drifted back to how Kade comforted her after her meeting with Mr. Carlisle. She knew Artemis was hiding something but didn't try to force it out of her once. It had worked at the time, but there was still a feeling of betrayal she couldn't shake taking root beneath her skin. It grew larger with every smile a squad member sent her way, its poisoned bark scraping at her insides the longer its branches grew, and Artemis feared she'd never rid herself of it.

She knew something her friends didn't.

Mr. Carlisle and Dr. Telford knew it, too.

Was it so selfish to not want anyone to look at her like a freak? Though Artemis knew it was bad, each time she tried to get the words out, they superglued themselves to the lining of her throat. Some naïve part of her thought there was a chance she wouldn't need to tell The Sevenfold what was wrong with her—what Mr. Carlisle was so fascinated with.

The real reason she was invited to Carlisle Academy.

Releasing a silent breath, Artemis slowly sat up in the bed. Dr. Telford would be coming in any second now. The window wasn't fully open—it only hung slightly ajar, yet it was enough for her to slide through if she timed her jump right.

Here we go.

Artemis leaped off the bed, making a break for it, but it was like the guard had known what she was planning to do all along. Her nails scraped at the windowpane, cracked paint flying into her eye as the man latched onto the waistband of her combat trousers and threw her back onto the bed.

"Get off me!" A scream ripped from her throat. Though she kicked and punched him as hard as she could, his grip was firm and unwavering, and he held her down as he called for backup. More guards poured into the room in a matter of seconds, each one grabbing a different limb and pinning it to the bed.

Tears streamed down Artemis's face, and she could barely make out Dr. Telford's figure in the blur. She stuck a needle in her arm and clicked her tongue. "Look what you made me do, Artemis. If you'd have just stayed calm, none of this ugliness would've happened."

"Let me go," she mumbled, whatever she'd been injected with already taking effect.

"You know I can't do that." Dr. Telford sighed. "Mr. Carlisle's invested too much in you to just let you go."

Artemis's eyes kept getting heavier and heavier no matter how hard she fought it. "What does that even mean?"

"Now that we've found you, there's no way you can escape us."

Artemis wanted to protest, but her limbs weren't listening to her brain, and her mouth refused to move. In the back of her mind, she imagined Kade and the others kicking down the door, beating up all the guards and carrying her back to their dorm, and a single tear rolled down her cheek.

"Make your peace with that however you want."

That was all she remembered before everything went dark.

31

ABYAN

Kade and Hassan joined her next to the ledge, flanking her as they sat down and let their legs dangle over the street below. Yet Abyan remained silent as the seconds passed between them all. The words had settled on the base of her tongue and refused to budge no matter how hard she tried.

She couldn't say it first.

The only person she'd ever willingly told about her past was Hank, and being forced to lay the most scarred and mangled parts of her bare wasn't something she was used to—it was like being stripped naked in the middle of a room. Abyan had blurted the truth out in the heat of the moment, and all she'd cared about in that split second before she spoke was getting one up on Kade.

Screw it.

"We all have our own baggage, and I've been trying to work through my stuff," she finally said. "I didn't go about it the right way, and I'm sorry for that."

A disbelieving laugh left Hassan's lips. "Didn't go about it the right way? I can admit that we were wrong to force you to tell us about Khalo, that we should've given you time to tell us on your own, and that we were bad friends for doing that," he said. "But you left us for dead on our Peeping Tom and then turned on us at King's Cross—you'll sacrifice your friends for a slice of revenge without thinking twice about it."

"He's right, Yan. I'm sorry for how we went about things, but can you really blame us?" Kade said, shaking her head. "It's like nothing matters to you anymore, not even our family. I feel like I can't trust you to have my back because you've become this . . . different person."

Though Abyan's heart hurt at their words, she couldn't really refute them. "Maybe I have changed this year. I don't care about the squad placing first, and even though that's the last thing you guys want to hear, it's the truth. And for what it's worth, I don't think first place will matter anymore with everything that's going on," she said, looking at them each in turn. "I really am sorry for all of it: the half apology from before, abandoning you both, fighting you for Khalo, and not being brave enough to have this conversation with you guys sooner. I promise that from here on out, my friends come first."

Kade wrapped her in the tightest hug and a slow smile spread over Hassan's face as he said, "This new Yan might not be so bad, after all."

"What did you mean before," Kade asked, pulling away from their embrace, "when you said that first place wouldn't matter with everything that was going on?"

The attacks on Carlisle.

"We need everyone here for that one." Abyan pulled out her phone, instructing the rest of the squad to meet them on the roof. Abyan figured if she was going to unload baggage, she might as well get rid of it all, and that meant telling the others what she and Hank had discovered, and more important, what they planned to do about it.

The boys came quickly enough with the recruit shuffling in behind them.

Once everyone was seated, she spoke. "I've been hiding something from you guys over the past couple of days."

Abyan saw Kade's brow crease from the corner of her vision,

and if she wasn't already sure they'd be annoyed when she came clean, the suspicion in the rest of her squad's eyes only solidified it. She didn't *want* to keep things from them. It was for their own good—if anything went wrong, they would've had plausible deniability on their side.

"*We've* been hiding something," Hank interjected, half raising his hand like the idiot he was.

It was just like him to do that, and Abyan had to make a conscious effort not to punch him. She didn't wear her martyr hat often, and it would've been hard enough to get the squad to believe she'd discovered the impending attacks on the London branch and kidnapped a first gen alone—the last thing she needed was him ruining her plans.

Tolly leaned forward. "What is it, Yan?"

"I kidnapped a first gen and found out why the Nosaru are fighting. Hank and I also discovered that the hosts are planning to hit all three buildings of the London branch soon." Abyan paused at the expletive-laced outcries from her friends and waited until they got the shock out of their systems. "Before you say it was risky, we should've known better, and all that, I need everyone to remember that none of us can change what's already been done."

"Does anyone else know you kidnapped a first gen?" Mason asked, searching her eyes for any sign of regret. "The school's been keeping an eye on all of us—they have to know you're up to something."

"No, they won't suspect a thing. I covered my tracks, and Harry's the one who led the operation, so I'm good on that front," she assured him before going on to tell them all what Matteo had revealed about the originals and the inter-Nosaru war. "Matteo could've been lying, but if he wasn't, it would mean that Soros thinks Mr. Carlisle is hiding something in one of our buildings and is going all out to find whatever it is."

There were five hives in total surrounding the London branch of Carlisle Enterprises. Three around the academy and one beside each of the intelligence and research wings. From what limited information they gathered, it wasn't clear whether the hosts were going to hit the wings separately or all at once in a coordinated attack, but the Nosaru were far from stupid.

The two lone hives could easily have been decoys meant to distract them from the three boxing in the school in an almost perfect triangle—not to mention there could've been other hives in the area Carlisle Enterprises was unaware of.

They discovered new ones all the time, and it was perfectly plausible that the five known hives were the least of their worries and an entirely new beast, one with more teeth and the sharpest of claws, awaited them in the dark.

Kade leaned forward then. "You want to hit their hives, right? Take them all out together to save the London branch."

"It's the smartest play." Abyan nodded. "To use one of our BLCC orders as a cover and neutralize the extra hives on the side, but there's a problem: There are five hives around our buildings, and that's too many to take on alone."

While one Year 14 was worth three Nosaru on average, first-degree hives typically held twenty-odd hosts each, and The Sevenfold was still outnumbered. Two hives they could take easily, three could be handled with some difficulty, but they had to neutralize five.

It was a suicide mission.

"So, you want to bring in another squad as well?" Hassan cocked a dark brow. "And for us all to join you on these missions?"

"Not if you don't want to," Abyan quickly said, and she meant it. "I'm not keeping any more secrets from any of you, so I wanted you all to know what Hank and I were planning."

A hush fell over the roof as they took in her words, and to Abyan's surprise, it was broken by Kade. "I'm in."

Two words. So simple in theory, but Abyan's chest swelled, and she shot her a grateful smile.

Mason spoke up next. "Me, too."

Tolly shrugged. "Same here."

Artemis agreed, and they were all left waiting for Hassan's verdict. He looked to the ground for a few moments, the clench of his jaw making it clear he was torn on the issue.

Hassan shook his head a little before giving a heavy sigh. "If you're all going to get expelled, we might as well get expelled together, right?"

They all laughed, and Abyan couldn't help but feel a tiny glimmer of optimism. She was going to save the London branch, and her team would be by her side when she did it.

———————————

Though the Great Hall could seat five hundred people at capacity, it wasn't half full by the time Abyan entered. She and the squad snagged seats right in the middle, and the students all gave them a wide berth the moment they caught sight of her.

She scanned over the never-ending rows of seats, and from what Abyan gathered, there were only Year 13s and 14s in the room—some of the best squads in the whole school were present, and she didn't have the slightest idea why. Her eyes repeatedly drifted to her phone, but she hadn't received any school alerts aside from the one telling her squad to go to the hall. There were no teachers in the hall either. Not a single member of staff in a room with this many students, and Abyan doubted that it was an accident. She only hoped that what was coming wouldn't be anything that could interfere with her plans.

Not when she was so close.

Her eyes snapped to the recruit's leg. It bobbed up and down so fast in the corner of her vision, it made Abyan twitchy herself. Her hand clamped down on Artemis's thigh when she couldn't stand it anymore.

"Stop it, recruit."

Pink spread across her light-brown skin, and she looked to the ground. "I can't help it. You can't tell me you aren't nervous, too."

"More cautious."

Of course, this was dodgy. Assemblies were always held in the morning, and other than the first and last ones of the year, they were never for a mixture of year groups. The last of the students shuffled in, and a quick glance around the room showed that it was just under half full. Noise bounced off the walls, and Abyan could barely hear herself think. She gazed at the empty podium before them and watched the dust particles swim across the air before it.

Then, it all made sense.

There was only one person who could silence two hundred rowdy students. One person capable of ensnaring the entire room with nothing but their presence. He didn't need teachers to control the crowd because he commanded more authority than all the faculty in the school combined.

The door behind the stage opened, and a figure stepped out into the glare of the lights in full view of them all. The smart black suit and tufts of red-brown hair confirmed Abyan's suspicions.

Sebastian Carlisle.

The silence that engulfed the room was suffocating and heavy enough that she heard someone swallow from the row in front of her. The exalted patriarch of Carlisle Enterprises put both hands on the podium and looked over the sea of students once before speaking.

"Good afternoon." He smiled, flashing two perfect rows of blinding white teeth. "I know many of you are wondering what terrible thing you must've done to be invited here and come face-to-face with me, but don't worry. None of you are in trouble."

It was like the room itself breathed a sigh of relief, the floor lifting as the taut brick-and-mortar walls gave way, and more than a few students leaned back into their chairs while Abyan only raised a brow.

This wasn't the angle she'd prepared herself for.

"In fact, this is a congratulatory assembly," he said, his blue eyes blazing with an otherworldly energy. "This has been an eventful year, and many things are changing. For example, the backlog of WLDOs has finally been cleared so they are no longer being issued at the academy, and as of this morning, all BLCC orders are being suspended until further notice. Yet rest assured, it's not anyone's fault. In fact, I wanted to personally thank you—the best students, handpicked by your teachers—for persevering through these trying times and staying your course."

It was an act.

Abyan shook her head a fraction, her bullshit meter blaring warning bells in her ears and damn near malfunctioning under the weight of Mr. Carlisle's drivel. The BLCC orders. Why on earth would he get rid of them?

He had to be planning something.

Shit.

Abyan was going to beg De Costa for a BLCC order on the day of their hive attacks as a cover, and she couldn't do that if they were being "temporarily suspended." She hadn't even had the opportunity to tell her about the Nosaru war because De Costa had been off sick for the past couple of days. Abyan didn't trust any of the other staff at Carlisle as far as she could throw them and had agreed with Hank to wait until De Costa got back.

Yet now Mr. Carlisle was out here drumming up support, puffing up every one of the already inflated egos in the room, and if her history books were anything to go by, this kinda thing only happened when leaders expected things to go sideways.

Abyan tightened her jaw. She was going to destroy the hives that threatened the London branch and find out whatever it was Mr. Carlisle was hiding with his fine-tuned words and intricately carved smile no matter the cost.

"And last but certainly not least, I would like to thank Maria De Costa for her services to the academy." Abyan sat up abruptly at that. Why the hell was he thanking her of all people? "After fifteen long years teaching here, she has decided to retire, but I know I'm not alone in believing she'll be dearly missed."

Abyan squeezed her eyes shut, blocking out his lies. De Costa wouldn't just up and leave. *Something happened to her.* Abyan's mind drifted back to her surprise meeting with Mr. Carlisle and Artemis, at how he made a point to ask if De Costa and Harry were the only other people who knew about what they saw. Was Harry gone, too? That would've explained why she'd heard nothing but radio silence from him ever since they'd captured Matteo. Abyan's heart stopped as she realized that whatever happened to them was done on direct orders from Mr. Carlisle.

He was behind it all.

32

ARTEMIS

THE ENTIRE SQUAD ASSEMBLED IN THE LIVING ROOM. HANK had to be dragged out of bed, and Artemis couldn't help but laugh as Tolly pulled him into the room by his ankle with only his boxers on. He grumbled under his breath, folding his arms under his head, and tried to sleep on the carpet right in the middle of the room. Abyan covered her eyes with her shawl, while the squad erupted in wolf whistles.

"Damn, Hank," Mason called in an exaggerated voice from the sofa. "Have you been doing squats?"

"Hank's thick as hell," Kade added, looking him up and down. Hassan and Tolly took out their wallets and started throwing money at him, and Artemis's heart almost skipped a beat at the sheer number of fifties they were dropping.

Sometimes she forgot they were rich.

Hank sat up, red in the face from laughter. "Screw all of you."

"Hurry up and cover yourself before our guests come." Abyan unwrapped the shawl from around her shoulders and held it out to him. "We don't have time for this."

She didn't laugh once at their jokes. Her eyes were focused on something beyond any of them, and Artemis wasn't sure if she wanted to know what was on her mind. Abyan wore a patterned long dress Artemis figured was a cultural thing, and with her hair covered in an African head wrap, it wasn't hard to describe her as beautiful.

Artemis's brows furrowed. "Guests?"

"I told you we can't handle five hives on our own," she replied, taking a seat next to Hassan. "So, I asked another squad to come over today and discuss a proposition. They don't know about anything yet, but it's the only squad I trust to help us out and keep their mouths shut if everything goes wrong."

Hank groaned. "The Renegades."

"For what it's worth, they were our only option." Abyan's voice softened, and she put a hand on his arm. "Promise you'll try your best not to throw something at Steph."

He gave a heavy sigh before looking at her. "The things I do for you."

Abyan nodded at him before turning to the rest of them. "Same goes for you guys, too. We need their squad on our side if we want to get any of this done."

Just as the words left her mouth, the doorbell sounded.

Kade led their guests into the living room, and with The Sevenfold all gathered on one side and all five members of The Renegades on the other, the tension was so thick Artemis feared breathing too loudly would shatter it.

Artemis's palms gathered a sheen of sweat as she took the girls in, and at the center, sitting with her boots propped up on the coffee table was none other than Stephanie Marshall herself. She'd seen Stephanie trying to catch Abyan's gaze a few times over the past few weeks, guilt written in her eyes, but Artemis didn't think Abyan had forgiven her just yet even though there was no way anyone could've known their BLCC order would turn out to be a Peeping Tom.

Stephanie cocked a brow. "What do you want, Yan?"

"You screwed us over by giving us that Peeping Tom." Her words were curt. "We have a proposition for you, and since you owe us, I think you should take us up on it."

There was a moment of silence; both squads sized each other

up, and Artemis didn't really know if they were meant to be allies or enemies anymore.

Stephanie crossed her arms. "Will this get us into trouble?"

"Only if we get caught."

"Expulsion?"

"Possibly."

"Is it life or death?"

"Without a doubt." Abyan stilled and looked at her with eyes so intense even Artemis's pulse jumped under their weight. "I wouldn't be asking if it wasn't serious."

Stephanie nodded and held her gaze for a second, a silent conversation happening in the sliver of time before she turned to her crew. The Renegades huddled, and although Artemis tried to lean closer, she could only make out a few words from their furious hushed whispers. From what she managed to hear, the conversation wasn't going in their favor, and Stephanie's next words only confirmed it.

"The team isn't unanimous," she said, turning to The Sevenfold. To her credit, her clenched jaw made it clear she wasn't on board with the decision. "Sorry, Yan."

Though Abyan opened her mouth, it was Artemis who jumped in, forcing the words out before her better judgment kicked in. "You're making a big mistake. The Nosaru are going to attack the school, and Abyan chose your squad because she trusted you to help us stop them. Please, help us save Carlisle."

Stephanie blinked at Abyan, who only shrugged. "What she said."

She didn't even look at her squad this time round. "Tell me everything I need to know."

This is it.

Abyan's phone stared back at her on the kitchen counter, and Artemis watched her turn around and stir the pot she had boiling on the stove. This was the perfect opportunity. The countertops were covered in potatoes, onions, tomatoes, and all of Abyan's dozen other ingredients—it would've been at least an hour before she realized her phone was gone.

Artemis's limbs shuddered with anticipation.

She breezed into the room, silent as the wind, and snatched it the second she was close enough. Artemis had to find out for sure; at least that way when she told The Sevenfold she could say it with her chest.

Though the general anesthesia from her biopsy had worn off ages ago, she didn't have any memory of that afternoon besides the bandages and the phantom grip on her limbs any time she closed her eyes. Artemis's hands shook, her mind drifting back to the hospital room. *I have to know.* She gulped, blinking hard, and unlocked the phone—she'd seen Abyan do the code so many times she'd lost count.

All of them had the Carlisle Enterprises student app, but there were different features unlocked in each year at the academy. Abyan's version had the locations of a selection of first-degree hives as well as suspected Nosaru attacks, and it was just what she needed to find herself a fourth gen. She glanced over her shoulder; even knowing that no one was home wasn't enough to settle her frazzled nerves.

Westbourne Park.

There was a hive in one of the estates: Brunel House. Artemis set the phone back down on the counter how she found it and waited until after dinner to leave. Once everyone seemed busy enough not to notice her absence, she took her chance. She grabbed her discarded jean jacket before heading out the door. The single dagger in her bag made her heart race. Releasing a breath, Artemis stilled her shaking hands. The last thing she needed was for some old lady on the train to think she was "suspicious."

Brunel Estate was between Royal Oak and Westbourne Park train stations. Artemis pulled her hoodie over her head as low as it would go, tucked her phone into her pocket, and held out the radar attached to her wrist the closer she got to the estate.

There was no way she was attacking a hive by herself.

But she might find a stray walking around and . . . Jesus, she still didn't know what she was going to do. Her fingers wouldn't stop shaking, and it wasn't from the cold. She kept clenching and unclenching her hands, trying to snap them out of it as her heart hammered against her rib cage.

Somewhere between Stonehouse and Portishead House, Artemis decided this wasn't her. She wasn't cut out for the whole midnight-murder thing. She couldn't do it. Bile rose in her throat at the thought. Yet her skin blazed, an intense itch making its way up her arms, and no matter how hard Artemis scratched at it, it never seemed to go away.

She turned on her heel and went back past a line of wheelie trash bins to the front of the estate, trying not to gag at the stench, but she stopped in her tracks at the dark figure blocking her path. The man's head and shoulders twitched violently, something between a gargle and growl leaving his curled lips. Artemis didn't have to check her radar to know what was standing in front of her.

A fourth gen.

Her dagger was in her backpack, and she couldn't reach for it without setting the host off. Sudden movements were a death wish when it came to uncontrolled fourth gens. Usually they were too busy warring with their human, trying to stop them regaining sentience, but a quick jerk of the hand fired up the host's base instincts: fight or flight.

Artemis's feet melted into the ground. Her body felt like it had been set alight, all prickly and inflamed. The host staggered forward, and she couldn't get the dagger even if she wanted to. She blinked at the Nosaru, willing her limbs to run, to jump—to do anything besides what they were doing in that moment.

The host lunged at her, and she squeezed her eyes shut, her whole body bristling. But the thirty-six-tooth bite never reached her neck. A deafening screech cut through the air, making all the hairs on her arms stand on edge, and Artemis cracked open an eye. The man had crumpled to the ground and writhed, agony etched into every fine line of his face.

Artemis took a tentative step forward, her mouth hanging open in horror. Her skin tickled, pulsing to the tune of his screams, and she raced to calm it. *He's not a threat anymore, he's not going to hurt me.* Taking deep breaths, she drowned out the noise and repeated it to herself until the itching stopped.

A twig snapped somewhere to Artemis's left, and her head immediately snapped in the direction of the noise. She couldn't see anything. It was too dark to make out if anyone was there, all the shadows seemed to blend, morphing into a hundred different shapes so quickly Artemis didn't know if it was her eyes playing tricks on her.

Maybe she'd imagined the whole thing.

The Nosaru groaned, the sound shattering the silence of the night, and curled up on the pavement in a fetal position. Though everything in her told her not to, Artemis took another step toward the host. He had midnight hair, Mediterranean skin, and looked like he was in his midtwenties.

When he wasn't twitching and snarling, you wouldn't be able to tell the difference between the host and a regular human. It was jarring, and Artemis couldn't help reaching out a shaky hand. Yet the host shot up from the ground before she could blink, teeth bared, and lunged at her.

Artemis screamed and fell back onto her hands. Before the host could take another step, a dagger struck him square in the side of the head, and his body crashed onto the ground beside her. Artemis's head slowly turned to the side like an old creaky hinge, and she came face-to-face with Kade and Abyan.

"Don't take this the wrong way, recruit," Abyan said, a blend of fascination and horror twirling in her honey eyes. "But I knew it."

33

ABYAN

HANK WAS THE ONLY ONE AWAKE WHEN THEY GOT BACK. HE paused the action movie blaring in the living room as Abyan entered, taking a huge bite out of his Snickers bar. Her gaze drifted over to the other three boys splayed out on the furniture, sound asleep.

Half of Hassan's body was hanging off the edge of the sofa, and there were so many chunks of God-knows-what stuck in his hair Abyan lost count, while Mason's neck was bent at such an uncomfortable angle that she hurried to place a small pillow beneath his head just so he didn't sprain anything by morning.

"I thought we told you not to stay up for us," Kade said, motioning for Artemis to help her peel Tolly off their ridiculously expensive Persian rug, now covered in the crumbs of his discarded crisps and drenched in his drool.

"Did you?" Hank cocked a brow, the amusement in his eyes betraying his feigned ignorance. "I don't remember you saying anything."

Abyan had been agonizing about how in the hell she was going to tell the boys about the recruit's revelation all through the taxi ride home and still couldn't figure out how to break it to them. "Hey guys, Artemis has powers and can somehow control the Nosaru" just didn't seem like the best way to go about it.

She was almost grateful most of them were asleep by the time they got back to their dorm. Abyan still hadn't mustered up the courage to tell them what she thought Mr. Carlisle did to De Costa either because there was no telling how they would react.

But Hank needed to know.

"Roof," she said, and the two of them immediately made their way there, leaving Kade and Artemis to deal with the boys.

The scent of Hank's shitty perfume calmed her in no small capacity as they sat in their usual place, on the ledge with their feet hanging over the side. Abyan clasped her hands against the cold and took a deep breath before speaking. "Mr. Carlisle killed De Costa."

His head snapped to her. "What are you talking about? She retired."

"No, she didn't," Abyan said. "In my meeting with him and Artemis, he asked specifically if De Costa and Harry were the only other people who knew about all the weird shit we've seen, and now he's trying to tell us she 'retired' at a moment's notice? I don't believe that for a second."

They'd all seen Harry in the recruitment building on the day after Mr. Carlisle's big speech, but no one had heard anything from De Costa. "Why wouldn't he kill Harry as well if he was trying to tie up all his loose ends?"

"He's connected to Mr. Carlisle through his dad, Richard. After our BLCC order in King's Cross, Harry mentioned something to me about being saved by Richard Carlisle when he was younger."

Abyan's mind buzzed. She couldn't find anything on Harry no matter how hard she tried, every file she tried to peek into was either heavily redacted or classified, and the last thing she needed was to rouse anyone's suspicion.

"What if Harry was assigned to us by Mr. Carlisle himself?" Hank asked. "Holy shit, Yan. We have to tell someone."

She sighed. "They'll just disappear, too."

The Sevenfold were completely alone. Her heart twisted whenever she remembered how they would never hear De Costa's voice, see those graying curls or her coffee-stained smile. De Costa was tough as nails, and she didn't deserve what happened to her.

She was innocent.

"Goddamn it!" He threw a discarded piece of scrap metal as far as he could, and Abyan couldn't blame him. They were drowning with their arms tied up in a straitjacket, and there was no help on the way.

Mr. Carlisle was untouchable.

"We can't trust Harry anymore," Abyan said. "I've tried to see if I can find out more about him, but there's nothing there."

Hank shook his head. "No, there has to be something. I'll check in with my contacts in the intelligence wing and see if they know anything."

"That's not the only thing I have to tell you." She gulped as he ran a hand over his face, bracing himself for the next bombshell. "I finally found out why Artemis is here."

"Why?"

"She has a power over the Nosaru, Hercules." Abyan placed her hand over his mouth the second his lips parted to speak, ignoring the way his eyes almost fell out of their sockets. She needed to get it all out in one go. "The recruit can control them somehow. She doesn't know how she does it because it only ever happens when she's really scared, but it explains what you saw her do to the host back when she was in The Choker and why Mr. Carlisle has that creepy obsession with her."

She slowly removed her hand, and Hank barely got his first syllable out before she slapped it back into place. "We only just found out an hour ago. I wasn't keeping it a secret."

He cocked his head to the side and looked at her pointedly before she realized her hand was still very much attached to his face. Abyan whispered a quick apology before finally retracting her arm, and he released a heavy sigh.

"What do you think caused her powers, then? The only explanation is human trials."

Abyan shook her head. "That's never been proven though."

Officially, the research wing of Carlisle Enterprises was there to study the creatures, manufacture weapons to help operatives defeat them, and most importantly, to try and find a cure for the infected hosts. They'd been people once, after all, and killing them was supposed to be a last resort to stop Nosaru numbers getting too high.

There was no way of successfully separating a Nosaru of any generation from a human once they were bonded. No matter what methods researchers used, the outcome was the same: The host died. Much like how squid secreted ink when in fear, when Nosaru detected something trying to pull them from their human, they released a toxin into the host's bloodstream which caused rapid organ failure that no doctor could stop in time.

Yet people always speculated that, unofficially, the company tried to synthesize Nosaru genetic material into something compatible with the human genome. Human trials. But they never had a shred of evidence to back up their claims, so Abyan never entertained the thought of human trials actually taking place.

"Do you honestly not think she could've been a part of some kind of experiment, though? I know you don't *want* to believe it, but how else could she have gotten her powers?" Hank said. "That could be why Harry's our shadow: to keep an eye on her for Mr. Carlisle."

It made sense in a way that Carlisle Enterprises had been conducting human trials, since there were a ton of biological advantages Nosaru had—Abyan couldn't imagine what it would be like if a human had their mind-control ability.

It would've been groundbreaking.

She blinked, her mouth moving too fast for her brain to catch up. "I wouldn't put it past them."

Shit.

"If that happened, how likely do you think it is that she was part of them? It had to have been when Artemis was a kid or something, since she clearly has no memory of it."

"Too likely," Abyan said. "If there were real experiments on humans and Artemis was part of them, why the hell would they let her go? You don't just let a successful human test subject walk out the door for seventeen years for shits and giggles."

"That's true." Hank ran a hand through his brown waves. "But what other reason is there? That she was born like that?"

Just as Abyan was about to reply, Hank's phone vibrated, and he quickly fished it out of the front pocket of his purple basketball shorts. His features darkened as he took in whatever it was on his screen, and Abyan's pulse skipped several beats.

"What is it?"

Hank moved from the ledge. "My mom is here."

"What the hell is your mum doing here at two in the morning?" Abyan asked as she hurried to catch up to him.

"I don't know. She just sent me a message saying her men are outside our dorm and not to panic." While his strides were always much longer than hers and she had to take two rapid steps just to match one of his on a good day, his deliberate speed walking had her almost jogging to keep pace. When they eventually reached the elevator, Abyan could feel the blood rushing in her ears. She stepped toward the wall Hank leaned against as he glared daggers into the carpeted floor.

"Don't lose your cool," she warned, placing a hand on his shoulder. "She probably just wants to talk to you—you haven't seen her in over a year."

He scoffed. "She's ten years too late, Yan."

"Aren't you tired of hating her?" She crossed her arms. "If you don't care about her, just give yourself a break and let this go. Move on with your life."

"Believe me, I've tried." He sighed. "My stepdad never says it, but I can tell he wants me to forgive her, too. All those sly lectures about how important it is to forgive people aren't for no reason."

"That sounds a lot like him."

"I've told him to stop trying. I don't think I'll ever not hate her."

Abyan's eyes softened. "You don't mean that."

"I do, Yan. I really do," he said, straightening. "John was ten when he had to start taking care of me, and she shut down on us. I made do without a mom then, and I'll make do without one now."

The elevator dinged, and Abyan cocked a brow. "I thought you said it was your mum?"

"Wherever her henchmen are, she's usually not too far behind," he muttered as they came upon five black-clad, burly men all huddled in front of the door to their flat. Abyan scanned the foyer once more for the unmistakable silver hijab of Rosemary Mulligan and came up empty again.

"What do you want?" Hank asked the men, standing firmly beside her. Abyan's fingers instinctively moved to her sides before remembering the men were human, and she didn't need daggers to take them down.

One of them, pale and blond, stepped forward. "The League would like to speak with Abyan Farax Guled."

She tried not to cringe at the way he butchered all three of her names as she took in the guards. Something told her this wasn't a polite request she could simply reject. The League wasn't really *asking* her for anything.

Hank remained silent and waited for her reply, and she didn't need to ask whether he was coming along. Each member of The League was formidable enough on their own, but if all twelve were going to be in the same room, she was relieved to have at least one ally by her side.

She walked back to the elevator and pressed the button. "Let's go."

34

ABYAN

CANARY WHARF WAS DIFFERENT AT 3:00 A.M. THE high-rise towers and sprawling streets were usually full to the brim with people in dark suits and pencil skirts, bankers and the like.

Where the 1 percent got richer and everyone else got screwed.

The intelligence wing of Carlisle Enterprises sat in the middle, a sleek building guarded at all hours by seasoned operatives. When she and Hank were first loaded into a black Bentley, Abyan thought they'd be going to the research building, since Marble Arch was closer.

It didn't take long for her to realize how wrong she was.

Going to the intelligence wing was a privilege awarded to very few students at the academy, and Abyan could count the number of times she'd set foot in it on one hand and not even use up all her fingers. Although she fought to keep her cool on the outside—the last thing Abyan needed was for Hank to see her panic—she'd already read Ayatul Kursi approximately twenty-three times.

In all her years at Carlisle, she'd never seen the twelve members of The League in the same room. If they'd found out who hacked them weeks ago and wanted to do whatever it was they did to people who broke their cardinal rules, she and Hank were walking straight into an ambush.

There was no way of escaping.

Unlike the research wing, Abyan didn't know the layout of the building well enough to think of a possible escape route. She had no idea how many variables there were that could factor into her impossible plan, and that was assuming the two of them could get past the dozens of senior operatives patrolling the halls and exits.

Abyan crossed her arms so her left hand was hidden beneath her right arm, keeping her gaze trained on the windshield. She extended her forefinger so it grazed Hank's side before beginning her series of taps. Morse code wasn't a requirement at Carlisle. The Sevenfold only decided to learn it in their early days as a team-building exercise, since they were miserable at pretty much everything when they were first thrown together.

The only squad to be formed by an algorithm rather than choice.

The school's personal pet project.

Abyan still remembered how in the beginning The Sevenfold couldn't do anything without it turning into a dick-measuring contest between the boys or a fight breaking out. She remembered how Jared always used to moan at her for breaking his left thumb because it looked so ugly after it healed and no doctor could figure out why.

"No escape. Don't save me." Abyan tried to condense her sentence to save time, but the way Hank's head snapped in her direction, the half-light of the streetlamps illuminating the blaze of defiance in his eyes, made it crystal clear he understood exactly what she meant and intended on ignoring every word.

She shot him a pointed look, silently asking if he'd left his better judgment back outside their dorm, and the moment he sent one back confirmed he most certainly had.

When the car pulled up in front of the building, one of their guards instructed Abyan to follow them inside. She exited first and Hank followed, keeping pace with her as they meandered through the hallways. Five doors they walked through needed passcode authorization, none of which Abyan caught a glimpse of, while the other three needed a key card.

With every beep and scan, her heart rate increased.

Her prospects looked bleaker and bleaker the closer they got to wherever The League was waiting. By the time they arrived at their destination, the steel door leading to The League looked more like the front gates of a slaughterhouse, and any small shred of hope she had of escape was a distant memory.

One of the henchmen who'd brought them over from the academy stood beside her and Hank while the rest guarded the exits of the corridor. The moment he entered to announce their arrival, Abyan released a slow breath.

Something bad was going to happen.

She knew it in her bones.

"You got this," Hank whispered, bumping her side with his arm.

She didn't have the heart to look at him straight. "What if I don't?"

It was easy for him to be so calm. There was no way Rosemary would let anything happen to her son despite their rocky relationship; Abyan, on the other hand, was fair game. She didn't have a safety net of money and an important family name or someone to yell "STOP!" when the gavel came down and sealed her fate.

"I know you do."

She shook her head, the navy carpet beneath her feet becoming more interesting the more her hands shook. "You don't understand—"

"Look at me, Yan," he said, angling his head downward as she met his gaze. "If you want to go in there and find out what the hell this is all about, I'll be right there next to you. If you've changed your mind and want to run, we'll go out in our impossible blaze of glory together, okay?"

Abyan didn't need hope when The League knew what they did. What she did.

Hacking Carlisle didn't just mean expulsion from the school, the loss of all her progress, and the derailment of her plans—there were worse things The League could do to her. Much worse things. Abyan didn't doubt the plethora of resources they had could've easily ruined her, but Hank was giving her that annoyingly cute grin of his, and she couldn't help but want a tiny slice of the faith he had in them for herself.

God.

This boy was going to be the death of her.

She didn't fight it when the corner of her mouth tipped up. "You're so annoying."

"Don't thank me, it's what I do." Hank smiled, tipping an imaginary hat to her.

Before Abyan could reply, the guard from earlier returned and ushered them into the room. She took one look at the reassurance in Hank's eyes and the determination in the set of his jaw, and that was all she needed.

Abyan stepped into the room.

The twelve members of The League sat in plush leather chairs around a huge wooden table. Mr. Carlisle was at the head, his sinister smile wiped clean from his face, and an inferno burning in the pits of his eyes. *Murderer.* The rest sat on either side, a single red file before each of them. Abyan caught sight of Hanshiro Nakamura, Kade's dad, clad in a turtleneck and dark suit, and the glint of Rosemary Mulligan's silver hijab at Mr. Carlisle's right might as well have been a glaring police siren.

"Miss Guled," said Amina Saeed, the patron League member of the Ankara branch. "Do you know why you're meeting with us today?"

She knew exactly why she was there. "No, miss."

Amina pursed her lips as she opened the red file before her and took out a piece of paper. "Do you remember the mission your squad took on the evening of the third of October?"

It took everything in Abyan not to let her jaw drop or shoulders sag with relief. Alhamdulilah. Hank stiffened at her side, and she fought the urge to turn her head as she spoke. "It was a BLCC order in King's Cross Saint Pancras station."

"We have a few questions we would like you to answer honestly."

Why did they want to know about what happened at King's Cross? Abyan had already sorted it out with Mr. Carlisle. She couldn't believe it. They damn near gave her a stroke just to ask about a failed mission they already knew of.

This was a waste of her time.

Abyan made the mistake of looking at Mr. Carlisle then. He sat with his jaw clenched and his back unbearably straight, yet it was the red-hot singe of his glare that was the final piece of the puzzle. The reason The League called on her, why they were asking about that specific mission, and why he looked two seconds away from exploding.

Abyan almost wanted to smile as the rest of The League opened their files. "What do you want to know?"

It was Rosemary who spoke next, her voice calm as the Thames and deadlier than the tip of Abyan's favorite dagger. "The after-mission debrief drafted by Maria De Costa stated there were indeed three Nosaru at the station, and that you managed to successfully apprehend them."

She paused and scanned Abyan's face; her eyes drifted to Hank for a heartbeat, something darting across them too fast for her to catch. "However, according to our sources, that was not the case. How many Nosaru were there that night, Abyan?"

"Yan," Hank warned under his breath.

He knew what she was going to do. Mr. Carlisle had lied to The League and made De Costa doctor her original debrief, but they'd found out. He was going to be in hot water now. If Abyan wasn't in Mr. Carlisle's crosshairs before, her betrayal would certainly put her there, and sooner or later he was going to take his shot.

Sorry, Hank.

"Sixteen, approximately." Abyan kept her gaze steady and trained on Rosemary as silence enveloped the room. Hank's hand drifted to his side, and he tightened his jaw upon finding it absent of weapons. They were searched twice in the lobby, and the closest thing Abyan had to a weapon left was her hijab pin.

Hanshiro locked eyes with another League member, disbelief written clear in their mahogany depths. It seemed some of them hadn't believed Amina's suspicions, and her confirmation of them wasn't something they were prepared for.

"Please recount the events of that mission as accurately as you can."

Abyan exhaled before speaking, glancing over at Mr. Carlisle again. There was a tinge of red to his face, his fist was clenched, and she wondered how much longer he could hold back the tempest before it tore through the room and left him in pieces, too.

"My squad and I heard a commotion coming from two of the platforms." A thin layer of sweat gathered on the surface of her palms, and her pulse was thundering in her ears. "The Nosaru were killing each other with a faction-like divide between them. There were two first gens in the station also: Khalo—one of the targets of the BLCC order—and another female we couldn't identify. The first gens both escaped. We captured three of the others and killed the rest."

"Impossible." It was Fatou Diop who spoke, a League member Abyan was seeing for the first time in person. Her sharp brows were furrowed as she leaned forward, the light dancing across her dark brown skin.

"We have no reason to lie," Hank said. Murmurs took hold of the room, everyone having something to say yet none finding the courage to do so with their chests.

Abyan didn't dare look away from Fatou. "I was also called to a meeting several days after the mission with Mr. Carlisle and was told to forget about what we saw."

That was for De Costa.

Mr. Carlisle didn't deserve her loyalty.

Rosemary cleared her throat and held up a hand. "Thank you, Abyan. You've given us much to discuss. You may return to the academy. We'll bring you in again if we have any further questions."

She nodded, turning on her heel. A weight lifted from her shoulders as she exited the room. Though Abyan had made an enemy of Mr. Carlisle, she couldn't care less. She did the right thing. Whatever was going on was serious and most likely a threat to them all, and he didn't get to play with all their fates however he liked.

The guard from earlier showed them out, and the moment the door closed behind them, Hank turned to her. "Do you know what you just did, Yan?" he asked, each of his words heavy with disbelief. "Mr. Carlisle's going to come after you now."

A fire ignited somewhere deep inside her. "I'll be ready when he does."

35

ARTEMIS

THE WHOLE SQUAD WAS WAITING FOR ARTEMIS IN KADE'S room. Abyan texted her just as she left her 6:00 a.m. training about the group meeting, saying that she and Hank had something important to tell the squad. And although Artemis knew it wasn't about her, that the entire squad knew about her powers now, she couldn't shake the uneasy feeling in her bones.

She still couldn't forget how each of the boys reacted: Tolly looking at her like she'd grown two extra heads like some hydra, Mason's skin going paler than she'd ever thought possible, and the way Hassan full-belly laughed until his eyes watered.

Everything will be fine.

They wouldn't start hating her again.

They couldn't, could they? Artemis thought. They were all friends now. She refused to go back to square one with them all now for yet another thing that was out of her control.

Kade's room looked like the inside of a pink bath bomb, with bodies strewn over every piece of furniture in sight. Hank and Abyan stood in front of everyone as Artemis shuffled in and sat between Tolly and Mason on the plush carpet.

She wiped the sheen of sweat from her brow and tried not to pant too loudly—she'd run all the way from the other end of campus to get to the meeting, and her lungs still hadn't adjusted yet.

Hank asked, "Do you want the good news or bad news first?"

"Good news," came Kade's voice from the bed behind her.

Artemis glanced at Abyan's solemn face and knew that whatever the bad news was, it was way worse than anything they could imagine. She was a light sleeper, and since her room was adjacent to Hank's, Artemis was used to getting woken up by the sound of his laughter or teasing during one of his phone calls with Abyan.

However, last night they woke her up at 4:50 in the morning with thunderous steps, all hushed whispers and drawn-out silence. Although they were talking too quietly for Artemis to hear in her groggy haze, if it was bad enough to make Hank and Abyan fight over it, part of her didn't even want to find out what it was.

"The League hasn't discovered who hacked them," Abyan said.

There was a brief silence before Tolly leaned forward. "How do you know that for sure?"

"That's the bad news."

"We met The League last night," Hank added. "My mom's guards came here at 2:00 a.m. and told Yan to come with them, so they took us both to the intelligence building. All twelve of them were there."

He was cut off as noise erupted in the room. Curses and other sounds of disbelief bounced from wall to wall, and even Artemis struggled to wrap her mind around it. It made perfect sense, and yet not one tiny part of her wanted to believe it.

Abyan held up her hands to quiet everyone. "Listen, they were asking about what happened at King's Cross. Mr. Carlisle lied to them about it and tried to pass it off as a normal mission, but somehow they found out, so I told them what really happened."

"That wasn't smart, Yan." Mason ran a frustrated hand through his hair. "He's going to be so pissed."

"It was the right thing to do."

"I agree." Artemis cleared her throat as all eyes turned to her. "Now that the board of the organization knows what really happened, they'll be keeping a closer eye on Mr. Carlisle, and maybe they'll figure out what he's been up to before we do and save us the trouble."

"I don't regret it either, so there's no point moaning at me about it." Abyan sighed. "Trust me, Hank's already done it for you like a hundred times."

Hank shook his head. "It was the wrong call. You put yourself in danger just to get back at Mr. Carlisle."

Abyan's eyes narrowed. "I didn't ask for your opinion, did I?"

Artemis had never seen them so heated before. If she didn't know any better, she could've sworn Abyan's voice was venomous. Hank's jaw was clenched so tightly, she thought his teeth might just snap in half, and red was creeping fast up his neck. She glanced at Mason, worry shining clear in his eyes as they all watched the horror show unfold.

"Well, someone's got to at least try and talk some sense into you since you've obviously lost your damn mind." Hank's voice was rising with every word, and fury blazed in Abyan's eyes. "You're going to get yourself hurt."

Artemis didn't know what to do. Should she get up and step between them?

Hank and Abyan wouldn't physically fight—would they?

"I don't need you worrying about me, Hercules."

Hank looked at her like she'd just run him through with her thorniest dagger and salted the wound for fun. Even his jaw dropped before he managed to recover. "You're my best friend, and I care about you, Yan. This is for your own good, whether you can see it or not."

"Is that why you keep acting like my mother?"

"He'll kill you!" Hank yelled. "Sorry if I'm the only one who cares about that."

Kade jumped up from the bed in a whirlwind of pink silk and stood between them. "Guys, stop it. We've all seen and heard enough, all right? Stop talking before you say anything else you'll regret later."

Abyan released a slow breath before reaching for a small pile of papers behind her. She gave out two pages to everyone, and Artemis didn't miss how she avoided Hank's gaze when she handed him his.

"What's this?" she asked, skimming the pages.

Abyan walked to the door and paused just before it. "The final plans for our hive attack tomorrow. Your individual instructions are written on the pages I gave you. Learn them, memorize them, and then shred them. There's no room for mistakes."

———————

Artemis was already doing her stretches by the time Abyan joined her at the edge of Holland Park at 6:00 a.m. sharp. She waved as she lowered herself into a split, and Abyan offered her a small smile in return, quickly throwing her training bag to the side and rewrapping her headscarf so it was a little tighter.

Abyan mirrored her stretches. "You never ask about my hijab or say anything about my hair. Most people are a little bit curious."

"There were a lot of Somalians where I grew up." She shrugged. "I know you don't need to wear your scarf in front of girls."

"It's Somalis, not Somalians," Abyan corrected, and Artemis wanted the ground to swallow her up whole, her golden-brown cheeks flaming.

"My bad."

She figured Abyan came from somewhere in London, judging by her accent, but her usual indicator of the general parts of the city—north, south, east, or west—didn't work in her case, since Artemis hadn't heard her speak anything other than proper English. For all she knew, Abyan was just another rich kid from South Kensington who owned a Ferrari and two boats.

Abyan got to the question before her. "Where are you from?"

"My family moved to Birmingham a few months ago, but I grew up in Ladbroke Grove near Latimer."

"I didn't know you were from ends." A smile spread across her lips as she held her fist out to her. "My family live down the road in Shepherd's Bush."

Artemis returned the spud. "I just thought you were rich like everyone else."

"Wallahi I thought the same about you." She laughed, falling out of her split and into the grass. "Thank God, someone I can talk normally to."

Artemis grinned, shaking her head. "Mad."

It was strange finally speaking her dialect. Her vernacular switch was always flicked off the moment she entered the school's lifeless stone walls. It was automatic—she never noticed the change and only ever missed her words after they were long gone and the barest shadow of them remained on the tip of her tongue.

"How come you never talk like this in front of the others? You don't slip up once."

Artemis distinctly remembered the first and only time she let a few words escape her filter in front of Mason, and he still jokingly called her a ting sometimes. It was hard to explain how it felt . . . it was more than just cringy or disrespectful.

It made her blood boil.

"Don't get me wrong, I love them all," Abyan started. "They just don't understand where I come from. They'll come to me for advice on what car to buy for their birthdays when they already have like three each, and I can't even afford driving lessons." She sighed. "I let a few words slip once when I was angry, and they didn't let me live it down for weeks. I know they have good hearts and shit, but being the punch line of all their jokes for a good month ain't something I'm trying to relive."

"Sounds tough." Artemis picked at her combat trousers. If she struggled with it after just over a month with The Sevenfold, she could only imagine how Abyan felt.

"We just aren't cut from the same cloth at the end of the day." Abyan rose to her feet. "I hope you've been practicing your defenses because there's no way you're coming along for our hive attacks if you're not ready yet." It took her a second before she hastily added, "And I mean that in the nicest way possible."

She followed suit. "Oh, I'm more than ready."

Abyan shrugged. "We'll see."

They faced each other and stood in fighting stance, knees bent with one foot forward and their fists raised, with the morning wind on their skin. The park was blissfully empty, so it was easier to think of it as just another kind of training room. Everything else faded into the background quick enough. Abyan released a breath before stepping forward, closing the gap between them, and launching a straight punch to her face.

It was simple and easy to deflect.

When Artemis's palm came up inside the crook of Abyan's arm, redirecting her blow so it missed its mark completely, the corner of her mouth perked up. Artemis came at her with an uppercut, and she easily blocked the punch with her forearm, twisting her torso and never stepping out of stance once.

They kept going like that for so long back and forth, hit and block, that Artemis didn't even bother to check how much time had passed. Her skin was slick with sweat, her throat dry and burning. Yet Abyan was relentless and Artemis had something to prove, a deadly combination that left no room for the luxury of giving up.

She feigned right, ignoring how her skin suddenly prickled all over, and grabbed Abyan's forearm so she didn't have time to retract it. Artemis inhaled sharply and brought her foot behind Abyan's front leg, sending her plummeting to the ground on her back.

Artemis didn't try to stop the exhausted laughter bubbling up inside her.

I told you I was ready.

"Bloody hell, recruit." Abyan's groan turned into a chuckle as she rubbed the back of her head. Yet just as Artemis was about to reply, Abyan's features darkened as panic flashed in her eyes. "Dive left, now!"

Artemis did as she was told, heart in her throat, and landed on the ground roughly. The tiny stones in the grass scraped at her skin, drawing blood. *What the hell?* A blur of a man descended on Abyan in a flurry of fists, and she scrambled to catch up and deflect his never-ending blows—Artemis didn't know what to do.

Why would someone randomly attack Abyan?

She narrowed her eyes on him, taking in every detail as she finally scratched her burning arm. Young, dark hair, cuts and bruises over every inch of his exposed skin. *The first gen she kidnapped.* It had to be him. The haze of vengeance in his eyes was too red and raw not to be personal.

"Your word is as worthless as you are, human," he bit out between punches. "Is that the thanks I get for trying to help you?"

"Help me? You were stalking me for God knows what reason, and I did what needed to be done." Abyan managed to block the last punch, but the force of it threw her off balance, causing her to stumble back a few steps. "How did you even get out, Matteo?"

She'd told the squad that Harry had helped her keep the first gen locked up in a secure location. Did that mean that he was aware that Matteo had escaped? Maybe he didn't know at all, Artemis thought. The first gen wore a shirt that looked like it could've been gray once and jeans that would've looked good if they weren't soiled with blood, sweat, and muck.

"You need to come with me, human," he said.

Abyan laughed in his face. "In your dreams, maggot."

"Foolish girl, you are in danger, and I am the only one who can protect you from it."

Artemis had to stop this. Abyan was already worn out, and she was losing more ground to the host with every passing second. Yet Artemis knew she'd be no good getting between them; they moved too fast, cutting across the grass like tornadoes.

She didn't have a chance.

My power.

Artemis had never used it on purpose before and wasn't entirely sure if it could work on command, but that wouldn't stop her from trying. She closed her eyes, holding out a hand in the host's direction, as if it would make it easier, and tried to imagine the burning sensation across her skin as a raging bonfire.

She clenched her hand into a fist, picturing the flames being snuffed out like a candle, starved of oxygen and weak. And the second the inferno started dwindling in her mind, Artemis opened her eyes to see Matteo drop down to one knee.

Was that me or Abyan?

She wasn't sure, and no matter how hard she tried to channel her powers again, Artemis couldn't picture anything in her brain. *Crap.* Matteo turned to where she was crouched then and looked at her like he was seeing the sky for the first time before squinting and sniffing the air a few times.

He opened his mouth to say something, but whatever it was died on his tongue because Abyan knocked him upside the head with a rock the size of Artemis's fist and he slumped to the ground.

After checking for a pulse, Abyan wiped at her face with shaking hands and took out her phone. "I'm texting Harry our location so he can pick up Matteo," she informed her. "Maybe he'll actually keep him locked up tight for once."

"What about what the first gen said?" Artemis pressed, thinking back on his cryptic words. "Shouldn't we talk about it? Or tell Harry about it? He probably knows more than we do about all this."

"No. Matteo was talking rubbish," she replied, slipping her phone back into her pocket. "We won't be telling Harry shit either—he's another walking unanswered question, and we don't need him sniffing around us anymore. The only reason I texted him now is because this is his mess, not mine, and he's the one who has to clean it up."

Artemis stayed quiet, not wanting to agitate her further with her dissenting opinion. She didn't think Harry was the bad guy here. Surely there was just as much on the line for him because he helped them with an off-books mission? He'd suspected The Sevenfold were up to something with the hack from the start and probably had enough grounds to have their dorm searched from top to bottom, and yet he didn't do anything.

He was on their side in his own kind of twisted way, and while Abyan refused to see it out of stubbornness or her own dislike of him, Artemis tucked what she'd learned away in the back of her mind. Some niggling feeling in her chest told her that having Harry on their side might come in handy sooner rather than later.

36

ABYAN

THOUGH IT WAS NOVEMBER, AND THE SIGHT OF THE SUN was almost foreign, a few defiant rays broke through the thick cloud-wall that shrouded them and bounced off Hank's brown locks in a way that struck Abyan speechless. He was jogging on the spot to combat the cold, and a tuft of gray smoke left his lips with every breath.

Abyan wanted to tell him what had happened with Matteo so badly it hurt. She needed to know she was doing the right thing, and Hank would always give it to her straight. The others had to know, too, but it was weird not being able to tell her best friend first.

She and the recruit decided to wait until after the hive attacks that evening to give everyone the rundown of what Matteo said— they didn't want anyone getting cold feet because they mistakenly thought Harry might come and investigate whatever nonsense Matteo was spewing.

Stop worrying.

Abyan cursed internally and focused on the recruits again.

Hank trained them alone because Ms. Bruno was sick, so they were doing the bleep test in the Astroturf behind the residential building. Abyan raised her binoculars and looked on from her position in the foyer. It wasn't hard to feel sorry for them, running from one side of the grass to the other while the bleeps coming from the stereo beside Hank only increased in speed.

Abyan couldn't help the grin that took hold of her lips as she watched Artemis. Though more than half the class had been eliminated, the recruit was still running—and ahead of the others, too.

Something swelled in Abyan's chest she didn't dare think was pride.

Still, she couldn't shake her unease despite the progress she'd seen the other day in training and now. Artemis told her she'd tried to use her power on Matteo, but if it had any effect on him, Abyan didn't notice at the time.

The thought of bringing the recruit on their mission to attack the five hives that evening—the sheer number of things that could've gone wrong with only the original members of The Sevenfold alone—sent her nerves into a frenzy.

But it wasn't her choice anymore.

Abyan waited in the foyer, perched on a stool, until Hank blew the silver whistle around his neck and yelled that training was over. As the recruits dispersed, each of them red-faced and looking two seconds away from collapse, she made her way to Artemis.

Despite Abyan wearing four different layers under the hoodie she'd stolen from Hank weeks ago, she was shivering within seconds of stepping outside. She clenched her fists and crossed her arms, silently praying she didn't die of hypothermia. Artemis sat in the middle of the Astroturf beside Hank, alternating between taking swigs of her water bottle and laughing at his jokes.

Abyan wanted to shake her head at the pinch in her chest.

She was being ridiculous.

Hank noticed her first and immediately looked away. Abyan didn't know what was so fascinating about the dying blades of grass, but evidently, they were easier to look at than her face. She'd worn his hoodie on purpose, for God's sake. That morning, his eyes drifted to it a total of seventeen times, but he didn't say a word to her.

Abyan hadn't gotten so much as a smile from him all morning, and it was doing her head in. He whispered something to Artemis just before she reached them and took off not a second later, not looking back once as he walked away.

"We need to talk," Abyan said, sitting cross-legged in front of her and shoving all thoughts of Hank into a tiny box in the back of her mind.

Artemis cocked a brow. "Did I mess up again?"

"No, you're good." She tried to sound reassuring, but her teeth were chattering so much, she could barely get the words out. "It's about whether you come on the mission with us or stay behind."

"I think we should do a vote," Artemis said. "That way everyone gets a say. If the majority of us don't want me to go, I don't mind staying."

"We already had one while you were in first period physics." Abyan sighed. "It was a tie. Me, Tolly, and Hank voted for you to stay here. The rest wanted you with us—they think your powers might come in handy."

Artemis's eyes bulged, a small laugh escaping her lips. "Even Hassan?"

That dickhead.

"Even Hassan."

He was one of Abyan's safer bets when she'd called the impromptu group meeting that morning. She figured he and Tolly would've most likely sided with her, Hank was a pleasant surprise, and even Mason hesitated before declaring his side. Abyan knew Kade was going to be split fifty-fifty and had hoped flipping Mason or Hank would get her to see reason, but the moment Hassan said he wanted the recruit on the mission, Abyan knew Kade was going to go with him.

"So, am I going to be the deciding vote?" When Abyan gave her a solemn nod, Artemis released a slow breath. "I'm not staying behind. I want to be with the squad."

She ran her hands over her face, their icy touch stinging her cheeks. "No matter how much you've progressed so far, you're still a recruit, Artemis. We don't know what the hell's waiting for us in Holland Park. There could be a hive full of first gens, and do you know what's gonna happen? You'll get yourself or me or someone else killed—that's what."

"I'll stay in the back, behind you and the others. Just tell me what to do, and I'll do it."

Abyan shook her head. "I shouldn't have to tell you what to do all the time."

They were doing an unauthorized operation, jeopardizing The Renegades as well as themselves, without the cover of BLCC orders to hide their tracks, and they didn't need any added risk. The whole operation hinged on none of them leaving anything identifiable that could tie them to the hives. Carlisle Enterprises wouldn't send operatives to check out a few hives going dark unless they had reason to suspect something was up.

So, The Sevenfold would give them nothing worth turning their heads for.

The recruit leaned forward and grabbed Abyan's hand, the sudden rush of warmth bringing the faintest shadow of feeling back into her numb fingers. "Please, Abyan. Give me one chance."

Though she wanted nothing more than to refuse and override the team's vote, the desperation in the recruit's eyes knocked the swift rebuttal Abyan had ready clean off her tongue, and she couldn't bring herself to do it.

Abyan released a defeated breath. "Fine, you—"

The words were cut off as the recruit leaped into her arms and squeezed her hard enough that Abyan's breath momentarily escaped her. "You won't regret it, Abyan."

"Calm down." She laughed, hugging her back. "We'll see what happens. You only have permission to get excited when we win, recruit."

While her words were light-hearted, Abyan was dead serious. Until the mission was done and dusted, none of them could rest easy. It was risky, in unfamiliar territory, and she didn't have a clue as to what she'd dragged her friends into.

———+———

The Sevenfold gathered in the parking garage. They huddled next to their cars, swords sheathed and tranq guns holstered. Her squad looked ready for war, and the determination in their faces made Abyan's heart swell. Steph and her squad had already left for the Greenwich hives closest to the intelligence wing, and all that was left for The Sevenfold to do was say their goodbyes.

Abyan pulled Mason and Tolly in for a tight hug. "If you idiots die, I'll kill you."

Tolly laughed. "That's not how it works, Yan."

"Shut up."

The rest of the squad exchanged final words and embraces before loading into their separate cars. Abyan and Hank artfully dodged each other, nothing but weighted gazes passing between them. "I'm sorry," she wanted to say, and the way Hank lingered before going into the other car told her he wanted to make amends, too.

Or, at least, she hoped he did.

It would have to wait until the mission was over now anyway. He, Mason, and Tolly were going to the Marble Arch hive while Abyan and the rest of The Sevenfold were taking the Holland Park one. Abyan's pick was far from the safest bet. All the hives were in residential buildings with a high potential for civilian casualties and multiple exits for the Nosaru to escape from.

While it wasn't ideal, it was the best chance they were going to get.

"This is it," Hassan stated, pulling up in front of Janes House in Norland Square. Though it was pitch black outside, you could practically smell the money radiating from the houses in this part of the city.

The Nosaru must've killed someone extra fancy for a hive to be in a place like this.

"Looks like it, traitor."

He rolled his eyes and exited the car. "Let it go, Yan. Sometimes votes don't go your way. That's the thing about democracy."

Abyan crouched by some bushes, switching on their jammer and hiding it under the shrubs. "I'm sorry, were you saying something? All I hear is hissing."

"Guys, focus." Kade stepped between them and held up her tracker. "Look at this."

They all peered at the screen. The mass of green blobs was enough to silence them all. It was impossible to count how many there were when they were all huddled so close together.

Abyan turned to her squad and whispered, "The radar says they're concentrated in that house, so we'll go in through the front door. Kade and I go first, then Hassan, and Artemis last. Kill them all, understood?"

When all three of them nodded, Abyan put a hand on Artemis's shoulder. "Remember what I told you about the tranq?"

The recruit nodded. "Point, aim, and shoot."

"At?"

"Anything that's not one of us."

"And never?"

"Play hero or shoot if I'm not sure I'll hit my target."

"Remember to always?"

"Call for help if I need it and hold my gun with both hands."

Abyan warned, "Whatever happens, Artemis, don't freeze."

It would put them all at risk.

Abyan held her eye for a moment longer before making for the door. She took a pin from her pocket and picked the lock in eight seconds flat. In areas like this, just being Black was enough to rouse suspicion, but because of their jammer, regular police wouldn't be interrupting them any time soon. Nevertheless, Abyan hurried into the building before any nosy neighbors got too curious for their own good.

The lights on the ground floor were all off, and it was freezing inside. Audhubillah, the smell. Rotting flesh and a mountain of steaming dog xaar couldn't come close to whatever stink was emanating from upstairs. Abyan stifled a gag as she crept up the wide stairs, Gacan Libaax in hand, with Kade and Hassan at her back. She held her breath as she pressed her body against the wall and poked her head into the dimly lit hallway.

No sign of any Nosaru.

She took a slow, tentative step forward, careful not to make a sound. One look at her radar showed they were all in the three rooms at the end of the corridor. Abyan only had to decide which one they were going to hit first. She held up a closed fist and kept the others behind her in place for a few seconds as she weighed up their odds, making up her mind the second her probabilities aligned. She signaled to her squad, her hand high in the air with two fingers pointing left.

The floor plans Tolly managed to get from the building architect's computer showed that the room on the left had a balcony, so they wouldn't be boxed in by Nosaru on all sides. Abyan stood in front of the door, pressing her ear to it and hearing nothing but eerie quiet. She stepped back, foot poised high in the air, and counted in her head.

One.

Two.

Three.

37

ARTEMIS

THEY WERE SURROUNDED.

Though the room was dark, and she couldn't make out much in the thick shadows, Artemis could feel their presence. It was suffocating. An itch she couldn't scratch no matter how hard she strained. A thousand fire ants dancing across her flesh.

There were so many Nosaru around them, waiting in silence like dormant volcanoes. She wanted to slap Abyan's hand away from the light switch she was about to turn on and scream they should get out while they could, but the words refused to come.

Clutching her tranq to her chest with shaking hands, Artemis held her breath as the lights flickered on. Her whole body froze. Over twenty Nosaru surrounded them, with eyes black as night and their teeth already elongated. Even Abyan and Hassan momentarily stood stock-still. The Nosaru had knocked down the walls between the three rooms, so it was now one huge one. The trails of coagulated blood on the chestnut floor led to three bodies hanging from the ceiling.

Human bodies.

Meat hooks hung where the chandeliers once were and sliced right through their flesh. Artemis didn't even have time to gag before the chaos began. Abyan hurled her first dagger at the female Nosaru closest to her, hitting her square between the brows.

Snarls and labored breaths filled the air as Kade and Hassan threw themselves into the fray. The rest of the creatures wasted no time closing in on them, blocking the door they'd come in through and forcing them step-by-step into the center of the room.

Artemis couldn't move.

Her feet were pinned to the ground, and her arms were bound in a straitjacket only she could see. She couldn't peel her eyes away from her friends. The Sevenfold were a blur. It didn't take them long to realize Artemis had shut down, so they formed a protective triangle around her, doing whatever it took to keep the Nosaru back.

Artemis knew she should be helping them. Tears filled her eyes when her limbs refused to move. They were pinned in the middle because of her, and every time her squad killed one, three more hosts seemed to take their place.

She was going to be the reason they all died.

"Artemis, snap out of it!" Kade yelled, the desperation in her voice making it shrill.

Artemis's head snapped in her direction.

She was behind her, surrounded by four Nosaru, her limbs moving so fast Artemis struggled to keep up. Shots rang out from her left; the sharp series of bangs made her heart skip several beats. Abyan was out of daggers and was rotating between her sword and her tranqs. Hassan was down to his last one, stabbing it into the skull of a Nosaru running for her, and the squelch as he pulled it back out made Artemis's skin crawl.

There was one behind Kade. Artemis could see him ready to pounce on her. *No.* Her arms moved on their own, raising the gun. She didn't even realize she'd pulled the trigger, only blinking as the Nosaru slumped to the ground. Kade shot her a grateful look and nodded at her once, and that was all Artemis needed.

She turned on her heel and shot at another one. The gun shook in her hands, its kick reverberating up her arms, but she held it steady each time she fired. *Point, aim, shoot.* There were only ten Nosaru left—they could do it. Every member of The Sevenfold was down to their tranqs and swords, but they didn't seem fazed.

Abyan was a whirlwind, firing her dual-wield guns. She tore through the remaining Nosaru like a tempest, twisting on her back foot, and never staying in one place for more than a second.

A hand shot out of the corner of her vision before Artemis could react and gripped her throat, hoisting her high in the air.

The female Nosaru ripped the gun from her hands and tossed it like discarded rubbish, her fingers getting tighter around her neck with every passing moment. Artemis couldn't breathe. She scratched and clawed at the hand to no avail. For a brief moment, the creature's black eyes swirled blue and her grip loosened, but the black color and crushing strength came back so quickly Artemis thought it might just have been some asphyxiation-induced hallucination.

Let me go. Let me go. Let me go.

Artemis squeezed her eyes shut. The words raced through her mind repeatedly. She couldn't do anything. Her lungs burned, and her entire head pulsed to the beat of her straining heart. Suddenly the hand around her throat loosened, and she crashed to the ground.

Gasping for breath, Artemis reached for her gun and shot the frozen Nosaru without a moment's hesitation. The host's brows were furrowed, its mouth hanging open, before it slumped to the ground.

Artemis placed a hand on her neck, the feeling of the Nosaru's fingers still fresh. Her head snapped to the other members of her squad who were finishing up the last two creatures and seemingly hadn't noticed what just happened. Artemis's voice failed her as she tried to call Kade's name, nothing but a frail croak leaving her lips.

Kade plunged a dagger into the last Nosaru's head and released a low whistle. "Now, that was something."

"It wasn't as bad as I thought it was going to be." Hassan shrugged, making his way to where Artemis was sitting and extending a hand. "You all right, recruit?"

She nodded, not trusting her voice. If they didn't see what happened, it meant she didn't need to explain anything. Maybe it was a blessing in disguise. They all knew about her powers, or at least, what she thought her powers were, but that didn't mean she was comfortable talking about it with all of them yet.

She'd just used them on the female Nosaru.

Artemis didn't want to believe it.

Even though it was by accident, she'd done it all the same. Hassan and Kade were talking, but all she saw was the Nosaru's face. It was stunned. Artemis was, too. How did she do it without even trying? She just wanted to breathe. It was different from what happened on Ben Nevis. Artemis caused them pain, made screams rip from their throats until they left her alone. *Not me,* she remembered thinking. Over and over. *Not me.* The same thing happened when she went looking for that fourth gen in Brunel Estate.

Maybe that's why her power didn't work on Matteo.

She hadn't been terrified for her life, then.

"Something's wrong." Abyan had been silent, in deep thought, ever since the fight finished. "This was too easy."

"What?" Kade cocked her head to the side. "Sure, we've had tougher missions, but that doesn't mean this was easy either."

"No, you're not seeing it." She pointed at the bodies. "They were fourth gens. All of them. Why would you have a hive full of fourth gens ready to attack Carlisle with no superior Nosaru to keep them in line?"

She was right.

They were the weakest Nosaru, effectively nothing but mindless robots, and without a leader, they were useless. Though the Holland Park hive was closest to the academy, it didn't take a strain of her imagination for Artemis to know the school could've held off an attack from not one but several fourth gen hives just like this one.

"Maybe the first gens are at one of the other hives," Hassan said, but Artemis could hear the doubt in his voice.

They were all thinking the same thing and desperately hoping it wasn't true.

Abyan took out her phone, hitting a few buttons, and then raised it to her ear. "Are you okay? And everyone else?" She paused for a moment. "Good, we'll tell you what happened back at home, I promise, but did you guys have any first gens in your hive?"

Abyan fell silent again and then said her goodbyes, turning to them. "Hank said they only had fourth gens in their hive, too."

If all the hives had fourth gens, it meant they'd gone wrong somewhere in their thinking. But that wasn't possible. Artemis knew in her heart they were right—they had to be.

Too many lives depended on it.

"I'll call Steph." Kade tapped furiously at her screen, and Artemis held her breath as she asked how Steph and her squad were. "Did you have any first gens in your hives?"

The curse that left her lips not a moment later told them enough. They only had fourth gens, too. Abyan balled up her fists, fury taking hold of her features. "We did this for no reason. These Nosaru weren't a part of their plan."

"It's not that bad," Hassan said. "We just have to recalculate."

"With what resources, Hassan? Everything we had led us here. We haven't got anything else to go from."

Silence befell them. Abyan was right again. They didn't have any other information, no clues—nothing. Logic and common sense led them here, and they'd failed. The Nosaru were still coming for Carlisle Enterprises. The only difference was that now Carlisle's only line of defense was back to square one, and next time, the enemy would know they were coming

38

ABYAN

ABYAN PACED BACK AND FORTH. THEY'D DECIDED TO MAKE a pit stop to get changed and debrief before heading back and ended up in Shepherd's Bush Green.

Kade, Hassan, and Artemis were splayed out on the World War I memorial in the center of the deserted park.

Abyan, on the other hand, couldn't stand still.

The dozens of shuttered shops and barren streets around her all faded into the very back of her mind. Their mission was a flop, the Nosaru were still one step ahead, and she couldn't pinpoint where the hell she went wrong.

The hives they'd hit were the closest ones to the three Carlisle Enterprises buildings. All of them were fresh, created in the last year, and the intelligence wing had recorded high levels of recent activity in each of them. It didn't make sense that they'd all be full of fourth gens.

Maybe she was wrong and there wasn't going to be an attack. Maybe someone was changing the floor plans and just hadn't had a chance to update the system with the new ones yet.

It was entirely plausible.

Although every fiber in her being recoiled at it, she could've done all this, jeopardized her friends and herself, for no bloody reason. But Abyan couldn't bring herself to believe it. God, she clenched her teeth at the thought. She replayed her steps in her head: the WLDOs, the hack, the plans, the hives—all of it.

The boys were meant to be meeting them in the park. They couldn't go back to the academy still looking like they'd just come from a fight because their teachers would see it in their eyes in a heartbeat.

They needed time to get their act together.

Back in the hive, her fingers dialed Hank's number without thinking, and the moment she heard his voice, way deeper than what should be legal, a wave of relief washed over her.

He was okay.

Her boys were fine.

The three of them were blissfully unaware of how royally they'd messed up. Tolly had even texted her to say they were stopping at McDonald's to pick up victory food. Though her stomach rolled at the thought of breaking the news and seeing their faces drop, Abyan knew she'd have to tell them sooner rather than later.

The recruit had been eerily quiet since the fight. She figured it was a natural reaction to her first proper mission, but the instant Artemis froze up, Abyan regretted letting her come with them.

She knew it would happen.

She'd called it from the start.

There was a reason recruits always started with the easiest BLCC orders and gradually worked their way up to the more intense missions, and Artemis's case was a perfect example why.

Abyan ran her gloved hands over her face, the tuft of smoke from her heavy sigh twirling in the air for a second before dissipating. She was going to have to give the recruit a talk after they got home to help her fully understand what happened.

"I hope you're not trying to sneak up on me, Hank." Abyan kept her back to him, and his hushed curse made her want to laugh. "That would be very rude."

He stood beside her, looking out at the traffic lights, a full bag of McDonald's in his hand. "You're a jinn, Yan. That's the only logical explanation for how you always see me coming."

"Actually, it's because you breathe like Darth Vader, and I could literally smell your perfume from Manchester."

Hank raised a hand to his chest. "First of all, I have better breath control than you, and second, it's called *cologne.*"

"Same shit, Hercules." While he was lying about the breath control, he was also finally talking to her, and Abyan wouldn't jeopardize that for anything.

"Well, your right side is weaker than your left, and I'm so eating your Filet-O-Fish."

"You can't see anything without your contacts. It must be tough not being part of the twenty-twenty vision club." She brushed nonexistent dust from her shoulder. "And don't you even think of eating my food."

Hank paused and met her playful gaze, both of them erupting into laughter not a moment later. "This wasn't how I imagined our first conversation going."

When she sobered, Abyan spoke again. "Me neither."

"Let's not fight again." He gave her a reassuring smile, and a weight lifted from her shoulders. "I like it better when I can tell you to your face to stop stealing my hoodies."

"Shut up; sharing is caring," Abyan said, lowering herself to the grass. "Now give me my food, so I can tell you the bad news."

Hank set the bag down between them and sat before her. "How screwed are we on a scale of one to ten?"

"Fifteen." Abyan didn't hesitate as she spoke and took both of their Filet-O-Fish meals out in turn. She plopped a still-warm fry into her mouth before launching into her suspicions of the fourth gens, how they'd somehow missed the mark with the hives, and how they were back to the drawing board all over again.

Kade was busy telling Mason and Tolly what happened, and the string of expletives coming from somewhere behind her made it crystal clear how they felt about the situation.

Hank, on the other hand, simply shrugged.

"At least we have all those other files we hacked," he said, scarfing down his last few fries. "There's still a few thousand we haven't looked at, and they might have something we can use."

"That's exactly what I was thinking."

Abyan cleared her throat. "There's another thing I have to tell you," she said, taking a moment before telling him everything that had happened with Matteo yesterday and what the first gen had told her. "I don't believe a word that comes out of his mouth. If he's so hellbent on 'protecting' me, then why not tell me what I need protection from?"

"Agreed," Hank concurred, though a deadly haze settled over his eyes the second she'd mentioned Matteo. "Did you wait for Harry to pick up the host?"

She nodded. "The only thing he said to me was that he was 'handling' it, and then he threw Matteo into a car and drove off."

"I think it's for the best. It's his problem to fix, after all, not ours."

Abyan threw her hands up. "That's exactly what I said!" He was eyeing the fries in her hand with so much intensity, she eventually rolled her eyes and held them out to him. "Hurry up and take it before you give me the evil eye by accident."

"It was going to be on purpose, but we can go with accidental if it makes you feel any better."

She punched him in the arm. "Prick."

"What the hell?" Hank cradled his injury. "I think I'm dying."

Hassan called their names—apparently their car was waiting. Abyan stood and dusted off her jeans, extending a hand to Hank. "Stop being such a drama queen, Hercules," she teased. "This isn't a Greek tragedy."

"I don't know what's worse, Yan, that joke or the fact that you actually thought it was funny," he said, taking her hand and pulling himself up.

"Oh please, that was a great joke."

She and Hank strolled through the park for a little while before going to join the others. They walked in silence, savoring each other's company like it was the last piece of their favorite chocolate bar. Hank's features caught the light of the streetlamps in a hundred different ways, every single one stealing the breath from her lungs. He kept trying to sneak a glimpse of her out of the corner of his eye, and Abyan's stomach fluttered each time their eyes met.

"Holy shit." He stopped abruptly, his mouth falling open. "I couldn't tell you this before, but my friends over in the intelligence wing finally got back to me about Harry."

Abyan asked, "And what did they find?"

"His real name is Nicholas Armitage, and he graduated the academy the same year as The Cardinal Six, so I think it's safe to say he and Mr. Carlisle knew each other in school."

That explained why Harry wasn't killed along with De Costa. He and Mr. Carlisle were working together on whatever their plan was, and no one was the wiser. And because of Abyan, Mr. Carlisle now knew about Ora and Soros's war and the threat of a second Nosaru invasion.

"Is that it?"

There had to be more.

Hank released a breath. "That's all they could get without drawing attention to themselves."

"Okay, when we're in the car we'll tell everyone else about Harry, Matteo—all of it."

Hank agreed and they joined the others in the black BMW with tinted windows waiting for them. The ride back to Carlisle Academy was short. They'd dumped their soiled clothes in the nearest public bin and kept it moving so there was no way any of the teachers would find out what they'd done.

They had a weeklong window before anyone noticed the hives were taken out—dead hosts still gave out radio waves for seven to ten days after death, so everything would appear normal to Carlisle's satellites in that time.

Abyan's mind buzzed with ideas on how to move forward. They'd go through all the files they hacked, and knowing the intelligence wing, there had to be some information about recent Nosaru activity patterns. They could do their own digging on Harry and see what they could unearth now that they knew his real name, and Abyan knew they could get to the bottom of whatever it was he was hiding. She was just grateful her squad weren't fixating on their loss and were on board with her and Hank's new plan as soon as she told them.

Abyan didn't know what she'd do without them.

As they meandered through the halls of Carlisle Academy, she was stopped by a custodian. "Miss Guled, Mr. Oluwole has been waiting for you. There's a personal matter he would like to discuss."

Her brow creased. It was one in the morning. What problem was so big it couldn't wait until a proper time? Nevertheless, she shrugged and told her friends to go on without her. Although they hesitated, Abyan assured them she was fine because her bones ached and she just wanted to get it over with.

Abyan knocked on the door to Mr. Oluwole's office twice before entering to find him standing with his arms crossed, nothing but ice-cold rage in his eyes. "Remain standing, Abyan. You won't be here long, so listen carefully because I will not repeat myself."

"Sir?" she asked, still not getting what this was about.

He inhaled sharply. "The Sevenfold took an unauthorized mission today. We were warned by Mr. Carlisle that you might be up to something, so we had you followed. Enough evidence has been gathered to expel your entire squad."

Her eyes bulged. Abyan couldn't get expelled. Carlisle was all she had. Khalo and the others were still roaming free, leaving nothing but chaos and death in their wake.

She couldn't leave.

She had a fucking score to settle.

"No, sir. You—"

"Do not interrupt me when I'm speaking!" he boomed, the veins in his neck protruding. She was going to get expelled for a failed mission, and her whole team was going with her. "While I would have you out of here, The League has stepped in on your behalf this one time."

Abyan's whole body sagged, and she fought the urge to grip the bookcase next to her.

His jaw tightened. "Nevertheless, Mr. Carlisle has insisted you be punished. No one doubts you're the ringleader in this, and for that reason, I'm removing you from The Sevenfold, and you are hereby suspended from any and all missions until you graduate."

She clutched the bookcase, bile rising in her throat. "You can't do this."

"Actually, I can," he said. "To prevent you from colluding with your former team, your electronics will be confiscated, and you will be given a Carlisle-monitored phone and laptop. You will continue your training with a personal trainer according to the schedule you will find in your new dormitory."

"New dorm?" Her voice was a ghost of itself.

Abyan's pulse was in her ears, the room rotating before her eyes.

"Retrieve all essential items now and then go to this room." He held out a piece of neatly folded paper. "The rest of your things will be collected for you tomorrow."

Her stiff fingers wrapped around the paper. "You don't know what you've just done."

Mr. Oluwole's brows furrowed for the briefest moment. He didn't know Carlisle was going to be attacked. The Sevenfold were the only ones who had any idea, and the company's only chance at getting out in front of it. Some part of her wanted to tell him there and then, but she figured expulsion would be the least of her worries at that point, and no member of The League would protect her from Mr. Carlisle's wrath.

"Any breach of your new rules will result in immediate expulsion. You may leave now."

Abyan didn't say a word and staggered out of the room. She sprinted to the nearest toilet and threw up all the food she'd just eaten, rinsing her mouth out with tap water when she was done. She breathed slowly in and out enough times to calm herself down, though her hands still trembled.

How was she going to tell her friends?

Tears filled her eyes at the thought. *Don't cry.* They'd notice in a heartbeat. She wiped away the few traitorous tears and forced the rest back. This wasn't the end. She wouldn't let it be. Abyan released a slow breath and returned to the dorm she'd called home for the best part of two years to find her whole squad waiting for her in the living room.

Allah ba'ay.

"What did he say?" Mason asked.

She wished they'd all be asleep, so she could break the news to them later on.

Hank jumped up and was in front of her in an instant, his eyes scouring her features. "You've been crying, Yan. What happened?"

She stepped back.

This was suffocating.

"I've been kicked out of The Sevenfold."

39

ARTEMIS

"What?" Artemis blinked.

Though it took a moment for them all to process what Abyan said, everyone rose to their feet the instant it sunk in. Half of her wanted to believe it was a lie, that she was joking and just waiting to tell them all the punch line, but Abyan's hands were balled, and Artemis didn't doubt it was to hide their trembling.

"Why the hell would they do that?" Hank demanded.

Abyan said, "They had us followed. They know everything."

"Those snakes," Kade spat.

Artemis didn't want to imagine what she and the others were going to do.

Tolly's brow creased at the revelation. "Why would they only punish you and not the rest of us, too? It's not like you went on the mission all by yourself."

Probably because they were all either children of The League or from filthy-rich families who'd been attending Carlisle Academy for generations, bar Artemis and Abyan. And she figured Mr. Carlisle would stop anything happening to his prized lab rat. The only one of them with no form of protection was Abyan, but without her, the rest of them would fall apart. It was the cruelest, yet most certain way to cripple the squad, and the school knew it.

"You know why." There was no bite to Abyan's words. Cold

and wrong as it was, it was the truth all the same. "They would've expelled me completely, but The League stopped them. Apparently, it was Mr. Carlisle who wanted me to be punished specifically."

Artemis wanted to put her head in her hands. She remembered the day Abyan and Hank went to their meeting with The League. He'd warned them all that Mr. Carlisle was going to find a way to get back at her for ruining his plans. Then again, Abyan just said The League stepped in on her behalf and stopped the school from getting rid of her, which meant she had to have made allies as well as enemies during that meeting.

They could help The Sevenfold fix this all.

Abyan had told them it seemed like there was a divide between most of The League members and Mr. Carlisle, and this was further proof of it. Artemis's breath caught. They could try to tell The League about the impending attack. The board members would be lenient when they managed to stop it before it was too late.

"That bastard," Mason said through gritted teeth. "If he's the reason you've been kicked out, there's nothing we can do."

Kade was taking measured breaths, but from her quivering fingers to her clenched jaw, Artemis could tell she was seething. "I'm going to kill Mr. Oluwole and Mr. Carlisle in no particular order."

Hassan squared his shoulders. "I'll help."

"Do you guys need an alibi?" Tolly asked.

The corner of Abyan's mouth perked up, but the humor died before it reached her eyes. They were so guarded when she'd first walked in—before she'd told them what happened—yet Abyan's eyes were hollow now, as if being around the squad for the last time had broken down every single one of her fortifications and emptied her of all she had left.

They couldn't just sit back and let her be treated like that. Not without a fight. Artemis's chest ached just looking at her, and she was speaking before her mind even registered what was happening.

"I think we should tell The League about the attack and what we did."

"Then only you, Mason, Hank and Kade would still be here while the rest of us got kicked out along with Abyan." Tolly raised an unimpressed brow, and the rest of the squad echoed his sentiment.

"No, there's obviously a rift in The League," Artemis pressed, keeping her eyes on Abyan. "Otherwise this would've been worse. Maybe we can use it to our advantage and tell the few members who are willing to listen exactly what's going on: the ship parts, the originals, and the attack on the London branch—everything. They'd be grateful we informed them about it and could put you back in the squad."

Abyan shook her head. "It won't work, recruit."

"This doesn't have to be the end—"

Tolly interrupted, "When the other members that we didn't tell find out, they'll think we were just making up lies to stir up trouble between them. Then, we'll all end up in a deeper mess than we were in at the beginning."

"Just let it go, Artemis," Hassan said, shoving his hands into his pockets. "Our hands are tied."

How were they just going to give up like this? Couldn't they see how wrong it was? Artemis looked at them each in turn: Mason, Tolly, Hassan, and Kade. Their faces were sullen, heads low and resigned to defeat. She looked to Hank last. He'd been quiet for so long, eyes glued to the carpeted floor beneath their feet, that Artemis half wanted to call his name just to make sure his head was in the same room as his body.

"Screw this." Hank turned on his heel and left the room, slamming the door on his way out. Abyan didn't hesitate before running after him, leaving the rest of them still huddled in the middle of the living room.

Kade let out a sharp breath and grabbed Hank's two signed

baseball bats from the wall to her side.

Artemis's eyes bulged. "What are you going to do with those?"

"I'm going to freaking destroy Mr. Oluwole and Mr. Williams's fancy-pants offices." She set one of the bats on her shoulder and held the other out to Hassan. "Do—"

He grabbed it straight out of her hands before she could finish her sentence. "I'm in."

"Have you lost your minds?" Tolly demanded, stepping forward.

"What, Tolly?" Kade asked. "They can't touch me, and when we get caught, I'll say I forced Hassan. If they have a problem with any of that, they can take it up with my dad."

"Mason, talk some sense into them."

"No, the school did this to themselves," he replied, and Tolly only face-palmed in reply. "Which one are we going to first?"

"We'll figure it out on the way," Kade said, striding to the door with the boys in tow.

Artemis and Tolly shared a panicked look.

Their friends weren't thinking straight anymore.

She was first to recover. "Go after them. There's not much I can do to change their minds."

"I'll try my best." Tolly ran out the door, leaving her alone in their dorm.

Artemis's eyes burned. Her squad was spiraling, and they wouldn't let her help them. The plan she'd come up with could work if they'd give it a try. If they'd believe in her just a little. That was all she was asking for. She didn't know exactly when the tears began to flow, only that she couldn't seem to stop them once they started.

She wiped at her face furiously with her sleeve and went back to her room. Artemis needed to find a way to help the team. If she wanted to go to The League with their suspicions, they needed further evidence to consolidate it: changes in Nosaru behavior, more cover-ups by Mr. Carlisle—just *something*.

Pulling her laptop onto her bed, Artemis dabbed the last of her tears away. *No more crying.* She had to fix this before it got out of hand. Tolly had sent all the files they'd hacked to a secure and encrypted email that only The Sevenfold knew the password to. Instead of regular naming, the folders had numbers corresponding to what contents they held.

She clicked each folder pertaining to the Nosaru, going through everything they held one by one. The intelligence wing had information on Nosaru outward migration from the Austrian Empire, where they first crash-landed, dating all the way back to the 1700s. They had graphs on estimated population growth and hive numbers for every major city in the UK.

Hours later, Artemis decided to finish the files in the folder she was currently on and then call it a night—or morning, as the sun was peeking out of the horizon. She hadn't found anything concrete yet and still had a couple thousand more to go, but what she found was another folder within the one she was currently on, hidden right at the bottom, with a number she'd never seen before.

Despite everything in her telling her not to click it, Artemis's fingers hit Open before her brain could stop them. There were twenty-three thousand files, and every single name began with: #HTS. The reference number she'd originally seen on Dr. Telford's folder. Her breath caught in her throat as she scanned the list for one in particular, everything in her twisting and turning in equal parts anticipation and dread.

There it was.

#HTS1806B was the 1806th one on the list, separated from the number #HTS1806A by a forward slash. Artemis had no idea what it meant but clicked it anyway. A gasp escaped her lips as she took in the photo before her, all the text beside it blurring for a moment. Red hair the color of the sky at sunset and eyes greener than green could be.

It was Hannah Garrett.

Artemis's birth mum.

She let the tears flow when they came and tried to read the document through the blurry haze. It was a case file. Next to her mother's name in the corner it read: Human Test Subject 1806. A sickly feeling overcame Artemis the more she read, but she couldn't tear her eyes away from the screen.

They'd been doing tests on her with Nosaru nFNA, namely gene-editing techniques on both her somatic and germ-line cells that even Artemis knew were illegal. The report said her mum was a volunteer for the study, but she couldn't wrap her head around it. Why on earth would her mum volunteer for experimental gene editing of all things?

The final page of the report stated she was released after her trial because she was perfectly healthy, and her trial period had ended with no visible effects of the Nosaru nFNA being introduced to her genome. She was instructed to return to the lab once every six months to monitor her if there were any changes, but none of her visits were recorded in the report.

The date caught Artemis's eye. It was approximately twelve months before the day she was born. She still remembered her Auntie Joy telling her she was a "pleasant surprise," which was a nice way of saying her parents weren't planning to have kids so soon. She kept scrolling down, and her heart stopped.

There was another report titled: "Human Test Subject 1806B: Artemis Garrett-Coleman."

It detailed how her existence was previously unknown to them until a year before the incident on Ben Nevis. Her jaw dropped when Jared's name popped up in the midst of all the genetics jargon, and everything inside her died.

The boy who first bumped into her at her favorite coffee shop and accidentally dropped her vanilla Frappuccino. The boy who offered to buy her a new one and asked her out on a date—her first ever date—in the same breath. The boy she'd loved with her whole heart . . . was a liar and a fake.

He'd been assigned to a mission the day before their first meeting to observe and get close to his target: Artemis Garrett-Coleman.

40

ABYAN

ONE WEEK HAD PASSED SINCE HER SUSPENSION FROM THE Sevenfold.

Though she'd tried to lose her annoying chaperone hundreds of times, Abyan had yet to find a way to get her off her tail. She hadn't spoken a word to any of her friends since their hive attack because if her squad so much as looked at her, they were all punished with double training sessions.

They'd learned that lesson the hard way.

Hank, Mason, and the others tried everything: passing notes, Morse code, and they'd even sent her a box of chocolates with invisible ink writing on the lid. Abyan only knew of the note since her monitor, Karen the demon—a tall jinniyo with an awful attitude—held a UV-light over it right in front of her and subsequently gave her three days of extra intensive training.

The demon was an operative and had graduated from Carlisle Academy a while ago, and Abyan guessed she was in her early thirties. At first, she thought it was strange for her to be given a menial task like babysitting. That was when it clicked. Abyan's monitor had messed up somehow and was being punished just as much as she was.

It explained why she was so bitter all the time.

The demon followed no less than two paces behind her wherever she went and not only checked the school toilet cubicles for any hidden messages before Abyan entered but also stood inside with her back turned while she used it.

The only place Abyan was ever free of her was in her new bedroom.

It was smaller than her other one, with walls of ashen gray and a tiny TV in the corner. She'd only been there a few days, but it was already a mess. Dirty clothes and junk food wrappers littered the floor, and there were papers strewn all over the desk. Abyan's head hurt at the sight, but she couldn't bring herself to do anything about it.

Peeling her body from her bed, showering, and brushing her teeth in time to get to her 6:00 a.m. combat training sapped enough of her strength. By the time she got back, her muscles hurt in a thousand different places, and she just wanted to sleep. Abyan had forgotten to eat at least twice every day, only realizing her lapse when she began to feel dizzy after training.

She didn't know what to do.

Usually when she knew it was going to be a bad depression day, she set reminders on her phone to tell her when to eat, but it was like the school was doing its utmost to let her know just how much they hated her for breaking their rules.

That school-issued laptop she was meant to receive? Abyan had yet to see it. The school-monitored phone? It was a Nokia brick from bloody 2005. It didn't have anything useful on it, and she was only allocated thirty minutes of call time a month and no texts.

At first, she thought it might have been a joke. They couldn't have been serious. But seven days had passed, and she'd accepted that whatever joke they were playing on her, she was the punch line.

It was the second week of December, and all of Year 14 was slated to attend their annual Christmas assembly in the Great Hall. Abyan tied her curls into a low bun and wrapped her usual black hijab around her head, sighing to herself in the mirror.

Abyan had been doing her utmost to avoid the rest of her year.

The thought of all their intrusive questions made her stomach turn. Even from an outsider's perspective, it wasn't hard to see that something had happened to her squad. And in a few minutes, she was going to have to enter the Great Hall—full to the brim with her peers—and walk straight past The Sevenfold's usual seats in the center of the tiered room.

A brisk knock at her door snapped her out of her thoughts. The demon. Though there were many things Abyan would've rather done than deal with that shaydaamad and her bullshit that she lost count, she swallowed her hatred, gathered her things, and exited the room as instructed.

The walk to the hall with the demon practically breathing down her neck, scuffing the heels of her shoes twice, was agonizing. Several stray students loitered in the corridors, and despite their hushed whispers filling the air as Abyan passed, she made sure to keep her head up.

She wasn't their entertainment.

As they entered the back entrance of the hall, the demon turned to her. "Sit right at the front, in the middle seat."

Abyan forced her feet down the stairs. The room was almost full, and she could feel everyone's eyes on her like lasers searing her flesh. She caught sight of her squad, sitting right in the middle row. She had to admit when she'd heard about a few offices being vandalized the day she was removed from the squad, Abyan wanted to both punch them all in turn for being so stupid and hug them for caring at the same time.

Her heart twisted at the sight of her friends seated beside one another, looking at her with worry clear in their eyes. Hank met her gaze, and Abyan didn't know what she was expecting—a solemn nod, a look of anguish—but she wasn't prepared for him to pull the ugliest face she'd ever seen, contorting his features in unbelievable angles. She cackled so loudly, all those who weren't already staring at her turned to see what she was laughing about.

Abyan slapped a hand to her mouth as the demon shoved her forward, whispering sharply for Abyan to keep it moving. The giggles didn't stop even when they'd found their seats in the middle of the first row, and even the demon's foul attitude and quick temper couldn't dampen Abyan's mood.

Hank was the best.

God, she missed him so much. His goofy and too-attractive-for-his-own-good self, awful taste in perfume, and the smile that stopped her heart instantly. Abyan wanted to tell him about her day, listen to him crack a few terrible jokes, and laugh along with him, but she couldn't.

Not anymore.

The room quieted as Mr. Williams took the podium. His skin was especially pink today, and he wiped at the sweat on his brow with his handkerchief before clearing his throat. "Welcome students," he began, and the lights dimmed around them. "Today I would like to discuss two important topics: respect and the importance of order."

A scoff escaped Abyan's lips before she could stop it, and she was rewarded with a swift elbow to the ribs from the demon. She saw the jab coming the instant she moved her arm, but Abyan let it happen. The last thing she needed was to get into a fistfight with her monitor when she was effectively on probation in front of her entire year and their headteacher.

It was more trouble than it was worth.

While the demon looked pleased with herself when she retracted her arm, Abyan didn't care. She could have this one. If they were having a truly fair fight, Karen wouldn't have had any teeth left to smile with.

Mr. Williams pointedly ignored their exchange and continued droning on about respect in his insufferable accent. The more he went on, the more Abyan realized the message he was sending was directed to The Sevenfold rather than everyone else. The prized jewel of the school had switched up on them, and Mr. Williams didn't like it one bit.

He couldn't do anything to them without upsetting The League, key company shareholders, or legacy families. Even Abyan knew suspending her from the squad was creating more trouble for the school than they'd anticipated, and it was only a matter of time before all the other legacy kids realized the power they had over the administration, too.

She wanted to laugh.

They'd bitten off more than they could chew and were now choking on the mouthful. *Mac sonkor, bastariin yahow.* Those bastards deserved everything they got. The more Abyan thought about it, the more it became clear they weren't worth saving. She'd gone through so much just to protect them from Mr. Carlisle and his creepy backroom bullshit and the Nosaru attack he probably knew was coming, and what did she get in return? They took away the only good thing about their stupid school.

Mr. Oluwole was just a puppet. He and all the other useless, brainless faculty. They didn't even suspect what was happening. She wanted to grab Mr. Williams by his collar and scream there was something going on that was so much bigger than him or any of them, and if they didn't prepare themselves for it, they deserved whatever was coming.

Abyan didn't care anymore.

She'd tried to help, followed her instincts, and it got her nowhere. Harry had been lying to them and feeding Mr. Carlisle information on her squad, and she hadn't seen it coming. The Nosaru were coming for them all, and Mr. Williams could harp on and on about respecting authority figures and being dedicated to creating an orderly school environment as much as he wanted.

It didn't change the fact that sooner or later, shit was going to go down. And when they all turned to each other in disbelief, wondering how they didn't see it coming, Abyan would look Mr. Williams right in the eye and say three words: "You deserve it."

41

ARTEMIS

ARTEMIS WAS ROTTING FROM THE INSIDE OUT. THE knowledge she held festered and boiled beneath her flesh and pretty soon, she was sure her squad would start to smell the stink. The only person she wanted to tell what she'd discovered was Abyan, and their friends were lost without her.

The Sevenfold was in open rebellion. None of them were attending training, assisting the recruit combat sessions, or going to any school functions. The only reason they were at yesterday's assembly was because they knew Abyan would be there, and seeing her only cemented what Artemis knew to be true.

She needed her back.

Her file had given her final pieces of her puzzle, that she was a murderer and that Jared was a fraud. Artemis had suspected her powers at first and then found them to be true, but how did she not connect the dots between her powers and Jared earlier? *I didn't want to be a killer.* It was an accident, but that didn't really matter.

Artemis still hated herself for it.

Her room—Jared's room—haunted her. Everything about it screamed death in her waking moments and whispered "Murderer" in her sleep. She slept on a spare mattress in the living room, since Artemis originally thought she might just stay in Abyan's room until she came back, but Hank was always in there, and she didn't want to have *that* conversation with him. He barely spoke to anyone, stayed in Abyan's barren room or on the roof 24/7, and Artemis could've sworn she hadn't heard him laugh once in over a week.

Everything was all wrong.

She decided to keep her revelation to herself, letting it chew her up from the inside until she could speak to Abyan instead. Artemis didn't know how the others would take the news—as selfish as it was, she didn't want them all to turn on her. They were her friends. And she would do everything she could to fix the squad, to bring Abyan back to them, and hopefully they'd find it in their hearts to forgive her in time.

After racking her brain for days, she still hadn't figured out who assigned her mission to Jared or why and decided to finally confront the only person who would know the answer. Artemis paced up and down Tolly's room. The second he entered, still wearing his rain-soaked coat, she shoved a copy of her file into his hands.

"Did you know?" Artemis scanned every inch of his face as she pointed to the section detailing Jared's betrayal.

His brows furrowed the further he read. "You were a mission?"

"Oh my God, you didn't." She raked a frustrated hand through her hair. "The whole relationship was a sham, and your best friend didn't even tell you."

"He'd never kept secrets from me before." Tolly took a seat on his bed, an emotion she couldn't place flitting across his dark eyes. "We were brothers."

Artemis said, "All this time you blamed me for his death when he lied and hid a successful human trial subject from you."

"Everything makes sense now," he replied, speaking more to himself now than her. "All those things you told us about him, how he acted when he was with you—it wasn't the Jared we knew and now I know why."

"He was lying to both of us." She sat down next to him. "All this time I'd been mourning someone who wasn't real and probably didn't care about me at all."

He still didn't deserve to die.

Tolly fiddled with his hands, looking down. "I'm sorry for being so hard on you, Artemis."

"I forgive you." Artemis held a hand out to him. "I think we should start fresh with a clean slate. We don't have to become instant best friends or anything, but we can see how it plays out at least."

He stared at her hand for a second before shaking it. "Agreed."

She turned on her heel and went all out in the kitchen, some small slice of her hoping the food would wake her friends up enough for her to talk some sense into them. Although Artemis had been a member of The Sevenfold for just over ten weeks, she'd never cooked a meal for the squad. Abyan and Tolly had done it twice, Hassan three times, while Kade, Hank, and Mason had done it once each.

She was making one of her favorite dishes: curry goat with rice and beans. Just the mouthwatering scent was enough to make her miss her parents and younger brothers, the sound of Mum singing as she cooked, and Dad's smile.

Artemis hadn't spoken to Dad in days and couldn't bring herself to call him with all that was going on at Carlisle. Did he know about what happened to her birth mum? *He couldn't possibly have known.* He'd never lie to her about anything, let alone something so serious.

A tiny voice in her head whispered how raising Artemis to believe her mother was a perfectly normal person who'd died in childbirth was much easier than the truth of who Hannah Garrett was, but she silenced it.

Artemis had a plan.

The rest of the squad were all watching TV in the living room, surrounded by the empty pizza boxes from last night that no one had bothered to throw away. That was all they did for the past week or so. Wake up, eat, and then go to sleep. They hardly ever spoke anymore except for when they argued—not because they hated one another now—but if Artemis, who'd only known them for a few months, could feel the gaping chasm in their family left by Abyan's departure, the rest of them felt it a thousand times more.

The toll it took on them was plain as day.

It was like watching a headless body trying to find its way through a maze. She'd had enough of it. Artemis devised her plan over the last week, and she was sure there was a real chance it could work.

Her squad only had to believe in it half as much as she did.

She turned off the stove and began plating the food. Kade had already set the table, so there wasn't much else left to do but call them all in. The Sevenfold piled into the kitchen, steps sluggish and uneven, and thanked her in turn for cooking the meal before digging in.

Artemis waited until they were fixated on the food, and her courage was high enough that she could speak. "Um, guys?" Her voice came out smaller than she intended, so she cleared her throat. "I have a plan to get Abyan back so we can stop whatever the Nosaru are planning and get her reinstated."

Tolly sighed, fork raised in midair. "It won't work, Artemis. We've already tried everything."

"But if you'll at least hear—"

"Leave it, recruit." Hassan met her gaze. "She's gone and there's no way we can get her back."

Mason shrugged while Kade looked to the ground. They'd given up on her. She couldn't believe it. Her plan could work—it *would* work if they'd hear her out. She was sick of being dismissed all the time because she was a recruit; Artemis was resourceful, too, and she was damn smart. Her ideas were good. Would it have killed them to put a little faith in her?

She didn't think she was asking for much.

"I want to know the plan, Artemis." Her head snapped up at the sound of Hank's voice, the faint circles under his eyes telling her enough about how well he'd been sleeping lately.

Hank glanced around the room and silenced any objections with a sharp glare of warning before nodding at Artemis to speak. She swallowed the lump in her throat. "Tomorrow is open evening for prospective Year 12s, and we'll have a window to get a message to Abyan, since her dorm is right next to where all the guides will be taking people in."

"She'll be stuck in there with nothing being allowed in or out of her room unless her monitor checks it," Tolly interjected.

"That's the thing," Artemis said. "We won't be sending her a physical message."

Kade's finely arched brows furrowed. "What do you mean?"

"Stephanie's band will be playing in the courtyard, across from Abyan's room. I was hoping one of you knew a song that would have some meaning to you guys, and we could get Stephanie to change a word or two of the lyrics, so she'd know where to meet us."

"I know one," Hank said, the ghost of a smile tugging at his lips. "I'll talk to Steph."

"Are you sure that's a good idea?" Kade asked, her tone skeptical. "Mason would be a better choice." They'd all seen how much he disliked her back when The Renegades visited. Even Artemis bristled at the idea. It would do more harm than good, and they didn't need any more bad luck coming their way.

"If it's for Yan, she'll do it regardless," Hank stated. "But Artemis, what about the monitor? We still need to get rid of her."

She sighed. Artemis didn't like this part of the plan herself. "Abyan has to lose her monitor on her own. We can't help her without exposing ourselves, and then she'll get expelled for good."

Kade leaned forward. "How does this get her back in the squad?"

"We need all of us to figure out when the Nosaru are going to attack, and when we stop it, The League will have no choice but to reinstate her." The Sevenfold were silent for a moment before the first few traitorous smiles broke through the ice, yet Artemis was going to rain on their parade before it even began. "We can't all meet with her though."

"Why not?" Mason asked, his jaw momentarily dropping. "She'd be away from her monitor."

Artemis wrung her fingers under the table. "The second Abyan disappears, the first thing her monitor will do is call the academy and check where we are. If we're all missing, it won't take them long to know what we've done. Only one of us can go."

"So, Hank should go."

"No, it has to be someone who can fly under their radar, who the school would never suspect of doing anything against the rules." A fog settled over Hank's features. "It has to be Artemis."

The Sevenfold looked around at each other, realizing the truth to his words. Artemis was the newbie, the recruit, and no one at Carlisle would ever think she'd do anything wrong—she was the perfect person to do this. She'd meet up with Abyan and share all the knowledge she'd gathered and devise a new plan to save them all.

"Are you all in?" Artemis asked, fingers crossed under the table.

Hank didn't spare a glance at the others. "We're in."

42

ARTEMIS

Artemis waited in the football pitch of Wormwood Scrubs Park. Hank didn't tell her what song he'd told Stephanie to play, what lyrics he'd told her to change, or what they meant to him and Abyan. All he said was to get herself to the football pitch and wait for Abyan there.

It had been three hours.

She had no idea whether or not their plan had worked—Tolly thought their school was spying on their phones, so they couldn't communicate. Artemis was cold and tired, and her hope was dwindling fast. She focused on the ice-coated blades of grass beneath her feet. Maybe Abyan hadn't managed to lose her monitor, or maybe she didn't get their message in the first place. Artemis kicked at the ground. The Nosaru were going to hit Carlisle, and it would be her fault. Everything they'd worked so hard for would've been all for nothing.

I gave everyone hope for no reason.

Artemis scratched at the back of her hand, suddenly prickling all over, and would've dismissed it as totally normal were it not for the figure standing not ten paces from her. He was tall, with mid-length black waves, and one look at his eyes told her exactly what he was.

Matteo.

She put both her hands up and balled them into fists. "If you come any closer, you'll regret it."

I can use my power on him properly this time.

Matteo moved out of the shadows surrounding him like he didn't hear a word Artemis had said. How did he escape Harry again? "Listen to me carefully: You and your friends are in danger," he said. "All of the hybrids are in danger."

Hybrids?

Artemis paused for a second. "W-what are you talking about? How did you get away this time?"

"What matters is I tried to hide it, but Soros has uncovered the program." He drew nearer still. "All of your little group are at risk, so you should leave that school before any harm befalls you. You need to convince the others because my kind are the only ones who can protect you now."

"How do you know this for sure?" It was like her brain refused to process his words. "You could be lying through your teeth for all I know."

Hosts didn't speak to humans, not willingly at least, and now after being tortured Matteo comes out of nowhere to tell her that The Sevenfold are Nosaru hybrids? It wasn't adding up. Artemis didn't know how long this host had been watching them, but he was sorely mistaken if he thought she could convince the squad of anything.

She barely got them to go along with her plan to get Abyan back.

"Your friend, the pretty girl—quick in the mind and sharp in the tongue?" He looked at her expectantly and Artemis nodded, knowing exactly who he was talking about. "From the first time I saw her, I knew she did not smell like a normal human, but I could not place it until I met one of your other companions—the large fool—who smelled just like her. You, on the other hand, don't smell human at all; you smell like one of us." He ran a frustrated hand through his hair. "It took me some time, but I realized what you were, what that organization has managed to do after all these years."

Artemis didn't want to believe him. "My powers don't come from being a hybrid."

"I do not have time to nurse your pitiful internal crisis," he snapped. "I would not be telling you this now if it was not urgent. Soros cannot get her hands on your team, and if none of you are going to come willingly, my people will take matters into our own hands."

She exhaled sharply the second what he'd just told her really hit. *He has to be telling the truth.* The Sevenfold were hybrids, and none of them had any idea; it explained Artemis's powers and why the squad had always been freakishly good at everything, but why didn't they have powers like her? If they were all the same genetically, then they should've been able to control the Nosaru as well.

"I'll try and convince them," she lied, putting her best poker face on so he couldn't see her true intentions. "But you have to go before Abyan gets here."

Matteo nodded at her once before leaving her alone with her crowded thoughts, her heart pounding faster with every passing second. The human trials. Artemis was a Nosaru hybrid. Kade was a Nosaru hybrid. Jesus Christ, *Abyan* was a Nosaru hybrid.

Out of the entire squad, Artemis knew she could never tell her the truth because it would destroy her so completely—Abyan hated Nosaru with every fiber of her being, and she'd suffered so much and for so long at their hands.

She deserved some light for all that darkness.

Artemis didn't care what Matteo said because he didn't know The Sevenfold like she did, and she knew they could handle whatever was thrown their way. Her friends just didn't need to know this one tiny detail, this one glaring nuke camped out in each of their DNA strands, and Artemis swore to herself that she'd ensure it stayed that way.

She'd never let a host shatter her squad like that.

"Artemis?" someone asked, a pair of boots materializing in front of her. She had to blink twice when she looked up just to make sure she wasn't hallucinating before throwing her arms around Abyan and pushing everything she'd just learned to the back of her mind.

If she didn't acknowledge it, it didn't exist.

Artemis welled up. "It worked."

"I thought you'd be happier to see me, recruit," Abyan joked, patting her back lightly.

"I am, I really am." She untangled herself from her. "I have so much stuff to tell you, and you aren't gonna like any of it."

Abyan's brow creased for the briefest of moments before she composed herself. "Take a deep breath, and start from the beginning."

She linked arms with Artemis and began slowly walking. Artemis did as she said and dived into the story of how she found her birth mum's file, the genetic tests that were done on her, and how she herself got her powers. "So, that's the bad-but-not-*that*-bad stuff—"

"There's worse?" Abyan's eyes widened a fraction.

The only signs of shock Artemis registered as she told her tale were the occasional tensing of her muscles and stiffening of her posture. Other than that, Abyan was taking the news better than she thought. But what Artemis had to say next would ruin everything. She knew it in her heart. You couldn't just forgive someone for doing what she did.

Abyan would hate her.

"Um." She gulped. "Jared wasn't killed by Nosaru."

She froze. "What do you mean?"

"I killed him." Her voice trembled. "The report said I influenced the Nosaru—that I used my powers to get them away from me so they went to him instead."

"Recruit," Abyan said, but she couldn't stop talking.

"I killed him, Abyan." The words seared her throat as they passed through, each one more unforgiving than the last. "When they were on top of me, I remember thinking 'Not me, not me,' and then they went to him. It's my fault he's dead—I'm a murderer."

"Artemis!" She was in front of her, hands locked on both her arms. "It wasn't your fault. You didn't know about your powers back then."

"But—"

"No buts," Abyan said. "It was an accident, okay? I've met enough murderers to know one when I see one, and when I look around here, there's not a single murderer in sight."

She pushed back the argument making its way up her throat but knew she couldn't force herself to lie and say that she believed Abyan's words, so she kept quiet.

Abyan tightened her jacket. "How is everyone?"

"They're all right." Artemis didn't want her to worry about them with all that was going on. "We miss you."

It seemed so simple, so stupid to sum up everything The Sevenfold were going through in three simple words, but she didn't know what else to say.

A small laugh escaped Abyan's lips. "I miss you guys, too."

Artemis's eyes lit up. "We're gonna get you back in the squad."

"It's impossible."

"No, it's not. We just need to find out when the Nosaru are going to attack, stop it, and then The League will reward us for saving Carlisle Enterprises by putting you back in the team." Artemis couldn't wipe the grin from her face. The plan was so perfect, and everything would work out in the end. She knew it would.

Abyan set her jaw. "They don't deserve to be saved."

She blinked. "What?"

"Why do I always have to sacrifice myself for people who couldn't care less about me?" She looked away. "They can save their damn selves for all I care."

"You're right. Mr. Oluwole, Dr. Telford, Mr. Carlisle—they don't deserve your help." Artemis thought on her words, twisting the skin of her fingers. "But do it for your squad and all the other students who haven't done anything to you. I don't think we should leave them for the Nosaru when they're innocent in all this."

"You don't—"

"Your beef is with Mr. Carlisle and the senior teachers, not the rest of them," Artemis pleaded. "My plan won't go wrong, Yan, and we've already agreed as a squad that we're going to quit the school completely if they try to kick you out, so don't try and talk us out of it."

Abyan was silent. "That's the first time you've ever called me Yan."

"Is it?" Artemis blinked.

She turned on her heel suddenly. "Come on, then. Let's go back."

"Back where?"

"To The Sevenfold's dorm," Abyan said, like it was the most obvious thing in the world. "It's the last place they'll think I went."

"What are you talking about?"

A mischievous smile formed on her lips. "I'm going AWOL."

43

ABYAN

Abyan was in the east wing of the residential building. She knew the place like the back of her hand, and it didn't take her long to find a way inside. She'd parted with the recruit around Holland Park station in case there were already people out looking for them.

When Artemis returned to Carlisle without her, they'd assume Abyan wasn't in contact with her squad and buy into her going AWOL more. It was nine in the evening, so she was counting on there not being too many students about.

There was a service staircase with a lock pad next to it at the end of the corridor behind her. She pressed up against the cold wall, and the chill sent shivers down her spine. She couldn't risk poking her head into the hallway. There was a security camera mounted right in the middle of the ceiling, and the facial recognition software Carlisle Academy had would catch her in an instant.

Think.

Abyan pushed herself off the wall and sprinted for the stock room three doors down. It had another keypad next to it, but like all service-related utilities, the password was the same: 2-7-4-4. The stock room was empty, and she quietly thanked Allah for it.

The cleaners would've outed her in two seconds flat. The room was filled with supplies, aprons, and toilet paper. There was a rack of freshly pressed service uniforms on the side, and Abyan rushed to it in an instant. She slipped off her clothes and pulled on the closest-fitting one, taking off her hijab and bundling her hair into the white cap all the cleaners were supposed to wear.

She tried to ignore the purple and green bruises already forming across her knuckles and arms. Karen had finally got what was coming to her. Abyan had thought she might just knock her over the head and leave whether she got a simple concussion or a full-on brain hemorrhage to Allah, but the second the demon blocked her exit from her dorm, she saw red and couldn't hold herself back.

Turns out, Karen's bark was much worse than her bite.

Abyan's skin crawled the moment the breeze from the air-conditioning blew through her curls, but she gritted her teeth and shoved her hijab into the discarded bucket-shaped tray closest to her. There were no cleaners at Carlisle who wore hijabs—she would've stuck out like a sore thumb if she kept it on. She shoved the first cleaning supplies she saw onto her tray with a little too much force, cursing herself at the clamor when two bottles of detergent slammed against one another.

She hurried to the paper face masks hanging on the wall beside the goggles and other miscellaneous stuff. The rich kids at Carlisle were into some weird shit, and she'd seen the custodians rushing around with masks and thick gloves so many times it had gotten to the point where if Abyan saw one wearing a hazmat suit, she wouldn't blink twice.

She seized the tray, securing her mask and pulling her cap down as low as possible, and made her way to the door of the service staircase. Abyan wasted no time and punched in the code, keeping her head low enough that the camera wouldn't be able to discern any of her features through the shadows of her hat.

Vaulting up the stairs, she kept an ear out for anyone coming up or down. She'd already settled on talking with a fake Somali accent and pretending she didn't speak much English. Most people in the tax bracket of Carlisle students or faculty wouldn't give her a second look the moment they heard her broken English.

The residential building had five floors, and she knew her plan would fail the moment she reached the fourth. It was the noise. Barking. The rough sound bounced off the walls and sent her nerves into a frenzy. They had bloody sniffer dogs on the fifth floor looking for her. Abyan paused, gripping the railing, and made herself think as she forced air into her burning lungs. Why were they still looking through her old rooms? They should've gone there first and moved on by now.

Her breath caught in her throat.

The vents.

They led right into the living room of The Sevenfold's dorm. She was slender enough to move through the steel vents, and it would throw the dogs off, since her scent would be carried all around the building by the air currents.

Abyan made sure to spray detergent in the air as she went up one final flight of stairs and stopped in front of the vent. She hooked her fingers into the gaps of the metal and carefully lifted it off the wall, pulling her tray in and closing the vent behind her.

She hurriedly wrapped her hijab back around her head before crawling quietly through the shaft. The schematics of the residential building were splayed out in her mind. She'd seen them before in Mr. Oluwole's office when he was bragging about their newest building extension.

Abyan took a right and kept going until a yellow light shone into the vent.

Before rushing to the end, she waited. Abyan could hear Mason complaining to their intruders that they'd ruined all his things and warning them they'd all be without jobs in the morning. *Typical.* The last thing she heard was a brief apology from an unfamiliar voice and the shuffle of boots exiting their rooms.

Abyan waited a few minutes longer to make sure the people

had left. Silently, she shuffled forward and gave the opening of the vent a hard shove, catching it before it could hit the ground. She crawled out and stood straight, wiping the dust from her body.

When Abyan looked up, her entire squad was looking at her like she'd just come back from the dead, wide-eyed and mouths agape.

She cleared her throat. "I missed you—"

She didn't get to finish her sentence and only registered a blur of pink silk before Kade launched herself at her and said, "The plan worked!"

"Hey, stop keeping her all to yourself." Mason removed Kade from her gently, and she rolled her tear-filled eyes at him before stepping back. He lifted Abyan up when they embraced, twirling her in the air. "God, I missed you so much."

"I missed you, too." She managed to get out between giggles.

When he set her down, Abyan hugged Tolly and Hassan in turn, ruffling Hassan's hair and laughing when he swore at her not a moment later. Hank was staring, still frozen in shock. She gathered up all the courage she had and walked right up to him, crossing her arms.

"So, I come back after almost two weeks away, and all you're going to give me is that zombie look and a few blinks." Abyan placed a hand to her chest. "I'm hurt, Hercules."

There it was. That thousand-kilowatt grin. It crossed his face slowly—the slightest upturn of the corner of his mouth, the creasing of his cheeks, and that blinding twinkle in his eyes. Abyan hated herself for being such a sap, but she was grateful when he opened his arms because she was a second away from falling anyway.

"Come here, Yan."

She leaped into his embrace and couldn't help but think of how natural his arms felt around her waist and how perfectly her head fit into the crook of his neck. Subhan'Allah. Abyan knew she shouldn't care about him in that way, but he made it so damn hard.

It's haram, she reminded herself over and over in her head until she found the strength to let him go.

She didn't miss the longing in his eyes as she pulled away. Abyan turned to the recruit and held her hand out for a spud. They didn't need to exchange words. They both knew what this meant for the team.

Without Artemis, it would've never been possible.

"I know you guys have a lot of questions about what happened while I was away," Abyan started. "But I really don't want to go into it right now because we have more important things to talk about."

Hank nodded. "You're here now, that's what matters."

She swallowed the lump in her throat and moved to sit on the sofa. "So, where are we at with the Nosaru?"

The squad took their seats and Kade sighed. "Nowhere. We've been looking through the files but haven't come across anything interesting. And I've been listening in to the gossip around the school. Aside from yesterday's big score, no one's talking about anything else."

Abyan cocked a brow. She hadn't heard anything about that. "What big score?"

"Some operatives managed to capture two first gens yesterday, and the school won't shut up about it."

Abyan slapped her palm to her forehead. "Where are the first gens being kept?"

"The research building." Hassan's dark brows furrowed, a perfect crease forming in his tawny skin. "Why?"

"Because we didn't catch them." She sighed, wondering if there was anyone with common sense left at Carlisle. "They wanted to be caught. The Nosaru are going to hit the research wing, and it's going to happen soon."

"We need to check hive activity around Marble Arch," Hank said, pulling out his phone to check the Carlisle app.

The first gens had to have gotten themselves captured so that when their third and fourth gen soldiers arrived, they'd have people already on the inside who could keep a tight hold on them.

It would've been a landslide victory.

"Oh shit." Hank looked up and showed them his phone, pointing at the green blobs on the blacked-out map. "These are the newly formed hives around Marble Arch as of this morning." He flicked to a different page, showing the green dispersing steadily over the surrounding area. "This is what it looked like this afternoon. The system updates every eight hours, but we can guess what it'll look like then."

Abyan shook her head in disbelief. "Why haven't the operatives noticed it, too? It should've been flagged."

"Because hives in Leicester Square, Westminster, Greenwich, Tower Hamlets, Holland Park, Southwark, and Covent Gardens are also dispersing in the same way," came Harry's voice from the hallway.

Both Abyan and Hank immediately shot up from their seats, while the others looked on in confusion.

How did he get in without any of them noticing?

Hank was first to recover. "What the hell are you doing here?"

"Garrett-Coleman invited me, King," Harry said, moving into the living room. "I was expecting a warmer welcome."

Abyan glared daggers at him as everyone else turned to look at the recruit. "I told him about the possibility of an attack on Carlisle and nothing else. He didn't believe me when I spoke to him, so I had no idea whether he would actually come."

"He can't be trusted, Artemis." Abyan had to make a conscious effort not to yell at her. "Not with anything."

Though she wanted to kick herself for not telling everyone what Hank said after their failed hive attacks, Abyan quickly realized that there was no way she could've done so, since Mr. Oluwole booted her out of the squad that very same night.

Harry cocked a dark brow. "What makes you so sure of that?"

"You tell me, Nicholas. What's your connection to Mr. Carlisle?"

Annoyance took hold of his features, and in that moment Abyan realized something that made her stomach turn. Harry already knew they'd learned of his real name. "We'll save how you found out about the attack and my name for after the mission. Right now, there's an imminent threat against the research wing, and I don't think my past is what we should be focusing on."

"Either you explain or you can defend the research wing by yourself."

If The Sevenfold had to get in bed with the devil to protect the organization, Abyan would rather know him like the back of her hand. When the rest of the squad didn't challenge her, a mixture of intrigue and confusion on each of their faces, Harry gave a defeated sigh.

"Richard Carlisle took me in when I was sixteen after I helped his wife fend off some hosts. I was homeless at the time, so he took pity on me and let me enroll in the academy once he saw my potential."

"So, you were like a son to my grandad," Mason interrupted, and even Abyan couldn't read all the emotions flitting across his face. "He's been dead for years—I don't know why no one's ever told me about you."

"Probably because your father and I have never really seen eye to eye. The only reason he stopped trying to off me is because I have enough fail-safes in place that he wouldn't come near me with a ten-foot pole." Harry looked each of them in the eye, almost daring them to challenge him. "Now can we skip to the part where we save the research wing?"

Abyan nodded, deciding to reserve her personal opinion on Harry until after the mission. There was going to be a hive attack on nearly every major site in the city. Though all Carlisle's buildings were on the list, Abyan figured the operatives would put the public first and rush to help them. The Nosaru were hitting all those sites as decoys because they knew operatives would be spread thin trying to protect everyone else, not knowing that the research wing was the true target.

Harry told them his plan and no one disputed it. "If anyone asks why you were there when this is all over, tell them I commanded you all to do this mission with my squad and you were following direct orders."

"Won't you get in trouble for breaking the rules?" Artemis asked.

Harry only shrugged. "If the Nosaru succeed, there'll be no rules anyway."

With that, he turned and left their dorm. Abyan stood and the rest of the squad followed suit. The more time they wasted, the longer it left for doubt to settle in.

"Grab all the daggers and weapons you can find," she said. "Leave separately and take different routes out of the building. Meet me in the parking garage, and we'll all head to the research wing together."

The recruit steeled herself, taking a deep breath. "Okay."

"We got this." Kade stuck her hand out between all of them, and the rest of The Sevenfold put their hands in, too.

Abyan placed hers on top. "Yeah, we do."

44

ARTEMIS

THE SEVENFOLD PULLED UP ON EXMOOR STREET. IT WAS under seven hundred feet and four streets away from where the research building was located. The three classified sublevels of the research wing were surrounded by a complex network of tunnels only to be used in emergencies.

They weren't visible in any of the building schematics except the ones stolen by the Nosaru, but there wasn't any other route for them to get inside as Squad 2528 were going through the front entrance to box the hosts in.

The squad hurried to the park across the street, all of them dressed in black with each of their swords sheathed at their backs and daggers artfully hidden under long trench coats. There were two sewage drains in the park, and neither of them led into sewers. It was well after midnight and the wind, lightning fast and biting, whipped through Artemis's curls.

The daggers around her stomach poked into her sides, but thankfully, Abyan also let her have a tranq. It was a specialist handgun, nine tranquilizer-filled bullets to a clip, and no death in its kick. It felt secure against the skin of her thigh, and the four spare mags strapped to her other leg eased some of her fried nerves.

The dying December grass crackled and groaned under the weight of their heavy boots as they came upon the first manhole. Artemis gulped as Abyan turned to address them. "Once we go down there, fifty feet in there'll be a two-way fork and we'll have to split up."

"Won't all the tunnels lead into sublevel three anyway?" Tolly cocked a brow. "I don't see why we need to split up."

Abyan shook her head. "We don't know which route they took to get there, and we need to stop them before they reach sublevel three."

"So you, me, Tolly, and the recruit go left while Kade, Mason, and Hassan go right?" Hank asked.

"That's exactly what I was thinking," Abyan confirmed. "Whoever finds the Nosaru first needs to signal it, and the other group has to sprint to the opposite side of whatever tunnel it is and box them in, okay?"

The squad nodded in reply. Tolly knelt and lifted the cover of the manhole, exposing the ladder leading into the darkness below. Hank went down first, Abyan followed, and Artemis released a slow breath before going in next. She wasn't the most religious person—she went to church with her family and that was it—but a silent prayer left her lips as she descended into the tunnel. The metal rungs were so cold, the hairs on Artemis's arms stood on end.

The rest of the squad soon joined them, and they crept through the tunnel. Lights popped up on the walls the farther in they went, and sure enough, there was a two-way fork. They shed their coats and made the final checks on their weapons.

"Don't you even think of dying." Abyan pulled Mason in for a hug. "I mean it."

She turned to Kade and Hassan and hugged them as well. Artemis followed suit, and she realized that this could be the last time she saw any of them: the last time she saw Kade's beautiful smile, the last time she heard Tolly's laugh, or one of Mason's jokes.

Jesus.

"Don't cry, Artemis." A smirk tugged at Kade's lips as she wrapped her arms around her, her gaze lingering on Artemis's mouth. "There's no way God would let a face like this go to waste on some worms and flesh-eating bacteria."

Though fear crept up her spine, threatening to freeze her bones solid to the marrow, the shot of adrenaline that flooded her veins as she met Kade's eyes was enough for Artemis to get up on her tiptoes and plant a kiss on her soft lips.

The kiss was cautious yet certain, the first steps on a new world and the hundredth stroll down the street she'd grown up on all rolled into one. Not home yet but something that felt pretty damn close. Kade took a second to react before her lips parted slightly, her hand finding the nape of Artemis's neck, and she kissed her back.

It was strange. For the first time since meeting Kade, Artemis didn't feel guilty about wanting to be near her, wanting to see her smile—she kept waiting for that crushing weight to hit her like a tidal wave, but there was nothing. There was a different kind of guilt that washed over her now, but Kade was free from each merciless wave.

She was grateful for that at least.

Artemis pulled away first and whispered, "Don't let that be our only kiss."

Kade rested her forehead on hers, a slow smile taking hold of her mouth. "See you on the other side."

The Sevenfold split up.

Artemis made sure her safety was off, walking silently behind Hank. Abyan didn't want her to come on the mission. Artemis didn't really blame her either. She froze up and almost got them all killed back in the Holland Park hive. She had to show them she wasn't a liability, that her powers could serve a purpose, too.

It was a few more feet treading carefully through the concrete, domed tunnel before Artemis felt it. Her skin crawling. A thousand fire ants. The gun in her hands started to shake as she furiously hit the signal button on the radar wrapped around her wrist. She grabbed Hank by the arm. He, Tolly, and Abyan stared at her with questioning eyes, and Artemis didn't miss the "Oh no, not this again" look they shared in the split second they thought she wasn't paying attention.

"Nosaru right in front of us," she mouthed. While Nosaru were limited to the human body's capabilities, and therefore only had average human hearing, tunnels had echoes and she didn't want to announce their presence to the whole world. Artemis pointed to her radar as yellow rings pulsed across it. "I signaled already."

They didn't ask how she was so sure. They already knew. Hank walked ahead, drawing his sword. The metal shone in the dim yellow light of the tunnel, and Artemis wasn't sure if it was her nerves, but the glint of the sharpened edge made her heart race. It was really happening. The closer they got, the more Artemis wanted to shed her own skin.

She was choking.

There were so many of them, more than the twenty-odd ones back at the hive, but the Nosaru felt the exact same. Jittery. Unstable. They were fourth and third gens, Artemis knew it in her heart. She could hear the hosts—the snarls, labored breathing, and the scuffle of feet. They were less than thirty feet ahead; there was no point being stealthy now.

Hank took out a Carlisle-designed grenade that wasn't even allowed for anyone who wasn't a senior operative. *How on Earth did he manage to get that?* The quiet click of the pin being pulled was swallowed by the snarls, and he held it in his hand for two seconds before hurling it deep into the huddled mass before them.

Artemis ducked behind one of the metal boxes on the side of the tunnel, shoving her fingers into her ears as the grenade exploded and shook the ground beneath her feet. Dust and death filled the air as all the Nosaru who weren't killed or maimed by the explosion came at them.

Tolly and Hank charged forward, throwing daggers in every

direction. Bodies crashed to the ground all around her, and Artemis kept her gun raised as she moved through the tunnel, desperately trying to keep up with her squad.

The silent pulse of her radar caught her attention, and her heart plummeted to the ground as she took in the sight. Mason's team was signaling. They had Nosaru in their tunnel as well. There were about thirty hosts left alive, but as Artemis did her headcount, she caught sight of one of the males handing a briefcase to another and exchanging a few words before he took off farther into the tunnel.

Something was in that briefcase, and they needed to stop it.

"Abyan!" Artemis yelled over the noise. A Nosaru lunged at her, saliva dripping from the host's fanged mouth as blood poured from the gaping cut across its stomach, and Artemis's fingers squeezed the trigger without thinking.

She blinked as it slumped to the ground, only coming back to her senses when Abyan yelled back. "I'm going after him!"

Abyan carved through the Nosaru mercilessly, cutting down any who dared to step in her path with Gacan Libaax, and Artemis ran behind her, shooting at those she didn't manage to catch. The blond Nosaru who'd run off earlier turned a corner in front of them, and Abyan followed right behind him, a tempest carrying her steps.

They entered the room he'd ducked into, servers lining every wall, as the Nosaru pushed a button on whatever was in his bag and faced them. Abyan reached to the holster at her ribs and swore when she came up empty, but Artemis was one step ahead and quickly threw one of her own unused daggers to her.

She caught it effortlessly, swiveling on one foot and kicking the Nosaru across the jaw with so much force, he lost his footing. The second he tumbled, Abyan lodged the dagger through his eye socket and he went limp, the briefest of whimpers leaving his lips. She wiped at the blood that had spattered onto her cheek and walked to the open bag, a curse leaving her lips the moment she was close enough.

Artemis stepped toward it tentatively, though the noise emanating from where it sat should've told her enough. Her stomach turned. She peered into the briefcase and saw the plastic, the copper wiring, and the timer strapped to whatever deadly explosive was under it.

A bomb.

45

ABYAN

They only had fifteen minutes.

Abyan cursed again, running her hands over her hijab. She swore like a sailor, pacing back and forth, as she tried to jog her brain. Where was Harry when you needed him? Espionage was taught in Year 13, but it had never clicked with her. She didn't know what to do. The briefcase contained enough TNT to level the research building and take several others nearby along with it.

People were going to get hurt, and a lot of them, too.

We're gonna die.

She couldn't do this herself. The wiring was far from juvenile, and the last thing she wanted to do was set the thing off prematurely. One false move and they were all dead. Abyan put a hand to her mouth, fighting to control her breathing, and drowned out the sounds of battle and the rhythmic beeping of the bomb.

Cuts and bruises covered her body, and Abyan could barely feel a thing besides the bile rising in her throat. Her head pounded. How the hell was she going to fix this when Tolly was the only one more than half-decent at defusing shit? He was stuck out in the tunnel, surrounded, fighting for his life.

What if she couldn't get to him in time?

"Hey, you're going to be okay," the recruit said, materializing in front of her. "We'll figure this out."

"I can't defuse it, Artemis." Abyan shook her head. "We need Tolly."

And they needed him quickly.

In those split seconds, Abyan gathered the frazzled pieces of her—the fear, the anxiety, the dread—and threw them into the deepest pit she could find in her mind. *Pull yourself together.* She couldn't afford to lose it. Her friends needed her, and she'd keep herself together for them.

She tightened her grip on Gacan Libaax and moved to the door, speaking to the recruit over her shoulder, "Keep an eye on the bomb, Artemis."

The recruit tried to protest, but Abyan shut the door behind her before she could convince her to stay—they didn't have time to waste. She glanced around the tunnel to find Tolly and Hank fighting back-to-back a short distance away, covered in blood she desperately hoped wasn't their own.

Two hosts pounced on her.

Abyan brought Gacan Libaax up in time to slice through one of their arms, spinning and angling herself for a more precise blow. The satisfactory thuds a second later told her she'd stuck true. *I need to get to them.* She pressed forward, cutting down whatever Nosaru that tried to get in her way, sheer desperation making her forget about each of her shaking limbs and turning every injury she got in the process into a distant memory.

Shit.

Abyan was still too far away for Tolly to hear her over the clamor. She panted, the stuffy underground air clogging her lungs, and prayed that she could keep going for just a few minutes more. A few more minutes, that was all she needed to get Tolly into the server room. A few more minutes, and they could save everyone.

A few more minutes, Ya Allah.

She turned her head to check her six and gasped. Ginger hair, beady eyes, that ever-present smirk. Her body stiffened as she met his dark gaze, her mind taking her back to that night when she was fourteen years old—to how he stepped over the bodies of her parents and siblings without a care, to how their blood dripped down his ashen chin.

Abyan's lip curled. "Khalo."

He was almost at the end of the tunnel and Abyan knew it would take a lot to catch up to him, but that slim chance was all she needed. She could make everything right. Finally take the burden off her shoulders. He wouldn't be able to escape her anymore, and once he was dead, she could start to let it all go. Abyan could truly try and heal from what happened to her.

What Khalo *took* from her.

Yet as soon as she took her first step in his direction, Abyan paused. *The bomb.* She had to get Tolly to defuse it and save the research wing, but she could still kill Khalo first, couldn't she? Abyan had to have at least ten minutes left. Though it would've been tight, it was still very much doable.

Tolly and Hank looked exhausted the last time she'd looked their way and Allah knew what hell Mason and the others were knee-deep in on their side of things. Abyan made her decision in those precious heartbeats before Khalo turned away from her, a stray tear running down the side of her face as the balance in her mind tipped unquestionably to one side.

She chose her friends.

And she always would.

Abyan tore through the hosts that separated her from Hank and Tolly, not registering the snarls or the blood making her clothes stick to her like a second skin. When she was close enough for them to hear, Abyan yelled at the top of her lungs, "Guys, get over here! There's a bomb!"

Even though the boys looked like hell, they broke into a sprint and followed her back into the server room. Abyan pushed Tolly inside and shut the door, locking her and Hank out alone with the sea of hosts around them. "We have to hold them off while he defuses it, Hank."

Hank raised his red-stained sword, Excalibur, his voice rougher than usual. "How long do you think he has?"

"Not long enough." She turned, elbowing a host that had gotten too close for comfort. Abyan brought Gacan Libaax across the air in front of her in a flash and knew the creature wouldn't be getting back up any time soon.

Damn it.

Everywhere she looked there were fangs, eyes as dark as a starless sky, and the promise of death. A lump formed in her throat as a host clawed up her thigh. Abyan hissed, fire burning across her flesh, and shoved a stray dagger into its skull. She and Hank wouldn't last the next ten minutes no matter how hard they fought.

Her gaze flickered to him just as he looked at her.

There were so many things she needed to say to Hank, but they were all either lodged in her throat or stuck to her tongue. Her heart just didn't want to be laid bare, it seemed. He looked at her like he wanted to say something, too, and there was a sorrow to his gaze, a yearning heavy in the way he licked his lips.

Sorry, she wanted to say. For everything. Abyan was sorry she couldn't not love him, and sorry she made him love her, too. It didn't matter how much she wanted to kiss him, feel his lips on her skin, or drown in the warmth of his body. She couldn't do it. While she wasn't the most devout Muslim and would never claim to be so, she wasn't like him or Hassan—she couldn't break the rules she was raised with and act like it was normal.

Abyan couldn't help but think this was a punishment for something she'd done wrong.

"Why the blue sprinkles?" she bit out. Of all the things in her mind, it was the one question that stuck out from the rest. Whenever he brought her something to eat when she was sad, there'd always be blue sprinkles on top, and Abyan had always wondered why.

She just thought she'd have more time to ask.

Hank staggered toward the next host in front of him, speaking through labored breaths. "On my dad's bad days, it was the only thing that would get a reaction out of him."

God.

Although Abyan's eyes blurred for only a second, that was all it took for a fist to land on her jaw, throwing off her balance completely. Hank cried out for her, but she used Gacan Libaax as a crutch to get up when the overwhelming pain in her legs stopped her from rising. She had to keep going for Tolly.

There were just so many hosts left—Abyan counted dozens—and she and Hank looked and felt like death. Black spots appeared in her vision, increasing in size and number too fast to count, and the sharp pain in her head made tears spring to her eyes. They wouldn't be able to hold on for much longer, and the thin door behind them would offer little resistance if the two of them fell.

Hank put down the host that had hit her in a single strike. "Listen, Yan," he breathed, gazing at her for the briefest of moments before turning back to the enemies closing in around them. "You know how I feel about you, how I've always felt about you. I love you with everyth—"

The hosts around them suddenly stilled as if frozen in time, mid-leap and -growl, with nothing but their eyes following her movements. Abyan's jaw dropped, and even Hank stopped in the middle of his confession.

Audhubillahi mina shaydaani rajeem.

Abyan wavered on her feet and tried to make sense of what was happening through her agony, blinking hard as though it would stop the dark spots from swallowing the sight before her. Yet it only took a few seconds more for her eyes to close against her best efforts, and the panic in Hank's voice as he cried out for her would have sent a jolt straight through her if Abyan wasn't so exhausted.

She just couldn't fight it anymore.

46

ARTEMIS

Artemis didn't know what she was expecting to happen the moment she closed her eyes and tapped into the chaos raging under her skin. The fourth gens' energy was intoxicating—water that refused to lie still, rippling and splashing. She wanted to set fire to it and drown in it at the same time. It was hard to wrap her mind around it all at first, so much was happening inside her, and Artemis tried to picture the humming energy as an ocean.

A huge, terrifying ocean that only she understood.

She reached a hand into the thrashing water and willed it to stop with everything in her, picturing stone, ice, an ancient creature trapped in amber. Stillness in all its multitudes. And the instant her skin cooled and Artemis didn't feel like crawling out of it, she knew something had changed.

Had her plan worked?

Artemis glanced at the bomb Tolly loomed over, carefully prying the wires apart with his switchblade. Forty-five seconds left. Sweat beads trickled down his mahogany brow, his hands shook a little, and Artemis didn't envy him in the slightest. All their fates rested on his shoulders. She decided against saying anything that would mess with his concentration and moved to the door to check on Abyan and Hank.

Then, she heard it.

Boots.

Running.

The cavalry had arrived.

Took you long enough, Harry.

She cracked the door open a fraction and her breath caught. All the hosts were held in place by some invisible force, and operatives from the other end of the tunnel used it as an opportunity to finish them off quick and easy. Artemis could still feel the hosts under her skin, and it was like they were humming, rattling, aching to be free from whatever cage she'd trapped them in.

Hank called out from somewhere to her side, interrupting her thoughts, "Hold the door open, Artemis!" His voice was hoarse, panicked, and Artemis understood exactly why the second she realized he carried an unconscious Abyan in his arms.

Artemis hurried to get the door open wide enough for the two of them and made sure to lock it afterward in case the Nosaru ever broke out of her hold. Hank had propped Abyan up gently against one of the servers, the slow rise and fall of her chest indicating she was out cold. Her uniform was ripped in a dozen different places, cuts and blood covered her skin, and Artemis's heart burned at the sight.

She put up one hell of a fight.

Hank checked her vitals, cradling her face in his hand as he tried to find a pulse, and turned to Artemis when he was done. "She's okay," he said, though the panic never left his eyes. "But she got hit in the head, so it might be a concussion."

Artemis looked at the timer and gulped. "We only have ten seconds left."

Hank lowered himself next to Abyan, perfectly parallel to her. He wasn't touching a single part of her body, not her shoulder nor holding her hand, but the way he looked at Abyan felt so intimate that Artemis had to turn away.

Her vision blurred as she thought about Kade. Was she okay? Was she hurt? If Artemis was going to spend her last moments with anyone, she'd have preferred it to be with her.

"I did it!" Tolly cackled, the sound splitting the room asunder and stopping Artemis's heart mid-beat. "I did it, guys!"

Her head snapped in his direction. "What?"

Four seconds were frozen on the clock.

Death in neon red.

"I defused it." He grinned, his teeth gleaming under the blue-tinged light of the server room.

Artemis turned to Hank, eyes wide. "He defused it."

"I heard." He laughed with his whole body, boisterous and melodic, and turned to an unconscious Abyan. "Looks like we're not dying today, Yan."

Artemis ran to Tolly and gave him the tightest hug she could muster with her still-shaking limbs. "Thank you, Tolly. You saved us all."

He shrugged. "It was nothing."

She stepped back and peeled away the holster wrapped around her ribs, revealing the hard drive and tablet beneath. The last part of her plan. She hurried to the servers, ignoring the confusion in Hank and Tolly's eyes, and plugged it in.

"Can you open the door and take the bomb out to the operatives while I do this?" she asked. "Tell them what happened and keep them busy until I come out."

Tolly cocked a brow. "And when they ask what you were doing in here?"

"Leave Yan behind and tell them I was checking to see if she was okay," she replied, not missing a beat. "Send for medics, too. We'll need them to check her properly."

All of Carlisle's research database was concentrated in this one room. It was the perfect opportunity to get more information. The Nosaru who'd brought the bomb inside knew the nine-digit password for the door, and there was no way Carlisle wouldn't change it the moment they discovered the leak—Artemis had to do this now.

They could find out more about the trials with Nosaru genetics, both human and animal, and whatever else was being hidden from them all in the research wing. The Sevenfold couldn't be the only successful hybrids. Artemis wanted to know everything about the program: Did Mr. Carlisle do it alone? Were their parents in on it somehow? Did they all get powers?

She had too many questions to count.

The Nosaru were changing, getting smarter and more efficient. The humans had to change, too. The higher-ups didn't get to keep them all in the dark so the rest of them could become cannon fodder while they got data for whatever it was they were planning. Artemis knew Mr. Carlisle would fight her tooth and nail, but she didn't care in the slightest. She'd tear the organization down brick by brick, and there wasn't anything on this Earth or outside of it that could stop her.

He was finally going to lose.

47

ARTEMIS

THE LEAGUE WANTED TO SPEAK WITH HER.

Artemis had said it aloud so many times, and it still didn't seem real enough to be happening in a few minutes. Was it going to be all twelve of them like Abyan and Hank had seen? God, she felt sick at the thought. The Sevenfold had been asleep for all of two hours after their four-hour-long interrogations in the research building before they heard the pounding on their door.

Five burly men clad in black from head to toe said that Artemis and Abyan had to accompany them. A shot of ice-cold fear ran up her spine as their words sank in, but she didn't have time to speak before the rest of the squad demanded to come along, too. The men refused and informed them that The League's invite was only extended to her and Abyan for a reason.

One they had yet to tell them, of course.

Even as Artemis sat in their fancy car with Abyan repeatedly telling her to relax, walked through the intelligence building, and stood outside the door to where The League was waiting for them, she couldn't shake her nerves. It was only natural, she told herself—potentially facing the twelve most powerful members of a shady underground organization was literally terrifying.

Being scared was expected.

Matter fact, it would've been weird if she *wasn't* afraid.

It was impossible for The League to know what had really

happened the previous night because The Sevenfold had agreed not to say a word about what she did to the Nosaru before their interrogations started.

To lie through their teeth for her.

And they did.

Artemis hadn't known it at the time, but when she'd taken over the Nosaru in the server room, she'd done it to all the Nosaru in the tunnels, even the ones Kade's group were fighting. It was . . . odd. What she could do. And chilling. Her powers would've proven useful if The League ever found out about them, and they'd undoubtedly use her as a weapon—they'd probably try to copy her genome and mix and match whatever they wanted with her DNA.

There'd be no escaping them.

That was why they could never know. Artemis was done being anyone's specimen to be poked and prodded, and she was going to tell Mr. Carlisle that himself when she saw him. She was in control now, not him. He would never retaliate by kicking her out and risk her telling The League what he'd done. He also couldn't tell them about her directly because then they'd know of the human trials, and he'd face the consequences of his actions.

It was a zero-sum game, Artemis realized. Either way, one of them was going to lose, and she was going to make it her mission to ensure it was him every single time. No matter what it took, the great Sebastian Carlisle was going to fall before he reached the sun he'd been sacrificing everything for, and Artemis would be the one to set his wings aflame.

"You ready?" Abyan asked, straightening her back.

She'd stayed in Kade's room after they returned from their mission. The senior operatives from the intelligence wing understood that she hadn't gone AWOL and released her after the interrogation. And although many words were exchanged in all their cross-examinations, Artemis had yet to hear a thank you from anyone at Carlisle.

Artemis sighed. "I have a bad feeling about this."

"They're just people," she assured her. "Don't make it bigger than it is—it gives them power over you."

Just as Artemis was about to reply, yells erupted from the room in front of them. Mr. Carlisle's voice, she recognized, but she couldn't place the female one he was arguing with. A third, hushed voice swooped in, trying to calm them before Abyan and Artemis heard, but it was too late. She looked at Abyan, the same conclusion in both of their eyes.

There was definitely a division in The League, and Mr. Carlisle wasn't as invincible as he made himself out to be.

The steel door in front of them opened, and a guard ushered them in. Her brows furrowed when they entered to find only two of the twelve members of The League sitting before them. She was greeted by a metallic hijab with a point sharp enough to cut and green eyes with nowhere near the life and warmth of her son's.

Rosemary Mulligan.

To her left sat Mr. Carlisle, a storm raging across his features. God, he was angry. His pursed lips and tight jaw made it crystal clear he wanted a head put before him on a silver platter, and Artemis just didn't know if it was hers or Abyan's that was first on the menu.

"Hello, girls," Rosemary said, and continued speaking without even waiting for their reply. "I'm going to keep this brief since I know you've been through a stressful past twenty-four hours. We would like to formally thank you for helping Squad 2528 stop the attack on the research wing of Carlisle Enterprises and applaud you for seeing it before any of us did. We would also like to apologize to you, Abyan, for removing you from your squad and unjustly punishing you."

Artemis felt Abyan stiffen at her side.

"And as such, your ban from The Sevenfold is lifted with immediate effect, and you may go back to your regular scheduled classes."

"Thank you, miss," Abyan said.

"You're welcome." A hint of a smile passed across Rosemary's lips before she focused her attention on Artemis. "Miss Garrett-Coleman, it's my understanding that you've been undergoing examinations for grief counseling?"

"Yes, miss." Artemis cleared her throat, ignoring her racing heartbeat. It wasn't for grief counseling, and it never was, but she couldn't tell Rosemary that. Allies had a nasty habit of stabbing you in the back when it came to Carlisle.

"The League was unaware of this, and after a full review, we've decided that such examinations are not necessary and should not have been undertaken by staff in the first place." She folded her hands. "We apologize for any discomfort caused by what took place, and I can assure you, speaking with the full authority of The League, it will never happen again."

Artemis's eyes stung, but she forced the tears back. "Thank you, Mrs. Mulligan."

"You are dismissed." She gave a brief flick of her wrist in their general direction. "Enjoy the rest of your evening."

They had to take a cab home. Halfway through the journey, Artemis told the driver to stop at a gym in Notting Hill. She exited the car without a word, ignoring Abyan's confused expression, and was back not five minutes later with a wrapped bundle in her hands.

"What's that?" she whispered.

A portable hard drive.

Yet Artemis didn't so much as blink before she spoke. "The end of Carlisle Enterprises."

ACKNOWLEDGMENTS

This story has been with me for a long time. I first came up with the idea when my mum told me I had to put my younger sisters to bed. It was around 2013, when I wasn't more than fourteen or fifteen years old, and over the course of three nights the bare bones of *The Sevenfold Hunters* formed in hushed whispers and was intermittently interrupted by my mum telling me I was either being too loud or to wrap it up, already. According to her, bedtime stories didn't take three hours to tell, but I digress.

So I'd like to thank my three younger sisters for in a way being my first readers, for listening attentively and offering me feedback both when my story was just words in the dark and when it became ink on a page. Thank you for cheering me on through my publishing journey, celebrating the highs with me and picking me up during the lows. This book quite literally wouldn't be here without you.

To my wonderful mum, thank you for nurturing my love of reading even though you didn't really understand my obsession, for taking me to the library as a kid whenever I asked, and for buying me books even though we couldn't always afford it. Thank you, Hooyo, for believing that my writing was important and would get somewhere even when I didn't believe.

To my editor, Tamara, thank you for seeing the true essence of this book and taking a chance on it at a time when I'd genuinely given up all hope of it ever being published. I'm so grateful that my work found a home with an amazing editor whose vision aligned with mine and who elevated it to levels I hadn't even imagined were possible. Thank you also to the whole team at Page Street and everyone who helped get my story and me to this place—I'm so grateful to you all.

To my agent, Garrett, thank you for being this book's biggest cheerleader from day one. Thank you for being unfazed throughout our long and difficult journey toward publication, and thank you for having enough faith for both of us.

To Linda Epstein, whom I'd originally queried with this book what feels like a lifetime ago, thank you for sharing my work with Garrett. Thank you for taking that extra time when it would've been much easier to reject me outright because none of this would've been possible without you.

To Emily Skrutskie, my AMM mentor, thank you for taking on a glorified first draft and helping me make it into something that shone. Thank you for your direction because I'm so grateful for the lessons you taught me back then.

Lastly, to my high school English teacher, I'm not going to name-drop you here but thank you for having faith in me and giving me praise when I wasn't sure of myself. Thank you for making me believe I was capable of anything. You once said I'd make a great English teacher myself, and although I took a different route, I hope this counts as a close second.

ABOUT THE AUTHOR

Rose Egal loves autumn, sad poetry, and cats who humble themselves. *The Sevenfold Hunters* is her first novel, in part inspired by her MS in biochemistry from Queen Mary University of London. She lives in London with her family and their cat, her arch nemesis, Hercules Aethelstan Buni Massimo Pandemicus The (not) Great.